THE SHAKING

BY
CÉLESTE PERRINO-WALKER

Farenorth Press
Strait Truth Series: Book 1

Farenorth Press

Farenorth Press
P.O. Box 1005
Rutland, VT 05701

Except for God, of course, all characters, names, corporations, institutions, organizations, events, or locales in this novel are a product of the author's overworked imagination or, if real, used fictitiously. Any resemblance to real people, places, or things, living or dead, is a product of yours.

First Edition

ISBN-10: 0990836118
ISBN-13: 978-0990836117

Cover Design by Wicked Book Covers
www.wickedbookcovers.com

"You can safely assume that you've created God in your own image when it turns out that God hates all the same people you do." ~ Anne Lamott

"How many people have been lost because they had their eyes on sinful, erring human beings and not on the only sinless unerring Human that ever lived? For this reason, we need to separate our faith from anyone and anything, even and especially those in the church, and center it only on Jesus . . . In the end, when push comes to shove, when the day of testing will hit every soul, we need to be able to stand alone, trusting in the Lord and His Word and in no one else, because no on else can be entirely trusted." ~ Clifford Goldstein, *The Remnant*

"The work of judging his brother has not been placed upon any man. 'Judge not,' the Saviour says, 'that ye be not judged; for with what judgment ye judge, ye shall be judged: and with what measure ye mete, it shall be measured to you again.' He who takes upon himself the work of judging and criticizing others, lays himself open to the same degree of judgment and criticism. Those who are ready to condemn their brethren, would do well to examine their own works and character. Such an examination, honestly made, will reveal the fact that they, too, have defects of character, and have made grave blunders in their work. If the great Judge should deal with men as they deal with their fellow workers, they would regard him as unkind and unmerciful" ~ Ellen G. White, *Christian Leadership* (p. 59).

"His servants then asked, 'Do you want us to go out and pull up the weeds?' 'No!' he answered. 'You might also pull up the wheat. Leave the weeds alone until harvest time. Then I'll tell my workers to gather the weeds and tie them up and burn them. But I'll have them store the wheat in my barn' " (Matthew 13:28-30, CEV).

For Clifford who refused to be shaken.

"If a church kicks you out the front door," he used to tell me,
"come in the back."

"I have fought the good fight,
I have finished the race,
I have kept the faith.
Finally, there is laid up for me
the crown of righteousness,
which the Lord,
the righteous Judge,
will give to me on that Day,
and not to me only
but also to all
who have loved His appearing"
2 Timothy 4:7, 8, NKJV.

Chapter One

I'm trying to get a raspberry jelly stain out of my work blouse courtesy of a co-worker at the bakery. It's a white blouse, of course. My only one. Derrick said something really foul just before he squirted it at me, but I was the only one who heard him. If a lesbian is the only one who hears an insult in the kitchen, then it hasn't happened. At least that's what I've been told before. This isn't the first time my property has been ruined, or I've been harassed.

I miss Lily. Whenever I had a rotten day, she'd always make me feel better about it. She could see the humor in any situation, even the bad ones. And ever since I swallowed my pride and went back to college to get my degree in economics, there had been a lot of bad ones. Looking back, you could almost say it was the beginning of the end. Now I was back at the beginning.

I really hoped we could stay friends after we broke up, I really did. We were such good friends first, before we became partners, I guess I just fooled myself that we could keep part of our relationship even if we couldn't keep all of it. At first I blamed God when I lost Lily. I mean, I *really* blamed him. I screamed curses at him, and I just hated on him for awhile; but despite all that he never left. My anger wasn't strong enough to drive him away. Eventually, I could see that his plan was best, even if I didn't like it.

Sometimes I just wish I could go home and get away from my life, like the prodigal. The thing is, the last time Daddy saw me—when I came out to my parents—he got all pale and said something like, "Dear God in heaven, I've spawned a monster." Then he changed the subject and was all like, "Young lady, how dare you come into this house looking like that? What do you think Jesus would say about that get-up? I don't want to see your face again until you've changed."

That was back when I was going through my paramilitary phase. I had on combat boots and camo. Or maybe it was my dreads he didn't like. Or the piercings: eyebrow, ears, lip, and nose. Or the tats; I have some awesome tats. I keep them covered now, but back then I was proud of them.

Mom just stood there and bit her lip and looked like she wanted to cry or scream or both. But she didn't say anything. She didn't stick up for me. She didn't say, "Graham, you're being ridiculous. This is our cherished daughter, Brooke. How can you say such hurtful things to her?" But then, Mom never really had the backbone to stand up to him. To be honest, he *was* pretty scary when he got all "holier than thou" on us. He seriously freaked me out, that's for sure. I haven't been back since.

Oh, I send them cards at Christmas and their birthday, stuff like that. But I haven't seen them in years. I never hear from them, either. Not even Mom, though I'm pretty sure she would talk to me if I called. The problem is I can never be sure *he's* not going to answer the phone. And I know the only thing he'd want to know is if I'd *changed*, if I wasn't a lesbian anymore.

What he can't seem to understand, or maybe refuses to understand, is that even though I'm not in a relationship now, even though I'm committed to being "chaste" as they say at my church, I'll never stop being a lesbian. It's who I am, not what I do. I know he doesn't want to be blamed for contributing to the gene pool that could have created such a monstrosity, so he'll never accept me. Never. It would be like admitting he wasn't perfect, that maybe somewhere inside him there was a homosexual gene that could pop out at any moment and embarrass him.

The phone rings, and I automatically check the caller ID before I answer it. When you've been a kicking post as long as I have, you don't assume there's someone kind on the other end of the line. I breathe a little sigh of relief when I see who it is. Judah. Although I met him at college, he's from church; he's safe.

"Hey, what's up?"

"Brooke, I'm really, really sorry to ask you, but I've got an awful cold, and I'm supposed to lead Bible study tonight. Can you do it? I called everyone else first," he adds apologetically. I can hear snuffling as he blows his nose sloppily. "I know how busy you are, but no one else can do it, and I just feel so awful. Please?"

I sigh. I've got an exam to study for, and I really should be sleeping right now. My job at the bakery has me out of bed by two thirty in the morning. As soon as I get off work, I'm at school until the early afternoon. By dinner I'm ready to do a face plant in my supper. I rarely make it to Judah's Wednesday night Bible study. Instead I usually go to the one that's just before the service on Sabbath. It's easier for me to get up early on a day off than stay up late, ever.

"Sure, Judah, of course I'll do it. Feel better, okay?"

"Thanks, Brooke! I owe you one, girlfriend," Judah snorts into his tissue again, and I can't help grinning at his attempt to sound urban. He's fooling no one; Judah's a total nerd.

"Get some rest. Later."

A couple of years ago I would have stopped off at a convenience store for an energy drink to get me through the next couple of hours. Tonight, instead, I drop to my knees and pray. "God, I'm so tired. You know I really need to get some studying done and then get some rest, but Judah needs me. There are people who want to meet and pray together, and they need a leader, someone who will guide them into a closer relationship with you. I'm not the ideal person for that, Lord. You know that. But I'm available and I'm willing and I know you can work with that. I may only be a weak, flawed human being, but it doesn't matter what or who I am, only that I'm surrendered to you. Help me to be a channel for your Spirit tonight. Keep me awake and alert, and use me in whatever way you see fit. Amen."

I check to be sure I've got my national ID card (carrying it is mandatory and I've heard enough scary stories about what happens if you don't that I am paranoid about keeping it with me at all times) and my metro card before I leave, because I don't have enough cash to get another one tonight if I forget it. There's no time to prepare anything. I leave the blouse to soak and try to figure out what to wear. My wardrobe is pretty drab these days, but I try to make an effort to spruce up a little since I'm going to be the leader. I find a black skirt and a turtleneck. I look . . . okay. Not dressy, but pulled together anyway. I twist my dreads up and secure them on top of my head so they appear tidier.

Lately, I've tried to be more "girly." I even wear skirts sometimes. But I draw the line at ruffles and lace. And I have a hard time with colors. Most of my wardrobe is black. Sometimes I think I ought to try wearing colors, but on the rare occasions I go shopping for clothes, I can never make up my mind which color would look good on me. And it's not like I have any girl friends I can ask.

At times like those, I really miss my mom. She's a total "girly girl." I know she loves me, but I sometime think she wonders how we could be related. She's petite with a heart-shaped face, long, curly blonde hair, and tiny hands and feet. I, on the other hand, am tall. I'm thin, but not model-skinny, solid in an athletic way. My jaw is square and I have a faintly androgynous look if I make no attempt to soften my features by wearing makeup and plucking my eyebrows into delicate arches like most females would. I don't smile a lot which tends to intimidate people. They say I look grim and unapproachable.

"Don't look so formidable," Lily used to tease. "People won't try to get to know you if you come across as such a bear."

I put a few bucks in the bottom of my shoe in case of emergency, stick my metro card into my Bible like a bookmark, slip it into my messenger bag with my cell phone and other essentials, and head out. The subway is quiet at this time of night, just some stragglers. Most people are home by now if they aren't out partying with friends, or trying out the latest and greatest new restaurant. Still, there is at least one Terrorist Assault Officer in every car. They are grim and vigilant.

People call them TAOs as a joke because they're supposed to bring harmony to the natural order of things by their presence, like the Chinese philosophy of Tao. I'm not sure anybody believes they actually do, but after the last terrorist attack on the D.C. metro everyone's been on edge, and no one in any city likes to be underground much.

The TAOs aren't a joke though, and no one treats them like one. If you'd ever seen them take someone down and beat them senseless, you knew enough not to make jokes around them either. I saw a smart aleck kid treat them like they do those soldiers standing guard at the Tomb of the Unknown Soldier, the ones who don't move or laugh no matter what you do. The kid tried to bat the TAO's hat off. The TAO took him down and cracked him over the head with a bully stick so fast it was all a blur. They carted the kid away in an ambulance. No one reprimanded the TAO, and it didn't even make the news. They can pretty much do whatever they want. The best way to coexist with them is to keep your head low and your nose clean.

I'm grateful my stop isn't far along the line. The car squeals to a juddering halt, and I shuffle off with a few other people. The TAO narrows his eyes at me, taking in the hair probably, but he doesn't say anything. They don't talk much although I've heard a few bark orders for people to move faster, or shut up.

There are more of them on the streets. They're very visible with their black uniforms and that red insignia on their military-style, black caps. I think the government wants it that way as a deterrent. The local law enforcement is resentful of their presence, but even they make it a point not to antagonize them. The local officers nod curtly when they pass the TAOs, but there's no palling around like they do with each other.

I slant my body forward, hands in my pockets, making as small a target as possible, and move purposefully through the foot traffic meandering along the sidewalks. Church is a couple of blocks away, and I'm hoping to arrive a little early so I have time to pray and prepare. It's when I'm waiting at the first stoplight that I spot her. Lily.

She's standing on the sidewalk across the street studying the menu posted outside a restaurant. She's alone and looks small and vulnerable. I feel my heart speed up and my stomach clench. I want to run up and hug her and catch up. It's been almost a year since we spoke, and I miss her so much I feel physical pain at the sight of her. It's not that I miss the sinful part of our relationship. I just miss Lily, the person. And I want just a moment with her, just a moment.

Before I can react, I feel the Holy Spirit wrap around me, restraining me, cautioning me. I've turned my back on that life and speaking with Lily again, indulging in even a safe, wholesome conversation would be playing with fire. My sinful past flashes through my mind, the agony I walked through leaving it, the knowledge of how I'd hurt my Savior, and every fiber of my being is convicted that I can't even say hello to her. It wouldn't be fair to either of us, or to God.

God help me, my mind screams. *God help me walk away. Give me the strength to walk away. Don't let her see me.* The light turns green, and I'm crossing, praying Lily won't look over, when that's exactly what she does. Even at a distance I can see the pain darken her eyes. I wrench my gaze away, fixing it on the pavement in front of me, blindly following the feet ahead of me, wishing I hadn't run into her. By the time I reach the church I'm shaking, and instead of being able to quietly pray and prepare myself to lead the prayer meeting, I have to lock myself in a stall in the bathroom and sob quietly into some toilet paper until I calm down.

When I think I can control myself, I wipe my face off with some fresh tissue and exit the stall to wash my hands. They tremble as I hold them under the water and I watch it, mesmerized, as it flows around and through my fingers. It's crazy but it reminds me of the water in the baptismal tank and the day I was baptized, and I hang onto the thought like a woman drowning. This pain I feel, this is worth it. And it's nothing compared to the suffering Christ went through for me. The suffering *I* caused Him. It's a small price to pay.

I'm drying my hands on some paper towels when the door flies open, and Diana Wallace bustles into the small space. She's visibly taken aback when she sees me. But when she notices my red eyes and flushed face, her lips button up uncomfortably. I can almost see the struggle going on in her mind. Here is a distraught girl. She should feel pity. She should be sympathetic, ask me what's wrong. Instead, she feels nothing but revulsion, and she's afraid what I've got might be "catching."

I can see the struggle end, her mind made up, she says, "Yes, well," pats me awkwardly on the arm, and pushes past me to a stall. I shove down the tears that threaten to start up again, count to five to regain my composure, and head for the small room where the Bible study will be held.

As I look around the room at the carefully guarded faces of the people who have gathered for the prayer meeting, I know I am being sized up and categorized. I can almost see the "L" word printed across their irises as though I might as well be wearing a name tag with "Hello: I'm a lesbian" written on it. Their collective gaze sweeps over my flat, serviceable, black boots, up my plain, long black skirt, over my black turtleneck, across my dark complexion, registering the scars from my piercings with disgust which only deepens when they take in my dreads. I have been weighed in the balance and found wanting. Again. It's a little ritual I go through every time I step through the door. It's like they are surprised to see me, surprised I came back, and their little inventory of my shortcomings only strengthens their disapproval.

I can't face them alone. Their wall of condemnation and judgment is more than I can humanly bear. I pray, desperately and earnestly for strength, and I don't open my mouth until I feel the power of God's presence fill and reassure me. As I busy myself passing out hymn books and straightening chairs, I pray fervently and praise God for his faithfulness. My racing heart suddenly becomes peaceful, and I am reminded that it's not about me. Jesus' church crucified him; can I expect better than that from mine? I can face their visual crucifixion the same way Jesus faced his physical one: by the grace of God. This thought comforts me like a warm, soft blanket around my heart, and I am able to take my seat and even smile a little as I open the meeting.

"Are there any prayer requests?" I ask, forcing myself to glance around at the unwelcoming faces.

"Where's Judah?" asks Sarah, bluntly. A young woman, perhaps a decade older than I am, she's clearly afraid that she could be judged by association, and she is careful never to get too close to me.

"Yes," I say with forced cheerfulness, "let's pray for Judah. He's sick tonight. Thank you, Sarah. Anyone else?"

Before there's time to speak up, Diana pokes her head in the door. At first I think she's going to join us, so I'm about to motion her inside, but instead she's joined by an elder wearing a scowl. They whisper together for a few minutes and then leave. Rocko (whose parents called him Ricardo), the teen son of our pastor who is clearly rebelling against his upbringing by dressing like a thug and acting out, slumps back in his chair. As soon as Diana and Elder Fortin leave he leans forward and gives me a searching look.

"Can we pray for my friend Sibby? She tried to kill herself last night. They took her to the hospital and put her on the nutty floor."

"Absolutely." I nod encouragingly. "Is Sibby in your class at school?"

"Nah," he says. "I met her at the homeless shelter. I help out serving dinner there most nights. Sibby's a regular. She's like nine million years old, but she's cool, ya know? She ain't got no family. Says she might come to church here sometime." He glances back at the door where Diana and Elder Fortin had been standing. "Not sure that's such a good idea," he mutters under his breath.

This kid might fool other people, but he doesn't fool me. He's rebelling outwardly, but there is a whole lot more going on inside of him.

"Anyone else?"

A middle-aged woman in the back with her Bible propped open on her knees raises her hand timidly.

"Mrs. Swift?" I smile encouragingly. I don't know her, but I like her. She seems sincere and while she's not friendly, exactly, I don't get the impression that it's because she's critical, just shy.

"I would like us to be in prayer for my sister and her son. He's autistic and she doesn't have the money for expensive treatments, any treatments really, and it's hard for her to take care of him. Her husband deserted them . . ." She looks abashed, as though she's been caught telling tales out of school. "Well, he's not around anymore," she amends, "so it's just her and Jimmy."

"And what's your sister's name?"

"Amelia," she says quickly. "I'm sorry. It's Amelia." She offers me a shy smile which I return.

There's a long, uncomfortable silence during which not a single person offers a prayer request. Most of them avoid my gaze and keep their eyes drilled on the floor. A few stare at me belligerently. Praying out loud is not one of my strengths, but I start the prayers off by praying briefly for each request. A few people are brave enough to follow me, offering a sentence or two. Mr. Talbot, though he didn't have any requests, offers a lengthy prayer during which he touches on most current events and eventually gets around to a cursory mention of the prayer requests.

It's a short meeting, but it feels long. We sing a few hymns. There's a brief period during which I try to initiate some involvement by having people take turns reading scripture and commenting on what it's saying to them personally. By the end of the allotted period, I'm more exhausted than if I'd worked a double shift at the bakery and taken exams all day long. I barely have enough energy to pick up the hymnals and stack them neatly away while everyone filters (or bolts) out of the room. As I'm struggling with the stack of hymnals I feel wiry arms lift my burden and am surprised to find Rocko at my side, relieving me of the books.

"Thank you, but you don't have to do—"

"It's no problem." He lifts them easily and carries them to the shelf where they are stored. "You know," he says, turning to me, his eyes serious, "that was the best prayer meeting we've had here in a long time."

I am stunned. "You think?" I ask incredulously.

"Yeah."

I shake my head, dubious. "I don't know. They didn't seem to really . . . like . . . me." I hesitate over the word, not wanting to come off sounding petulant or needy. I don't *need* them to like me, but it would be nice. It seems like it would facilitate things.

He shrugs. "Doesn't matter. Something about it felt, I dunno, real, I guess. Thanks. 'Night."

He slouches out the door, and I find I'm alone. I collect my things, turn out the light, and follow them all outside. Fortunately, I'm not the last one out of the church, so I don't have to worry about locking up. On the sidewalk, I take a deep breath and collect myself. I'm so tired

I feel a bit unsteady on my feet. I know I should hurry or I'll miss the next train and have to wait around in the dark station a half hour for the next one, but I hesitate. I know it's silly, but some part of me is afraid Lily's still there, on the sidewalk, crying.

So I do what I always do when I'm facing a situation that baffles me or seems impossible, which is most of the time. I bow my head and pray. I'm so engrossed in my own thoughts, pleading with God to take my fear away and be with Lily and a million other requests, that I don't even hear them coming. From the sound of them when I do finally take notice, I could've probably heard them a block away if I'd been paying attention.

But I hear nothing until the very last second, and of course, by that time it's too late. I look up, startled; I imagine the bewildered look on my pale face, the only thing that must be visible against my black clothing in the darkened street. The bottle is moving so fast I don't see it. I don't even feel it when it strikes me on the temple. I just see their screaming, joy-filled, reckless faces as the car careens on down the street, the whistles of the TAOs just beginning to scream in protest as a curtain of nothingness falls over me.

Chapter Two

When I wake up, the light feels too bright. I'm on a gurney in the hallway of a hospital, probably Mercy General which isn't too far from the church. I gingerly raise myself up to get a better view of the hallway, but the splitting pain in my head convinces me I'm better off where I am. I do notice a TAO sitting on a metal folding chair at the foot of the gurney. He sees the movement and gets up to come stand by the head of the gurney.

"Ma'am?" His voice is respectful and his face is kind. Two things I wouldn't have expected. "How are you feeling?"

"I've been better, Officer." I grimace. It feels like someone has pickaxed me in the head. Even though my own voice is soft it sounds like a shout. I lift a tentative hand to examine the spot where the bottle made contact, but my head is swathed in bandages.

"Do you remember what happened?" His eyes are alert, his fingers grip a pen he's holding poised over a pad, ready to write down whatever I say.

I will my brain to think back. "Some kids, I think, they threw something at me."

"A bottle, yes, but do you remember anything about them? Can you describe what they looked like? What kind of car they were driving? Did you get a license plate number?"

I can see flashes of their laughing faces, like snapshots in an album, but it's like trying to see pictures at the bottom of a pool. They're just blurs of color. I start to shake my head, but the movement increases the pain so I say, "No, I'm sorry," instead.

The TAO looks disappointed and closes his pad. He slips a card into my hand and says, "If you think of anything, you call me. Okay? Ask for me. My name's on the card."

"I will. Thank you."

After he's gone people pass through the hallway, but no one stops to check on me. I'm not sure if I should stay there or try to get up. Eventually an orderly stops and looks at me in surprise. "You're awake again," he says, picking up my wrist and checking my pulse almost mechanically. His head is shaved in that "I'm bald because it's cool and not because my hair fell out" way and his face is relaxed in gentle lines, his manner soothing.

"I'm awake," I repeat. My head hurts so much I wish I wasn't.

"My head hurts."

"I'll bet it does," he agrees cheerfully. "Seven stitches, but don't worry, the doc who put them in is practically an artist." He contemplates the scars from my piercings thoughtfully, and I think he's about to add that I probably won't care either way, but he doesn't. "You had meds earlier for the headache. They should kick in soon. It's a miracle, you know."

"What's a miracle?" I ask feeling stupid.

"Well, first of all, you were hit with an empty bottle, not a full one which would probably have fractured your skull. That would have been worse. Second, it was a glancing blow. You only have a minor concussion, and a cranial CT scan didn't turn up anything serious."

"How long was I out?"

"You mean the last time?"

"Last time?" I repeat, not getting it.

He drops my wrist and checks the chart hanging on the gurney. "You arrived four hours ago, but you were awake and talking, well, more babbling about Jesus and lilies. We did the CT scan but had to wake you up for the stitches. You were coherent then, but fell asleep again right after. Looks like you've been in and out of it since you got here."

"I don't remember that. Any of it. And that shouldn't worry me?" It does worry me. I haven't got a single memory from the moment the bottle hit me.

He shrugs. "A little amnesia; it's not uncommon after a traumatic injury like this. If it continues, come back in for an evaluation. Like I said, CT scan didn't show any serious injuries. You're good to go."

"Just like that?" I'm surprised they don't want to hold me for observation or something.

"You got someone at home to look after you?"

"No, no one." Just saying it makes me want to cry which he seems to sense.

"How are you going to get home?"

"Train, I guess."

He thinks about this for a minute. "Not a great idea." He digs around in the pocket of his lab coat and pushes some money into my hand. "Look, I really shouldn't do this, but take a taxi, okay? It'll be safer. It's late, too late to be waiting at the train station or riding alone. Not in this city, not this time of night, not in your condition."

"I can't—" I start to protest, but he gets all businesslike again.

"You can, and you will. Doctor's orders."

I try to smile, but it hurts. "Are you a doctor?"

He chuckles. "Will be. Some day. Just take the money and get a taxi. Got it?"

I nod and I can feel tears well up in the corners of my eyes. "I will. Thank you." Kindness always surprises me. But kindness from strangers even more so.

He squeezes my arm and hands me my paperwork. "Bring this to that desk over there, and you can leave. Make sure they give you back your national ID card. We needed it to identify you, and it's with your paperwork." He strides off down the hallway.

I manage to roll off the gurney somewhat awkwardly, no points for grace. My head is protesting loudly, and I feel a little nauseous. The girl dressed in violet scrubs sitting at the desk I've been directed to hands me a mile long printout of things I should watch out for: vomiting, blackouts, seizures, vertigo. And there's a helpful warning that I can't bump my head again anytime soon, or I risk disastrous consequences. I have to sign a number of documents before she'll let me leave.

It's a relief to step outside into the cool air. The pounding in my head eases a little. I'm grateful that I don't have long to wait for a cab. They can be few and far between at night. I settle myself carefully into the backseat and try not to watch the lights outside go whizzing past. The dull thump in my head quiets a little. A miracle, the orderly said. "Thank you, Jesus," I whisper into the stale air of the cab. "Thank you for protecting me. Thank you for giving me a safe way to get home."

I must have dozed off because the next thing I know the cab is jerking to a stop in front of my apartment building. The cabbie is looking around nervously. I don't blame him. It's not a safe neighborhood. It's not a safe street. It's not even a safe building. I hand him the money the orderly gave me, but it's not quite enough, so I have to dig around in my shoe for the bills I stashed there which covers the fare. "Thank you," I tell him, but he only grunts and waits impatiently until I heave myself out of the cab. He squeals away the moment my feet hit the pavement.

It's a little hairy getting up to my apartment. It's no use pretending my apartment building is anything more than it really is: a flophouse. Apparently the guy who owns it has some sway with the city because the police usually leave it alone, although the TAOs search it on a fairly regular schedule. Every now and then there's a drug raid, but no one seems to notice the overcrowding, the people sleeping in the hallways, the blatant building violations.

My apartment is on the top floor which is a blessing because not many people want to climb that many stairs. (The elevator quit working months ago.) Usually I don't mind the climb; I think of it as my unofficial, free gym. Tonight every step feels like a kettle drummer has taken up residence in my brain and is counting out the steps. By the time I reach my door I'm so weak I have trouble retrieving my keys even though they are only in my pocket.

I don't remember changing out of my ripped clothes or even going to bed but that could be because I didn't do either. Instead, I apparently collapsed on the couch where I'm woken a few hours later by my phone shrilling beside my ear. I'm half asleep when I answer it to find my screaming boss on the other end wanting to know where I am. I manage to mumble something about an accident and hospital and finally he calms down. He's not happy, but he grudgingly tells me to feel better soon. Fortunately, I have the next couple days off anyway. I don't even have time to worry whether or not I'll be able to go back to sleep after that exhilarating fiasco before I'm out again.

When I finally surface, the sun is pouring through the dirty window, pooling around my couch, and getting behind my eyelids. Mercifully, when I open my eyes the headache is a shadow of its former self. I roll off the couch and sink cautiously to my knees half expecting it to return in all its glory, but nothing happens. I bow my head, close my eyes, and begin to pray.

"Heavenly Father, thank you for keeping me safe last night. Thank you that I wasn't hurt worse, and thank you for letting me serve you at the prayer meeting. Please bless all those who attended, and be with Sibby in the hospital. Help her to know you, Lord, because only in you will she find true peace and know real love. Give her a sense of your comforting presence today, and help her to find hope in Jesus."

I go on, praying for every one of the prayer requests from the night before. When I run out of them, I pray for each of the people who were in the prayer meeting. Before I finish, visions of Lily's tragic face hit me like a punch in the gut, and I falter. I want to pray, *and please let Lily and I become friends*, but I know that can't happen. Not now, not ever. So instead, I pray for Lily to find Jesus just as I did. I pray for her salvation. And I pray that she will find true joy and happiness in God rather than searching fruitlessly for it in others.

When I finish praying, I take inventory of my situation. My pantry is well-stocked because I'd just been shopping the day before. I have the next few days off from work. There's nothing particularly vital happening at school since we just finished midterms. After I find some breakfast I'll use my ancient computer to e-mail my professors and let them know what happened. I'll send them a copy of my hospital discharge form which clearly states I should get some rest for a few days. Then I'll check Blackboard, the college website portal, to get my assignments so I can keep up while I'm out.

While I'm poking through the refrigerator deciding what to eat for breakfast, I praise God for the timing of my accident. It's Thursday, so I have four whole days to recuperate before I have to get back to my life. The bliss of being able to rest and leisurely do my school work is unspeakable. I'm beginning to see this accident as a blessing.

Judah calls me on Sabbath because he's feeling well enough to go to church, and he's wondering why I'm not there. When I tell him about the accident, he's horrified.

"Why didn't you tell me?" he demands. Like he's my mother or something. "I feel so guilty. I feel responsible. If I hadn't asked you to fill in for me . . . it could have been me." This revelation seems to sober him right up, and he's silent for a moment. "You should have told me, Brooke," he says quietly. "I would have come over to check on you. I would have brought you soup or something."

I laugh, which feels good for a change; I don't laugh very often. "Judah, honestly, it's okay. I'm okay. It's been a nice vacation, actually. The headaches are almost gone. Besides, the guy at the hospital told me it was a miracle. Call me selfish, but I would have been jealous if a miracle had happened to you instead, and I'd missed it." I'm joking, but Judah is still too shaken up to register that.

"It's not funny, Brooke," he insists stubbornly. "I care about you. I'm sorry someone hurt you. Did they catch the guys who were responsible, at least?"

"I don't know." I try to make my voice gentle, to pacify him. It's not hard, because I'm touched by his concern. In fact, I'm so touched I struggle not to cry. "The TAO officer at the hospital asked me to identify them, but I couldn't. It all happened too fast. I couldn't remember what they looked like, so I couldn't help them at all. He gave me his card in case I remember anything."

He hangs up after making me promise to call him if I start to feel worse and promises he'll come rushing over to help. This is amusing because I've never seen the mother hen side of him. It's touching. I assure him that if I feel the slightest bit woozy, I'll call him before I pass out, and this seems to mollify him enough that he can finally bring himself to hang up.

The rest of the weekend is uneventful. I sleep as much as I can, and when 2:30 Monday morning comes, I feel ready to take on my life again. At least, I feel ready until I arrive at the bakery and discover that Derrick intends to punish me for my unscheduled time off. The fact that I am wearing a bandage to cover the gash on my forehead doesn't seem to faze him.

He's taking dough out of the proofer when I arrive. "Well, well, decided to come in to work today? It's nice you could be bothered."

I am used to Derrick by now. If he isn't picking on me because I am a lesbian, he's picking on me because I am a Christian. He seems to think "lesbian Christian" is an oxymoron. He is never overwhelmed by the choices though; he switches seamlessly between the two, disparaging them equally.

If it weren't for Derrick, I'd enjoy this part of my job. I love arriving in the darkness. I love the quiet, the routine, the smell of the ingredients as we get everything prepped. I love the variety of the baked goods we make: donuts, bread, croissants, cakes, cookies, muffins, fancy rolls. I love creating the special orders knowing they will add to someone's celebration and give them joy. I even love waiting on the customers; most of them are wonderful.

My job is to keep track of all the special orders, help Derrick get everything out of the proofer first thing in the morning, and prep it. We put on egg washes and toppings depending on the item, and then we start baking. While I clean up and get the special orders ready, Derrick starts making cookies. By the time the morning bake is over, the customers begin to arrive so I transition out to the counter to wait on them with another counter girl, Mel, who comes in later than I do.

If it gets slow, we help Derrick who has moved on to The Board: a constantly evolving list of things we're running out of, or getting low on, like fillings, frostings, cakes, etc. We try to knock off at least half of the items on The Board every day so we don't get too far behind. My replacement, Angie, shows up just before ten when I have to leave to go to my first class. After I'm gone they work on decorating the cakes which I'd love to learn because it looks like fun. There's a woman who comes in just for that because she's specially trained. She sort of runs the cake decorating show and orders the others around.

Everyone else is called by their given name (or sometimes, in my case, "hey you"), but Odile is called Madame Thibeaux (which is pronounced, apparently, "tee-bow") by virtue of the fact that she is an actual French woman who moved here as a young woman, and she insists on it. No one crosses her, not Derrick, not even the owner, Julian Coulter, who usually drops in at some point during the day. He's got other bakeries besides Bake Nation so we don't see him for very long, but he likes to be sure everything is running smoothly, or to check up on us, depending on whether or not you share Derrick's cynical, suspicious nature.

Derrick is not a morning person, so most of the time I just have to steel myself against the awful screamo music he likes to listen to, and if I keep my mouth shut, he'll ignore me. But sometimes he's sullen, doesn't have his music on, and seems bent on seeing how many scars he can give me before I leave. His personal best had me sobbing in the restroom for fifteen minutes before I could pull myself together enough to return to the counter.

"Did we have a nice vacation?" he's asking snottily, as though I'd taken a month off to go on a cruise, rather than a day off to recuperate.

I want to say that, but I know it will only rile him up. In my head, I recite 2 Timothy 2:23-26 to myself. "Don't have anything to do with foolish and stupid arguments, because you know they produce quarrels. And the Lord's servant must not be quarrelsome but must be kind to everyone, able to teach, not resentful. Opponents must be gently instructed, in the hope that God will grant them repentance leading them to a knowledge of the truth, and that they will come to their senses and escape from the trap of the devil, who has taken them captive to do his will." I'm grateful that I started memorizing scripture months before because God uses it during teachable moments like this one to guide me and sometimes to keep me from saying or doing the wrong thing. I'm praying, thanking God for giving me this word of wisdom, so I miss what Derrick says next.

"What are you muttering about?" he demands, his face hot and flushed. "If you've got something to say then speak up or shut up."

"I'm . . . I'm sorry. I wasn't saying anything. I was . . ." I know if

I say that I was praying, I'll never hear the end of it. It'll just be more ammunition to use against me. But I won't deny it either. I lift my chin a bit, not so much in defiance as to bolster my courage. "I was praying."

He laughs, but it's not the kind of laugh you like to hear. It's not the kind of laugh anyone would join in on. It's the sort of laugh an evil villain would utter, and it makes my skin crawl. "Praying, oh, that's right. Pray to your dead God, Jesus Girl. Jesus freak, more like. You're going to have to do a lot of praying if you expect to make up for all your sins, homo. You're going to be burning in hell a long time before you can do enough penance to graduate into purgatory, even."

While this statement is so far from the realm of my own beliefs that it's like a fairytale, it does give me insight into his own upbringing. Apparently Derrick does believe in God, but it's the vengeful, vindictive, hateful God a lot of people are terrorized by the idea of, rather than the loving, just, and fair God I know personally. Oddly, the fact that he believes in God at all, that he is even aware of the existence of God, gives me hope that someday he'll come to actually know the real God.

He continues ranting along in the same vein as the morning wears on while I do my best to block out his words by singing hymns in my head and reciting scripture. The weird thing about Derrick is that even though I don't participate in the conversation, I don't react to anything he's saying, I don't try to defend myself, he just continues to rant. It's just this long, monotonous diatribe that attacks me personally or homosexuality and God in general. It's ironic, but I prefer the screamo.

When Mel arrives, his persecution gets more sporadic and subtle. He says things under his breath when I'm nearby, but barely speaks to me in Mel's presence. She thinks we get along just fine. Once in awhile he forgets himself and says something derogatory in the hearing of others, but it's usually a slip up, and he doesn't do it often.

"Hey, Jesus Girl," Derrick jeers, jerking his head toward the counter, "you've got a customer."

I groan inwardly when I see that my customer is also one of my professors. He teaches my Economics and Psychology class, a class I'd dreaded because psychology isn't my strong suit. But he's a decent guy and even responded to the e-mail I sent all my professors explaining the reason for my absences after the accident. He was the only one who responded. He flinches now at the moniker, and one bushy eyebrow lifts slightly, but he doesn't say anything.

"Hello Professor McCormick. What can I get for you?" I paste a smile on my face and pretend I haven't just been humiliated.

"Coffee, thanks, uh, Brooke, right? Economics and Psychology, B+?"

I smile for real. "Yes, sir. Does that B+ mean you graded our midterms?" I'd been struggling to raise my grade in that class.

"It does. You did well. Your arguments on the limitations on standard economic models were . . . persuasive."

"I'll take that as a compliment," I say, handing him his coffee.

"You should." There is no accompanying smile, but as I ring up his order and count out his change, he gives me a thoughtful look before deliberately placing a ten dollar bill in the TIP jar.

I open my mouth to protest, but he cuts in before I can say anything, nodding to my forehead where a bandage peeks through despite my efforts to cover it with the arrangement of my hair. "Glad to see you're on the mend. Have a nice day, Jesus Girl." His voice is low and respectful, elevating the nickname to an almost honorable title, like "Your Grace." In an odd way it makes me feel like standing a couple inches taller.

I stutter a "thank you," but it is to Professor McCormick's retreating back. Derrick glares at me as I return to my duties, answering the question of whether or not he'd overheard. I hear him whisper "freak" under his breath, but even his nastiness can't penetrate the warm, happy feeling that envelopes me.

That's one of the things I like most about being a Christian, I reflect as I walk to my first class. I never feel alone. God is with me every moment of the day and for the first time in my life I don't feel desperately lonely. Even when I've spent six hours being berated and abused I feel content and happy. That sounds stupid, or naïve, or something, but it's true. Even though everything outside of me is dark and hurtful, inside is light and peace and safety because God is there. It isn't as if the bad things don't exist; they're still there. But they don't have the power to make the same impact. It's like the difference between the barely discernible sting of an icy snowflake and the annihilation of being pelted by meteors.

If I am with God all the time, it's like we're sitting together in a beautiful garden. He's holding my hand and telling me how much He loves me. When the hateful words come they kind of deflect off the love He's surrounded me with. They don't even really hurt unless I try to defend myself, and there are days when I'm feeling low in spirit that I don't do the right thing. I don't react the way a Christian would; I react the way a defenseless human being would. Those days are never good. It's kind of like trying to go out into battle without any armor. It's insane, but that's what life is like when I let go and let Satan have at me.

I wrap my arms around my torso remembering days and years when I was out there alone being smashed by Satan's meteors. "Thank you God for finding me. Thank you for loving me. Thank you for patiently pursuing me." I'm aware that people are passing me on the sidewalk, looking at me, thinking I'm a nut job, and wondering if I'm someone who could be a threat to their safety. But I don't care. I would sing, I would *shout* if it wouldn't get me thrown in jail.

God has saved me! God loves me! God walks with me! I look around, wildly ecstatic, grinning from ear to ear. My eyes fall on a figure standing near a notice board, watching me. It's Professor McCormick. He's tacking up a flier. He nods slightly at me, acknowledging recognition or my insanity, I'm not sure which, and walks off.

I veer to the side so I can read the flier. There is a picture of a zombie and the words: "Get a kit. Make a plan. Be prepared." It's put out by the Centers for Disease Control and Prevention. In a blank space under the wording, someone has lettered in: "Are you prepared for the zombie apocalypse? Join us to discover how to protect yourself. Thursdays from 3:00-5:00, Starr Pavilion, Room 213. For more information contact Prof. McCormick."

It's my turn to stare. As I watch Professor McCormick saunter down the sidewalk posting and handing out fliers I marvel that a grown man can believe in something so crazy. And yet, I suppose he'd think my beliefs are crazy, too. And that sobers me up quickly.

Is it possible, I wonder, *to share them with him?* And that gives me something else to think about.

Chapter Three

I'm surprised at how long it takes me to heal from the concussion. The headache went away, and then it came back. We have a stretch of sunny weather, and it just seems too bright outside. I have trouble thinking clearly. I lose my train of thought easily.

I don't even realize these are symptoms of the concussion until I go in to have my stitches removed. It's the same orderly I had before (who turns out not to actually be an orderly, but a med student), and he asks me questions about my symptoms from a checklist. Apparently I have a bunch of them.

"It's perfectly normal," he tells me. "It can take months to fully recover from a blow to the head."

"So I'm normal?"

He glances up from his paperwork and gives me a critical once-over. "I don't know if I'd go that far," he says mildly, "but you should make a full recovery anyway." After a pause he says, "That was a joke."

Which just goes to show you how accustomed I am to being insulted; I didn't even notice. I smile to show him I get it, but inside I'm thanking God for protecting me from greater injury during the attack.

"Did they ever catch the kids who did this?" I ask.

"If they did, they didn't tell me." His hand is poised over my forehead. "This is going to sting a little."

I brace myself. "You said it was a miracle," I say, more to distract myself from the feeling of the stitches slipping out of my skin than to strike up a conversation. "That I could have been hurt a lot worse. Do you believe in God?"

His hand hesitates before he starts to pull the next stitch. "I didn't mean it like that," he says, which isn't really an answer. "It was just a figure of speech."

"And?"

"And . . . I see an awful lot in here. I guess I'm not sure if God is a monster or indifferent or just not very powerful."

"Because he doesn't save everyone?"

"Because I see too many people suffering every day: parents losing children, people brutally murdered, horrific accidents, and I have to wonder what kind of a God would allow this. If he's so all-powerful he could put a stop to it."

"And because he doesn't he's not powerful? Or he doesn't love us?"

"Something like that, I guess." He pulls the last stitch out and snaps off his latex gloves. "You're all set." His face isn't formidable, exactly, but it's not especially open and inviting of more conversation along this line, either. I've seen this before. The last thing I want is to be confrontational.

"Thank you," I say, and before he can leave, I reach into my messenger bag and hand him a booklet. "I have a gift for you."

He reaches out automatically, most people do, and takes the booklet from my hand. It's a gospel of John. On the cover is a picture of someone in a wheelchair with their arms upraised and the words, "Set free by grace." He looks it over for a minute and then puts it in his pocket. This is usually a good sign. If people are really resistant they will simply hand them back. It happens sometimes. When I first started passing out these little Pocket Testament League booklets of John's gospel every rejection shook my confidence. I'm still not crazy about having them flung back in my face, but now, at least, I retain enough control of my emotions to pray for them rather than willing the earth to open up and swallow them.

He looks me in the eye, nods slightly, and says, "Thank you."

I want to press him, to ask if he'll really read it, or if he'll toss it into the nearest trash can, but I restrain myself. Instead, I smile, touch my fingers to the slightly bumpy scar on my forehead, and say, "Thank *you*."

He smiles and walks away. As I leave the hospital, I realize I've just given away my last pocket testament. I wonder if Judah has any more.

This little project of ours was his idea. He had to present it to the church board and get their approval. It was granted, but they said he'd have to fund them himself. So Judah made announcements that he was accepting donations to purchase the booklets and volunteers to pass them out (he received neither). In the end, he and I scraped together enough money of our own to buy thirty. We divided them up equally. Three weeks later we'd given them all away, so we ordered more.

We'd been handing them out for about six months now. It was still just us, but Judah, the eternal optimist, kept on promoting the idea at church, certain that it would eventually catch on.

We had dedicated all our change to the project. Judah called it "partnershipping with God" which was a term that I really liked. We agreed, in prayer, that we would pass out as many gospels of John as God gave us money and opportunities for. In exchange, we would contribute all our change—our own and any that we found—we would look for openings to share the gospels, and we would pray for the people who accepted them.

After we did that, I was amazed at how much change I started to "find." It was everywhere. It was never very much: a penny here, a nickel there, a quarter in a couch cushion, but it added up quickly. At first I was tempted not to pick up the pennies; they seemed too small to bother with. But one day, as I spotted one on the sidewalk and debated whether or not I should pick it up, a verse from Luke flashed through my mind. "Anyone who can be trusted in little matters can also be trusted in important matters. But anyone who is dishonest in little matters will be dishonest in important matters." I decided to be trusted with something as small as a penny, so I picked it up. I haven't passed up a coin since, no matter what the denomination.

I wanted to call Judah before church that week to see if he had any extras, but somehow I never made the time. It isn't until I run into him on the stairs at church that I get the chance to talk to him.

"Brooke! Girlfriend!" Judah pushes his heavy black glasses up his nose before bending down to give me a bear hug. Then he holds me out at arm's length and scrutinizes my forehead. "Ouch."

I maneuver a dreadlock over the scar self-consciously. "It's fine, really. Hey, have you got any more pocket testaments? I gave my last one away a few days ago."

"Nope. Sorry. Guess it's time we ordered more." He sighs heavily. "I wish the church would get on board. Then we could order more than a few at a time."

I shrug. "Partners with God, remember? He provides the money and the testaments. Not our department."

He grins.

"Wish the church would get on board with what?" growls a deep voice behind me. It's our pastor, Javier Marrero, who is a great guy, very compassionate. He's short and squat and looks like a human bulldog, which could be why he has the kids call him Pastor Pug. They all really love him, from the little ones right on up to the college kids. His wife Evie is a tall, willowy woman who is so soft-spoken she barely speaks above a whisper.

Judah shifts his weight from foot to foot clearly uncomfortable being caught saying something that could be construed as critical of the church. "I only meant that I wish . . . ."

I cut him off before he can finish. "We've been giving away a lot of the gospel of John books," I explain. "We're all out. We just wish there was a stockpile in one of the closets or something, so we could stock up again."

"Isn't there?" He looks puzzled. "I thought I saw some in the pastor's study."

We follow him as he charges down the stairs and bursts through the doors of the pastor's study, his study. From the closet he pulls down a medium-sized box. Ripping the flaps open he reveals stacks of little gospels. He looks positively tickled as Judah and I stare at the treasure trove with stunned expressions.

"But I thought the church decided we had to do our own fund-raising for the money to buy them?" Judah asks, trying to make sense of what's in front of us.

"Oh, you do," the pastor agrees. Then he holds up his hands like a traffic cop. "Not my decision. I would have given you the money in a heartbeat. If I had to, I'd rob Peter to pay Paul any day if Paul was handing out the gospel."

"Then where did these come from?" Judah blurts out, apparently unable to stand the suspense any longer.

"I ordered them," Pastor Javier says. "With my own money. I didn't rob Peter, Paul, or a bank. Evie and I prayed about it, and we like what you're doing. We wanted to help. They came just this week, and I've been so very anxious to show them to you. Please, take as many as you want."

Judah and I grab bundles, big, stupid grins on our faces. I stash them in my messenger bag. And then I can't help it. I throw an arm around Pastor Javier and give him a quick one-armed hug. "Thank you so much!"

"So is it still only you the two of you?" he asks, frowning.

"So far," Judah says, "but you never know when God will move someone to join us."

"Indeed you do not," Pastor Javier agrees heartily. "Meanwhile, keep up the good work you two. These will be in the closet in case you run out."

Pastor Javier always moves fast, and he's out the door and barreling off somewhere else before Judah and I have even started to leave the study.

"See? What did I tell you?" I ask Judah, punching him in the arm.

"Ow, stop. What? What did you tell me?"

"God will provide the testaments. And he did, didn't he?"

He grins. "He did," he agrees. "And we didn't even need any money."

"If God can make stones into children of Abraham, I guess he can make gospels of John from thin air."

We laugh as we make our way to the room where a bunch of us meet before church to study the Bible and pray. At least, that's what we're supposed to be doing. What mostly happens is that the leader will pontificate while everyone else listens. Sometimes that's not a bad thing; it depends on the leader. But most of the time it's not ideal. The prayer is usually along the lines of, "Does anyone have a prayer request? Raise your hand. God sees all those hands, and He knows what's on your heart. Let's pray." And then a blanket prayer is offered. This was apparently because someone decided it was taking too long to pray for requests. That's when they started this method instead. The thing is, when you have a prayer request and your heart is hurting, you want someone to really *pray* for you.

I just can't help wishing it was, I dunno, a little more *real*. That makes me think of Rocko and how he'd described the prayer meeting I'd lead as "real." I wondered if he felt the same way I did about the way church was conducted in general, though I doubted anyone would really care what either of us thought about it.

Today, Pastor Javier is leading. We settle back to listen, which is about all we're expected to do unless the leader asks a question, but we're in for a surprise.

"I'd like to do things a little differently today," Pastor Javier says. "Let's pull our chairs into a circle. Starting on my left, I'd like us to take turns sharing just one Bible verse that God used to speak to you this week."

I feel a frisson of excitement shoot through my body. Immediately my brain starts sifting through all the Bible verses God has used to communicate His truth to me throughout the week. There are so many choices; which will I share?

Before I can settle on one, Pastor Javier turns with a smile to the person on his left who happens to be Diana Wallace. She's shifting uncomfortably in her chair, but as soon as everyone's attention rests expectantly on her, she sits bolt upright, her lips pressed into a thin line.

"For God so loved the world that he gave his only begotten son that whosoever believeth in him will not perish but have everlasting life," she recites, her words coming out with the staccato of machine gun fire.

Pastor Javier's smile falters a little, but he nods at her encouragingly. "Yes, thank you Diana. And how did God speak to you through that verse this week?"

Instead of answering him she turns and stares pointedly at her husband Trevor in the chair next to her. He's been fumbling in his Bible, and he looks up when he registers the sudden, uncomfortable silence. When he sees that the attention in the room has shifted to him, he goes a little red. But he smiles and closes his Bible slowly.

"I'd have to say that the verse about God helping those who help themselves really spoke to me this week," Trevor says.

"That's not in the Bible," Judah whispers loudly in my ear, incredulous. "That's a Benjamin Franklin quote!"

I shush him, but not before a couple people look our way.

"I've just really felt God working with me this week," Trevor is saying. "I've had some big projects that had to be finished at work. I really pushed myself, you know? And God was there for me. He didn't let me down." He smiles, looking relieved, and turns to the person next to him.

The circle limps around eventually to Judah who waves one of the little pocket testament books before he starts speaking. I can tell he's going to give our little project a plug while he's at it.

"Yeah, I've been reading a lot from the gospel of John this week because we've been passing them out to people. I just really love that gospel, you know? I love how it emphasizes how Jesus was fully human and fully divine because he was filled with the Spirit of God. Man, there are some really inspirational verses in that book. It's hard to pick just one.

"Diana had a good one," he says, nodding at Diana who snaps to attention at the sound of her name. "But I guess the one that spoke to me the most this week was John 14:3: 'And if I go and prepare a place for you, I will come again and receive you to Myself; that where I am, there you may be also.' God's preparing a place for me; that's just so awesome. I mean, you know, he's preparing a place for all of us. Knowing that really helped me through some tough times this week. We're not stuck here; we've got somewhere else to go, a place where there is no pain, no sorrow, no stupid attacks on innocent people." His hand rests briefly on my shoulder and for a second everyone looks at me, probably wondering what he's talking about. "In the Contemporary English Version, at the end of that verse Jesus says, 'Then we will be together.'" He sighs heavily. "I can't wait to be together with God in heaven."

"I'm having a difficult time with a co-worker," I say when it's my turn, "and God's been using 2 Timothy 2:23-26 to help me." I flip open my Bible and read it out loud. "He's been showing me when an argument is stupid and foolish and when it's something I should stand up for. And it's nice to know he's in my corner, cheering me on. It's hard to pray for your enemies in the middle of a battle, but when I keep this verse in mind and try to understand that maybe God will save them because of something I say, or don't say, during a confrontation, it keeps me focused on their ultimate salvation and helps me try to say and do only things that will lead them to Christ."

One by one everyone around the circle shares something. Admittedly, it's touch and go; some people seem much more willing to participate while others resist, their answers stilted and rote. It seems more like they are trying to regurgitate the correct answer for a professor than share a moment from their relationship with God. I remind myself that sharing personal things doesn't come easily to everyone. It doesn't come easily to me, either, but I've discovered that the more interactive my relationship with God is, the easier it is to share it with other people. I'm not passing on something I've read in a book; I'm introducing someone to the God of the universe and that's so exciting I tend to forget all about myself.

Next, Pastor Javier leads us all through a responsive reading of Psalm 136. He reads the first part of each verse and we respond with the conclusion, "For his mercy endures forever." It's a powerful reading. By the time we get the last few verses I want to shout. "Who remembered us in our lowly state, For His mercy endures forever; And rescued us from our enemies, For His mercy endures forever."

I can tell I'm not the only one affected by the reading. The collective volume in the room has risen as the Psalm progressed. Even the people who seemed uncomfortable at the start of the session appear more relaxed. Mrs. Swift, who is sitting directly across from me, has tears in her eyes.

I wish we could sing a praise song next, but Pastor Javier closes us with prayer and people start to shuffle out of the room. Judah bolts out first because he needs to get something set up for the service. I pick up my things and turn to leave, but before I can follow Judah out, a soft touch on my arm stops me.

"Brooke?"

It is Mrs. Swift. Her voice is so soft that it is really more a feat of lip-reading than hearing that I know she's spoken my name at all.

"Yes?"

"I . . . I wanted to thank you for leading out at the prayer meeting last week. It was very . . . that is, I received a blessing from it. And I wanted to ask you, there was a Bible verse you mentioned. I meant to write it down, but I was distracted. Can you tell me what it was again?" She fumbles in her purse for a pen and paper. "It was very comforting to me at the time, and I wanted to share it with my sister."

I sift through my mind wondering which one of the Bible verses I shared that night, a week and a half ago, might have comforted her, when a verse rises effortlessly to the top. "Was it, 'Sing to God, sing praises to his name; lift up a song to him who rides upon the clouds—his name is the Lord—be exultant before him. Father of orphans and protector of widows is God in his holy habitation.'? That's Psalm 68:4 and 5."

Her eyes light up. "That's it! The very one. Thank you!" She scribbles it down and then her gaze travels up to the barely visible bandage on my forehead. I touch it self-consciously.

"What happened to you . . . to your, ah, head?" I can tell she has to struggle to overcome her natural shyness in order to ask, and her concern touches me.

"I was hit in the head with a bottle. Some teens, apparently on a rampage. It was right outside the church after prayer meeting, actually." I try to say this lightly. I'm not looking for sympathy.

Mrs. Swift's mouth drops open. "That's terrible!" she says, somewhat louder than she intended apparently because her hand flies to cover her mouth, and she drops her voice to repeat, "That's terrible! Are you okay?"

"I'm fine," I assure her. "In fact, at the hospital they told me it was a miracle. I could have been hurt much worse. So, you see, God was watching over me."

She clucks her tongue and pats my arm consolingly. "Well, I'm glad you're okay, dear." She's repeating, "That's just terrible," under her breath as she turns to make her way into the sanctuary.

Before I can leave raised voices freeze me in my tracks. The doorway where I'm standing is partially concealed from the rest of the room by a bookcase. Out of my line of sight I can hear the angry voices of Diana Wallace, her husband Trevor, and Elder Fortin. They are apparently complaining to Pastor Javier about the change in format.

". . . is not the way we do things around here," Diana is saying stridently. "If you are going to make a major change like that you need to clear it with the board. I happen to know they would never have approved what you've done here today."

"The church puts out materials for the members to study for a specific purpose," her husband argues reasonably. "What would happen if every member went off on their own and studied whatever they liked? There'd be chaos. No, they need someone to guide them, someone official. That way no error is taught and everyone is on the same page. Am I making sense?"

"I've been a member here for 40 years," Elder Fortin puts in, not to be outdone, "and we have certain . . . approved . . . ways of doing things. This is not one of them. I resent being put on the spot here today. Not only that, but this chanting of Bible verses is highly inappropriate."

"And it had better not happen again if you want to keep your position here." Diana's voice is so angry she can barely speak, and her words come out with a hiss.

Pastor Javier starts to reply, but his voice is so low and so calm that I can't hear him, and before I can strain my ears to try, I realize I'm eavesdropping and that I need to leave. I spin around quickly and almost run into Judah who has come back to look for me. Before he can say my name and reveal the fact that we're both close enough to hear the conversation continuing on in the room, I grab his arm and hustle him to the sanctuary.

"What's going on?" he demands.

"Mrs. Swift stopped me to talk," I say. I debate with myself about whether or not I should share the gist of the conversation I've just overheard. I decide he probably ought to know. "And some people were giving Pastor Javier a hard time about changing up the class like he did."

Judah's face darkens. "I'm not surprised," he says morosely. "Any time we deviate from the set order of things it seems like someone complains about it."

I worry that I shouldn't have said anything. This falls under the purview of Judah's biggest pet peeve and is probably the very reason he actually seems to enjoy being friends with me, someone who seems to be on the fringe. He is opposed to how obstinately the church clings to formalism. He doesn't like how the service marches rigidly from start to finish never allowing God's Spirit to change any of it for fear of running over the allotted time. "I mean, what are we here for, anyway?" he'll demand if you give him the slightest opportunity to spout off on the subject. "To check off points in the bulletin or to worship God?"

I don't like it, but sometimes I agree with him. There are times when church feels weird, like it is apropos to nothing. Like all it exists for is some weekly roll call where everyone puts in an appearance and gets accounted for. We go through the motions of worship without actually worshiping. It's like we're playing church. I wonder why we bother. I wonder why *I* bother.

I sit near Judah, right up front in the center where he likes to be. As the service progresses I find my mind wandering. While the announcements drone on and the offering is collected and a little girl with an adorable lisp sings, "What a Friend We Have in Jesus" for special music, my mind keeps returning to one phrase and it rings through my brain like a clarion call. "For his mercy endures forever." Throughout the service I praise and thank God for his mercy toward me, and when the service is over I feel like Mary, like I've been camped out at the feet of Jesus all day.

It doesn't surprise me when the following week the Bible study before church is back to its old format. It doesn't surprise me, but it does disappoint me.

Chapter Four

I wake up screaming. Fortunately, when I gasp awake I realize the sound only exists in my nightmare. There are no irate, groggy neighbors pounding on the walls yelling at me to shut up. The darkness of my room is filled instead with a rasping, choking sound coming from my throat, and my face is wet with tears. My heart slams against my chest wall, and it is a few terrible moments before I can make myself realize that it is only a dream that has woken me up.

I've had this dream before, many times. I know there will be no going back to sleep, so I climb wearily out of bed and reach for a sweater duster that is draped over a chair at the foot of the bed. I shiver as I slip into it and clamp it around myself, more because of the remnants of the dream than the cold. It felt real because it had been real. Before, Lily used to get up with me, make me hot chocolate, and let me cry on her shoulder.

Now there is only the empty apartment.

No, I remind myself. Not empty. God is here. He is my comforter now.

I take my Bible off the kitchen table where I'd left it the night before and curl up with it on the couch. I go directly to the Psalms. King David seems to have spent as much time as I do awake in the wee hours agonizing over the past. I read psalm after psalm and only stop when the racing of my heart finally slows down.

In the dream, I had been a child lying on my bed, paralyzed with fear as I watched my bedroom door creak open, light from the living room beyond silhouetting my brother Neil. It was a scene I'd lived through dozens of times, and I couldn't seem to shake it. For a second, before I can stop it, my mind flashes back to my first awkward kiss with a boy and how much it felt like the unwanted kisses of my brother, until the guy had stuck his tongue in my mouth. I had almost thrown up.

But it hadn't salvaged the experience. I couldn't separate the feeling of being kissed by a boy from being kissed by my brother during the dark, terrifying nights when he'd slipped into my room and molested me.

I'd been so young—7 years old—when it started that all it had taken to keep my mouth shut was the threat of taking my cat for a drive and dumping him miles from home. After he'd gone, I'd cry myself to sleep with my ear pressed up against the cat's warm fur.

To this day I hate cats.

Lily wanted to get a kitten when we had our first apartment. One cat was allowed and a co-worker of hers was trying to unload some kittens. Lily wanted one so much she'd brought it home as a surprise. Unfortunately, the surprise was in how vehemently I'd objected. She'd been crying when I made her return it immediately.

I still feel badly about that. But I can't even think about cats without feeling my skin crawl.

I don't think my parents ever knew what he'd done. Fortunately, once he graduated from law school we never saw much of Neil. He moved out west and didn't come back. Not even for Christmas. I'm not sure he even called Mom and Dad. If he did, they never mentioned it.

That didn't stop them from idolizing him. I suppose it was impressive that he got a job with a prestigious law firm in Seattle directly out of law school. He became a named partner faster than anyone in the firm's history and had a reputation for being a hotshot attorney. Some of his cases were so large they made the national news. It was strange seeing glimpses of him on television. Strange and terrifying.

It was inevitable that my parents compared the two of us and that I always came up short. I flunked out of college my first time around, and I came out not long after that. They tried the "why can't you be more like your brother?" line, but needless to say, it never had its intended effect on me. The last person on earth I wanted to be like was my brother.

People who don't know I'm gay sometimes discuss what makes someone a homosexual when I'm around. They debate nature versus nurture. I don't say much, but in my case, I don't think there's much doubt about what formed my homosexuality. I do sometimes wonder if I would have been gay anyway and Neil just helped me along that path, but I can't see past the abuse. I can't remember the innocent girl I was before he raped me, so it's impossible for me to know.

Lily is bisexual, and her story is similar to my own only it was her grandfather who molested her when she was a teenager. I guess he had been quite the ladies' man in his day, charming and rich, and he'd bribed her for what he called their "special time." Lily told me that she'd grown up in such poverty that she'd found it impossible to resist his offer even though she felt soiled afterward and continued, even when I knew her, to struggle with her self-esteem.

It wasn't until she'd aborted her grandfather's child and the procedure went badly that her mother found out. Preferring to believe her father's side of the story and accusing Lily of sleeping around with her boyfriend instead, her mother had kicked her out of the house at sixteen. According to Lily, she'd spent a few years homeless, trying to finish up high school. She'd gotten into the usual trouble: drugs, sex, petty theft. Eventually she turned herself around enough to keep a job at a local co-op which is where I'd met her. She'd had a few girlfriends in high school, she'd told me, when she'd "experimented with her sexuality" while bored or high and decided that she liked being "flexible," as she called it.

Lily and I are by no means poster children for the LGBT community. I believe I had been shaped by circumstances; perhaps others are shaped by genetics. What I did know was that no matter the sin, and I mean any kind of sin, sexual or not, the only means of salvation is the blood of Jesus Christ. So in the end, it doesn't really matter what caused my homosexuality, it only matters what saves me from the practice of it. And that is a day by day, sometimes hour by hour, commitment to follow Jesus and his Word as he leads me to understand it.

There are days when I spend the majority of my time praying for God to deliver me from an overwhelming urge to contact Lily. At times I almost wish I was a recovering drug addict or an alcoholic instead of a homosexual. Other vices or handicaps always seem preferable to the ones we struggle with. I envy others their support group; there is no one I can lean on except God. But ironically, I think that very reliance is what strengthened my relationship with him to the point that he is my first and best friend. The more I rely on him for strength, the closer we become.

There is a flash of lightning from outside that lights up the sky for an instant. Great, I'll probably get rained on going to the bakery this morning. I check my watch and see that it's almost time for me to leave. I forsake the warmth of the couch to press my nose up against the window and try to determine if it's raining yet. I don't have a television; I don't have time for it, and it will take too long to boot up my cranky computer to check online, so I'll have to make my best guess. Better bring my battered umbrella.

I'm preoccupied with my thoughts, so I'm almost glad that Derrick has his screamo blaring when I get to the bakery. He's surprisingly quiet, and we get through the morning without incident. It's almost a pleasant experience, and if I wasn't so tired I'd be doing a little dance as I leave for school.

With a fresh stock of gospels in my messenger bag, I head to class knowing that one of them has Professor McCormick's name on it. I don't even have Economics and Psychology today, but I am so determined to give the professor a gospel that I make a detour to his building on my way home even though I'm bone-tired by then. As I walk into his classroom I realize I have completely forgotten the zombie meeting. I'm on the verge of making an about-face when Professor McCormick sees me and motions me in. Reluctantly, I come in and take a seat near the back. They seem to be wrapping things up.

One of the kids is passing around a handout and thinking I'm just late to the meeting he sets one on the table in front of me. It's a list of disaster preparedness gear. Professor McCormick is telling everyone they should bring a pack containing at least some of the items by the next meeting. It's when they begin to file out that I realize some of them have come in actually made up as zombies.

The professor himself looks nothing like his usual tall, bookish, rather distinguished-looking self. It's like he's dressed for casual army Friday in wrinkled khaki shorts, a rumpled camo T-shirt, and running shoes. In fact, he looks as though he might have gone for a quick jog before the meeting.

"Hello, Jesus Girl," Professor McCormick says as the door shuts behind the last student. "Are you here to get ready for the zombie apocalypse?"

I walk to the front and sit in a chair directly in front of his desk, the place we secretly call the "hot seat" because if you're in it, you're usually getting a lecture on not giving your Economics and Psychology work your best effort. "Is that what they're doing?" I tip my head in the direction of the exiting students.

"Sure, we're all getting ready for the zombies. Don't you know there's going to be a zombie apocalypse? Run for your life." His voice gets high and false as he mocks the idea. Then he leans toward me and says in an undertone. "I grant you, that's what some of these guys are here for, and I let them think that's what it's all about. We're getting ready to defend ourselves from the zombies. But really," his eyes twinkle, and he winks at me, "they're sitting through disaster preparedness training. And they *want* to learn this stuff. It's awesome.

"I used to hold plain old disaster preparedness seminars, but you know what? Nobody's interested. I'd get a handful of kids, mostly survivalist or humanitarian types. This is not going to save us in the event of a major disaster. We need training on a much bigger scale." His face loses a little of its animation for a moment, and I can see a deep sadness in his eyes. "Believe me, I've studied many cultures whose existence was extinguished as a result of a natural disaster. I don't want to watch it happen to my own. Not if I can help it."

"You think we're headed for a major disaster?" I ask.

"You don't?" he counters. He holds up his hand and starts ticking points off on his fingers. "Look at the superspreading that happened with SARS. All we need is another coronavirus to morph one tiny little bit, and we're toast. A pandemic only needs to win once, you know what I'm saying? Of course, if a virus doesn't get us, it's likely the environment will. Storms are getting more powerful, pollution is . . . I can't even talk about pollution without getting angry at what we're doing to this planet. You see where I'm headed here? Earth has one foot in the grave and the other on a banana peel, if you get my drift. It's not going to get any better than this, I can assure you. But it's bound to get a whole lot worse before it's all over." A red flush has started to spread up Professor McCormick's neck, and his voice is rising in volume.

I bob my head in a neutral way that I hope is placating. He seems to realize he is working himself up because he suddenly looks chagrined.

"I'm sorry," he says, and laughs nervously. "I'm a little passionate about this topic. Can you tell?"

"No need to apologize," I assure him. "I can see you care a great deal." I join his laughter to put him at ease and diffuse any tension. "I didn't realize there was more to it than zombies. So you don't actually believe we'll be forced to protect ourselves from zombies, then?"

"Of course I believe that," he corrects me quickly, completely serious. "Oh, not your Hollywood type of zombie necessarily. But do I think a coronavirus could mutate into something that infects most of the population and spreads from person to person causing us to turn on one another? Absolutely. No question."

"Was it a joke? The poster? Claiming to be from the CDC?"

"That? No, it's real. You can download them right off their website. Of course they don't believe in the popular zombie view any more than I do, but that's where I got the idea to hold zombie apocalypse workshops instead of plain old disaster preparedness ones. Same trick they pulled; it makes it more fun and gets people interested." He shrugs. "Really, when it comes to something as important as this? Whatever it takes, you know what I'm saying?"

I laugh. "It's certainly a novel approach," I agree. "You've put an awful lot of thought into how the world might end. Do you believe in God?" The question seems to catch him off guard and he hesitates. One beat, then two.

"No," he says finally, but without conviction.

"Why?" I ask quietly.

His eyes don't meet mine. "I did. A long time ago. But I don't anymore."

"What happened?" Even though my question is gentle I see his face close up and become guarded and hard.

"It was a long time ago," he says again.

I pull a gospel of John out of my bag and turn it over in my hands, my fingers running along the edges. I'm suddenly having doubts about offering it to him. Maybe I should wait until another time, a better opening.

"What's that?" he asks, jerking his head at the book, forcing my hand. I pray quickly for the Holy Spirit to guide me, to give me the right words.

"It's the gospel of John," I say, deciding it's best not to cloak my intentions. I think he will appreciate it if I'm forthright with him.

"You've got a lot of nerve," he sneers. "Is that why they call you Jesus Girl? You go around converting people like John the Baptist or something?"

I swallow hard, praying for God to take the sting out of his words. I'd been enjoying our conversation. I thought we had a rapport. I was beginning to like him as a person. His scorn is difficult to bear.

"Jesus is my Lord and Savior," I say evenly. "That's why they call me—Derrick calls me—Jesus Girl. He means it as an insult, of course, but it's a name I'm proud to own."

Professor McCormick starts picking up his papers, shoving them hastily into his briefcase. I take it I'm dismissed. I stand up and turn to go.

"Leave it," he barks.

I hold my breath, afraid that the slightest move on my part will change his mind. Slowly, as if I am approaching a rattlesnake, I reach out and place the little book as invitingly as possible on the corner of his desk.

"Goodnight," I whisper as I walk away, still afraid I might undo the Holy Spirit's work with one false move. He doesn't reply, and it's not until I reach the sidewalk outside that I dare to take a full breath of air. I spend the entire walk home praying for God to lead Professor McCormick to read the gospel and reveal himself in such a way that the professor will have no doubts about how much God loves him and wants a relationship with him.

Judah calls me the day after his Wednesday night prayer meeting. "They like you better than me," he announces in a hurt tone that sounds, frankly, a tad melodramatic.

"They do not," I reply mildly.

"They do," Judah counters. "Rocko said that when you were the leader it was 'real'. He wanted to know when you were coming back. What I want to know is, what did you do?" he demands.

"I didn't do anything, honestly." I have to admit, even the possibility that they liked me *as much as* Judah feels like a warm blanket around my heart. "We just prayed and stuff."

"Well, will you come with me and 'pray and stuff' again next week so I can see how you don't 'do anything' that is 'so real'?"

I can't help it. He makes me laugh. Despite the fact that it's a punishing time of the day to do anything, and I know I'll pay for it the next day at work and at school, I agree. "I'll be there."

"I knew you'd do it!" Judah crows triumphantly. "Thanks, girlfriend!"

I roll my eyes even though he can't see me. "You're giving me a ride home afterward, though," I inform him, thinking of my last trip home from Wednesday night prayer meeting via the hospital.

"Deal!" Judah isn't hard to persuade.

It feels strange to find myself at the church the next Wednesday. Everything is the same, but different. I'm not so nervous this time. Nobody expects me to lead out for one thing. The wall of disapproval is just as high, just as strong, but now I sense gaps through which light shines. I feel like a prisoner who has been kept in darkness so long that those pinpoints of light are almost as good as full sun.

Rocko catches my eye and flashes me a hand sign that I take to mean, "glad to see you" or something along those lines. He is almost smiling.

"How is Sibby?" I ask him, and an actual smile manifests itself.

"Dude, she's good. She's back at the shelter. They got her on meds, ya know, but I think they're helping. They let her help out in the kitchen and the worst thing that happened was that she burnt the toast. She said it was on account of she couldn't see the toast very well." I laugh with him about this, and he seems genuinely happy that I asked.

On her way to a seat, Mrs. Swift drops a soft bundle in my lap.

"I made you a little something," she says, her smile faltering and hesitant.

"Thank you," I gush spontaneously. Her gesture is so unexpected that I hug the package to my chest in gratitude. Diana is glaring at our exchange, but I don't care. Mrs. Swift appears pleased to have made me happy. She takes her seat, opens her Bible, and looks up expectantly, waiting for the meeting to start.

As Judah gets the meeting underway I'm pleasantly surprised to see that people are much more open asking about prayer this time. As we pray for each other it feels like the Holy Spirit moves powerfully and people share even deeper as they are praying, asking God for help with very personal problems. I am moved to tears by the time we are finished. The atmosphere in the room seems so fresh with the presence of the Holy Spirit that I want to take deep gulps of it.

When I open my eyes, I see Diana scribbling away in a notebook. She looks very determined and not at all happy, and I feel a flash of fear. I try to signal my concern to Judah, but he's been swept away by the power of the meeting, and he's busy asking people to form prayer partnerships so they can continue to pray for each other and support each other during the week.

Rocko raises his hand, but before Judah has a chance to call on him he says, "Dude, isn't it about time we take this show on the road?"

"What do you mean?"

"Witnessing, that's what I mean," Rocko says. "There's a lot of hurting people out there, ya know? I say we pick a few places, the shelter or someplace like that, and we get out there and do some good."

"We could do that," Judah agrees, his voice rising with

excitement. "In fact, that's a great idea. We could form a couple groups, see what the needs are, and split up to cover them."

"After you get the board's approval," Diana interjects like a challenge.

"Uh, sure, after that," Judah falters, probably wondering, as I am, why the board would object to an outreach project. Still, it's always best to move through official channels. Judah seems to reach the same conclusion. "I'll make sure that suggestion goes before the board."

Rocko slumps back in a gesture of disgust and frustration. "Yeah, whatever."

I understand where he's coming from. Immediately following my conversion I was so excited and full of ideas I tried to instigate a number of outreach projects. They all failed miserably. At the time, I was disappointed, but I never considered it was because the church didn't support them. I had always assumed it was because they didn't support *me*. It made me gun-shy about proposing any more. Now, looking at Rocko's face, I'm not so sure. Maybe I'm not the only one who has been thwarted in outreach attempts.

I smile at him encouragingly, but it does nothing to remove the scowl from his face. Diana is underlining something fiercely in her notebook, and I wonder uncomfortably what exactly she's writing down in there. Why is she making notes at a prayer meeting? She hasn't been participating in the meeting, and she seems pretty upset. I wish I could approach her after, ask her what's going on. But we don't exactly have that kind of relationship.

When I ask Judah on the drive home if he knows what was going on with her scribbling, he gives me a blank look. "What do you mean?"

"She was taking notes through the whole prayer meeting. And she didn't look very happy, either."

"Seriously?" His brow furrows, and I realize he was on such a spiritual high he didn't even notice. That makes me kind of jealous. I feel a bit like I've been robbed of some happiness I could have had tonight, like I've been pickpocketed by Satan.

There's no doubt in my mind that we're involved in spiritual warfare, that Satan and his demons are trying to turn us from our allegiance to Jesus. I believe literal spiritual battles are fought every day to get us to change sides. But when Satan peeks out from behind the curtain like this and sticks his tongue out at me, I get really mad about it.

"It went well, though. Don't you think?" Judah is asking.

"It was very moving. Very powerful," I agree, deciding that it would be best to put Diana and her possible nefarious motives right out of my mind.

"You'll be my prayer partner this week, won't you?"

I smile. "Of course I will."

"And you'll come back for prayer meeting next week?"

I groan. "Judah, you know how hard it is for me to stay up this late."

"You'll try?" he presses. He's not the type of person to take no for an answer.

"I'll try." I sigh.

At home, I slowly peel the paper off the present from Mrs. Swift. A colorful pair of socks, gaily sporting splashes of raspberry and spring green, plop onto my lap. I'm so touched by her generosity that I actually start to cry. I'm practically sobbing as I pull the beautiful socks onto my feet and gaze at them admiringly. It's one of the nicest things anyone's ever done for me.

I can't bear to cover them up when I go to bed, so I leave my feet sticking out from the covers like twin beacons of kindness, and I fall asleep praising God for nice people like Mrs. Swift, and I ask him to watch over her and to bless her.

The next morning, when my alarm goes off at two thirty, I feel surprisingly refreshed. Usually, I'm halfway through my shower before I even start to wake up. This morning I feel as though I've overslept, and I check my alarm clock against my wristwatch to be sure it hasn't lost time.

As I'm spooning applesauce into my granola, I start to wonder if this is God's doing. If he has honored my participation in the evening prayer meeting by making me more refreshed today. I love it when God works in my life like this; I love discovering his acts of benevolence toward me. Most people would call them coincidences, but I know better.

"Thank you, Lord," I say out loud. "You know that Judah wants me to be at Wednesday night prayer meeting every week, and I feel as though you're beginning to bless it. I'd really like to be there, except you know how tired it makes me. But as long as you help me wake up on Thursday mornings, I'll keep going."

As I step out the door to head to the bakery, I feel not only as though I'd gotten my normal amount of sleep; I feel as though I'd gotten *extra* sleep. The short walk to the bakery doesn't seem like nearly enough time to praise God for such a blessing.

Chapter Five

The holidays hit me—or rather anxiety about the holiday season—the first week of December. Judah had invited me to his folks' for Thanksgiving, so I managed to get through that without being too lonely on my own. I haven't been back to celebrate the holidays with my own family since I left home. But December is different. I can feel it almost the same way I feel a shift in the weather. So the morning I wake up having one of "those days" is not exactly a surprise. They hit me sometimes, and I dread them.

I don't know how it is for other people, but when I have a "bad day," I am overwhelmed by the guilt of my past and the unfairness of my current situation.

No one will ever love me!

I will be misunderstood and vilified until I die!

I will never have my own family!

This is all the work of Satan, and I know that in the same way I know that the sky is blue. The trouble is that when that weight of guilt and unfairness hits me, it's so breathtakingly painful that I just want to curl up into a little ball under my covers and cry until I fall asleep hoping that it will be gone the next day.

That's not exactly helpful, so instead, I pray my way through it. The first time it happened I was confident that God would just remove it. After all, intellectually, I *know* that Jesus died for my sins. I know that nothing I have done can prevent me from being with him someday in heaven. I know that he's enough for me in every situation I face; he makes up every deficiency in my life. I have no spouse? Jesus is my spouse. I have no children? I have Jesus. No one really understands me? Jesus understands me. People despise me? Jesus loves me. There is nothing in my life, no situation or circumstance, that having Jesus doesn't compensate for a thousand times over.

I know this in my head. But the pressure on my heart is more than I can bear. Satan bombards me with my guilt. Scenes of my former sins play out relentlessly in my head. Dire projections about my future present themselves to me: myself, alone and unloved as I age inexorably onward. I see myself on my deathbed, dying of AIDS (not that I even *have* AIDS), totally alone. I imagine Lily, in another relationship, happy and in love, and I feel a surge of jealousy. The knife edge of pain slips between my ribs when I imagine the children

I *could* have had but won't.

Images like this run through my head on a constant loop. On good days, I pray and the thoughts are banished. I can walk away from them. On bad days, they practically incapacitate me with their ferocity. It's not that I think prayer works some days and not others. I think some days I'm just more vulnerable than others. Some days I'm more willing to give it over to Jesus to carry and other days I have this morbid compunction to give it to him and then take it back and worry over it some more.

Or maybe he is developing in me the ability to be persistent in prayer despite a seeming lack of results. Or maybe the result is that God is developing in me my "prayer muscle". Maybe he is teaching me to lean on him even when I don't seem to get any immediate gratification or results out of it. All I know is that on bad days I pray. A lot.

They say we shouldn't judge others because we don't really know how we would act if we were in their shoes. That if we had been formed by the same circumstances that made them vulnerable to their temptations, we might fall as easily as they do. I try to keep that in mind when I'm having a bad day, because my thoughts tend to naturally go back to my brother Neil. Satan suggests all kinds of ways for me to get back at him from outing him to outright killing him. There are times when my hatred is so fierce I think I could kill him with my bare hands, and that scares me.

One thing I try to keep in mind is that Satan can taunt me about my past or my future all he wants, but my past is covered by the blood of Christ, and my future is safe and secure in his hands. As long as I remember that, the only thing Satan can effectively torment me over is my present. If I stay faithful to God, he can't touch that, either. I don't even have to pay attention to him when he beats me up about my past because I am forgiven.

I say that into my empty apartment. "In the name of Jesus Christ, I command you to leave me alone. By the grace of God I am forgiven!" I shout the last part in a hoarse whisper so as not to arouse the ire of my neighbors, some of whom have been out carousing half the night and wouldn't appreciate being woken up early in the morning which is often the time Satan chooses to attack. That's when I'm the most vulnerable because I'm often tired.

This morning I feel as weak as a kitten and Satan's oppression wears me out further. I have the morning off from the bakery, but I have to get it together to go to class later on. By the time I pick up the phone and call Judah I'm having panic attacks. I'm holding the phone with one hand while the other is clamped to my chest trying to keep my heart from banging its way right through my sternum.

"Are you busy?" I ask him. "Will you pray with me?"

Something in the quality of my voice must indicate that it's urgent. "I'll be right there," he says and hangs up on me.

I didn't expect him to come over. I don't really have the energy to pick up my apartment. Fortunately, with just me here it doesn't get that dirty. While I wait for him, I put on some praise music and make an effort to at least wash my face and pull my dreads up into a tidy knot. I put the breakfast dishes away and stack the textbooks into a pile on the corner of the table. I finish making the bed just as he knocks on the door.

"I brought red tea," he says, offering me a cardboard mug with the logo of our favorite café where I like to get the double red rooibos. "You okay?"

I clutch the tea and shake my head. "No. I don't . . . I just . . . I feel so worthless, so condemned."

"Right." Judah propels me over to the sofa, and we sit down. He pats my knee comfortingly. "Brooke, I'm going to tell you something, and it's very important so I want you to listen carefully. Are you listening?"

I turn off the praise music so it won't be a distraction, nod dutifully because he seems to expect it, and wait with anticipation, giving him my full attention, willing myself to fully absorb whatever he's about to say.

"For God so loved Brooke that he gave his only begotten son so that if Brooke believes in him she will have everlasting life." His paraphrase of John 3:16 almost makes me smile. "Do you believe in Jesus, Brooke?"

"I do."

"Then you will have everlasting life. And that life starts now. We both know that. We know—we agree together like the Bible says in Matthew 18:20—that Satan can't harm a child of God. 'We know that anyone born of God does not continue to sin; the One who was born of God keeps them safe, and the evil one cannot harm them.' We are both children of God here, born of God in our new birth. We both claim the blood of Jesus Christ to cover our sins. Sin is sin, Brooke."

"I know, Judah, but my sin was so great . . ."

"And Jesus is greater. Brooke, listen to me, sin is sin. The Bible says, 'For all have sinned and fall short of the glory of God.' It doesn't say, 'For all have sinned, but some have sinned really bad sins and fall even shorter of the glory of God and he might not be able to save them.' How much we have sinned isn't important. How 'bad' our sin is on a scale of one to ten is not important. Jesus is bigger than any sin we can commit. His blood covers it all."

I know all this, of course, but hearing Judah say it reinforces it in my heart. He's the one who taught me that praying for each other is the most important thing Christians can do for one another, and I've become a firm believer in that truth. When Jesus sent his disciples out, he sent them two by two for a reason; they were stronger in pairs. If one fell, his brother could help him up. I am so thankful to Judah for helping me up.

He's looking at me for some sign that I've heard what he's been saying, that it's making an impression on me. " 'There is therefore now no condemnation to those who are in Christ Jesus, who do not walk according to the flesh, but according to the Spirit,' " I quote from Romans 8:1.

Judah smiles. "I love that verse," he confesses. "Someone put it to music once, and I find it running through my head for no reason or any reason at all." He starts singing it and after a couple times through I am able to join in. We move on from that song to another praise song. Judah's got a really nice voice; mine is not much more than serviceable, but he doesn't seem to mind.

When we're done singing, we pray some more and then Judah says he has to go, and I need to get ready for class. I put on a thick sweater and wear my pretty wool socks that Mrs. Swift knit for me; I've found that they're extremely warm. It's spitting snow as I make my way to class.

For some reason there are an extra number of TAOs patrolling the streets today. I'm not sure if it's because there's just generally more bustle on account of the holiday season, or if they've been tipped off about a potential incident. They're clustered together in groups of three and four, but not until I am almost at the campus do I realize they are bristling with weapons.

The TAOs can come onto the campus—they can go anywhere they

want—but there are relatively few of them wandering around. They seem to be concentrated near the metro stations, and my suspicion is that they've been warned of a possible attack. According to the news there have been some pretty violent demonstrations lately over our growing interference in the Middle East which many claimed was resulting in the mass murder of Christians in that area. Some analysts believe that Christians there would have been wiped out by now had there not been vast numbers converting every day and replacing their fallen brethren.

The campus looks cheerful in the falling snow. There are twinkly lights in the trees and garland has been strung on the brick buildings making them look particularly festive. There's a big wreath hanging on every oak door. I look at it all and wish I felt something besides a dull ache in my midriff. I can't remember if I ever got excited by Christmas, or if that's just one more thing Neil ruined for me.

Most of my classes are light today. I think the professors are as anxious as we are to avoid homework so they'll have less to correct at home. In Economics and Psychology, Professor McCormick is walking around distributing corrected papers. He doesn't make eye contact with me as he drops mine on the desk. I suppress a groan. There's a big D+ at the top in angry red ink. Next to it his scrawling handwriting says, "See me after class, Jesus Girl."

I feel a jolt of fear course through me. I can't afford to flunk out of this class. Is that what he wants to tell me? I give myself a mental shake. I can't be flunking. It's the first time I've gotten a grade lower than a C. True, I am averaging in the high Cs, low Bs, and I'd like to be getting a solid A, but that's not flunking. I barely hear what he says for the remainder of the class, and it's a relief when it's finally over, and I make my way down to the front.

"You wanted to see me, Professor?" I sit in the hot seat, wincing.

He's busying himself with papers on his desk, and it takes a long minute before he looks up. "That's right," he says. He throws the little gospel of John that I gave him onto the desk, and it slides partway across toward me. From the looks of it he's been reading it to tatters. Either that or he accidentally ran over it with his car. "Tell me why you believe that."

"The whole thing?" I squeak in surprise.

He sits down, crosses his legs, and props his chin on his fingers which he's laced together. He studies me carefully through his somewhat smudged glasses. "The whole thing," he confirms. "I want to know why someone like you—by all accounts a bright, intelligent, in some respects, remarkable human being—believes that there's a God up there who not only created us but came down here and lived among us and then died for us and rose from the dead to make up for all our misdoings. What makes you think any of that is real?"

The tornado that's been building in my chest all day suddenly ceases. It's like when Jesus looked out at the storm and said, "Peace, be still." Suddenly, everything is calm and quiet. "I don't think it's real," I say simply, but before his smile of triumph can reach its full potential, I add, "I know it's real."

"You can't *know* it's real," he counters testily. "You can't *prove* it."

"Yes," I say, "I can. It's proved every morning when I wake up, and I'm not living the way I used to; I don't even want to. It's proved when God gives me the strength to get through each day, the strength to ignore insults, forgive people who have hurt me beyond what I am capable of forgiving on my own. When I need answers, and God gives them to me in the Bible, I know He's real. They aren't just random words. He uses them to speak to me; he tells me what I need to hear. I can prove it because I have a relationship that proves it. You can have one, too."

He stares at me, and I'm not sure if I've been weighed in the balance and found wanting. Before he can respond I hear shouting followed by gunfire outside. The big glass window above the professor's head explodes and shards of glass rain onto us. I react before he does; I don't know how. I live in such a sketchy neighborhood I think I'm always poised to flee, but only divine protection can account for what happens.

I reach across the desk, grab the professor by the arm, and yank him sideways. He's much bigger than I so this really shouldn't get us clear of the majority of the glass spray, but it does. We both hurtle off to the side. I am so off balance by the force of our locomotion that I find myself flailing through the air, landing in a heap to the side. The professor lands half on top of me and unfortunately takes the brunt of the blast when the homemade bomb—which is what came sailing through the shattered window—explodes. I realize what it is an instant before it goes off and manage to cover both our heads with the edge of my sweater which, needless to say, shouldn't have been much protection at all, but instead seems to spare us the worst. A chair, the one the professor had been sitting on, is ground zero for the bomb, and the blast sends it rocketing toward us, hitting the professor. I don't see where or how because of the sweater, but when I look up after the explosion he's covered with blood, the source of which I can't locate because I don't dare move him, and he's unconscious.

I dig around in my messenger bag for my cell phone and dial 9-1-1. In a voice that is calmer than I feel capable of producing, I manage to give the operator the details of our emergency and our location. I find out later that the incident—a protest that is actually unrelated to the one that the TAOs had been gearing up for—originated in a different area on campus, so ambulances are already at the college. It is only moments, though it seems longer, before paramedics are rushing into the classroom with a stretcher.

When they turn him, I see a piece of jagged glass lodged in his neck. It's slick with blood, and the only reason I can see it now is that a shaft of light catches it. I expect them to rip it out immediately, but they leave it in instead and pack bandages around it. One of them starts an IV, and they literally sprint for the ambulance with the stretcher.

As the paramedics came in one of them sheared off from the others who began working on Professor McCormick, and he approaches me. "Are you okay?" he asks. "Are you injured?"

I tear my eyes away from Professor McCormick long enough to evaluate myself. I'm covered with blood, but I don't know if it's mine or his. I don't feel any pain. "I don't think I am," I tell him finally. "Nothing hurts."

"Let me check you over just to be safe," he says. By the time he's done, Professor McCormick is gone, and I hope the siren I can hear wailing faintly outside is that of the ambulance rushing him to the hospital. "Where did they take him? Which hospital?" I ask.

"Mercy General, it's closest," he says, after a pause during which he's taking my pulse.

"I want to see him."

"You family?"

"No, just a student. But I want to see him," I insist.

He shrugs. "You can try. He'll be in surgery for awhile by the look of it. Go in tomorrow and see if he made it." The way he says it sounds callous, and he seems to realize that. "He'll be fine," he assures me. "We made it in time. Trust me."

He helps me to my feet and then hurries off, barking a response into the cackling walkie-talkie he whips off the belt at his waist. I take a few wobbly steps before I feel as though I've got my feet back under me. The halls from the classroom to the foyer are completely empty, but outside it's total madness.

There are only two days until winter break, many classes are having tests and special programs so the campus is more crowded than usual. Everywhere I look there seems to be TAOs, police, paramedics, even firefighters and what looks like students from the school's medical program. There is blood spatter on a bench along one sidewalk and more of it stains the trodden snow nearby. A few occupied body bags are lined up along the Boyer-Baden Lab building.

It doesn't occur to me that I'm probably in shock. I just start walking and praying. I pray for the victims. I pray for the medical personnel who are helping. I pray for the families of the injured or dead. I pray for Professor McCormick. And I thank God for intervening. By all rights we should have been hurt a lot worse than we were.

It's chaos at the hospital, too. When I finally make it to the front of the line, the nurse at the desk informs me that since I'm not family I don't have any right to find out how Professor McCormick is doing. She advises me to come back tomorrow (or never) and see him during visitor hours if he makes it (not her exact words). Before I can even inhale enough breath to protest, she hollers, "Next!" and the person behind me body checks me to the side.

I don't know what to do, so I sit down in a chair in the waiting room near the surgical ward, where I figure he must be, and pray. I don't know how long I'm bent over, hands clasped, praying fervently, when I hear a familiar voice.

"You again?" someone exclaims incredulously. I look up to find the med student who removed my stitches when I'd had a concussion come to a dead halt in the corridor down which he had apparently been bustling. "What did you do to yourself this time? Were you in the attack?"

"It's not me; I'm not hurt," I blurt out. "It's my professor, Professor McCormick. We were talking after class, and there was a bomb. No one will talk to me. Can you find out how he is? If he'll . . . live?"

He looks harried and none too happy with the request. "Look, we're really busy. We're treating nearly fifty patients from that incident." At the sight of my crestfallen face his voice softens. "I'll see what I can do. Okay? No promises."

"Thank you."

It's at least an hour later before I see him again.

"He's in recovery. Still in critical, but they think he's going to make it." He cocks an eye at me. "That was quite some injury. They almost lost him twice on the table, but it looks like you got another miracle, huh?" He gives me a funny look. "Seems to happen a lot when you're around."

"It's not me," I mumble. "It happens a lot when God's around."

He laughs. "All right, I walked into that one. Look, there's no way they'll let you see him tonight even if he does regain consciousness which is highly unlikely. Go home. Get some rest. Come back and see how he's doing tomorrow." His eyes narrow. "You got money for a cab ride home? Because it's definitely not safe to be walking anywhere tonight."

I shake my head sheepishly, and he sighs and digs some money out of his pocket.

"This is becoming a habit," he says. He holds some bills out to me, but when I attempt to take them from his hand, I meet resistance. "I want this back," he says sternly. "It's just a loan. Tomorrow, right?"

I nod with a ghost of a smile. "Tomorrow," I promise and he lets go.

The first time Professor McCormick wakes up and sees me sitting by his hospital bed, a few days later, he doesn't look pleased. In fact, he looks downright hostile with a side of frustration. He looks very much like a man who has placed a bet and lost a substantial amount. He very deliberately closes his eyes and appears to go right back to sleep.

The next time he wakes up when I'm there it's two days later. He sighs heavily as though he is resigning himself to something. He isn't allowed to speak yet the nurses have told me. He has a little whiteboard that he uses to scrawl messages to them. He doesn't make an attempt to use it with me.

I had been reading my Bible, and he sees it in my hands. He indicates with a jerk of his head and raised eyebrows that I read aloud. At least, that's how I interpret the gesture. Clearing my throat, I comply.

We continue on like this over the course of a week, working our way through the New Testament, until one day when I show up he says, his voice barely above a ragged whisper, "Where?"

"Where what?" I ask, totally at a loss.

"Where do you go to church? You do *go* to church, don't you?"

"I do," I agree. "Yes, I do. I go to the Remnant Church. It's not far from here."

"When I'm back on my feet, I'd like to go."

I try not to show my shock and pleasure, but I can't help grinning. "Sure! Absolutely. Just say when."

"This doesn't mean you win," he informs me tartly.

"Who said we were fighting?" I ask, my voice so arch that it gets a twitch of the lips out of him that could be mistaken for a smile if you knew him well enough.

Chapter Six

It's not a knock that wakes me up. It's shouting and pounding and then a blood-curdling scream from one of my neighbors who objects violently to being rousted from their bed in the middle of the night. Even though it takes me a few minutes to gather my wits, I'm already in motion scrambling to get dressed. It's a raid, probably by the TAOs. They do this now and then. Apparently it's completely legal. They don't need a search warrant. They don't even need to have probable cause. They are free to act on suspicion, just a vague tip, or no tip at all.

I've seen the one who bangs on my door somewhere before, but it isn't until they are rummaging through my things that I remember he is the one who questioned me at the hospital after my attack. His name tag says "Huang." He doesn't acknowledge remembering me, so maybe he doesn't. There are five of them, and they work their way methodically through my apartment.

I know the drill, so I seat myself at the kitchen table and keep my mouth shut. The first time it happened I made the mistake of offering them coffee or tea. I also went around opening drawers to be helpful. That had just seemed to make them mad, and they ripped the drawers out and dumped everything all over the floor.

Now I just sit quietly and wait for it to end. It's sort of like a very invasive form of airport security. Fortunately, they don't do body cavity searches, although they are allowed to. They've been here a couple times before, and they don't usually stay long. I'm not sure if it's because I don't seem subversive enough to interest them or because my possessions are few, and it simply doesn't take long to examine them.

The one I recognize has come over to the table and is rifling through my books: the textbooks and my Bible. He gives me a long, appraising look when he sees it. Then he picks up one of the gospels that are stacked neatly to one side.

"Do you want one?" I ask him quietly.

"No!" he barks, his head shaking a negative as if to emphasize his point. But moments later, when he seems to think no one is watching him, I see him slip two into his pocket.

"Cold in here," he comments later as the others are finishing up.

"Yes," I agree. "The landlord doesn't like to heat the place. Too expensive."

He doesn't say anything about this, simply files out with the rest of them. They don't even bother to close the door behind them. It's not until later that evening that I realize the temperature in my apartment has risen and that I can take my big woolly sweater off and not shiver. I check the thermometer thinking that maybe it's gotten warmer outside, but it's, in fact, colder than it has been all winter so far.

I start laughing so loudly that I'm afraid I'll disturb my newly warm neighbors. "Heavenly Father, you're incredible! You can even use TAOs for good. Thank you! And please bless Officer Huang as he reads your Word."

I'm still chuckling as I fall asleep that night, warm for the first time since fall.

There are a couple of surprises awaiting me at church that Sabbath. The first is standing possessively beside Judah when he introduces us.

"Brooke, this is my girlfriend, Marissa." Judah has a look on his face that's half abashed and half proud.

Marissa is a tiny little person striving for height on the tallest heels I've ever seen. She has brown hair that falls like a silk sheet across her face and halfway down her back. Her smile is wide and genuine, and she has the frankest brown eyes I've ever seen. There is something very no-nonsense about her, as if you'd have to be very cunning to pull one over on her.

Looking at her, I'm overwhelmed with pain. I think of it as something like phantom limb syndrome, the pain an amputee feels in a missing limb. It isn't that I'm not happy for Judah, I am. It's just that his happiness is due to something I'll never have. I feel pain in my phantom spouse. It's the same when someone I know has a baby. I have phantom children pain. They aren't there and the missing of them causes me pain.

"I'm so happy to meet you," I say, trying to mean it.

"Judah has told me so much about you," she responds in the obligatory way, her voice not at all as I imagined it. She has the smooth, controlled tones of a lawyer. Later I find out it's because she *is* a lawyer. "I hope we can be friends." She seems sincere, and I like her already.

When I reach the room where we have our little before church study group, I find that it's grown. In addition to Marissa, Rocko has brought some friends, one of whom he introduces me to before the meeting starts.

"This is Sibby," he says, a big smile on his face.

A wizened little woman is regarding me through watery blue eyes. She grins, displaying a smile uncluttered by teeth. "I'm very pleased to make your acquaintance," she says, as if I am the queen.

"I'm pleased to make your acquaintance, too," I reply enthusiastically. "I'm so glad you could come today."

"God is my friend," Sibby informs me. "He looks out for me."

"That's what he does," Rocko agrees and pats her on the shoulder. "He watches you real good. You need a lot of looking after."

"Ain't that the truth," she chuckles, blushing modestly. "It's true, it's true. I get into a mess of trouble sometimes, but God always comes and gets me out. He's faithful," she informs me soberly. "He's always faithful."

"That he is," I say.

The second surprise is that apparently the board has "conditionally" accepted our idea for outreach, and we are to be split up into two groups to go out and do a little outreach. Some of us will be going to the battered women's shelter for a Bible study, and the rest of us are going to pack care packages and bring them to the homeless shelter where we will supervise the children for an hour to allow their parents time to work on their résumés.

When we split into groups, Judah says he'll take the battered women's shelter; Rocko is taking the homeless shelter since he knows everyone there.

"Brooke, you coming with me?" Judah asks, but it's more a statement and less a question.

"Actually, I'm going to go with Rocko," I say, trying to keep my voice nonchalant. It doesn't help. I can tell I've hurt his feelings.

"Oh," he says quietly. I know he doesn't understand. Sending a lesbian to a battered women's shelter is like sending a pretty girl to do prison ministry. Sure, good can come of it, but why make things harder than they have to be? The last thing I want or need is to be surrounded by emotionally vulnerable women who are justifiably hating on men. But I can't explain that to Judah, so I keep my mouth shut.

Rocko looks kind of pleased that I've decided to join his group, as if having the lesbian in his group gives us more street cred with the homeless or something. I try to remind myself that he's just a kid, and he means well. To tell the truth, I find it refreshing that someone likes me without reservation, no matter what the reason is. It's kind of nice.

There is yet another surprise awaiting me when we return to church. Professor McCormick is sitting bolt upright in a pew closest to the door as though he wants to be sure he can escape if they threaten to lock us in. He's been buttonholed by Diana Wallace who is peppering him with questions about why he's here.

When she asks him what his interests are, it's like watching a train wreck in slow motion. I see the glint in his eye and know he's about to be perverse just to spite her. "Actually," he's saying as I walk up hoping to prevent the next words out of his mouth, "I'm a doomsday prepper. I teach the students how to prepare for the zombie apocalypse. That's something we all need to be ready for, don't you agree?"

Diana's mouth has formed into a little moue of disapproval. "Why, no, of course not! I don't think that at all! The Bible is very clear on what will happen during the end times, and there is absolutely no mention of zombies or any other hideous creatures. If you'll take the time to read Revelation you'll know exactly how it will all end, I assure you. There is no talk of abominations like, like, zombies in the book of Revelation! That is a made-up creature of the world, and it might lead uneducated people astray, but it won't fool us. We've read the Bible, and we know what's coming, and if you think . . ."

I can tell she's not finished, not by a long shot, but the pianist has begun playing, and her voice drops to a hiss. "If you think for one minute that you can come in here and spread those lies, well, I'll tell you . . ." Before she can finish her threat the pastor and deacons begin their walk down the aisle to the platform, and the congregation rises to its feet to sing the first hymn. Diana is forced to give ground and return to her own seat, but she's shooting daggers at Professor McCormick that generously include me.

Rather than looking abashed or chastised, Professor McCormick seems pleased with himself. Like a little kid at the zoo, he's poked the bear and gotten a good show for his trouble. I can feel my heart sink as I slip into the pew next to him. With an innocent expression he offers his open hymnbook to me so I can follow along. Neither one of us sings, and I spend the entire time wondering if he's here to mock and ridicule or if he's truly searching.

He pays attention to the sermon and even uses the Bible from the shelf in back of the pew to look up the texts, though I have to help him find them. Like one of his students, he takes notes in a small, black Moleskine notebook, and I wonder if he's planning on studying them in more depth later or if he's going to use them to formulate a rebuttal. I make a mental note to ask him if he'd like Pastor Marrero to study with him.

I miss most of the sermon between helping him find the verses and praying for the Holy Spirit to be with each of the new people in the congregation, to speak to them and draw them closer to God. Oddly enough, I don't mind. I'm so excited at this evidence of the working of God's Spirit in the church that I almost miss the vicious whispers between Diana Wallace and Elder Fortin as people begin to file out.

"We can't have people like that here," Diana is saying. "What will visitors think? He might infect our own people with that nonsense."

"I'll speak with the pastor," Elder Fortin agrees. "You're right. This can't go on."

I swallow hard and glance up at Professor McCormick's face, but it is inscrutable. "I'm . . . I'm sorry." I know it is a pathetic attempt.

His lips tighten. He doesn't look pleased any more. He looks angry. Abruptly he stands and exits the church, pushing past people. I debate whether or not I should go after him, try to apologize more. Diana and Elder Fortin watch him leave, smug expressions of accomplishment on their faces. Diana looks over at me and raises one eyebrow in a mute challenge. *Try to bring your riffraff in here again,* it seems to say. *We know how to take out the garbage.*

"Brooke?" Judah asks, stopping by my pew on his way down the aisle with Marissa. "Is everything okay?"

I want to tell him. Judah will understand. But when I see Marissa's sharp eyes, I know I can't. A Bible verse flashes through my mind. *"Stay away from stupid and senseless arguments. These only lead to trouble."* If I tell Judah what happened, it would be like Diana and Elder Fortin's poison infecting not only its intended victim but also Marissa as an innocent bystander.

"No," I answer truthfully, "but it will be . . . someday," I add under my breath.

I see Professor McCormick two days later at the bakery. Derrick has been particularly nasty to me all morning, and I think the professor can tell by my red-rimmed eyes that I've been crying in the ladies room.

"Professor McCormick," I say, forcing a smile, "how are you?"

"Better than you, by the look of things," he says tartly. He raises his voice which is still pretty scratchy, "I'd like to place a *large* order for a *big* party, and I don't care to do it standing up. Can you join me at a table, please?"

I shoot Derrick a nervous look for confirmation. I can only leave the counter if he's willing to cover it for me because we're short-handed today. Grudgingly he nods. I grab the special order clipboard and scurry around the counter to join the professor at a table where he shoves a donut toward me.

"Ah, I really shouldn't. I'm working. But thank you."

"Brooke, eat the donut."

"Ah, well, okay." It's funny; I work here, but I never eat what we bake. The donut is actually very good, and I haven't had breakfast yet. "What did you want to order?" My free hand is poised over the order pad, but the professor doesn't seem to be in any hurry.

"What happened the other day, at your church," he begins, and then seems to struggle with how he wants to continue. I try to ignore Derrick who is glaring daggers at me from behind the counter where he's waiting on an elderly man who can't seem to decide what he wants to order.

"Brooke, you shouldn't be there, in that place, with those people. Isn't it enough that you have to put up with this?" He jerks his head in Derrick's direction. "You're a good kid, you seem to have a kind heart, although how is beyond my comprehension. I know I'm not your parent or your guidance counselor, but I do owe you . . ." He absently touches the scar at his throat. "I never even thanked you for saving my life."

"I didn't save your life," I protest.

"Several people at the hospital—medical professionals—disagree with you," he counters, and then waves a hand dismissively. "Anyway, the point is that I feel as though I . . . owe . . . you."

"You don't," I object flatly.

"Regardless, I'd like to save you from some pain if I can. Maybe you have to work here, I don't know your circumstances, but you don't have to keep going to that place."

"I know I don't, Professor. I go because I want to."

"How can you want to go to a place where the people are such, such . . . hypocrites?! Christians aren't supposed to light into people, even I know that. They're supposed to turn the other cheek, not give people a piece of their mind. If they can character assassinate me, whom they don't even know, I shudder to think how they treat people they feel entitled to criticize. Can't you see they have nothing to offer you?"

"Maybe I have something to offer them," I suggest quietly, and this stops him in his tracks as surely as if he'd hit a brick wall. He sputters for a moment, trying to work his way around my logic, but eventually he sits back, shoulders slumped, and shrugs.

"I can't argue with that," he says. He laughs a little. "You know the funny thing? You could very well be right. Maybe you *do* have something to offer them." So quietly that I can barely hear him, he says under his breath, "You've sure given me more than I bargained for."

When I return to the counter and hang up the clipboard, Derrick notices that it's empty. "I thought you were taking an order," he says, surly.

"I thought so, too." I can hardly tell him that apparently Professor McCormick had never intended to place an order at all, as he informed me after our little talk.

It's so quiet in the bakery, most of the morning coffee-drinking, donut eaters have come and gone, that the string of abuse he lets loose on me is nearly deafening. I take a step back, wanting to put some distance between us physically as he continues to accuse me of taking an unscheduled break to flirt with my "boyfriend" and threatening to dock my pay. What he doesn't see is that Professor McCormick is just out of his line of vision but still very much in the bakery, and he is livid.

He steps around the shelf that's blocking him and confronts Derrick. "Young man, what is your name?" he demands.

Derrick looks like someone slapped him across the face. "I'm sorry," he gushes, "I didn't see you there. I didn't know anyone was here."

"Apparently you did not," Professor McCormick agrees. "This isn't the first time I've heard you abuse this young woman, but I swear to you it will be the last. I want to speak to your supervisor immediately."

Derrick is obviously cowed, but not ready to relinquish ground. "He's not available, but if you want, you can leave him a message. I'll be sure he gets it," he smirks.

Professor McCormick obviously knows this will never happen. "Oh, he'll get the message," he says in a menacing tone. "You can be sure he'll get the message." And he stalks out the door.

Derrick turns on me. "If I lose my job over this, I will kill you." His voice is low and deadly calm. "I will literally kill you."

"Is that so?" asks a smooth voice from behind us. I'm afraid to turn around, but Derrick spins on his heel, his face gone white.

"Julian?"

The owner of the bakery is leaning up against the doorjamb. He doesn't usually come in this early. Most days he stops by to check on things after I've gone for the day.

"Hello, Julian." Still stinging from Derrick's abuse, I try to keep my voice from shaking.

His eyes never leaving Derrick's pasty face he asks me, "Where's Mel?"

"She called in sick today. Angie said she'd come in a little early to help cover. She should be here any minute. Madame Thibeaux stopped in to pick up cake samples, but she was meeting a wedding client at a venue. She'll be back soon."

Julian nods. "Brooke, would you join me in the office for a minute, please?"

Derrick licks his lips, and I can feel his eyes boring holes in my back as I follow Julian into the tiny, cramped office in the rear of the bakery. He sits heavily in the chair behind an enormous desk piled with paperwork and leans back, the springs creaking in protest. He indicates with a wave of his hand that I should take a seat as well. I have to shuffle paperwork out of the only chair available, and then I sit down gingerly. No one spends much time in here, so the reliability of the furniture is questionable.

Julian laces his fingers behind his head and stares at me in an appraising way.

I decide to bite the bullet. "How much did you see?"

"Enough," Julian says. "Enough to know that Derrick seems to have let his position go to his head. He's acting like he owns the place. I wouldn't mind that so much; I think he'd probably run it better than I do, to be honest. But I don't tolerate abuse in my workplaces. No sir,

I have zero tolerance when it comes to abuse. What I want to know is why you've let this go on? I assume this isn't the first time he's acted like this? I heard that customer say so, for one thing, and for another he seemed pretty comfortable doing it. Like he'd had practice."

"Yes," I agree reluctantly, "he's had plenty of practice."

"How long? How long has it gone on? And why didn't you come to me when it first started?"

"I did, but it was my word against his. I was new. You took his word for it."

Julian digests this information. "And when it happened again?"

I shrug helplessly. "I assumed you didn't care."

"I see." He sighs heavily, then he leans forward and looks me directly in the eyes. "Here's the thing, I can't have this going on in my bakery. I'm sorry. I'm going to have to terminate you."

I actually reel back as if he slapped me. "Me? You're firing me? But I didn't do anything! I didn't even complain. I took the abuse. I'll keep taking the abuse. I'll deal with it. It's okay. Please Mr. Coulter, I need this job. Please!"

"I'm sorry, Brooke. I can't replace Derrick; he's good at what he does. You? You're a dime a dozen. I'm sure I can find someone who can get along with Derrick, and we won't have to worry about this sort of problem." He starts flipping through a stack of papers. "You can go now," he says without looking up.

Derrick watches me carefully as I walk out of the office and carefully close the door behind me. I'm too numb to even care. The old Brooke would like nothing better than to curse him out like he deserves. Old Brooke nearly wins. Instead, as I collect my things I pray for Derrick, and Julian, and the rest of my co-workers at the bakery, a place where I had hoped to make a difference for God but where instead, it seems as though I've done nothing at all to further His cause.

I slip out the door as unobtrusively as I can. Seeing the triumph on Derrick's face would, I think, be more than I can bear. My shift was nearly over, so mercifully, I have my regular routine to keep me distracted and my feet moving. The day marches relentlessly onward until finally I reach the safety of home.

The letter arrives the next afternoon in a plain envelope and sits on my kitchen table for a few hours before I even get around to opening it. I'm not expecting mail from anyone. There is no return address. It's not very exciting. It could have sat there for days before I got around to caring what was inside.

But I happen to notice it when I take a break from studying. I'm having a cup of chamomile tea, and when I sit at the table, I spy it there, sticking out from beneath a stack of books. I open it idly, not really expecting anything in particular, certainly nothing that will rock my world.

It's from church, and it's on official church stationary. There is a brief letter informing me that all the members are being asked to sign a loyalty pledge. Furthermore, if anyone is unwilling to sign it, their membership status will be placed on probation until they meet with the pastor and the board members for questioning. Failure to sign the loyalty pledge will result in having your name removed from the church books.

Beneath this is a section that says "Further Action Required" and it states, "Member must conform to church dress policy. The hair is not worn in a manner that is befitting a church member and the style must be changed. Membership is in probationary status until such time as this requirement is filled."

I don't know how long I sit there blinking at the words, trying to comprehend what they mean. Eventually they blur together on the page, and I can't even read them.

Chapter Seven

I don't know why I think I am the only one who has been singled out with a letter. I guess it is because I am usually singled out. This time, apparently, I'm only one of many. Most of the church members have received one. Judah is all worked up about it the next day when he calls me.

"Did you get one?" he demands. "Did they send you one, too?"

"A letter from the church, you mean? Yes, I got one."

"Did you sign it? Tell me you didn't sign it."

"Not yet," I admit.

"But you're going to?"

"I don't see what choice I have. I don't want them to take my name off the books." I have been struggling with this for almost 24 hours now, and it still makes me want to start sobbing. My hair . . . I haven't had it cut in 10 years. I love my dreads, and the only way to get rid of them is to shave my head. I'm mortified at the thought of what I'll look like bald. The humiliation of this is not something I've been able to make peace with yet. But God hasn't been talking to me about my peace; he's been talking to me about love.

"You're crazy," Judah says. "Don't do it. Don't sign it, and don't do whatever it is they want you to do." There's a pause and then he asks, "Do they want you to do something? What do they want you to do?"

I sigh. "Cut my hair."

"No!" I can hear him screaming on the other end of the phone, but I can't make out what he's saying. "Brooke, look, some of us want to get together and talk about this. The thing is, we can't meet here. The plumbing is backed up and the landlord says the plumber can't come to fix it for a couple days. Can we come to your place?"

I glance dubiously around my tiny little apartment. "Sure, if you want. It's not fancy, as you know. But I'll make snacks."

It feels strange to wake up late, study at leisure, and have nothing to do except attend classes. My new schedule gives me plenty of time to get ready for the meeting. I'm a little worried about it, actually. I understand that people have legitimate gripes about what the church has done. I definitely don't agree with their actions myself. But I don't think that getting together and dissing them is going to make anyone happier or change anything.

That's why I spend all my free time before the meeting looking up verses on getting along with people we disagree with—"We love because he first loved us. Whoever claims to love God yet hates a brother or sister is a liar. For whoever does not love their brother and sister, whom they have seen, cannot love God, whom they have not seen. And he has given us this command: Anyone who loves God must also love their brother and sister" 1 John 4:19-21; "If it is possible, as far as it depends on you, live at peace with everyone" Romans 12:18; "Make every effort to live in peace with everyone and to be holy; without holiness no one will see the Lord" Hebrews 12:14; "The start of an argument is like a water leak—so stop it before real trouble breaks out" Proverbs 17:14—and praying that God will direct the meeting and cool heated tempers, and if there is any action to take, that we are able to take it calmly and in a way that honors him. I feel a little silly doing it, but I sit in each chair that I have set up in a circle around my "living room" area, and I pray for whoever sits in that chair, that they will be filled with wisdom and God will work through them in a powerful way.

By the time people start arriving, I feel as though I've done everything humanly possible to cover the meeting with prayer and leave the outcome in God's hands. I'm relieved that Judah and Rocko are the first ones to arrive because as others slowly filter in, I realize that I don't know many of them, not well anyway. I recognize them as faces in the pews each week, but I don't know their names. Some of them shake my hand in a friendly way and seem happy to meet me, or at least not violently opposed. Others duck past me to avoid a formal meeting and find a seat as quickly as possible.

The only people present are members of our church; none of the many visitors I've seen lately are in attendance. I'm thankful for that since I would hate for them to get turned off about God because of squabbling in his church. So far there are some animated discussions going on, but it's hard to get a sense of how the meeting will go. The seating, I realize, is woefully inadequate. People continue to pack into my little apartment until there's standing room only.

Judah takes the lead by opening with prayer. Usually his prayers are short and to the point, but he lingers here, entreating God to be present, asking him to give us understanding and compassion for the people in the church who wrote the letter, and asking God to bring something positive from it. He closes, but before we can get off our knees other people begin to pray, taking turns, building on what Judah said, adding their own requests, pleading for the spiritual condition of the church. By the time everyone who wants to pray has spoken there is an air of hushed reverence in the room.

"Can I just say," Sarah says finally as everyone sits expectantly waiting for someone to take the lead, "that I was really upset when I got the letter. I was hurt. I mean, what gives them the right to ask me to sign a loyalty pledge? What have I done that they would suspect that I'm *not* loyal to the church? So on one hand, I have no problem with signing the pledge because I do support the church. On the other hand, it's offensive to me that they asked."

Heads begin nodding solemnly, but Judah puts his hands up like a traffic cop. "I think we can all agree that it wasn't the best thing the church could have done," he says. "But we need to bear in mind . . ."

"Did they add stipulations to yours?" Rocko interrupts, turning to Sarah. "At the bottom, was there a list of things you have to do in order to keep your membership, so they don't kick you out or whatever?"

"N-no," Sarah stutters, looking stunned. "What do you mean?"

"Did anyone else have stipulations on their letter?" Rocko demands, looking around the room. Hands reach tentatively for the ceiling. I raise mine along with them. The people whose hands are not raised look around in shock.

"What did they say?" Sarah ventures finally, asking the question that is probably on all their minds.

Answers come from all over, mostly pertaining to the way people dress, but some to the type of food they eat, or entertainment they watch. One guy's car is too expensive, in the church's opinion, and should be sold and the money given to the church. "That car was a junker when I bought it," he says, fighting to keep the anger out of his voice. "It's my blood, sweat, and tears from spending my free time with my son restoring it in the evenings instead of watching TV that have made it worth anything at all. It's not my fault that it has value now. Too much value, apparently."

There's a low murmur building in the room as people begin to share their grievances with one another. Judah's eyes look a little panicked as he attempts to redirect them again. "Look, look, it's not a question of whether or not we have the right to feel hurt about what the church did," he says reasonably. "It's a question of how will we work through this? I mean, just because we disagree doesn't mean we have to part ways. We can disagree on how the church handled this, even among ourselves, and still pull together for the greater good. I mean, we're members; we aren't "dating" the church. We're in a committed, 'monogamous' relationship with it."

He looks around, appealing to people with his eyes. "We're not sampling denominations anymore, right? Nobody twisted our arm to join this church. We chose it. How would a marriage make out if couples broke up every time they disagreed? Just like married couples are one flesh but two separate people, we can exist in the church as active, productive, vibrant members even when we don't completely agree, right?"

"He's right," says a man I don't know. "We're supposed to be adult Christian believers, aren't we? Shouldn't we 'reason together' rather than walking away just because we don't like the way something was done?"

"Yeah," Sarah pipes up. "We should reason with them. If we let them know how their letter made us feel, they'll probably apologize and tell us to file them in the circular file."

Sarah's term for the garbage almost makes me laugh. Lily always called the garbage the "circular file," too.

"I guess the question we have to ask ourselves is whether it's more important to be right as we understand it, or to be Christ-like?" Judah suggests thoughtfully. "I think the only way we can do that is by letting God lead us, whether he leads us forward into the problem or in a retreat away from it."

"You mean just give in and let them push us around?" Rocko demands. "Dude, you know my dad's the pastor, and he don't even agree with what they did. This is our own church board done this to us. It's not like this is coming down from the higher-ups somewhere. They did this all on their own."

"Who's on the church board, anyway?" Sarah wonders out loud.

Judah holds his hands up and butts in. "That's not important."

A bit of disagreement erupts at this statement as clearly some people think it is important while others don't. During a lull Sarah looks at me, her gaze predatory and perhaps a little gloating. "What did they ask *you* to do?" she asks, the words so demanding they are almost a challenge.

Suddenly all eyes are fixed on me and a hush falls over the room.

I swallow hard and force myself to say, "They want me to get rid of my dreadlocks."

"Are you going to do it?" Sarah's eyes never leave mine, it's as if she's determined to catch me out if I lie about my intentions.

I draw a shuddering breath. "Yes."

Pandemonium breaks out again. Some people I don't know are yelling that I'm crazy, that I shouldn't give in to their stupid demands, but their phrases are much more colorful than that. I'm hearing Paul's admonition in my ears, *"Do not let any unwholesome talk come out of your mouths, but only what is helpful for building others up according to their needs, that it may benefit those who listen,"* and it drowns out the general roar of people supporting me trying to shout down the ones who are demanding that I give no quarter, as if we're in a war, which, I guess, we are. We're in a spiritual war.

The thing is, I don't want to be the prize on either side. I just want my response to the church to be Christ-like. After all, that's what I've spent the last few hours praying for.

Sarah's voice again cuts through the rest like a knife slicing through butter. "Why?" she wants to know.

Again I face a wall of silence. My words ping against it like pebbles bouncing off brick. As I begin to speak I can't tell if they're making an impression or not. I've always wondered what Paul meant about praying in the Spirit, but I think that's what I'm doing as my whole body yearns to say the right words. It is a wordless plea to God to direct what I'm saying even as I'm speaking out loud.

"Jesus is supposed to be our example in everything, right? Well, what did Jesus give up for the church?" I look around, my eyebrows lifted in question. "Everything. He gave up *everything*. He didn't hesitate. Paul tells us to, 'Repay no one evil for evil, but give thought to do what is honorable in the sight of all. If possible, so far as it depends on you, live peaceably with all.' The way I see it, I can get upset and make a stink; I can get mad and leave, or I can not give Satan the win and do what they ask."

I smile sadly. "How many people do you think have been lost over the years because they look at other people in the church instead of Jesus? In my experience, people will always let you down, but Jesus has *never* let me down. Does it upset me to be treated this way?" I look around and meet their eyes as they regard me soberly. "Yes, of course. But my Christian experience isn't based on what the people in this church do for me or to me. It's based on my relationship with God. If it wasn't, I would have left a long time ago. Maybe I wouldn't be here in the first place." My voice drops as I admit, "Very few people in this church have ever been kind to me; it's a total miracle that I'm here at all. Jesus loved me into the church, not people."

I look frankly at Sarah. "So maybe I have a different perspective on this than you do. Maybe my obedience—my *love*—will help someone else come closer to Jesus, to want to love more themselves." Sarah holds my gaze and her eyes are moist with tears. She gives me a curt little nod, as if acknowledging that she understands what I've said.

The roar rises again as I finish speaking, and it's probably a miracle that I hear the sudden knock at the door. It's tentative though, and I expect it's someone who is very late, probably got lost. I ease around the perimeter of the room to answer it. Pulling the door open, excusing myself to the people standing closest to it, I smile and start to say, "Come on in," before it registers that the man standing on my doorstep is Officer Huang.

My blood runs cold. He's here because someone complained about the noise, surely. "I'm so sorry, Officer, are we disturbing someone?" Behind me a hush is falling, but in addition to the noise I suddenly become aware of the fact that I've got a lot of people in my apartment. I'm probably violating some building code that I don't know about. Worse, he could think we're meeting for some subversive reason. After all, I don't live in a great part of town. They're already here a couple times a month, at least, looking for *something*. Maybe he'll think he's found it.

It takes longer than it should for me to realize that Officer Huang looks nervous. Also, he's in street clothes rather than his TAO uniform. Clutched in his hands, rolled into a tight cylinder, is the pocket testament he swiped from me the last time he was in my apartment. "You're busy," he says finally. "I'll come back."

"It's okay," I assure him, opening the door a little wider, inviting him to come inside. "These are people from my church. We're just having a meeting. What can I do for you?"

He doesn't move. Instead he beckons me out into the hall. I step outside, not quite closing the door behind me. He looks as though he desperately wants to say something, but he's not sure if he can trust me. Behind him is a young girl, maybe seven or eight years old. Her eyes are wide and frightened, and she's clutching the second Gospel of John that Officer Huang swiped only hers is not rolled up, but flat and pristine. I offer her a smile, but she doesn't return it.

I reach out one hand tentatively and cover Officer Huang's, which are twisting the little testament into an even tighter cylinder. "Officer Huang, it's okay. Whatever I can do for you, I will."

"Why?" he demands, suddenly, "why would you do anything for me? I am your enemy."

"We aren't enemies," I say with conviction.

"We are," he insists. "I have invaded your home, gone through your personal belongings. You *must* hate me." He averts his eyes, and in a whisper, he adds, "*I* hate me."

"Office Huang, I don't hate you. I don't." I will him to look at me, to meet my eyes, and finally he does. It's as if he can't believe what he sees there. "I don't," I repeat, smiling. "You were kind to me at the hospital after my attack. That's what I remember."

His stiff shoulders seem to relax a fraction, and he almost smiles. "We caught them," he says. "I wanted to tell you the last time we were here, but . . ." He trails off, and I nod. "We caught them," he repeats. It's almost as though he's offering it to me as a gift, a peace offering to make up for the many times they've invaded my home.

"Thank you," I tell him, more because I think he needs to hear it than that I really care whether or not the culprits have been apprehended.

He unrolls the gospel with difficulty and opens it to a dog-eared page. Pointing to a highlighted passage he asks, "Is this true?"

I turn the book around and read the words out loud. " 'I am the resurrection and the life. The one who believes in me will live, even though they die; and whoever lives by believing in me will never die.' Yes," I say, looking up at him. "Yes, it's true."

"And this?" He flips through the booklet and shows me another text.

I read, " 'Jesus answered, "I am the way and the truth and the life. No one comes to the Father except through me." ' " I nod. "Yes, it's true."

His eyes are full of tears. "My wife believed this, but I was too arrogant." He looks at me, pleading, "I have to know if it's too late. Is it too late for us?" He indicates the little girl with a sweep of his hand.

"No," I tell him, "no, it's not too late. Come inside with me. People from my church are inside. Let us pray for you. We would be happy to answer any questions you have." He hesitates for only a moment. I can see the struggle going on in his eyes. On one hand, he doesn't want to barge in. On the other, the offer is akin to holding out a pitcher of water to a man dying of thirst. In an instant, his mind is made up, and he nods gratefully. Taking the little girl's hand in his he follows me inside.

When I push open the door, I practically hit Sarah who scoots out of the way, a slightly guilty look on her face. I have the distinct impression that she's been eavesdropping. The room is quiet, and Judah makes his way over to us, a big, welcoming smile on his face.

"Judah," I say, "everyone, this is . . ." I turn to Officer Huang, "I'm sorry, I don't know your first name."

"Kyle," he supplies, then indicates his daughter. "And Sadie."

"Kyle Huang and his daughter Sadie," I repeat to the others. "They would like to get to know Jesus."

The hubbub is almost worse than it was before as everyone moves toward us in a crush to shake Kyle's hand and welcome Sadie. Any hostility that was present in the room seems to have vanished. All around me are smiles and genuine joy that a seeker has arrived. It's as if everyone wants to be part of the welcoming committee. I thank God under my breath for providing such a warm and loving experience for the Huangs, and I melt into the fringes.

"I'm sorry," a low voice says beside me. Startled, I turn toward it and find Sarah at my elbow. "I'm sorry I wasn't kind to you. I'm sorry I wasn't loving. I was afraid," she admits regretfully. Then she sighs. "And I guess I was, well, I guess I felt a little superior."

Her eyes slide to meet mine and then slide back, embarrassed. "I grew up in the church, and you're the big, bad sinner." Her voice mocks her words to lessen the sting, and I realize she really feels badly. I put my hand on her shoulder and give it a squeeze.

"It's okay," I tell her. "Really."

"I admire you," she says. "If they asked me to give up a part of myself, I don't think I could do it."

"You could do it with Jesus' help," I tell her.

She looks at me again. "With Jesus' help," she agrees, but I'm not sure she believes it.

The purpose of our meeting forgotten for the time being, some people begin to trickle out while others group around Kyle and Sadie answering their questions, Bibles open, pointing out and explaining texts. Someone has handed Kyle their own Bible, and he's following along, the misshapen pocket testament discarded.

Judah wanders over to me, a glass of water in his hand. "Is he a friend of yours?" he asks curiously.

"Kyle? He's a TAO," I tell him. "I don't really know him."

Judah stiffens, and I see fear flash in his eyes. "You mean, he could be here spying on us?"

My blood runs cold. Could he be here spying on us? Maybe he came here to try and catch me out and look what he found: jackpot! He'd get a real sweet promotion catching this many subversives. "No," I shake my head, "no, he wouldn't do that." But my voice lacks conviction. I don't know Kyle at all. I don't know *what* he would or wouldn't do. Could he be compiling a list of religious people for some future strike? Had I just put everyone in my apartment in jeopardy?

"It's okay," Judah says, placing a hand on my arm. His touch brings me back to reality and my fears skitter away into the dark places. "God brought him here, no matter what his original purpose was or is. Someone who didn't have real questions wouldn't ask the things he's been asking us. If he wasn't seeking before, he sure is now. God's in charge; we don't have anything to worry about."

I relax. "You're right. God's in charge." I look over at Kyle. He's holding his daughter's hand. His face is open, unguarded. He appears keenly interested, hopeful, joyful, even. It isn't until he leaves, one of the last people out the door, that he addresses me again. What he says gives me an ominous feeling of foreboding.

"We will be back," he warns me, "and when we come back, I can't do anything for you. I can't even acknowledge that I know you. It would be dangerous for us both, but especially for you. Do you understand?"

I glance from Kyle's intent face to Sadie's sleepy, innocent eyes and back again. I lick my lips. He's telling me that no matter what happens on any future raid he will deny all association with me. "I understand."

"Thank you," he says, reaching out to shake my hand. "Thank you so very much."

Judah is the last to leave. He hugs me wordlessly and closes the door softly behind him. I feel exhilarated and satisfied. The meeting hadn't resulted in any concrete answers that I knew of, but I think it gave people a lot to think and pray about. In that way alone, it had been a success.

Before I turn in for the night I spend some time on my knees praying for Kyle and Sadie. As I drift off to sleep, I'm pondering where I can buy a little girl's Bible. Something pink and flowery. Surely they sell something like that somewhere. I'll check online in the morning. Ignoring the warning bells in my brain about my hemorrhaging bank balance and how I can ill afford to spend my money on things that don't contribute to my survival (like food and rent), I turn over and drift off to sleep praising God for touching the hearts of Kyle and Sadie and for allowing us to introduce them to him.

I'm sitting in Economics and Psychology a few days later when I see the familiar scrawl on one of my papers being passed back from the front of the class. "See me after class." I've brought my grade up to an A-, so I don't think it could be about my grades. As everyone pushes past me to leave, I make my way to the front and sit down in the hot seat. The window above, the one that shattered when the bomb was thrown through it, has been replaced. It's easy to tell because it's so much cleaner than the ones on either side.

"You wanted to see me, Professor?"

He's packing his briefcase, his back is to me. At the sound of my voice he turns around as if surprised. "Brooke!"

"You wrote a note on my paper? You wanted to see me?"

"Yes! I'm sorry; I had forgotten. I wrote that note over the weekend when I was grading. It was late at night, and I had a crazy idea . . ." He stops and looks conflicted.

"Yes?"

It seems like forever, but finally he sighs and says, "Look, I know we talked about this, and it's none of my business, but I know you got fired from the bakery." He gives me a guilty sideways glance. "When I didn't see you around anymore, I asked where you were. They told me you'd been let go. I figured I knew why, so I contacted the owner and let him know what I thought of that." He looks pleased with himself for a moment. "Anyway, the point is, do you need a job?"

"I do, but I don't see how . . ."

"Then I'd like to offer you one," he says, cutting me off.

"Doing what?" I'm confused. Does he have children and need a nanny? What?

"Teaching assistant," he fills in. "My TA left a couple weeks ago, and I need someone to fill in for the rest of the year. Normally, as you know, you'd have to apply, and there's a lot of competition. However, because of the special circumstances, I need to hire someone, effective immediately. I thought of you. Are you interested?"

"Absolutely! But I don't know if I'm qualified."

"You're qualified," he says bluntly and returns to packing his briefcase. "Come in a little early tomorrow, and we'll go over your duties, what I expect, blah, blah, blah. It's not hard work, there's just an awful lot of it. Nicole's only been gone a couple weeks, and I need a break already. Expect to take some work home with you tomorrow. I'm a little behind at the moment."

"I will, and thank you, Professor. I really appreciate it."

He waves me off. "I'll see you tomorrow." Before he clears the door he barks over his shoulder, "And don't be late!"

People who think there is no God would chalk this up to coincidence or karma or fate. They would credit luck that I lost my job working for a brutal supervisor and almost immediately afterward got a better one working with a professor I admire, one whom, frankly, I was looking for opportunities to share Jesus with. They would say that my stars were all lined up or that Lady Luck was smiling on me. But I know none of that is true. I know, because I know that God is in control of my life, and whatever happens to me happens for a reason. I may not always like it, but I can always trust that God allowed it, so therefore, it must be of some benefit to me or to someone else.

It's easy to say that, of course. It's a lot harder to live like you believe it.

Chapter Eight

One of the most immediate benefits of my new job—aside from the fact that Professor McCormick gives me my first paycheck the very next day ("Brooke, shut up and take the check. I walked all the way down to accounting and hassled some poor woman, practically made her cry, just to get it. I probably broke every rule in the employee handbook. But I know you've been out of work for a couple weeks. Rent doesn't pay itself. Take the check; believe me, you'll earn it.") along with a stack of papers to grade that makes me stagger home beneath their weight—is that since I don't have to get up so early in the morning, there is no obstacle making it difficult to attend the Wednesday night prayer meetings. Judah is so triumphant when I tell him my news that he does a little dance right there next to his "I'm the leader tonight" chair in the front of the room.

"Praise God!" he keeps saying over and over. Aside from Lily, Judah is the only one who knows how Derrick treated me, and that's only because he caught me crying about it one time and made me tell him why. I hadn't even told him yet that I was out of work because I knew he'd try to give me money for rent even though he is a penniless seminary student.

It actually took some spiritual strength not to tell him, not to share with someone, anyone, my raw panic about having no income. I mean, it wasn't like I even had family I could fall back on. Instead, I confided my fears to God alone and left my fate in his capable hands. They call it practicing your faith, leaning only on God, learning to trust him for everything in your life. I'm new at it, and I'm sure there are plenty of people who are much more adept than I am, but God spoke to me, he actually spoke to me, and after that, I was filled with peace, so I really didn't worry about it.

The way he spoke to me was really cool. A couple days after I'd been fired I'd been balancing my checkbook, watching my already meager capital plummet, and quietly panicking, when I'd been impressed to reach for my Bible. It was sitting on the table next to where I was working, and I'd needed to get some distance, physical distance, from my checkbook, so I picked it up and went to curl up on the couch for a few minutes. I'd prayed for awhile; I remember that instead of pouring out my panic on God I'd simply praised him for his faithfulness to me. I'd started to feel peace then because I realized God *had* always been faithful to me, and I could trust that he *would* always be faithful to me. Then I'd opened the Bible, and my eyes had fallen on this verse: "You will keep him in perfect peace, whose mind is stayed on You, because he trusts in You." It was already highlighted, so I underlined it and wrote the date in the margin.

"Everyone," Judah is saying loudly, his face literally split in half his grin is so wide, "Brooke has some awesome news! She lost her job!" There's a general confusion of people pulling compassionate faces and groans of, "Oh no!" Mrs. Swift, who has just entered the room, reaches her hand out to pat my arm sympathetically even as Judah starts waving his hands for attention. "No, no, you don't understand. She lost a terrible job, and God replaced it with a fantastic job. This is *great* news! *And* this makes it easier for her to join us every week." It's like someone has pulled a switch as countenances brighten and a few people make their way to the front of the room where I'm standing to congratulate me.

The only person who doesn't look happy is Diana, but then it doesn't really look as though she's heard what Judah said anyway. She's holding herself very carefully as she perches on the edge of a folding chair toward the back of the room. Her complexion is ashen, and she's dabbing her lips with a tissue. She looks for all the world as though she's just eaten something that very much disagreed with her.

I make my way to her chair to see if she's all right. She's sitting with her eyes closed, and I almost hate to disturb her. "Diana?" I say quietly, "are you okay?"

Her eyes fly open and her face immediately closes up on itself. She tucks the tissue out of sight into the cuff of her cardigan and pushes a stray wisp of hair back into place in her tight chignon. "Yes," she replies shortly, irritation making a muscle just above her eye twitch. "Why do you ask?"

"It's just . . ." My voice trails off. "You looked as though you didn't feel well," I finish lamely.

"I feel just fine, thank you very much," she says with a tight smile.

"Okay, then." I try to smile, but I'd really rather cry. Why does she hate me so much? I want to ask her, but I don't. I can't. Instead, I pray for her as I go find a seat. It's hard, but it used to be harder. When I first started praying for her, obeying Jesus' command to "love your enemies! Pray for those who persecute you! In that way, you will be acting as true children of your Father in heaven" all I could manage was a, "Dear Lord, please bless Diana," which I repeated over and over again like a mantra. Later I learned how to pray scripture for people. My favorite verses to pray for Diana are Colossians 1:9-14: "God, please give Diana complete knowledge of your will and spiritual wisdom and understanding. Then the way she lives will always honor and please you, and her life will produce every kind of good fruit. All the while, she will grow as she learns to know you better and better. I also pray that she will be strengthened with all your glorious power so she will have all the endurance and patience she needs. May she be filled with joy, always thanking the Father. You have enabled Diana to share in the inheritance that belongs to your people, who live in the light. For you have rescued us from the kingdom of darkness and transferred us into the Kingdom of your dear Son, who purchased our freedom and forgave our sins." Just saying these words eases the hurt in my heart, and by the time I reach my seat, I have recovered enough of my equilibrium that I can enter into the meeting with a joyful attitude.

And I love Judah's meetings. I praise God (literally, I thank him every time I think about it) that I'm able to come to them now. I'm really impressed with how much Judah knows about the Bible. And a little jealous, if I'm honest. I wish I knew half as much. I'm really learning and growing since I started coming to the meetings. It's probably traitorous to say it, but I enjoy them more than I do the actual church service. The meetings feel so vibrant, so alive with the presence of God, that sometimes I get goose bumps.

I've noticed a shift in the way many people treat me. It's been a gradual transition, but it seems to be a trend. It's as if the edge of their hostility is slowly being worn away. I'm not getting warm and fuzzy vibes, exactly, but I also don't feel as though most of them would cheerfully drag me outside by my offensive dreadlocks and energetically stone me to death on the sidewalk, either. Just this level of amity is a breath of fresh air, and I feel as though I'm starting to blossom from it. True, the number of people attending the midweek prayer meeting is minuscule compared to the membership of the church at large, and a majority consists of people who weren't outright hateful toward me in the first place, but it's a start.

Judah's message tonight is so interesting that I find myself on the very edge of my seat as I listen to him. Because he knows Greek and Hebrew (although he insists he's barely passing those classes) he can really understand what a scripture is talking about. And that *does* make me extremely jealous. Tonight he's dissecting Philippians 1:19, "For I know that this will turn out for my deliverance through your prayer and the supply of the Spirit of Jesus Christ."

"I don't know about the rest of you," he's saying, "but this week I ran out of gas in a major way."

My ears perk up because I haven't seen, or come to think of it, even heard from him for a few days. I wonder what he's been facing that he hasn't been sharing with me.

"I know I'm not the only one who has been bothered by the recent communication the church board has sent to the members . . ."

Rocko interrupts loudly with, "Amen!"

Judah gently pacifies him with an acknowledging smile and carries on. "Satan was working on me overtime about it. It literally shook my faith. I let myself start to wonder why I'm even here." He spreads his hands, encompassing the church with his gesture. "I even wondered why I'm spending every penny I have to earn a Master of Divinity just so I can go forth and promote more of this sort of strife. That's not what I'm about; that's not what I believe the church should be doing. It's not what I believe *Christians* should be doing.

"Quite honestly, I felt such a sense of defeat that I just wanted to throw my hands up then and there and say, 'Uncle'. I'm so sick and tired of getting mixed up in this kind of hassle that I really didn't feel as though I had the strength to go on. I literally didn't feel as though I could wake up one more morning and face this kind of attitude in the church. I love this church," he confesses, "but I'm tired of fighting with it. I'm tired of trying to get it to stop persecuting its own members and go out there and share Jesus before it's too late."

This time Rocko isn't the only one who says, "Amen." Behind me I also hear a sharp intake of breath. I shift enough that out of the corner of my eye I can see Diana, rigid with anger, nostrils flaring, and fingers white as she clutches her Bible.

Judah runs one hand through his hair, rumpling it adorably, and settles his glasses more firmly up on the bridge of his nose. "As I was praying, God directed me to this verse in Philippians that we just read. Now, the word for 'supply' that's used in this verse is the Greek word *epichoregeo* which literally means 'on behalf of the choir.' " He pauses for just a moment and smiles at our blank, puzzled faces. "I know that doesn't make any sense. I have to tell you a story first. Way back in ancient Greece there was this drama company that put everything they had into a production they wanted to perform. By the time they were able to take it on the road, they were flat broke. After all that time and expense they were dead in the water; they couldn't do anything.

"But then this wealthy guy, probably some ancestor of Bill Gates, donated a bunch of money so they could go on. And get this: he donated it anonymously 'on behalf of the choir.' He gave them such an enormous donation to get back in business again that they couldn't even spend it all. He gave them enormously, abundantly, exceedingly more than they could even use." He pauses to look around the room at us significantly. "That's how much of the Holy Spirit God gives us so *we can go on* when we find ourselves dead in the water like I did. He gives us more than we could possibly ever need or use. That's why I'm here tonight," he says simply, "because Jesus supplied the strength I needed to keep fighting the good fight."

This time the "amens" are unanimous. Even Diana, when I squint unobtrusively at her, seems touched by his words. She's frowning thoughtfully. She seems to brush a tear from her eye, and then gives the side of my head a thoughtful scrutiny. We have a wonderful "season of prayer" as Mrs. Swift calls it and even sing my favorite hymn, *We Have This Hope*. I carefully note all the new prayer requests in a little notebook I've been carrying around and rejoice along with everyone else over the prayer requests that God has answered. Mrs. Swift, sitting next to me, can barely keep her voice steady as she joyfully introduces her sister and nephew who have joined us for the first time.

When Elder Fortin makes his way to where Judah is standing after our meeting is over, Diana doesn't join him at the front of the room where he holds his hands up in the universal sign for "stop" and "simmer down." He makes an impatient motion in her direction, but she appears oblivious. It seems intentional, but I can't be sure. It occurs to me that it's unusual for her to sit in on our prayer meeting at all. She usually prefers the one that is held in the sanctuary of the church and is much more traditional and sedate than ours tends to be, which is precisely the reason I avoid it.

Elder Fortin clears his throat and finally proceeds without her. "I just wanted to remind everyone that the deadline for actionable items in your letter from the board is fast approaching." His smile is congenial if a little strained. He's met with a frosty silence. "You'll want to get those things taken care of, so we can all be right with the Lord. We must all be prepared to finish the work here so we can go home. I know everyone wants to hear the words 'good and faithful servant' as much as I do." He ducks out the door—probably so no one can throw anything at him—and the room begins to stir again, but the peaceful, loving atmosphere has been replaced by a resentful, angry air. Everyone quickly gathers their things and slips out the door, dispersing into the night without a word.

I climb into Judah's car; he's been driving me home after prayer meetings because it's always so late at night. After a few weeks, I told him that I'd be fine; the attack was a fluke, a matter of being in the wrong place at the wrong time and I could get myself home. "Yeah, and from now on you're going to be in the right place," he had retorted firmly. "You'll be in my car; now get in."

He seems sad, deflated even. "You okay?" I ask him. "I really appreciated your talk tonight. I wrote down that Greek word you said in my Bible. Probably spelled it wrong though."

"Thanks," he says, but his heart isn't in it. "I wish we didn't have to waste so much energy on things that don't matter."

"Are you talking about the letters?"

"The letters," he agrees, "the bickering, the judgments, the criticism, the squabbling over ways of doing things. Why can't we all just get along?" His words, echoing the famous plea by Rodney King during the 1992 Los Angeles Riots, hang in the air poignantly, and I wonder if, in the history of the planet, there has truly been a time when a group of people have been able to work together in harmony toward a goal and for a cause they all believed in. I say this to Judah, and he shakes his head.

"That's just the point. The church isn't just any old group of people working for a common cause. The church is God's body, his body, Brooke. God's body isn't supposed to be at war with itself! God has always existed as a Trinity—three distinct persons in one being—and has never had so much as a tiff. Has, in fact, worked together with awesome power and authority, accomplishing great and wonderful things, creating universes, worlds, galaxies, saving humanity. We only know a fraction of what God has achieved, but it was all possible through unity. Can you imagine the chaos if the members of the godhead started squabbling about whether the planets ought to be square or round, if people should have two legs or four, whether ocean water should be salty or fresh? It would have taken them a lot longer than seven days to create the world. Not to mention more complicated things such as the plan of salvation."

His word picture makes me smile, but I know he's serious, and I know he's hurting. Before I can say anything he continues, banging his palms on the steering wheel for emphasis. "The whole purpose of the church, the reason it even exists, is to demonstrate unity to the world precisely *because* it's not possible for humanity to experience unity without God. Our very lack of unity screams that we don't have God in our midst. That message is the exact *opposite* of the message God is trying to bring to the world. We are failing in our mission, Brooke, and it makes me tired and angry." He grins slightly. "And I know that doesn't help."

He's pulled up in front of my building, and I know it's not safe to idle a car in this neighborhood; they'll have his car stripped while we sit inside it chatting. "Look, Judah," I plead, "I know we aren't where we should be, but can't you see that we're making progress? Maybe not with the church as a whole, but individually and in smaller numbers? Sure, it would be great if the whole church was able to work together, but remember, even Jesus said the wheat and the tares will grow together. The wheat can't give up just because it's surrounded by weeds; it's got to go on growing and becoming wheat. It's hard," I agree, "but we *are* making progress. Even if the church as a whole isn't where it needs to be, I think your small group is moving there on its own. Work with what you've got."

"You're right," he says with a real smile this time.

"I know I am," I respond, "and you know, it's possible that God will work through the ones who are being faithful to turn those tares into wheat before it's all over."

"Right again, girlfriend," he concedes.

I roll my eyes, but I'm not sure he can see it in the dark. "Now go home and get some sleep. God's got a lot for us to do."

His low chuckle reaches my ears as I let myself out of the car. I thump the hood with my palm and slam the door. He pulls away from the curb slowly, and I make my way toward the door of my apartment building, taking a moment to appreciate the first mild weather we've had. A sure sign that spring is coming. Eventually.

"Brooke?" a soft voice asks from the shadows, and I freeze. I know that voice. I know that voice like I know my own heartbeat.

"Lily?" I can barely get the strangled whisper out of my throat.

Lily steps into the circle of weak light cast by the tired streetlight. She looks terrible. Her face is drawn, cheeks sunken; dark circles make her eyes seem like cavernous pits in the shadows. "Yeah. I thought I saw you go in here one day. You live up there, huh?" She jerks a shoulder toward the apartment building. "Nice place," she says, her voice dripping with irony. I can't speak, and eventually she goes on. "Whatever. I just wanted to see . . . I just wanted . . . Forget it." She turns and hurries away down the sidewalk.

I watch her go, wanting to call her back, needing her to go. I can feel a silent wail begin at the core of my being and well up inside me until it's filling my head with such an intensity I wish my head would explode and give me some relief. *God*, I'm begging inside, *please help!* The emotional pain is so intense those are the only words I can formulate. I stagger over to the side of the building and reach out one hand to brace myself, leaning heavily against it for support. My whole body is shaking.

God, please help! The prayer is on repeat in my head. Somewhere a very rational, and critical, part of my brain is saying, *She looked awful, didn't she? She looked like she was in some kind of trouble. Maybe she came here looking for help. And* you *turned her away. You didn't even offer her a morsel of comfort. Some Christian you are. All your talk about loving others, but when it really counts you don't care at all, do you?*

I do care! I want to scream, *I do! It's not safe!*

So, the rational voice jeers, *Christians only help others when it's safe? That's convenient. In that case, don't worry about it. I'm sure she'll be fine. I'm sure she's not using again. I'm sure she's not in a bad place, a dark place, maybe a suicidal place. Nothing to concern* you *anyway. You just stay . . . safe.*

I'm not sure how long I stand there sagging against the building, panting and wrestling with the sneering voice before I realize with a start that it's not my conscience that's speaking to me; it's Satan. He's goading me, trying to push me into going after Lily, bridging the gap between us, luring me back into the old relationship. Oh, sure, not at first. In the beginning, it would be all about helping Lily. My motives would be pure, noble even. But eventually I'd fall. It would be inevitable. There is a very good reason for physically removing yourself from temptation; it makes it all that much harder to give in to it. That's why recovering alcoholics don't frequent bars, gamblers working the 12-Step program don't go to Las Vegas, and dieters don't stock their refrigerators with chocolate cake.

"Satan, I bind you in the name of Jesus Christ who is my ruler and king," I say out loud, not caring who should happen to walk by and overhear me. They'll only think I'm some strung-out druggie having hallucinations anyway. "I command you to get out of my life, leave me alone, and shut up! I serve the God of the Angel Armies; you have no power here. Jesus Christ is the lord of my life, and he lives in my heart. Get out!"

Pushing myself away from the building, I make my way resolutely up to my apartment. Dumping everything I'm carrying onto the table, I stagger to an armchair in the corner, but I don't sit in it. Instead, I kneel down and bury my face in the seat cushion, my shoulders shaking with soundless sobs. I don't know how long I'm like that, surrendered to grief and pain, before I finally feel as though it's out of my system. It's as though it all drained out with my tears, and there's nothing but empty resignation inside.

Drying my eyes, I retrieve my Bible from the table, curl up in the chair, and flip it open to Psalm 145. I read aloud, "I will exalt you, my God the King; I will praise your name for ever and ever. Every day I will praise you and extol your name for ever and ever.

"Great is the Lord and most worthy of praise; his greatness no one can fathom. One generation commends your works to another; they tell of your mighty acts. They speak of the glorious splendor of your majesty—and I will meditate on your wonderful works. They tell of the power of your awesome works—and I will proclaim your great deeds. They celebrate your abundant goodness and joyfully sing of your righteousness. The Lord is gracious and compassionate, slow to anger and rich in love.

"The Lord is good to all; he has compassion on all he has made. All your works praise you, Lord; your faithful people extol you. They tell of the glory of your kingdom and speak of your might, so that all people may know of your mighty acts and the glorious splendor of your kingdom. Your kingdom is an everlasting kingdom, and your dominion endures through all generations.

"The Lord is trustworthy in all he promises and faithful in all he does. The Lord upholds all who fall and lifts up all who are bowed down. The eyes of all look to you and you give them their food at the proper time. You open your hand and satisfy the desires of every living thing.

"The Lord is righteous in all his ways and faithful in all he does. The Lord is near to all who call on him, to all who call on him in truth. He fulfills the desires of those who fear him; he hears their cry and saves them. The Lord watches over all who love him, but all the wicked he will destroy. My mouth will speak in praise of the Lord. Let every creature praise his holy name for ever and ever."

As the praise rings out into the quiet room I feel it flood into my heart as well. I underline the lines that say, "The Lord is near to all who call on him, to all who call on him in truth. He fulfills the desires of those who fear him; he hears their cry and saves them." In the margin, I write the date. Then I bow my head, "Thank you for being near to me, Lord," I pray. "Thank you for answering my call. Thank you for saving me."

I don't know how long I sit thanking God and asking him to protect and save Lily, but when I finally make my way to my bed, instead of pain and panic, I'm filled with a sense of peace and love. God is in control. I can trust him, not only with Lily but with myself. He will honor my commitment to follow him, and he will pursue Lily with the same love he has lavished on me. With all of my heart, I hope she'll accept it.

Chapter Nine

I guess it's a testament to my newfound sense of, if not acceptance than at least, tolerance that I forget to look at the caller ID a week later and find myself speaking to a very curt, very irate man.

"*Miss* Brooke Merrill?" He emphasizes the "miss" as if he's afraid I might be in doubt.

"Speaking," I reply, trying to place the voice and kicking myself for not checking first.

"Miss Merrill, this is Mr. Nash. I am a member of the church board, and I am calling in a follow-up to the letter you received four weeks ago, a letter which you have, apparently, most blatantly ignored."

As soon as he says his name a picture floats into my mind. This is the first conversation I've ever had with Mr. Nash, but I recognize him now. He's always in the background at church, never in the spotlight. He's not really what you'd call a leader, except that he is. He just leads by manipulation and coercion rather than, well, actual leadership. He carries a copy of the church manual with him right along with his Bible. It wouldn't surprise me to find that he's got it memorized. I'm about to tell him that I haven't ignored the letter—as if that would be possible—when he seems to interpret my lingering pause as a defying silence instead.

"Miss Merrill, this is serious business. The church will not tolerate rebellion of the most blatant kind. Members must be unified in their conduct and appearance in order to represent Christ to the world. This is our Christian duty. From what I've heard about you," his voice gets even chillier, "you're on shaky ground as it is. Frankly, I'm not convinced people like you *can* be saved. But if you expect God to even want to try to save you then you *must* sign the loyalty pledge, and you *must* conform to the dress standards. Anything less than that flaunts your blatant disregard for God's values and requirements, proving that you are not even *worth* being saved." The way he throws the last part in makes it sound as though I would also be proving his opinion of me.

As he has been speaking, I've been praying. The anger and the hurt I feel are almost overpowering. I want nothing more than to let him have it. Who does he think he is to say that I can't be saved? *Though your sins are like scarlet*, I hear a calm voice speak in my mind, *they shall be as white as snow*. The words and their ringing assurance affect me like a cool breeze on a hot day. I am not calm, but I am composed. I'm about to tell Mr. Nash that he has nothing to worry about. My pledge is signed and tucked in my Bible for delivery the next time I'm at church, and I've set a time for shearing my dreads off, but before I can say anything at all, he makes a disgusted noise into the phone and hangs up on me. I'm pretty sure that just before the line goes dead I hear him mutter, "Good riddance."

It takes all day—during which I recite Scripture to myself—but my feelings finally subside, and I stop having panic attacks every time Mr. Nash's cutting words echo in my mind. But when I see Judah's face later at the homeless shelter where everyone has gathered to serve the evening meal, they come flooding back. "He called you, too, didn't he?" I don't really need him to answer me; I'm certain.

Judah sighs and steps into the serving line beside me, picking up the serving spoon and loading it with mashed potatoes. "Mr. Nash? Yes, he called me."

Suddenly I'm curious. I can understand why the church board would pick on me, maybe even on Rocko and a few of the others. But Judah has never said what the letter asked *him* to do. "Judah," I ask casually, "did the letter ask you to do anything?"

His eyes cut to me and then flit back. "Yes."

"Do you mind telling me what?"

His shoulders sag. It takes him so long to answer that I begin to think he's not going to. "They want me to take Bible study lessons with a member of the board."

At first I think he's joking. He's in seminary studying to be a pastor. Why would the church board feel the need to study the Bible with him? "I don't get it," I finally say, unable to think of any reason why he would need Bible lessons.

"Apparently I'm, what was the word they used?" He looks up at the ceiling as if he might find it there. "Oh, yeah, subversive. My methods create 'strife and discord,' and my choice of company is questionable."

He doesn't look at me, but I feel my face flush. He means me; *they* mean me. He's being censured for being my friend, for not shunning me as so many others do. He's being disciplined for associating with *me*. I feel sick to my stomach and the odor wafting up from the conglomerated sludge of vegetables and meat in front of me that I've been spooning on top of the piles of potatoes Judah has been slapping onto plates makes me gag. Judah seems to sense my reaction because he drops the spoon, turns to me, and wraps me in a bear hug.

"I'm so sorry," he whispers into my neck. "I didn't want to tell you. I shouldn't have told you." He pushes me back at arm's length and looks me directly in the eyes, making me meet his gaze even though I'd rather not right now. "They are wrong. Do you hear me? They are wrong, and what's more, they have no biblical ground to stand on."

I nod, but my throat is so constricted that I can't speak. Someone across the table from us clears their throat, and Judah pushes away from me to take up his station again. "Sorry," he says to the man. "We needed a hug."

"Me, too," the man replies wistfully. I gape as Judah drops the mashed potato spoon again and leans across the table to give the homeless man a hug. The man clings to him as though he's drowning, and when they pull apart, there are tears in his eyes. "Thank you," he whispers, moving along down the line.

I see Rocko sitting next to Sibby at one of the long tables. She's spooning food into her mouth quickly, as though this is her last meal. He's talking and gesturing, but his face looks like a thundercloud. I'm guessing Mr. Nash got to him as well.

"Judah," I say softly.

"Hm?"

"Are you going to do it?" I mean "take the Bible studies" not "stop being my friend," but I can't manage to speak the words.

"No," he says, his voice sad. "No, I'm not. It's not right, and I won't do it. They can take whatever steps they feel are necessary. If they want to take my name off the church membership list, so be it. But they can't stop me from coming to church."

"But how will you be a pastor?" I protest, cold fear washing over me as if someone doused me with a bucketful.

He chuckles. "Brooke, you crazy girl, I work for God, not the church. If I'm doing his work, don't you think God will take care of me if the church won't? Maybe I'll have to learn how to sew tents, like Paul."

"And they won't let you lead out any more?"

"I don't think so, but it's okay," he says gently. He sweeps one arm out to indicate the homeless shelter. "They can't stop me from serving here, or at the women's shelter, or any other outreach venue I choose. The church may have walls but God doesn't respect them. *His* congregation, his *church* is everywhere and includes everyone, not just a privileged few who are allowed on a membership list." Amusement creeps into his voice. "Something tells me when we get to heaven, we'll find that God's membership list is a whole lot longer than ours."

I think about that for awhile. Part of me wishes I could be that strong, that I could defy the church board the way Judah is, but I can't. And I don't think I should. Judah's response is different than mine, but it's for a different reason, too. If he complied, it wouldn't demonstrate love; it would just falsely justify the church's error. My compliance, on the other hand, can show the church outwardly what they fail to recognize inwardly, that by the power of God I am a changed person, a new woman in Christ. Like Paul says, "Anyone who belongs to Christ is a new person. The past is forgotten, and everything is new."

If I sign the loyalty pledge and shave off my dreads, they will have nothing with which they can condemn me, and I will have lost nothing except my pride. If Judah were to sign the loyalty pledge, stop associating with people like me, and submit to Bible studies with the church board, he would only be contributing to the judgmental, critical attitude that has crept into the church and we have been trying so desperately to change. It would be like Jesus becoming one of the Pharisees instead of standing up to them and refusing to be like them.

Rocko slouches over to us, a glum expression on his face. "Yo," he says.

"Hey, Rocko, I hear you're moving," I say, hoping to brighten him up. I'd heard his mom talking to someone at church, and she'd seemed excited to be moving out of the tiny house they were crammed into to a much more spacious place. She'd called it the house of her dreams. "Everyone will have their own bedroom," she'd gushed happily. "And my kitchen is to die for."

He shrugs. "Yeah, whatever. I'll be moving out soon anyway, so it doesn't really matter to me. Besides," his face grows even darker, "what right do we have to live in a nice, big house when these people are living on the street?"

"They aren't living on the street," I tell him in a stage whisper. "They're living *here*." But this does nothing to put a smile on his face.

He scowls at me. "You know what I mean."

"You're moving out?" Judah asks, a mock concerned look on his face. "Where are you going? You're a little young to be going out on your own, aren't you?"

Rocko's scowl deepens. Clearly he doesn't appreciate our attempts to shake him out of his foul mood. "I'm a junior in high school, but I'm the oldest kid in my class," he retorts. "Actually," he adds quietly, "I'm thinking of dropping out of school and living on the streets to minister to the homeless."

Judah frowns now in earnest. "I can't believe your parents approve of that."

Rocko looks shifty. "Not exactly, no." He picks up a wet dishrag and starts wiping the serving table down energetically. "Sibby says she knows a guy I could hang with. He lives in an abandoned building on the other side of town, and there's plenty of room there. It's sort of like a whole community of homeless people. They stick together and take care of each other. I could maybe start Bible studies, encourage people to go to church." His face, which had started to brighten at the thought, darkens again. "Except what good would that do? They'd only get driven out by the narrow-minded members."

Judah puts a hand on his shoulder, but Rocko shakes him off. "Our responsibility is to plant the seeds, Rocko," he tells the boy, "not to make the plant grow. You can only do what you can do; you have to trust God to do the rest."

"Yeah, well, it's discouraging," Rocko says sourly, "when you plant seeds and then have to watch other people trample on them."

"I know," Judah says sympathetically.

I want to add an "amen," but I keep my mouth shut. I know perfectly well what the Bible says: pray for your enemies. It doesn't say to bad-mouth them in retaliation so you can feel better about how they treat you. I swallow hard because the thought sticks in my gizzard, but praying for strength, I manage to say instead, "Can we pray for them? Right now? I think we should." Rocko looks disgusted, but Judah nods soberly.

"They're hurting just as much as anyone we're reaching out to," Judah agrees, "only they don't know it. I read something once that said the greatest deception in Christ's day was thinking that just agreeing to the truth was the same thing as having righteousness, but that only a theoretical knowledge of the truth never saved one soul."

Rocko flinches a little, like this hits close to home, but he doesn't reply. He doesn't pull away, either, when Judah takes my hand and places the other on Rocko's shoulder. We all bow our heads. To my surprise, before Judah can say a word, Rocko starts praying.

"Gracious Lord, heavenly Father, you know what's going on in our church. You see the attitudes of the people. You see the lack of love they show each other. Forgive them . . . they don't know what they're doing. Forgive us, too, for letting them get to us." He sighs deeply. "Forgive *me*. I don't know why it bothers me so much. You know I only want to serve you, and I want to help people know you, and they're preventing that with their stupid, ignorant attitudes." Rocko's voice is escalating angrily, and I sneak a worried peek at him only to see him struggle to get a grip on himself and take a few deep breaths before continuing. "Lord, you know the best way to reach them. And you know how to protect us from them. Help them to change their minds about the stupid letters they sent out, Lord, and welcome people instead, in spite of their differences, or the way they look, or whatever."

It's quiet for a few minutes, and just as it gets awkward Judah says, "Lord, please be with your church. As your representatives on earth it's our responsibility to demonstrate your unity. But we're only human, Lord, full of petty problems and ridiculous inconsistencies. On our own, we can't get along even with the people we love, let alone people we disagree with. Teach us to love, really *love* others so that we only want what's best for them. Teach us to lay down our own lives in service to each other and to forgive wrongs immediately and freely so they don't fester and snowball into even greater hurts.

"We all want the same things, Lord. We all want to see you return soon, and we want to see as many as possible saved. We look forward to being with you in the earth made new. You said that wherever two or three are gathered in your name you are in the midst of them. Thank you for loving us and for saving us. We love you, Jesus. Amen."

Rocko and I chorus amen and when I open my eyes I see Rocko quickly scrub tears from his. He nods curtly to Judah. "Thanks, man," he says.

I notice Sibby has joined us sometime during our prayer. Her hand is on Rocko's shoulder, and he pats it tenderly, giving her a smile. "You want more food?" he asks, tipping his head toward our serving pots, but she shakes her head.

"Nah, I'm full as a tick. Just wanted to hear the prayin'."

"Come on, let's go get you signed up for a bed tonight," he tells the old woman, raising his voice slightly. As an aside to us he adds quietly, "Sibby decided to go 'on vacation' for the past three days. We have no idea where she's been or what she's been doing. She showed up this morning and couldn't tell us, either. We're trying to convince her to stick around." He waves his hand slightly in parting, puts his arm around Sibby's tiny shoulders and hunched back, and leads her gently away.

I watch Rocko's retreating back and suddenly realize that he's never said what it is the church board wants him to do, if anything. I wonder if Judah knows. "Did Rocko's letter demand he do anything to keep his membership?"

Judah hesitates and then says, "They want him to stop calling himself Rocko. They think it's undignified for a pastor's son. They said if he wants to go by a nickname then he can use something traditional like Ricky."

I'm so stunned I can't think of a reply to this. Judah doesn't seem to expect one. He busies himself putting the food away, handing off dirty dishes and silverware to people in the kitchen manning the sinks, wiping down the tables. I join him, but neither of us speaks. There are so many hands helping that it doesn't take long before everything is cleaned and put away.

Most of the homeless people have either gone back to their rooms or into the living area in the adjoining room where a television is showing a program with a lot of action. A few are studying the Bible with some volunteers at one of the newly cleaned tables. I recognize the volunteers; they've recently started coming to the Wednesday night prayer meetings, but I can't think of their names.

The director of the shelter takes the time to thank us for our help as everyone begins to filter out. I follow Judah out to his car. "Where to?" he asks as we buckle up. "You headed home?"

I nod. "Yeah, I've got a ton of papers to correct and . . . some other stuff to do," I finish lamely as I recall with a sudden rush of panic what *else* I'm doing tonight. I haven't told Judah because I know he's against it, but tonight's the night Sarah is coming over to help me shave my dreads off. She's bringing some sort of hair shaver she's got, and she's going to give me moral support.

Judah just nods, not seeming to catch my hesitation or a tone in my voice that would suggest something is wrong. He doesn't talk much on the way to my apartment, just responds absently if I ask him a question or make a remark. "You okay?" I finally ask.

He sighs before he answers me. "I'm fine. Just praying. I'm worried about Rocko," he confesses finally after a long pause.

"Me, too," I admit. "He seems pretty raw."

Judah agrees, "Yeah, raw like a powder keg about to explode." He pulls up to my curb and turns to look at me. "Pray for him, would you?"

"Of course," I say. "Always."

"See ya."

"Later," I respond, getting out and slamming the door. He pulls away slowly, and I make my way inside which is a little tricky because someone is apparently having a party. There are strung-out people littering the hallways and one of the men makes a grab for me. I twist away and run the rest of the way to my apartment where I find Sarah waiting for me outside the door looking as shaken and pale as I feel.

"Nice place you live in," she says sarcastically.

I shrug. "Yeah, well . . . the angels work overtime around here."

She grins. "That explains it. I felt like I was running the gauntlet to get up here, but no one even seemed to see me pass by."

I usher her into the apartment and lock the door gratefully behind us. "You brought the stuff?"

Sarah nods. "Yeah, but aren't you going to offer me something to drink or eat?"

I think she's kidding, so I say, "Nope," but then realize maybe she's serious. After all, I don't know her very well yet. "Unless you want something?" I amend.

She throws back her head and laughs. "I was just yanking your chain," she says. "Trying to lighten the mood. No, I don't want anything; I'm good. Let's do this." Her face suddenly darkens, and she studies me with troubled eyes. "You know, you don't *have* to do this," she tells me. "No one will think less of you if you don't. No one important, anyway."

"I will," I reply softly. "I'll think less of me."

I get a towel from the bathroom, drape it over my shoulders, and sit in one of the kitchen chairs. Sarah opens the little case she brought with her. It has the words "Pro Hair Clipper Kit" on the side. She extracts the clippers. There are a bunch of little plastic plates in the case, too, and she examines them dubiously. "How short do you want it, exactly?"

I consider this for a minute. "I'm not sure; I guess the longer the better."

She selects a thick plate and snaps it onto the business end of the clippers. When she switches them on, I feel a rush of panic and reach down to grip the edge of the seat tightly, as though I may fall off. Sarah licks her lips nervously, lifts one of my dreads, and raises the clippers. Before the metal touches my scalp, my hand snakes up, and I grab her wrist, stopping her. She jumps as though she's been bitten by a snake.

"What?" she demands defensively.

"Can you pray with me first?" I ask shakily, on the verge of tears and hating myself for it.

Her face softens. "Of course." She turns the clippers off and the silence is almost deafening. Then she kneels down on the worn linoleum next to my chair, hesitates a second before taking my hands in hers in a brisk, no-nonsense fashion, and bows her head. "Lord, I come before you today with Brooke. She wants to do your will, Lord. She is prepared to sacrifice her vanity for your cause, and she needs your help. Be with her and give her strength. Fill her with your peace and the assurance that she's doing the right thing." She pauses for a moment, and I think she's done, but with a catch in her voice she continues, "Help her to realize that you love her and accept her no matter what she looks like. She's your loving daughter, and you are her best friend, *our* best friend. We love you, Lord. Amen."

Before she stands up, Sarah throws her arms around me, and I can feel her shoulders shake slightly. It feels so foreign to receive compassion from someone that I'm not sure exactly what to do. I've gotten used to Judah hugging me on occasion, but I know him pretty well, and besides, he hugs everyone. Sarah is not exactly a touchy-feely kind of person, and receiving a hug from her is like being the recipient of a rare gift, but a fragile one. As well, I'm always worried that physical contact with a woman, no matter how innocent, will start up the temptations again, and I've been mercifully free from them for awhile now. I cautiously allow myself to hug her back and force myself not to pull away first.

Eventually she lets go and climbs back onto her feet, wiping her eyes hastily, and composing herself. She takes a deep breath and looks at me resolutely. "Ready?"

"Ready," I confirm and with a weak smile manage to say, "and thank you."

She nods curtly and turns on the clippers. I close my eyes as I see them approach my head. I feel the cool metal scrap against my scalp. I hear rustling as my dreadlocks fall to the floor. The blades tug at the roots of my hair and it hurts, but I clamp my lips together tightly, forcing myself not to cry out. A verse goes through my head: "He was oppressed, and he was afflicted, yet he opened not his mouth; like a lamb that is led to the slaughter, and like a sheep that before its shearers is silent, so he opened not his mouth."

The agony I feel burning in my chest is slowly eased as the words repeat over and over. What I am going through is nothing compared to what Christ went through for me. No one is pounding a crown of thorns into my head. No one is scourging me. No one is flaying my back open with a lash. I'm not about to be marched from my apartment and crucified. All I'm losing is my hair, not a single drop of blood. And unlike Christ, hanging on the cross and feeling the presence of his beloved father withdraw from him as he bore the sins of the world, I can feel his presence wrap around my soul like a warm blanket. I feel his strength fill me. The more hair falls to the floor at my feet the lighter my spirit becomes.

I don't even notice the sound of the clippers has ceased until Sarah interrupts my thoughts with a tentative, "Well?"

My eyes fly open. "You're done?"

She nods, and I reach one hand up to feel my head. It's bristly and feels funny beneath my fingertips. "How does it look?" I ask her curiously.

"Well, if they were aiming to make you look more acceptable in a traditional sense, they failed miserably," she says, but she's grinning. "It's actually, I don't know, on you, it's almost . . . cute." She grabs her bag which she dumped on the kitchen table and fumbles around inside for a minute. "Here, I brought you a present."

I take the small package from her and open it. Inside is a brightly colored do-rag, and I laugh. "Thanks!"

While I go into the bathroom to assess the damage and try on the do-rag, Sarah deals with my dreads, discreetly sweeping them into a plastic shopping bag and depositing them in the garbage, treating them with as much reverence as you would a dearly beloved, deceased pet.

I've never exactly liked mirrors; I'm no great beauty at any time. But the person who greets me from the mirror in my bathroom looks like a holocaust survivor. My cheekbones are high and even more prominent than they were before without any hair to frame them. My lips seem too big for my face, and my ears, I suddenly realize, stick out from my head quite a bit. The scar I got from being hit by the bottle is glaringly obvious with no hair to hide it.

Sarah comes up behind me and stares over my shoulder into the mirror. Her curly red hair and flawless complexion are in such sharp contrast to my dark, shorn, bedraggled appearance that I want to cry. She takes the do-rag out of my hands and wraps it around my head. It's definitely an improvement, and I smile wanly.

"You look adorable," she says.

A laugh barks out of me before I can stop it. "I've *never* looked adorable," I assure her. "But if this is what it takes to make them happy . . ." I trail off and shrug. "So be it."

I make tea for Sarah and me, and she stays for awhile to chat. She tells me that she grew up in the church and has always considered herself a Christian. "I've never had trouble believing in God. He's always just been there, like some absolute, you know? Like air. I can't see that either, but I'm sure it exists. To me, God's like that."

I wonder what it must be like to be that sure of something, to be that sure of God whom you can't see. I feel as though I have a fairly good relationship with God, but sometimes a little niggling doubt creeps into my mind. I'll wonder, *what if none of this is real? What if God doesn't even exist, and this is all just a waste of time?* Then sanity returns, and I realize that, for one thing, God gives me ample proof, daily, that he does exist. And for another, even if it turned out that God was a hoax, I'd still rather live for him and believe in him. I'm still happier this way than I was without him. So it's a win-win situation.

When Sarah is ready to leave, I ask her if she wants me to walk down with her to the sidewalk just in case any of my lovely neighbors are still roaming the hallways. She laughs and opens her hand allowing me to see that she's clutching a small canister of pepper spray. "And I've got angels riding shotgun, remember? I'll be fine." She gives me another quick hug, and then she's gone.

I lock the door behind her and realize suddenly that's I'm emotionally exhausted. It's all I can do to brush my teeth and climb into bed. Professor McCormick's papers will have to wait until tomorrow.

Chapter Ten

People's reactions to my new look are varied. There are the people who look at me with the same apathetic blandness they always have, as though I could sprout another head and it wouldn't faze them. And then there are the people who stare curiously or give me pitying looks because they think I must be a chemo patient.

Professor McCormick does a double take when I arrive early for class so I can give him the papers I brought home with me. He glances up from his notes and his jaw drops. "What. Have. You. Done?"

I touch my head and ask facetiously, "Do you like it? It's deliciously cool." I'm finding that with the unusual heat wave we've been having this lack of hair actually has its advantages. "And I'm saving a lot of money on shampoo."

Professor McCormick shakes his head. "You beat all, honestly." He narrows his eyes at me. "That church of yours didn't put you up to this, I hope."

I plunk the stack of papers down on his desk, ignoring the implied question. "Here are the assignments you wanted back today. Do you have anything else for me to work on?"

He sighs and jerks his head toward an equally large stack on the opposite side of his desk. "You can take those," he says. "Oh, and I meant to tell you. I'd like you to come to the zombie prep meeting tonight."

Now it's my turn to gape. "What? Why?"

He avoids my eyes. "I just do, that's all. You can take notes for me and pass stuff out. And you can assist with the drills."

Sounds riveting. I squirm, but can't think of any graceful way to get out of it. "Okay," I finally say, "I'll be there."

When I go home to dump my books off and grab something to eat before the meeting, I find Kyle Huang in my apartment. He's sitting on the couch and doing something with the papers on my coffee table. I'm so startled I nearly drop my books on the floor. Panic floods me and my knees feel so shaky I want to drop into the kitchen chair in front of me. Instead, I grab the back of it to support myself. What is he doing *inside* my apartment . . . And how did he get in?

Kyle holds his finger up to his lips in the universal signal for silence. "It's okay," he says in a quiet, reassuring voice, the sort you'd use to calm a child. "I didn't know when you would be home, and in case they recognize me out of uniform, I didn't want everyone in the neighborhood to see a TAO camped outside your door." He lifts up a piece of notebook paper that I gather he's ripped from one of the many notebooks that litter my coffee table. I can see there are some words scrawled across it. "I was leaving you a note."

He's tensed, studying me as though trying to determine whether or not I'll scream, or bolt, and doesn't visibly relax until he sees me relax. "You scared me." It's not exactly an accusation, but he looks abashed.

"I'm sorry. I was trying to protect you."

"How did you get in?"

He smiles and it's almost a shock how much it changes his face. He's always had a kinder expression toward me than any of the TAOs, well, than most people in general, to be frank. But I never realized how he wore the sadness in his heart on his face in unguarded moments until it vanishes. "I'm a TAO," he says simply, his voice becoming mockingly sarcastic, "we can go anywhere, do anything."

I give up my death grip on the chair back and cross the room to sit in the one opposite him. "What did you need to see me for?"

"There will be a raid tonight," he begins.

"Is that all?" I say, relieved. "There hasn't been one for awhile, so I suppose it's about time." He's shaking his head impatiently.

"This time there will be arrests."

My blood turns to ice in my veins. "Who are they—you—arresting?"

"*They*," he corrects me with emphasis, "are arresting anyone they want. They are dragging people in for various reasons or no real reason at all." He runs his hand distractedly through his close-cropped, military cut hair. I can see the worry in his eyes. "They have been going on for about a week now. Some of the people they have arrested are religious, some are not. Some have been released and others are still in a detention facility outside of the city." He glances at me. "There are rumors of torture . . ." His voice trails off.

"So what should I do?" I ask after a brief silence. "I know better than to be either angry or friendly. They don't care for either response. It's not like I can pretend not to be home; they'd just bang the door down if I didn't open it. Is there something you think I should get out of the apartment before they arrive? Something incriminating?" I cast my eyes around wondering what the TAOs would find incriminating.

Kyle is shaking his head. "You don't understand. I don't want you to even *be* here when they come. If they decide to take you, I can't protect you. It's safer if you're gone. They'll probably trash your apartment, but they can't arrest you if you're not here."

I look at him blankly. "But where would I go? I . . . I don't have family I can stay with," I add quietly.

There is a long pause during which Kyle looks conflicted and uncomfortable. I wonder if he's sorry he told me since there is obviously no way to avoid the situation. "I hope this is not presumptuous of me," he says finally, "but would you be available to babysit in the evenings? It's no picnic," he rushes on before I can respond to the sudden change of topic, "Sadie never wants to go to bed when she is supposed to, and she is as messy as a small tornado. You have to bribe her to get her to eat her vegetables, and you'll get hoarse reading to her."

He stops and looks me in the eyes long and hard. "You would be safe," he says simply.

"I . . . I . . ."

"I'll be gone," he assures me, mistaking my hesitation. "My shift starts at seven, and I don't get back until breakfast. You won't have to sleep on the couch, either. There's a small suite of rooms at one end of the house that the cook and nanny are supposed to share. I only have a cook when I'm throwing a party, and there's no full-time nanny now, of course, because Sadie is at school during the day. But I have a collection of sitters who take care of her when I have to work and do a bit of housecleaning. You would just be one of those sitters." He keeps his voice light, but I can imagine how much courage and trust it took for him to ask me, practically a complete stranger, to take care of his daughter, someone he obviously loves more than anything in the world. And why? To protect me from people like him.

"Kyle," I say, finding the taste of his name in my mouth strange but pleasant, "why are you a TAO? You don't seem like one of them. You . . . have a conscience, for one thing. You don't even seem to agree with most of what they do."

"I didn't join up, if that's what you mean," he says. "I was already in the military. I had just returned from my fourth deployment to Israel. TAOs are selected. There's a very strict protocol. I was chosen for my particular . . . skill set." The way he says "skill set" makes me shudder involuntarily. Whatever it means, it can't be good. "But that doesn't mean I'm happy about it. I would never have applied. In fact, I was hoping to finish my military career and do something a little more," he hesitates, "mundane."

He sighs deeply. "I've wanted out for a long time, but unfortunately you can't 'quit' the military, and you definitely can't quit the TAOs. I'm just trying to hang in there until my discharge. It's so close, only a year now. Then I'll be free. I just . . ." He looks troubled. "I'm not sure my conscience will let me continue that long. Pray for me?" he says.

I nod. "I will." Curious, I ask, "Why are you helping me? Me in particular," I elaborate.

In response, he pulls out the crumpled pocket testament he stole from my apartment during a raid. "I am saved," he says simply, his face relaxing, almost glowing. "So is Sadie. We have heaven to look forward to when this all ends." He waves his hand vaguely, indicating the world outside my apartment. "We know Jesus now, and He has made all the difference in our lives, in *my* life. My little girl has her daddy back, and someday we will have her mom back." Tears spring into his eyes, and he blinks them away. "Because of you," he finishes, his voice breaking. When he looks at me, the raw emotion in his eyes wrenches my heart. "I owe you a debt I can never repay. Never. Let me try? Let me keep you safe?" he pleads.

I nod, not trusting my voice.

"I didn't know your schedule," he says, looking pleased, but keeping his joy at my answer in check by focusing on the business at hand, "so I briefed the other sitters. They know you could come any night. If you show up, they are free to go."

"I don't want to put anyone out of a job," I protest.

Kyle holds up a hand to silence me. "They are all on salary. Paid for by my employer. It is one of my 'job perks,' though, unfortunately," he adds, "I can't add you to the roster without firing one of them, which means that I can't pay you. They won't know that though. They will think I'm employing you the same as I do them."

Kyle stands, preparing to leave, and I remember that I have something for him. "Wait," I say, before he can make a move toward the door. "Here, I was going to let you 'steal' this the next time you came, but since you're here as a legitimate visitor I can just give it to you." I grin as I hand him the adorable pink Bible I bought for Sadie.

I've been dying to give it to her, but I haven't seen Kyle and didn't know how I was going to manage it. It's all soft, pink leather and filled with the most whimsical drawings. I practically want to keep it myself it's so cute.

He takes it in his hands as though it's fragile and might crumble if handled roughly. "Sadie will love this," he says, his voice all choked up. "She will love it. Thank you so much."

"Are you attending a church?" I ask, hoping he says no so I can invite him to mine.

He shakes his head, but before I can proffer an invitation, he says, "It's too risky right now. Sadie and I have been studying with one of the people who was here at your meeting a few weeks ago. Judah."

I stare at him blankly.

"He didn't tell you?"

"No," I reply, wondering why Judah didn't mention it.

Kyle shrugs. "Anyway, like I said, right now we can't risk it. They're starting to apply extra scrutiny to organized religion as a whole. I have to keep my distance. Soon it won't be safe for anyone. But," he says meaningfully, giving me a long, significant look, "there is nothing to prevent us from being invited to someone's private home, and if an impromptu 'meeting' happened to evolve, well," he spreads his hands disarmingly, "there is nothing I can do about that."

I grin. "Is that so? Well, if there isn't going to be a raid next Wednesday, and you aren't otherwise engaged, you're welcome to come to my home. I'm having a few friends over. Everyone is bringing a dish, but you don't have to."

"As it happens, I am free on Wednesday; it's my night off. And after tonight there won't be any raids for at least a week. They've run out of holding space," he says with mock chagrin.

"That's a pity," I murmur.

"But you should spend the evenings at my place anyway. No sense taking chances. I'll let you know when things settle down again. If they ever do," he adds under his breath, grimacing. "Oh, here." He hands me a folded piece of paper with directions written on it. "This is how to get to my apartment and the names and numbers of the other sitters, just in case you have any trouble or run into a problem. As far as the TAOs are concerned, if anyone asks, you work for me as a babysitter."

I nod. "Got it." I study the directions for a few minutes to be sure I understand them. When I look up, I catch an unguarded expression in Kyle's eyes. He reaches out and taps his fingertips lightly against my bristly scalp.

"What happened to your hair?" he asks gently.

I sigh. "It's a long story," I tell him. "It needed to go. It's only hair; it'll grow back. In the meantime, I'm practicing humility."

"That's one way to do it," he agrees wryly. He looks like he's trying not to laugh. Well, why not? I suppose I *do* look funny. "You have a great sense of humor, Brooke," he says, opening the door and slipping out into the hallway. He pulls the door shut behind him so decisively I don't even have time for a retort. When I open it to say something, he's already gone.

I feel grossly out of place at the zombie preppers meeting. These folks are deadly serious when it comes to zombies. The ones who aren't dressed as zombies, lurching into the meeting room and "attacking" people, are carrying realistic toy weapons they pretend to bash each other in the head with. The whole thing gives me the creeps.

Professor McCormick feeds into their rabid interest, hyping up the looming threat in order to get his disaster preparedness training into their heads. I know it's all part of his master plan, but I also sense that he enjoys the hype; he enjoys being part of this exciting end-time scenario. In a small sense, I think he buys into the "what if?" aspect of it all despite how intelligent he is.

If only they knew was really *coming*, I muse as I distribute one of his handouts.

With a jolt, I feel God speak to me. *Why not tell them?*

Me? I feel like Moses standing uncomfortably before the burning bush being instructed to go speak to Pharaoh. Why would they listen to me?

They won't be listening to you; they'll be listening to me, a calm voice in my head assures me.

Before I can even wonder how I might go about injecting a biblical view of end-times, a girl pipes up, "My parents don't really like me taking a zombie class," she admits. She's one of the few who doesn't play dress-up. "They're Christians, and they believe there's never going to be any zombie apocalypse."

This remark gets a few snickers, but Professor McCormick raises his eyebrows at her. "Is that so?" He jerks his head at me. "I don't think Jesus Girl believes in the zombie apocalypse either, do you?"

I'm so flabbergasted it takes me a minute to collect my wits and reply. "No," I say evenly, "no, I don't." I look at the girl. "Your parents are right. The popular view of Hollywood zombies isn't biblical. Dead is dead." In my head, I'm praying feverishly. Now what do I say?

Professor McCormick parks his butt on the edge of his desk and crosses his arms. He gives me an amused, thoughtful expression. "So you don't believe in dead men walking?" he asks.

"Literally as zombies? No. But if you're being figurative, sure, I guess I believe in that. The Bible says 'each person is destined to die once and after that comes judgment.' So, yes, dead is dead. I suppose, in a literal sense, people's bodies can live on after death in their organs, like in an organ transplant. But they aren't aware of that. It's not like Suzie's liver thinks Suzie's thoughts in Bob's body. It just functions as a liver. And no one has to bash Bob's brains out to kill Suzie's liver. When Bob dies, Suzie's liver just dies along with him." This gets a chuckle from the students, and Professor McCormick actually laughs.

"But figuratively, we're all dead men walking. The Bible says 'You were dead because of your sins and because of your sinful nature was not yet cut away. Then God made you alive with Christ, for he forgave all our sins.' Every person on earth has sinned, so," I shrug, "we're all dead men walking, zombies of sin, I guess you could say. Even then," I point out, "God doesn't club us to death to put us out of our misery. He saves us from it. Instead of killing us, he gives us new bodies and new minds. He makes us new creatures. We get a new start in life. Everything old and ugly is gone, and we're completely clean and restored."

There's a hush as I finish speaking. I'm on the verge of tears, and I realize my little speech has been pretty impassioned. I'm fervently wishing the floor would open up and swallow me when Professor McCormick, who seems strangely touched, says quietly, "Is that what happened to you, Jesus Girl?"

Every head in the class swivels toward me curiously. This class has suddenly gone from disaster preparedness zombie nonsense into my own testimony.

I remember Judah speaking once on some verses from 1 Peter: "Always be prepared to give an answer to everyone who asks you to give the reason for the hope that you have." He said we'd never know when or where we would have the opportunity to witness and that we just had to be prepared to do it on the spot. And then he'd asked for volunteers right then and there. No one had taken him up on it. We'd all just glanced around in embarrassed silence, but he'd made his point. We needed to practice beforehand so that we'd know what we wanted to say and then we had to let the Holy Spirit gives us the exact words with which to say it.

I had taken his words to heart, mortified that I might not be able to give my testimony when the time came. I'd gone over it and over it until I could recite it from memory. Before I say anything, I pray that God brings it all to the tip of my tongue. And then I open my mouth and recognize nothing that comes out of it. The Holy Spirit is not only speaking through me, he's using words I didn't even practice.

"Yes," I say, "that's exactly what happened to me. My whole life was a sham; it was a lie. I was so messed up inside, so wounded, that I couldn't wake up in the morning without wishing I could die. I tried therapy, I tried drugs, but nothing made me feel alive. You think playing zombies is fun? Try being one. Everyone wanted to take a swing at me." I glance up at Professor McCormick, thinking of Derrick and how he stuck up for me, and my eyes start to tear up again. "Only a handful of people in my life have ever been kind to me. I got really good at hiding myself away. It was the only way I could protect myself."

I shrug. "And then I got to the point where I didn't care if I lived or died anymore. I just wanted to feel something." I've never told anyone what I'm about to say. I never even told Lily. It happened not long before we met. "So I tried to kill myself." There's a collective intake of breath. I hold my arm out and pull my long sleeve back revealing a thin, long, jagged, white line that meanders across my wrist. "I used a kitchen knife," I say wryly, "because I wanted it to hurt. I wanted to feel it."

"*Did* it hurt?" someone pipes up.

"Oh, yeah," I admit. "The knife was dull, and I chickened out in the end; the cut was completely superficial. I didn't end up hitting anything vital, just made a big mess. I was in college at the time, and one of my friends was a nursing major. She managed to put me back together again with super-glue and butterfly stitches. Miraculously I didn't get any infection or anything, and it all healed up. Not very pretty, but I learned my lesson."

"So what happened to change your life?" a skeptical voice interjects.

I know he wants a pat answer, something along the lines of, "and then, God touched my life and everything was perfect, and now I'm happy all the time." I wish it was as simple as that, as concrete. I wish there was a moment I could look back at and say, "That's it. Right there. That's the precise instant God changed my life." But that's not what happened. It was a lot more complicated than that.

"My life happened," I say simply. "It just kept spiraling down. I thought I was at the bottom, but there always seemed to be another level I could fall. When I finally did hit the bottom, I realized I didn't need a patch, something just to fix me up, as I'd thought. I needed a whole new life. And that's when I found God."

"Found him?" someone asks. "I didn't know he was lost." This is followed by a general snickering, but there's no malice in it.

"I guess that does sound a little funny," I admit. "I was so lost I couldn't have found my way out of a wet paper bag. I know God was there all along; I just couldn't see him. It wasn't until after he opened my eyes that I realized he was even there to be found."

"So how's your life now?" someone shouts from the back of the room.

"Yeah, Jesus Girl, people treating you better these days?" Professor McCormick stares pointedly at my shaved head.

I give him what I hope is a beatific smile. "Not always, but my perspective has changed. I know that no matter what happens in my life, no matter who hates on me, God is on my side. He's in my corner. He loves me, and he fills me with strength and joy and peace and hope and love . . . so many gifts. And He wants me to share them with other people, and no matter how much of them I give away, he replaces them. It's a never ending supply of love." I chuckle. "For someone who never felt loved, that's beyond awesome."

I glance around. Some of the students are looking at me wistfully, as though they want what I have. A few look bored. One has dozed off. Professor McCormick shuffles paperwork on his desk, but he has a look of such stark yearning on his face that I impulsively want to give him a hug and sit him down for a thorough Bible study. I want to lead him right up to Jesus and introduce them.

He clears his throat. "Well, thank you for that. I'm not sure how that will help us with water purification during the apocalypse, but you never know." There's a smattering of laughter, and the class picks up where it left off.

I resume passing out papers, but I notice more of the kids seem friendly to me, so it doesn't surprise me much when a couple of them approach me after class and want to know more. I give them each a pocket testament and invite them to the Bible study that's scheduled for the following week at my apartment. And then I spend the entire commute to Kyle's in awed appreciation of God's work not only in my life but in the lives of all his lost children.

Almighty God, I pray silently as I step onto the metro car that will bring me to Kyle's, *thank you for using even my messed up, broken life to draw people to yourself. Please be with the students whose hearts were touched by my testimony and also with Professor McCormick. I know he's seeking, even if he doesn't want to admit his need for you. Reveal yourself to him in a way that will show him how very much you love him.*

I'm so absorbed in talking to God that I almost miss my stop. I have to catch the door as it begins to close and squeeze past a couple irritated passengers. A TAO standing just outside the door narrows his eyes at me. "ID please," he says flatly.

Chapter Eleven

I pull my messenger bag around to the front of my body and dig my card out. I know better than to smile or make chitchat as I hand it over. That just seems to aggravate them, and they end up harassing you even more.

The TAO scans my card quickly, and the corners of his mouth turn down. "Destination?" he asks curtly.

"Um, I'm, uh . . ." I fish around in my messenger bag again while he fixes me with an icy glare. I retrieve the address Kyle gave me. "I'm going to 121B, apartment 3 in Lex," I tell him, reading the address from the slip. He keeps me pinned with an intense stare as he repeats the information in the direction of his shoulder, and I can see some kind of communication device fixed there.

"Nature of your business?"

I haven't been stopped by a TAO in a long time. It feels more like I'm crossing into a foreign country than just a different—albeit nicer—section of the city. "Babysitter," I reply promptly. "For a TAO officer." I lift an eyebrow at him defiantly in spite of myself. I'd like to see him argue with that.

"That so?" His voice is as flat as ever. "Stay there." He moves a short distance away, never taking his eyes off me, and conducts a conversation with his shoulder. Finally he returns and says grudgingly, "You're free to go."

"Thank you," I reply politely. He hands me back my ID card, and I put it away as quickly as I can, moving on down the sidewalk and trying to blend in. Looking around me, I can see why he questioned my presence. The other pedestrians look . . . cleaner, somehow. Their clothes are nicer. Some of them are carrying take-out cups of coffee, something you'd never see in my neighborhood. They are wearing suits, carry briefcases, and are openly using electronics, something no one on my end of town would dream of doing even if they had the money to own expensive electronics.

Ever since the last tantalum mine in Rwanda was blown up by activists who opposed the bloody conflicts fueled by the mineral trade, only the well-off can afford to buy electronics which rely on the rapidly dwindling stockpile of the mineral. News reports continue to claim that technologists are close to finding a replacement mineral "any day now" to make electronics once again available to the masses, but they've been saying that for quite some time, and most people no longer believe them.

The biggest breakthrough they'd had so far was being able to synthesize a replacement mineral for cell phones, otherwise very few people would still have those, either. But according to the techies that had been an easy one, and since the new cell phones didn't need tantalum specifically, they could get by without it. The more sophisticated electronics, apparently, relied on it.

I feel severely under-dressed in my usual long black skirt, black top, and black Dr. Martens. Some people give me curious looks, but most are too wrapped up in their own lives to spare me a second glance. By the time I reach Kyle's apartment, I'm anxious to slip inside and escape public view.

A swanky girl answers the doorbell, takes one look at me, and demands to see my ID card before she'll let me in. I guess I can't blame her. I hand it over cheerfully, and once she's verified that I'm who I say I am she lets me in, happy I'm there to relieve her.

"I have a date," she confesses as she collects her things. "I was going to have to cancel, but Officer Huang said I might get the night off. What a stroke of luck. You won't have any trouble with Sadie," she promises. "She's a complete angel." She gives me a troubled glance. "Try not to be too scared of Officer Huang," she says with a shudder. "I know he can seem cold and harsh, well, I think he probably *is* cold and harsh, but considering what he has to do for a living . . ." She trails off and shudders again, wrapping her arms around her torso as though she's got a sudden chill. "I don't know how Sadie turned out so sweet; her mother must have been a complete saint."

She throws her designer bag over her shoulder, twiddles her fingers at me in goodbye, and slips out the door. Before I can lock it she pops her head back inside. "Lock the door," she says. "And keep it locked. Got it?"

I nod and lock it firmly behind her. It's like I've ushered a small tornado out the door. I wonder what she meant about Kyle's job— does she know what his "skill set" is? Before I can think about it too much I hear a soft sound behind me. When I turn, I find Sadie regarding me with her solemn, black eyes.

I give her a friendly smile. "Hi Sadie, do you remember me? My name is Brooke."

Sadie nods. She's hugging the Bible I gave her as though it's a stuffed toy.

"Do you like your Bible?" I ask softly. "Would you like me to read it to you?"

She nods again, and I follow her to the couch where she surprises me by snuggling right up with me as though we're old friends. It takes me longer than it does her to relax, but as soon as I get into the story of Zacchaeus climbing the sycamore tree in order to see Jesus, I discover that I have a talent for reading to children. I'm so invested in the story that I do voices and make sound effects without consciously realizing it. I have no idea where this latent ability comes from. I don't remember anyone reading to me like this when I was a child. Sadie eats it up and giggles in all the right places. When I finish, she demands another. I discover Kyle is right; I will be hoarse long before she's ready to let me stop reading.

Eventually, I talk her into giving me a tour since the other sitter—Elena, Sadie informs me—neglected it in her mad dash out the door. Kyle and Sadie live in a well-appointed, nicely furnished, beautifully decorated home, and I try very hard to block comparisons to my own squalid hovel by reminding myself that lots of people have it far worse than I do. The "small suite of rooms" for the nanny and sitters that Kyle referred to is, in fact, a compact apartment unto itself on one side of the larger apartment. It's bigger than my own apartment and a hundred times nicer.

Tacked to the refrigerator door I find care instructions. Reading them over, I realize I've already let Sadie stay up past her bedtime. Fortunately, she doesn't give me any grief about turning in as Kyle said she might. I pray with her, and as I'm tucking her in, my eyes fall on a photo in an ornate silver frame. It's on Sadie's nightstand. I pick it up and look at the women in the photo while Sadie watches me soberly.

"Is this your mom?" I ask gently. She nods. The woman in the picture does not look not Asian, like Kyle and Sadie, but she has dark hair and brown eyes. She looks serene and confident. I remember Kyle saying she'd been a Christian. "What was her name?"

"Mom," Sadie replies innocently. "But Appa called her Sylvia."

I chuckle at this. I suspect that "Appa" refers to her father, and later I find out that it's the Korean word for "Daddy."

"She died from cancer," Sadie volunteers. "Now I have

babysitters." She wrinkles her nose.

"You don't like the sitters?" I ask, bemused.

"I'd rather have a mom," she says matter-of-factly. I can't argue with her there.

Once she's in bed, I don't know what to do with myself. I wander aimlessly around the apartment for a bit trying to absorb the elegance of the place so I have something to take back with me when I leave. Everything here is so light and airy. I can't believe how starved for beauty I've been until I'm surrounded by it.

I didn't always live in squalor. For one thing, the city wasn't always like this; it used to be nicer, cleaner. But then the economy collapsed, and the wars—so numerous now it was hard to keep track of where we had peacekeeping forces—started to take their toll on the country both because of the sheer amount of personnel we deployed and the retaliatory attacks that had begun to escalate on our own soil—hence the TAOs. I actually grew up not far from Kyle's apartment in a neighborhood that wasn't quite as grand, but still plenty respectable. My parents still live there.

There are paintings on Kyle's walls that look like museum pieces. I took an art class in college one semester and while these don't look like anything famous, they do all look like originals. I fix myself a cup of tea in the beautifully appointed, bright and shiny kitchen, and carry it with me while I go methodically from one painting to another, as if I'm in my own private art gallery. I take my time, studying each one. It's like being on vacation in some new city. I have to keep reminding myself that I'm only on the other side of my own.

When I've seen every painting in the main rooms (there are only a couple doors that are closed, and I don't even try the knobs to see if I can open them), I curl up on the sofa and for the first time I notice a large, black screen set into the wall opposite me. It's the biggest, fanciest television set I've ever seen. I haven't owned one myself for years, but my parents had one, and I've visited people who have them. I look around for the remote control and find it on a small stand near the sofa.

It takes me a few minutes to figure out how it works; they've changed a bit since I've used one. The screen comes to life suddenly and startles me. It's so colorful and so vivid and so *huge* that it almost hurts my eyes to look at it. I flick through the channels trying to find something interesting, a nature program maybe, but I stop in horror as a picture flashes onto the screen. It's a burning building. *My* building.

It's a distant shot; the female news anchor is standing well away from the blaze. I squint my eyes at the screen, trying to determine if the fire is on the side near my apartment or somewhere else in the building, trying to figure out how bad it is. A fire truck is pumping water onto it, and it doesn't look as though the fire is spreading.

Over the news anchor's left shoulder people are swarming. Some are running away from the building, some are running away from the TAOs. There are gunshots as the TAOs fire into the crowd. People scream and some of them fall. Aghast, I steel myself and try to focus on what the camerawoman is saying. She's tapping on her ear piece and frowning.

"I'm sorry, Roger, there's a lot of interference. I couldn't quite make out your question, but I believe you asked if I knew what had caused this tragic outbreak of violence. We have only preliminary reports from bystanders at this time, but eyewitnesses say that the TAOs were conducting a routine check of this neighborhood . . ."

"Raid, you mean," I correct her.

". . . when vagrants in the building behind me," she indicates my apartment building with a wave of her hand, "opened fire on them."

This, I realize, is probably quite true. I can completely imagine someone getting so fed up with yet another raid that they opened fire. I can even imagine completely strung-out druggies, the ones who camp out for weeks at a time in the hallways, shooting at the TAOs, too. Especially if they tried to make them forfeit the territory they'd staked out. Chances are the TAOs had stumbled across them during their regular raid, only this time they'd decided to haul some of them in to the detention center and the vagrants had resisted, with force.

The news anchor shrieks and dives off screen for a moment before reappearing, her composure shattered. "That was *not* a stray bullet," she's screaming at someone behind the camera. "They're firing at us! I've covered Afghanistan, you idiot! I know what I'm talking about."

There's a soft grunt and the camera dips suddenly.

"He's hit! He's hit!" the news anchor is shouting. "Get a medic! Get out of the line of . . ."

The picture goes all staticky. I scramble for the remote and start punching buttons, hoping there's coverage on another channel. I can feel my heart beating wildly in my chest as I press the channel selector over and over, scrolling through endless, mindless drivel, desperate for more information. Did they get the fire under control? Did they get the crowd under control? Suddenly my brain stops dead. Kyle.

Kyle was the one who told me there was going to be a raid at my apartment building tonight. He is working, which is why I'm here in the first place. Does that mean *he's* out *there*? I try to remember the TAOs I saw, try to remember the way they moved, if there had been anything familiar about any of them. They all look so alike in their black uniforms, black hats, and black boots. The only splash of color is that red insignia on their hats.

My cell phone rings and gives me such a shock I nearly fall off the sofa. "Hello? Hello?" I'm speaking before I even jab the buttons, hoping it's Kyle to tell me he's on his way home and the news report was just a big hoax.

Before it can occur to me that Kyle doesn't have my cell phone number and if he really wanted to reach me he would call his own house phone, a male voice roars, "Brooke? Thank you, God, thank you for keeping her safe. You are safe, aren't you?"

"Judah?"

"I just heard about what's going on at your apartment building. Are you there? Are you okay?"

"I'm okay," I tell him. "I'm not home. I'm babysitting at Kyle's. I'm nowhere near there."

"Thank you, God," he says again. The relief in his voice makes me want to weep. "Wait, Kyle's? The TAO guy? How did you . . . What are you . . . Never mind. You can explain it to me later. I have some other people I need to check on. I'll talk to you later, girlfriend, okay?"

"Okay," I agree, smiling. "Thanks, Judah."

For a little while I scroll through the channels endlessly, but the story doesn't seem to have been picked up on any of the other channels, and the one I was watching it on is still off the air. Finally, I give up and turn the television off. I can't concentrate on a program right now. All I can think about is all those people, the shooting, the fire, and Kyle.

I slide off the couch and onto my knees. "Dear Heavenly Father, please protect Kyle and the other people involved in this situation tonight. Be with those who are injured, get them the help they need. Heal not only their physical wounds, Lord, but also reveal yourself to them. Show them that only with your help, with your *life* can they be whole. Only with your strength can they be free from the problems of this world, no matter how impossible it seems to us, because we know that with you *nothing* is impossible. You walked among us to show us how we can have a better life, a victorious life. We don't have to live like slaves to sin anymore. You set us free. Help us to live like free people."

For just an instant a shadow passes through my mind. *Where's your freedom?* it asks. *If you're not a slave to sin, then why are you living like one? Where's your victory? Sure, you're keeping away from a sinful relationship, but that's not the same thing as having a God-ordained relationship, a biblically sanctioned relationship, is it? Pretty hollow victory if you ask me.*

Until that moment it hadn't occurred to me to wonder if my celibacy was enough, if managing to keep thoughts of Lily at bay by sheer willpower alone was enough, if "managing" my "problem" was enough: compensating for my weakness, building a wall around myself for protection. Is it? Or am I living like a free slave? Still shackled, but ambling through life under my own steam. Is that truly what God has planned for me? Or could he have more in mind?

It wouldn't matter, would it? the shadow taunts. *You can't change. You'll never change. Not even God can change you. He doesn't have enough power to change someone like you, someone as dirty and weak as you.*

I feel as though I've been stabbed. Can that be true? Are there some sins God can't forgive? Are there some people God can't change? Am I living a lie? Is God up in heaven having a laugh at my delusions? Is he pitying me for thinking that we even *have* a relationship?

A Bible verse runs through my head. "Surely the arm of the Lord is not too short to save, nor his ear too dull to hear." Relief begins to trickle into my consciousness. Of course God's arm is not too short to save me! Another verse follows quickly, as if in response to my thought. "Be sober, be vigilant; because your adversary the devil walks about like a roaring lion, seeking whom he may devour," and suddenly my world shifts back on its axis. Satan is trying to devour my faith. He's trying to tear it down, destroying my soul.

"I am yours, save me," I pray. My hand reaches automatically for my Bible; I want to see the words of Psalm 119 in black and white. I want to trace them with my finger. I want to touch them and claim them. My grasp meets air, and I suddenly come back to myself, realizing I'm not in my own apartment. My own Bible is probably on my kitchen table, in my burning apartment building.

My eyes fall on Kyle's Bible. It's partially hidden beneath a stack of other books on a small end table next to the sofa. I pull it onto my lap and page through to the Psalms. There are notes written in many of the margins, verses—sometimes whole chapters—are underlined. It's clear Kyle has been spending a lot of time reading his Bible. I find the verse I'm looking for in Psalm 119 and read it aloud. Kyle's version is different than mine and the wording isn't what I have memorized, but I like this translation. "I am yours; rescue me! For I have worked hard at obeying your commandments."

I let these words seep into my soul. I feel them deep in my heart. I pray them again, out loud, with conviction. God's arm is not short! His ear is not dull! I am his child, and he will rescue me. I feel the darkness dissipate and a calm peace descends over me. "Thank you, Lord," I murmur, suddenly exhausted by the events of the day and the spiritual struggle.

It's the door slamming that wakes me. For a moment I don't even know where I am, and I begin to panic. My eyes slowly register my surroundings and rationality kicks in. Surely no place that looks this nice can be too bad. Then Kyle comes into the living room, and it all comes back to me.

"You're okay," I say with relief, struggling up from the floor. "I saw a little of the news report about my neighborhood on your television. Were you involved with that?"

Kyle looks at me with a hard edge in his eyes. He doesn't even seem to recognize me. I don't need his answer to know he was caught in the situation at my apartment because his uniform is smudged with soot and there are dark stains on his face. More soot? Blood? Slowly, the unmistakable odor of smoke reaches me. He doesn't seem to be bleeding, but his vacant, cold eyes are starting to scare me. After all, I don't know this man. I trusted him based on the fact that we're both Christians. That battle-weary, dead sort of look in his eyes frightens me.

"Where is Sylvia?" he demands, looking around, as if I've done something with her.

He's clearly in another place mentally. Is he asking about his wife because she died during one of his deployments? Does he think he's still over there, somewhere, in Israel or wherever they sent him all those times? I want to pray out loud so he can hear me, but I'm afraid to do anything that might provoke him, so I pray silently instead. "Sadie is still sleeping," I say, as though he had asked about his daughter instead of his dead wife. I keep my voice completely neutral. "She should be up any minute though. I'm sure she'll be hungry. Would you like something to eat? You must be starved."

I move slowly and deliberately toward the kitchen, and when I glance back over my shoulder I am relieved to see that Kyle is following me. Instead of sitting down at one of the stools at the counter, or seating himself at the table, he paces, agitated, around the perimeter of the room. Every now and then he barks something at me, usually an order not to use something I'm reaching for, or a direction on how to cook something, and I have to keep a tight grip on myself so that I don't jump or react in any way. It's unnerving. I see none of the kind, compassionate man I thought I was beginning to know.

I serve up the French toast on a plate with some sliced peaches and fried eggs and place it on the table. "*Bon appétit*," I say, forcing a smile.

Kyle stares at me blankly. "What did you say?" he asks, his voice not as harsh as it was.

"*Bon appétit?*" I repeat uncertainly. "It's the only French I know. It means, er, it's something like, eat well, or have a nice dinner . . . Or breakfast," I amend quickly.

He sits down, practically collapses, in a chair at the table and mechanically starts eating, wolfing the food down. I sink cautiously into a chair opposite him. Halfway through, he looks up at me, and I can see comprehension flicker. "Brooke?" he asks.

"Hi, Kyle," I reply softly, not wanting to startle him back into whatever dark place he's just come from. Up close his eyes are bloodshot, and as he begins to relax a little, I can see that he's exhausted. But at least now he seems to know where he is and who I am.

"Appa?" a small voice asks, startling us both. Sadie is standing in the doorway rubbing her eyes. She's holding a stuffed rabbit with the improbable markings of a zebra by the ear and she's got only one slipper on.

"Sadie, sweetheart," Kyle says. "Come here." She goes to him without hesitation, despite his grime, and throws her arms around him.

He holds her close, and I can see his shoulders begin to shake. He's weeping. Sadie seems to sense that something is wrong, and she wriggles out of his grasp.

"You smell bad," she observes, "and I have to go to school soon."

School! I realize I have no idea what her schedule is. I get up to check the instructions on the refrigerator and to give Kyle a moment to collect himself. Fortunately, everything is written down in detail. I manage to get Sadie fed, washed up, and dressed. By the time we're ready to head out the door to school Kyle has recovered his wits enough to give me directions on how to get there.

"Go on," he says wearily. "I'm going to take a shower." He rallies enough to wish Sadie a good day and brush a kiss on her cheek. I'm afraid to leave him alone, but it can't be helped.

Sadie's a regular chatterbox as we walk hand in hand to her school. She's clutching her lunch box in one hand with the lunch I made her— the first lunch I've ever made for a child, and I worry that I did it wrong—and has a flowered backpack on her shoulders. Some people we pass give us funny looks, but Sadie's presence seems to neutralize my own. The whole experience is so surreal that I can hardly believe it's reality; it feels like a very vivid dream.

When I return, Kyle has changed into clean clothes, a pair of black sweat pants and a white T-shirt, and his hair is wet from the shower. He's sitting on the couch in the living room, his Bible open on his lap. He doesn't look up when he hears me come in, if he hears me come in, and even at a distance I can see his lips are moving. I spend as much time as I can in the kitchen, tidying up and doing the breakfast dishes, before I check on him.

"Hey," I say softly. "How are you feeling?"

When he looks up at me, I see that he has a dark bruise on one cheek, and his eyes are full of tears. "Brooke." The word sounds jagged, but at least he knows who I am. "Will you pray with me?" he asks.

"Of course."

He slides off the couch and onto his knees still clutching his Bible. I kneel down next to him, and he reaches out, fumbling for my hand. I resist the urge to yank it away and realize that he's sobbing uncontrollably. "Please, pray," he manages to get out between gut-wrenching sobs. "Please pray for me."

His grief scares me, but it also strikes a chord deep inside my heart where it finds an equally fierce, equally desperate echo. I pray for Kyle, and I don't even know where the words come from. They don't feel like my words. I quote scripture without having to look it up, and I plead desperately for God to have compassion and mercy on both of us, to cover our sins, make us new creations in him, and forgive our inadequacies and failings.

When I say amen, Kyle begins to pray himself, and I feel as though I'm eavesdropping, but there's no way to escape. He has hold of my hand and there is nothing I can do to block the words as they shoot out of his mouth like bullets, slamming into my conscience, confessing to sanctioned murder and other war acts so atrocious that at one point I try to wriggle my hand from Kyle's in order to escape, but his grip tightens on mine, and I am forced to stay and hear everything.

"God save me! God save me!" he cries finally, when his words run out, and the cry is so like my own the night before that suddenly I see him not as the hardened war machine he's just confessed to being, but only as a broken man, a sinner in need of a savior, *just like me*. Sin is sin, I remind myself. My sin is no better or worse than his. Some people would forgive him more easily than they would me. After all, the things he did could be justified as acts committed during a time of war or service to his country, whereas my own sin looks like a lifestyle choice if you don't know my history and no one, except for my brother, does.

"Am I lost?" he asks me, raising tortured eyes to mine. "Can God forgive me?"

"Yes, God can forgive you; he *does* forgive you," I respond confidently. "God saves everyone who calls on him." Gently I pull the Bible from his hands. We sit on the floor, side by side, leaning back against the couch, and I start with Romans 10:13: " 'Everyone who calls on the name of the Lord will be saved.' " I look at him to make sure he understands that. "Everyone, Kyle, do you understand? *Everyone* who calls on the name of the Lord. That means you, that means me, which means everyone who asks God for forgiveness will be forgiven, and he will save us all."

Kyle scoffs, "You, what have you got to be forgiven for? You can't know how I feel."

I consider him for a long time before I answer. I am so frightened that I have to pray silently for God to give me the courage to speak. I don't go around telling my salvation story to people lightly, not in its entirety anyway, not the details of my past. But suddenly, I feel that it's imperative for him to know he's not alone. He's not the only "unforgivable" person in the world. So I tell him. I tell him everything about my brother, Lily, and how God saved me. And I watch the revulsion in his eyes slowly change to comprehension and then finally, as I know it did in my own, to compassion.

It seems stupid, maybe, but as we sit there, fresh with the knowledge of each other's deepest sins, I feel as though I know how Adam and Eve felt right after the fall. We're both damaged goods, and we can't do anything to change our pasts. And the answer to our brokenness is the same as it was for Adam and Eve: Jesus. They looked forward to his death and resurrection, and we look back on it, but it accomplished the same thing for all of us. It placed on Jesus the penalty for our disobedience and gave us the reward for his obedience.

I page to another section of the Bible and read, " 'I give them eternal life, and they will never perish. No one can snatch them away from me, for my Father has given them to me, and he is more powerful than anyone else. No one can snatch them from the Father's hand.' "

Kyle leans his head back on the sofa, and his hand finds mine again. "We're saved; we're saved," he whispers. "Thank you, Jesus; we're saved." In moments, he's asleep, freed from the demons that have plagued him all night. I hate to leave him alone, but I need to get to class. I have to check on my apartment and see if it's still habitable. I leave him a note and tuck it partway into his Bible, gather my things, and slip out the door, locking it behind me. For a moment I stand on the doorstep, relishing the warmth of the sun on my face and feeling as though I've left a dark, dark place and stepped out into the sunlight.

"Thank you, Jesus, for saving us," I whisper. And then I head for the wrong side of town.

Chapter Twelve

It takes me two hours to get to my apartment. The whole area is cordoned off. I have to surrender my ID card and submit to a thorough search and then they have to locate my name on a list of official tenants before they'll allow me to pass. The only reason I even get to enter is because my apartment is on the unaffected leg of the L-shaped building. The section that was burned is already boarded up, and guards are stationed outside all the entrances.

The hallways are unusually vacant and my apartment smells faintly of smoke. I think longingly of Kyle's nicely appointed, clean apartment before steeling myself to deal with my own. The work Professor McCormick sent home with me is stacked on the kitchen table, and I wish I had brought it with me to his zombie meeting last night. A quick check of my watch tells me I'm going to miss his class this morning. He's not going to be happy with me, I muse, stuffing the pile into my messenger bag along with all my books.

I take a quick shower, change my clothes, and scan the apartment wondering what else I should bring with me. Who knows what will become of this building? It's possible they'll shut the whole thing down. How would I return tonight? After the violence of the night before, I expect that it will be crawling with police and TAOs. Just in case, I pack a small backpack with a couple changes of clothes, a toothbrush, and my Bible. There's not really anything else I need. I don't wear makeup, and my hair is wash-and-go. I feel almost liberated not to be tied to worldly goods.

I miss my morning classes, and when I find a few minutes to drop in on Professor McCormick, he's irritated with me.

"I needed those papers," he tells me testily. "If you aren't going to be here for class, the least you could do is call. Don't make me fire you," he threatens.

I gulp. "I'm sorry." I try not to be stung. "My apartment building was partially burned last night. It took me all morning to clear security and even get inside."

He looks abashed. "You're okay?" he asks, giving me a swift once-over.

"I wasn't there at the time," I explain. "I was babysitting at a friend's. I'd left my books and the paperwork at the apartment, and . . ." I spread my arms helplessly. "Well, the place is crawling with security and cleanup crews. If it takes me that long to get into my apartment every time I go home, I don't know what I'll do." I have visions of myself catching catnaps at the Laundromat and in the college library, wearing the same stale clothes day after day. It's not a pretty picture.

"I'm sorry about your apartment," he says, and I know that despite his brusque façade he is. "Follow me."

Curious, I follow him as he threads his way through one of the aisles and makes his way to a corridor beyond. At the very end, just as I'm starting to get nervous, he opens a door and indicates I should look inside. I peer around him and find a small, cluttered, dusty room. Towers of books are leaning haphazardly on one wall; graduation gowns are strewn across a couple bookcases and small metal tables. There are a couple folding chairs toppled over and some old equipment that looks like it might have had something to do with displaying images on a screen long before my time.

"This is my designated storage room," Professor McCormick says. "As you can see, I don't use it. Get this cleaned up, throw it all away for all I care. You can store your stuff here for now. No one will mind. You could even sleep here in a pinch, but if you tell anyone I said that, I'll denounce you as a liar." He waves his hand down the corridor we just passed through. "This is all storage," he says. "You should even be able to find a desk in one of these rooms. Set it up in this room, and you can work here until the situation at your apartment improves."

"Thank you, Professor McCormick," I begin, but he shushes me with an abrupt motion of his hand.

"Just looking out for my own interests," he says gruffly. He heads back down the corridor leaving me to take stock of the room. I decide there's no time like the present. As I work, I can't help but praise God for his goodness. Not only has he provided me with work, he's protected me and given me not one, but *two* clean, safe places to stay. This room may not be very big, but there are no cockroaches in it, I don't have to climb over passed out drunks to reach it, and it doesn't smell like backed-up sewage.

By the time I'm finished it looks, not cozy maybe, but utilitarian; you could almost say snug. I couldn't find a desk in the adjoining rooms, at least not without having to move other large furniture to get at it, but I did find one of the student chairs with an attached platform arm that serves as a desk. Set up next to one of the cleared off small metal tables it makes a perfectly usable work space.

I'm halfway through grading my next batch of papers when Judah calls me and wants me to meet him at the small campus café for supper. "I want to see you with my own eyes," he says dramatically, "to be sure you're okay."

As soon as he mentions supper my stomach reminds me that I haven't eaten since that morning at Kyle's. I have just enough time to finish the rest of Professor McCormick's paperwork before meeting him. We fix a time, and then he's interrupted on his end and hastily wraps up our call. *Well*, I think, *there will be plenty of time to talk at the café.* Ignoring my protesting stomach I return to work.

To tell the truth, I'd forgotten that he hadn't yet seen my recently shaved head. So much has happened that it seems like weeks ago, not days ago that Sarah shaved off my dreads. I'm slightly taken aback when he doesn't even recognize me. He's scanning the café when I arrive, and I slide into the booth opposite him.

"I'm sorry," he says, glancing over at me, "that seat's taken. I'm waiting for a friend."

At first I think he's kidding, but when I don't leave he looks at me again, irritation obviously held in check. "I said . . ." He trails off as a puzzled look crosses his face. Several long moments tick by as realization slowly dawns in his eyes. "Brooke? Brooke! You didn't! You didn't do it . . . Why did you do it? Oh, Brooke!" He throws his upper body across the table top and crushes me in an awkward hug. People are staring at us, and I feel a fresh wave of grief and sympathy for myself at his obvious consternation.

After a bit he sits back and looks at me with anguish. "I'm so sorry you had to go through that," he says. "I wish you hadn't done it."

I shrug and try to swallow my own anguish. "It's okay, really. I felt that God wanted me to, that it was a small price to pay to preserve the peace. He gave up so much more for me . . . for us." I smile weakly and try to cheer him up, "It'll grow back, you know." It dawns on me that I've had dreads for so long I'm not sure I know what style I should eventually shoot for or how to do mysterious things like blow it dry or curl it.

Judah shakes his head helplessly, his lips compressed into a tight, displeased line. Then he takes a deep breath. "Love suffers long and is kind; love does not envy; love does not parade itself, is not puffed up; does not behave rudely, does not seek its own, is not provoked, thinks no evil; does not rejoice in iniquity, but rejoices in the truth; bears all things, believes all things, hopes all things, endures all things. Love never fails." He smiles slightly at me. "With God's help we can love everyone, even our church board, right?"

I know it's a rhetorical question, but I answer anyway, "Right." Just hearing the words has a soothing effect on my heart, and I can tell they've made Judah feel better as well.

"God will help us through this," he says with conviction. "He will. We just have to be faithful. It's his job to change hearts, not ours."

I nod. "That's right." I study him for a few minutes while a waitress comes over and takes our orders. After she leaves, I ask, "Judah, is something wrong? You don't seem yourself."

He's quiet for a few minutes before he admits, "I'm worried about Rocko, and I'm worried about the church. Don't get me wrong," he hastens to add, "I'm really glad we have so many new folks coming. I just wish . . ." His voice trails off. He glances at my shorn head and then away again quickly.

He doesn't have to say it; I know what he wishes. He wishes the church would stop gazing critically at its own reflection in the mirror and spread the gospel like it's supposed to be doing. We've had numerous conversations about this, some of them with Pastor Javier who feels as though his hands are tied by bureaucracy. Every time anyone tries to start an outreach program the board quashes it. Either they are unwilling to allocate funds to support it, or they find some potential legal or other unarguable reason why it can't be done or won't work. The few projects that make it off the ground are largely supported by a handful of people who, like us, are determined not to be deterred. Everyone else seems apathetic or downright too busy to participate.

On top of this, there is a steady trickle of people coming into the church, but it's being offset by the steady trickle of people *leaving* the church. It's like trying to fill a bucket that has a hole in it. I know Judah gets frustrated because all of these factors make it difficult to see any progress. In addition, watching people leave, sometimes after you've pleaded with them to stay, is heartbreaking. Some leave discouraged, and some are just plain angry, and you can't tell if they've given up on God entirely or just our particular church. I remind myself again that, "No one can snatch them from the Father's hand." We just have to trust them to his safe keeping.

"So," Judah says, clearing his throat and changing the subject, "are we still going to be able to hold the prayer meeting at your place next Wednesday?"

"I think so. It took me forever to get to my apartment today because of all the security, but that should slack off by next week, shouldn't it?" I think of all the people we couldn't reach if we had to move the meeting. Professor McCormick's students among them. I'd hate to have them show up and find no one there. What kind of a witness would that be?

Judah shrugs. "Hopefully. I guess if it hasn't we'll have to come up with a Plan B."

"Which is?"

"My place?" I've never been to Judah's apartment, but from what he says, it's cleaner and in a slightly better location than mine, but it's smaller, which is hard to believe. My apartment is six hundred square feet; whereas, Judah claims his is only three hundred.

"Let's hope we can use mine then."

Over dinner I give him all the details about the night before and how I came to be at Kyle's instead of my apartment. He's particularly interested in this. "I've been studying with him," he tells me around a mouthful of risotto.

"So he said. Why didn't you mention it?"

Judah looks puzzled. "Should I have? I study with quite a few people, you know. Do you want a list?"

He's joking, but I'm actually curious. "How many is quite a few?"

He thinks about this for a minute. "I've got about thirty Bible studies going at the moment."

I'm stunned. "Really? But when do you have time to study and go to class?"

His gaze shifts away from me guiltily. "I'm not going to class," he mumbles.

"What did you say?"

"I'm not going to class," he repeats, louder, almost defiantly. For a second he reminds me of Rocko.

"Since when?" I suddenly realize that we haven't spent much time together outside church activities for awhile now. Ever since . . . Marissa. I wonder if she knows. Maybe she even encouraged him to drop college.

Most of the time Judah projects an aura of confidence so polished that I take him to be years older than he is. But I'm older than he is; not old enough to be his mother, but I feel a maternal instinct rise up in me. I narrow my eyes at him while he squirms uncomfortably.

"The last couple of weeks," he admits. "What's the point? I'm going to graduate and then what? The church thinks I'm too radical to be a pastor. They'll never hire me." He sighs heavily. "I told you before, I work for God, not the church. And God doesn't require a degree before *he'll* hire me."

"What does Marissa say about this?" I ask casually.

He hikes up one shoulder noncommittally. "She's not happy about it."

"Really?" That's good. I have an ally.

"Do you really think I should go back?" he asks, dismayed.

I choose my words with care. "I think you should consider your decision carefully," I say, "and pray about it, too. God is already using you, that's clear, but maybe he has more to teach you here in college—Greek, Hebrew, and other subjects you can only learn here." I reach over and pat his hand. "Think about it. Please?"

He doesn't agree, but he looks thoughtful. His eyes travel past me. "What are they doing?" he asks abruptly.

I turn to look in the direction he's staring and see a group of TAOs herding a bunch of students and a couple bewildered looking professors ahead of them. Every now and then a TAO breaks off to round up another student, or dash into an adjacent building presumably to look for someone else to add to their growing group. *Are they working from a list,* I wonder, *or just picking people up randomly?*

"We should go," Judah says. He beckons the waitress over and settles the bill before I can protest that I want to go Dutch. He slips a tip into a pocket testament and leaves it on the table, pulling me to my feet and hustling me out of the opposite end of the café from the side of the building where we saw the TAOs. On the sidewalk, he regards me dubiously. "Are you okay to get home by yourself? Do you want me to walk with you?"

I wave him off. "I'm fine. I can get around them easily. Go. I'll see you at church in a couple days."

"Okay." He hesitates and I can tell he's torn between wanting to leave and not wanting to leave me in case the TAOs carry me off, so I start walking. I wait a hundred yards before I risk a peek back to see if he's still there and he's not. He's texting someone as he walks away. Marissa?

I slow down when I'm sure he's not paying attention to me anymore. I feel as though I've been set adrift. I do *not* want to go home to my apartment, but I was determined not to return to Kyle's so soon. For one thing, even thinking about everything we went through this morning still feels raw. For another, I don't want to take advantage of his offer. He said I could come whenever I wanted and that the other child caregivers would get the night off, but I feel embarrassed about turning up again so soon. Will they think I'm trying to edge them out of a job?

The other reason I hesitate is fear, I admit to myself. I'm afraid now that Kyle has had time to think about my confession the revulsion will return. The strong resistance to seeing him again so soon, I realize, is my equally strong desire not to see that in his eyes. After the storm we passed through together, I feel connected to him at a very deep level. I'm not sure I've ever felt so deeply connected to another human being. It frightens me, to be honest. I feel fragile and vulnerable. I'm afraid that if I see rejection in his eyes something inside me that is very delicate will shatter, and I want to protect it.

But after eying the approaching group of TAOs warily and cycling quickly through my very limited options, including the storage room, I find myself on the metro headed for Kyle's. Elena answers the door this time, and she's even more eager to leave than last night. I follow her into the little apartment where she's already got her things together. "I was hoping you'd come back tonight," she confides as she grabs my elbow and herds me back toward the front door with her. "Frankly, I don't envy you. He's home." She raises her eyebrows meaningfully and lowers her voice so Sadie, who I can hear playing in the nearby living room, can't overhear her. "He's *not* in a good mood, and I just heard him call in sick."

"Oh," I feel my hopes drop. The thought of returning to my dismal apartment is almost more than I can bear. "Should I go then since he doesn't need child care?"

"No!" Elena says, her voice sharp and insistent. She claps a hand over her mouth, her eyes wide with chagrin. "No," she repeats in a whispered hiss. "Someone has to cook dinner, get Sadie ready for bed, and get her to school tomorrow. Someone *has* to stay. If you don't, I'll have to and right now he scares me." She seems to realize she might scare me off as well because she hastily assures me, "I'm sure it's nothing, just a bad mood. It'll be fine. Just stay out of his way and keep Sadie quiet. Everything will be fine."

Before I can protest or change my mind, she slips out of the door, and it clicks shut behind her. I take a moment to pray before I go in search of Kyle and Sadie. I find Sadie in the living room playing with a herd of horses on the floor. She's got them all rounded up and is painstakingly moving them around the living room en masse which involves tediously inching them forward one at a time to join the leaders. "Hello, Sadie," I say, interrupting her concentration.

She glances up at me distractedly before returning to her task. "Hello."

I sit in one of the plush chairs and watch her for a little while, glancing surreptitiously around for any sign of Kyle. "Do you want me to help you?"

"No," she says without looking up. "They only like me."

I try hard not to smile. "Oh, okay. Do you know where your daddy is?" Might as well beard the lion in his den.

There's a long pause as she concentrates on lining the horses up exactly. "Appa's on the patio."

I kick myself for forgetting what she calls her father, and I didn't even know there was a patio. "I'm going to go talk to Appa for a minute, okay? If you need me, come get me."

Sadie doesn't respond to this, so I go in search of the patio and find it beyond some double French doors screened behind potted plants in the kitchen. There is a small, bricked area with the usual wicker and metal patio furniture as well as a cute little metal café table that looks like it came straight from some quaint little bistro or ice cream parlor. Beyond the patio is a small, walled lawn about the size of a postage stamp. Kyle is sitting awkwardly on one of the metal chairs. He's not a big man, but he dwarfs the dainty chair. He looks up when he hears the door close.

"Brooke," he says, but it seems like it takes great effort, and there is no corresponding animation in his face when he recognizes who I am. I feel my stomach clench. He's been thinking about what I said; he's going to ask me to leave and never come back. "Come. Sit." He pats the seat next to him, and it's not an invitation but an order.

"Hi, Kyle," I say, licking my lips. I sit down gingerly on a chair next to him. "How are you feeling?"

He turns so he can meet my eyes full on, and I try not to flinch away. I pray fervently that God will give me the strength to face his loathing and protect me from it. I brace myself and raise my eyes directly to his. I see only compassion and an overwhelming pain and sadness. My relief is so great that if I didn't feel so touched by his obvious misery, I might cry.

"I feel . . ." He shakes his head. "I don't know what to do. I can't go back, to the TAOs. I can't keep being someone I'm not. I go and I do what they ask me to do, but it's wrong. There was a time when I believed in what we're doing, all of it. I *requested* some of my deployments; I am good at what I do, and I wanted the opportunity to do it. But now?" He shakes his head again. "What I'm doing is not Christian. What I'm doing is not even *moral*. I can't live with myself. But I can't quit; you don't just 'quit' being a terrorist assault officer. There's no way out until my retirement, but I don't think I can do this for another year. What am I going to do?"

Tentatively, I place my hand on his shoulder. "Kyle, God is in control. We don't always see him working for good in our situations, but he's always there. The Bible tells us, 'Be strong and of good courage, do not fear nor be afraid of them; for the Lord your God, He is the One who goes with you. He will not leave you nor forsake you.' You don't have to figure this out on your own. God tells us that his thoughts are not our thoughts, and our ways are not his ways. As high as the heavens are from the earth are his ways higher than ours and his thoughts than our thoughts. If God wants you to leave the TAOs, he will make a way for you to leave them if there is no way.

"He got the Israelites out of Egypt, didn't he? Getting you out of the TAOs has got to be a piece of cake compared to that."

That actually gets a small smile from him. There is a flicker of hope in his eyes. "How will I know?"

"In my experience," I say, flashing back through my conversion to God's unmistakable leading out of homosexuality, "God is very capable of speaking to you when he has something to say. He will convict you, or provide an opening so large you could drive a tank through it. That's the wonderful thing about serving a living God; he speaks to us and he leads us because he is always *with* us. Your only responsibility is to give the problem to him and be willing to act when he leads. Who knows? Maybe God has placed you in the TAOs 'for such a time as this' like Queen Esther who saved her people because she taken against her will to be the wife of King Ahasuerus."

He perks up. "I don't know that story." He hands me the Bible he's holding. "Can you find it for me?"

I flip his Bible open to the book of Esther and leave him reading while I go inside to make dinner and check on Sadie. She's still absorbed in herding her horses, so I turn my attention to dinner. Kyle's refrigerator is well stocked, something I noticed this morning when I was making him breakfast.

I quickly discover that making dinner is a simple matter when you have an abundance of ingredients on hand. There's no need to cobble something together out of mismatched items like I'm accustomed to doing. The last meal I made for myself at home consisted of a handful of wilted Swiss chard, a piece of rock hard Parmesan the size of a golf ball, and half a can of black beans. By comparison, Kyle's cupboard feels like wealth beyond compare.

By the time I set all four steaming courses on the table, I wish I hadn't eaten earlier with Judah. "Aren't you going to eat with us?" Kyle asks, fork poised over his plate.

"I had supper before I got here," I say, pulling up a chair, "but I'll sit with you."

His eyes crinkle as he smiles at me. "*Bon appétit.*"

I laugh. "*Bon appétit.*"

"Bone appetite," Sadie chimes in, wanting to be in on the joke, which makes us all laugh. As I watch them enjoy the food, I'm filled with a sudden, overwhelming feeling of happiness and contentment that it makes me catch my breath. I feel . . . included, like family. It feels . . . good.

Chapter Thirteen

The rest of the week passes in a blur, and I've gotten so used to my new hairstyle that seeing the shock on the faces of people at church on Sabbath is almost a surprise. Mr. Nash is tight-lipped with rage when he confronts me in the foyer. "Well," he hisses, "I suppose you think this is better than that godless business you had on your head before. Are you not capable, Miss Merrill, of chaste, Christian behavior befitting a young woman of the Lord?"

"Mr. Nash," I protest weakly, "you asked me to remove my dreadlocks, and I did. I can't help it if the only way to remove them is by shaving them off. I did what you asked. Do you think I want to look like this?"

He considers me for a long moment. "Yes," he says finally with a smug little smile, "I can believe that. I think you would go to any lengths necessary to defy the church board. That's what I think, 'Miss' Merrill." His lip curls as he sneers my name, and he stumps off in the direction of the restrooms.

As I turn to enter the sanctuary, I realize Diana has witnessed the confrontation from a corner where she is straightening bulletins. She looks troubled, but I scoot inside to locate a pew before she can take a piece of me, too. Judah is already inside, sitting halfway up the aisle with Marissa, and I don't want to intrude. I slip into a pew near the back where hopefully no one else will be bothered too much by my shaved head.

Today is the Sabbath that the letters specified as the date for compliance with whatever demands the board made, and I notice that attendance seems to be way down. There are quite a number of new faces, those people who have started coming to church recently but aren't members yet, but looking around, I notice a lot of regular members are missing. I feel a pain in my chest at the thought that they may have decided to seek fellowship elsewhere rather than submit to the board's demands.

I open my Bible and my eyes fall on Matthew 15:13, "He answered and said, 'Every plant which My heavenly Father has not planted will be uprooted.' " *Is this, I think, what's happening here? Are the true believers being winnowed out? And if so, are they the ones who have left or the ones who have stayed?*

My heart is heavy thinking of all those who are missing. Were they not true believers? Some of them played very active roles in the service. This is even more glaringly apparent as the service progresses when strange faces are thrust into new positions to replace those who are missing. It's like trying to regroup the army after a bloody battle. The flow is stilted and the players awkward in their new, unfamiliar roles.

Lord, I pray, bowing my head in the pew and blocking out the service for a moment, *please be with every person who is not here today. Keep Satan from discouraging them. Heal their hurt, Lord. Draw them back to fellowship with other believers, so they can be strengthened and encouraged. Place your hand of protection over them and seek each of your lost sheep as if they were your only sheep. Bring unity to your church and love the fallen world through us in order to draw all your children home . . .*

I'm interrupted by a sudden sharp intake of breath that's echoed throughout the sanctuary. My head snaps up, and I realize I've missed something important. In the pew in front of me, Gloria Nash leans over and loudly whispers to her husband, "Did he just say he has a confession to make?"

He shushes her sharply and tilts forward to hear what Pastor Javier is saying. I follow his gaze and see that Pastor Javier is leaning heavily on the podium in front of him. His face is stark, and tears are running freely down his cheeks. He gathers his resolve and begins to speak again.

"My dear friends," he says, his voice shaky with emotion, "I can only pray that you'll forgive me for my error in judgment," he pauses a moment and then corrects himself, "my sin. I do not deserve your forgiveness although I am deeply sorry for abusing your trust."

He pauses a moment to collect himself. His lips move without making a sound, and I think he must be praying for God to give him strength. When he speaks again, his voice is stronger. "Most of you know that my family and I were planning to buy a new house. You may not know the struggles we have experienced as a family. My wife," a deep sob escapes his throat, but he plows on, "has been a model of patience throughout our married life, raising our children in one tiny apartment or cramped, run-down house after another, moved every few years by the church. She's never had any place to really call home in our 27 years of marriage.

"Earlier this year we found a house, the house of our dreams.

There was a yard for the children to play in and enough rooms for everyone to have their own. And two bathrooms," he adds lightly, but no one laughs. "We planned to finish raising our family here and grow old together waiting for the Lord to come and take us to our real home."

He pauses again and the congregation holds its collective breath until he continues. "The reason we were able to purchase this new house was because a relative of my wife's passed away and left her an inheritance. Unfortunately, the money was delayed, and we needed to move on the new house quickly before it was taken. It would only have been a matter of weeks; just a cushion really, was all we needed. The realtor was pressuring us, the owner was going to back out, and the lawyer kept promising that the money would come through any day.

"I needed the money immediately. I was so afraid we would lose this house, a house I felt God had promised us, had blessed us with. I . . . took the money from the church bank account to cover what we needed to close on the house. I only meant to borrow it. I was going to return it the moment we were in possession of the inheritance money."

He takes a deep breath and plunges on. "We closed on the house. We even moved most of our belongings to the new place. Evie had begun to decorate. It was such a blessing. Then last night . . . we were away from home, and I thank God that we were. Some electrical wiring started a fire, which is what the firefighters believe. Our beautiful house burned to the ground. We lost everything." He chokes up. "Everything is gone."

Another gasp ripples around the room before he drops the other shoe. "They are now telling us that there was some mix-up about the insurance. The insurance policy on the new house had not gone into effect yet. Without insurance we will receive no money for our loss. I cannot replace the money I borrowed . . . I stole," he corrects, giving himself a little shake to brace himself up. "My family and I have lost everything we have in the world. We are completely penniless and homeless."

"See?" hisses Gloria Nash to her husband. "Mexicans! I told you nothing good would come of hiring him, but you wouldn't listen to me. You wait," she finishes triumphantly, "I'll bet we find out he's an illegal alien to boot."

I want to tap her on the shoulder and tell her that Pastor Javier is, in fact, of Guatemalan descent and was born in Boston making him an American, whereas she had been born in India while her parents were in the mission field as she so proudly informs anyone who will listen every time she brings an Indian dish to potluck; she is, in fact, a foreigner. This, I know, will do no good, nor is she particularly civil to me in any case. She'd hardly welcome correction of her facts, no matter how true, from me.

Rocko, I suddenly notice, has stood up in his pew, and his face is flushed with anger. "Hypocrite!" he screams at his father, spittle flying out of his mouth with the force of the word.

Pastor Javier's head, which was bowed in humility, snaps up as if he's been physically struck. "Ricardo." The word is a moan of anguish.

Judah shoots upright and bolts out of his pew to reach Rocko, but it's too late. He's got a full head of steam behind him, and he's determined to say his piece. His mother Evie, hunched into herself on the pew next to him, weeping quietly, doesn't even attempt to stop him. His younger siblings, lined up from oldest to youngest next to her, look confused and scared.

"How could you do this? Shame us like this? Shame my mother? Shame God? And for what? So we could have a bigger, fancier house? Do you think that will make us happier? Jesus didn't even have a place to lay his head. What makes you think any of us deserve more than that, huh?"

A malicious edge sharpens his voice as he hurls it at his father. "Or were you going to open our big, fancy, new home to the people from the shelter, eh, Papa? Give the less fortunate," his voice drips with sarcasm, "a beautiful place to live? Were you going to share your 'coat' with your brother? Even that would not justify the disgrace you have brought on our family with your underhandedness."

Judah has reached him, and he's whispering urgently in Rocko's ear. Pastor Javier stands as still as a statue at the podium, his face as white as marble but infinitely more fragile. His whole body shakes as his face crumbles, warping onto itself as his mouth opens. No sound comes out. His grief is so overwhelming that I have to look away.

"No!" Rocko is shouting, pushing Judah away, "No! I've had enough." He waves his arms to encompass the whole church. "I've had enough of all of it. I'm sick of the pretense, the posturing, the politics. It makes me sick. You make me sick!" he screams at the congregation, turns to his father and repeats, "You make me sick!" Pushing past Judah, he hurtles out of the pew and down the aisle.

His eyes are hard and cold as he passes the pew where I'm sitting. I reach out my hand to catch his sleeve, but I know it's futile. He brushes me off without even slowing down. Judah, watching him helplessly, catches my eye, and I can feel his pain.

Pandemonium washes over the congregation slowly like a wave. People stand, arms are waved, a fist fight breaks out in one corner. It's as if the Holy Spirit has withdrawn and men revert to their base selves, the people we all truly are without God's intervention. Around me, faces reveal a mix of emotions: some appear hurt, some smug, some bored, some angry.

Diana is perched unsteadily on the edge of a back pew as though she'd been standing and suddenly felt her legs go wobbly and dropped down to regain her balance. Her face is ashen, and I realize she doesn't look good. In fact, she looks ill. Before I can wonder if it's something serious, I see Mrs. Swift sobbing quietly into her hands.

Edging my way gently past the people who are arguing in the aisle, I make my way to Mrs. Swift's pew and slide in next to her. "Mrs. Swift? Are you okay?"

Her head swings from side to side, and her shoulders continue to shake. "No," I hear coming from her hands in a thin, drawn-out, pitiful wail. I place my hand tentatively on her shoulder hoping that my touch is comforting. While I wait for her to regain her composure, I pray not only for her but for the entire congregation and for Pastor Javier and his family.

Judah is purposefully moving from one knot of people to another; I'm sure he's counseling and comforting. Pastor Javier has shuffled off the podium and is collecting his things, his face a mask of grief. His family is huddled miserably near the door as if they can't wait to escape, but I wonder where they'll go. Didn't he say they are homeless now? Do they have relatives in the area?

"He baptized me." Mrs. Swift's voice interrupts my thoughts, and I turn my attention back to her. "He's the one who gave me Bible studies, who led me into the church. He saved me."

"Jesus saved you," I correct with as much gentleness as I can.

"You know what I mean," she snaps, uncharacteristically brusque. "If it weren't for him, I wouldn't be here. I wouldn't even be a

Christian. How could he do something like this? He's no better than a common criminal. I believed in him, and he stole thousands of dollars. If he could be so dishonest maybe he 'saved' me to get me to go to church just so I could pay tithe and contribute to the very coffers he was planning to rob." She turns to me, her eyes fierce. "Christians don't steal," she states flatly. "Ever."

"Haven't you ever made a mistake?" I ask desperately, trying to help her empathize with Pastor Javier. I won't make excuses for him; what he did was wrong. But it is plain to see that he's sorry for it. He's confessed his sin, not only to God but his entire congregation. God most certainly forgives him; judging by the reactions I've witnessed so far, the congregation is going to be a mixed lot. "Haven't you ever done something terrible that you were sorry for?"

"No," she says coldly, her voice brooking no argument, "no I haven't, not even before I was a Christian. And I never will. I've always been a good person; I just wasn't a Christian. Now I know my Christian duty. I obey the Ten Commandments. I would never steal."

I'm at a loss. I don't know what else to say. A verse from Luke comes into my head: "But whoever has been forgiven little loves little." I feel so sorry for her that tears prick the backs of my eyes, and I'm afraid I'm going to start crying. She seems to notice this and sense that she's the cause.

"I'm sorry, dear," she says. "I don't mean to unburden all this on you. You have enough troubles of your own." Her eyes flick meaningfully to my head and then quickly away. She smiles weakly. "I wish you well." She gathers her things and scoots out of the pew before I can respond. Her back is ramrod straight, her eyes fixedly forward as she marches out of the church not pausing to speak to anyone. I have the distinct impression that she won't be coming back.

I look around and spot Judah speaking to Pastor Javier. They seem to be arguing. I make my way toward them.

". . . can't impose like that," Pastor Javier is saying adamantly, but tears are streaming down his face.

"It's not an imposition," Judah assures him. "And I insist." I give Judah a questioning look, and he explains in an aside to me, "The Marreros are going to stay at my place until they find somewhere more permanent."

"But the homeless shelter?" I ask, thinking of Judah's cramped apartment versus the many rooms at the shelter. "Wouldn't they be more comfortable there?"

"Rocko is there, and Pastor Javier is afraid of shaming him further."

I mouth a silent "oh" and nod to show him I understand. "I have a little room as well," I offer dubiously, "but it would mean splitting up unless you all want to go there instead, and you know the situation at my apartment right now. I'd be happy to have you, but there's got to be a better option."

Pastor Javier wipes his eyes. "I thank you, Brooke, but we must stay together as a family. Especially during this painful time." He puts his arm around Evie, and she lays her head on his shoulder. I can't imagine how she must be feeling. Not only has she lost the house of her dreams and all the dreams that went with it, but her husband has lost his job—I assume—and his reputation which casts a long shadow onto her own. The fault isn't hers, but the consequences will be.

Out of the corner of my eye I see Elder Fortin bustle toward the front of the sanctuary, beckoning to someone in the foyer. "He's in here," I hear him say. Two black-clad figures emerge through the double doors. Judah and I exchange a shocked look, and then I realize Kyle is one of the approaching TAOs. He doesn't react in any visible way at all when he sees us. His partner does all the talking and aside from a slight softening of his eyes when he glances at me, I could believe we'd never even met before.

"Pastor Javier Marrero?" Kyle's partner asks—Officer Oliver according to his nametag. He's overly tall and towers menacingly over Pastor Javier who doesn't top me much in height. In addition to his height, Officer Oliver is muscular which makes him even more imposing.

Pastor Javier looks stunned and it takes him a moment to respond. "Yes, I am he."

"I'm placing you under arrest for grand larceny." He doesn't bother to read Pastor Javier his rights; TAOs don't have to. They can arrest you for anything they like and detain you without a charge for as long as they like. I wonder if that's why Elder Fortin called them rather than the police.

"Javier," sobs Evie, clinging to her husband. "No!" Her thin howl cuts through my heart like a knife. The TAOs pay no attention to her. Officer Oliver grabs Pastor Javier roughly, turns him around, and slaps cuffs on his wrists so fast it's all a blur. He shoves Evie aside, and I grab her before she falls. She's about to throw herself at her husband again, but I hold onto her tightly, trying to soothe her. I don't even realize it until later, but I'm whispering the twenty-third Psalm to her.

Kyle says nothing, but as they march Pastor Javier out, I see him reach over and squeeze Pastor Javier's shoulder. Unfortunately, Pastor Javier hasn't yet met Kyle and seems to feel more threatened than comforted by this gesture. I want to tell him that it's okay, that Kyle will protect him, but I can't even know that for certain. Kyle's told me he will continue to do his job, whatever that entails, and wait for God to show him a way out. He'll try to help people in any way that he can without getting caught, but no one can be seen to receive any special treatment. Outwardly, he cannot appear changed.

Pastor Javier twists around, trying to see his family one last time. "I love you, Evie," he calls. "Remain faithful, my love. Pray for me."

"Javier!" shrieks Evie. "I will pray for you, sweetheart! Jesus will protect you!" She breaks down sobbing onto my shoulder. "Jesus will protect us all."

Judah and I stare at each other speechlessly. "We need to talk," he mouths at me.

I glance helplessly down at Evie, clinging to me and sobbing, and then back up at Judah. I nod, but shrug, knowing it will take awhile for Evie to calm down enough to let go of me. Judah gathers the children, some of whom are old enough to be scared and concerned. He gives them all little jobs to do: go collect your mother's things, put your toys away because we'll be leaving soon, find your coats, use the bathroom.

Eventually Evie calms down enough that I'm able to leave her, so Judah and I step into a small room off the sanctuary. "What?" I ask him.

He rumples his hair. "I don't know what to do," he confesses. "Without Pastor Javier there it isn't really appropriate for Evie and the children to stay at my place if I'm there. Maybe they *should* go to your apartment."

"They'd be more than welcome, but I'm worried about the TAOs. You know Kyle's worked it out so that I can stay with Sadie at night if I need to because they're making arrests now. I've actually been there every night since my building got burned," I confess. "He's got that separate apartment for his help, so I stay there when I'm not taking care of Sadie if he's home. It's kind of like having my own place. Well, a place that's mine, but not really mine, if you know what I mean. But I need to go back to my apartment soon before the other sitters start to get curious about why I 'work' so much.

"Anyway, the TAOs hit my apartment pretty regularly. What happens if they find Evie and the kids there instead of me? And what about safety? Can you imagine her trying to get the kids up and down from my apartment to the street past my neighbors?"

"What is going on?" an indignant, breathless voice demands as Sarah bursts into the room. "Where is Pastor Javier? I can't get Evie to make any sense."

Judah and I stare at her blankly. "Didn't you see the TAOs take him?" Judah asks.

"TAOs? No, I just got back." She's panting slightly. "I went after Rocko. I caught up to him, but I couldn't convince him to come back with me. TAOs took Pastor Javier? For what? Questioning? Will they release him or lock him up?"

"That's just it," I tell her. "We're not sure. The whole family was going to stay with Judah, but now that Pastor Javier can't be with them it's not . . . appropriate. We have to go ahead as if he won't be coming back. We need to find someplace for them to go."

"Well, they can't stay at your place," Sarah tells me with a snort. "The homeless shelter?"

"Rocko," Judah says by way of explanation.

"Oh, yeah, not such a good idea right now." She appears thoughtful. "They can stay with me."

"Do you have room?" I realize I don't know where Sarah lives.

"Enough," she says. "I live in a small apartment not far from here. In the opposite direction from you," she tells me in an aside. "It's really too big for me, but my husband's life insurance policy paid off the mortgage after he passed away, so I stayed."

"You were married?" I ask. Judah doesn't look surprised, but then, he's known her a lot longer than I have. "I didn't know that."

"Ten years," Sarah says wistfully. "We were very happy. Morgan died of cancer. I miss him every day." She becomes businesslike. "Now, let's go pack up Evie and the kids, and I'll take them over to my place."

Judah veers off from Sarah and me as we enter the sanctuary. While we help Evie and the children gather their things and explain to them where they're going, Judah seems to be having an argument with Marissa. I make a point of not staring at them, but soon their voices rise in volume, and I don't have to wonder what they're fighting about.

". . . not your responsibility," Marissa is saying. ". . . nothing to do with you."

"Of *course* they're my responsibility," Judah responds patiently. If I didn't know him so well, I might miss the edge of frustration in his voice. "We're *each other's* responsibility, all of us, the whole church. That's part of being a church *community*."

"Oh, yeah?" Marissa snaps. "And where is *that* written in the handbook? Face it, Judah, you've got a savior complex. You like going around saving people. It validates you. It's what makes you feel important."

I flinch at the malice in her voice. I want to stick up for Judah, but it's not my place.

"Is that what you really think?" Judah sounds incredulous. "Marissa, it's not like . . ."

"Forget it!" she says with disgust. "Just never mind, okay?"

Out of the corner of my eye I see her stalk down the aisle and out the front door. After a moment's pause, Judah follows her. Sarah and I exchange glances of sympathy as we herd Evie and the kids out to the parking lot. Sarah asks me if I want to go along, but I decline. I haven't been to my apartment in a few days, and I need to check on it and get things ready for the prayer meeting we're planning to have there on Wednesday.

Evie pulls up behind Sarah's little sedan in her dilapidated minivan. Even through the dirty windshield I can see her face is streaked with tears. I step away from Sarah's car so she can pull out.

"See you Wednesday," Sarah says, rolling up her window and inching her car forward.

"Wednesday," I agree. I wave as they drive off.

Behind me Mr. Nash is locking up the church. I check to be sure I've got my messenger bag and haven't left it behind in a pew. Thankfully, I do; I would hate to have to ask him to let me go inside to retrieve it. As I turn to walk to my apartment, I catch sight of Diana sitting in her vehicle. She's hunched over the steering wheel, sobbing.

I fight with myself. Part of me feels compassion and wants to help, the other part is terrified of getting my head bit off and wants nothing to do with her. As I stand there struggling with my feelings, watching

Mr. and Mrs. Nash drive off in their sleek car, I feel a strong urge to at least offer Diana my support.

I approach her car with fear and trembling and tap lightly on the window. She looks up, startled. When she sees who it is, she rolls the window down an inch.

"Diana? Is there anything I can do?"

Before I can say more she motions me away. "Go, just go," she chokes out, and rolls the window up again.

I swallow my hurt feelings, and after waiting a second to see if she'll relent, I turn and head resolutely in the direction of my apartment. She may be able to prevent me from comforting her, but she can't prevent me from praying for her. I spend the entire walk and wait at the security check—albeit a significantly shorter wait—praying for Diana and asking God to touch her heart and her life.

Chapter Fourteen

Kyle and Sadie are the first to arrive on Wednesday for the prayer meeting.

"I miss you, Brookie," Sadie says, reaching her arms up for a hug. "Elena and Jennifer don't read me the Bible stories when you're not there." She wrinkles her nose. "They read me other books. Sometimes Amy reads them to me, but she doesn't do the voices like you do."

I'm amused. "Is that so?" It tickles me that I'm a favorite.

Kyle draws me aside as Sadie tugs a tote bag full of toys out of his hand and heads for a corner of the living room to set up shop. "We should be okay for tonight," Kyle says, but I see concern shadowing his eyes. "I'm not sure how much longer this will be safe though. You should consider setting up a signal to warn people away, just in case. Maybe you could set up an alternate meeting place?"

"That's a good idea. Wait, there's Judah. Tell him and he can announce it."

I leave Kyle talking softly with Judah—who I can't help but notice has come alone, no Marissa in sight—and station myself at the door to let people in and direct traffic. My apartment fills up quickly, and I'm amazed to see there are even more people than last time. My heart lurches when I realize that many of them are people I haven't seen in a couple weeks, people I assumed had left the church. I praise God to see them again. Maybe many of them haven't fallen away as I supposed.

Sarah, Evie, and the children arrive and there's a tearful reunion between Evie and Rocko who comes in a short time later with Sibby and some of the other folks from the homeless shelter. I wonder whether or not Rocko knows his father is in prison, but I suppose that if he didn't before, he will now. Evie is speaking earnestly with him, though how they can hear each other above the hubbub is beyond me.

These impromptu, unorchestrated prayer meetings have really grown since their "beginning" on Wednesday nights at the church. For one thing, they shifted, quite naturally though inexplicably, to my apartment. Maybe people assume that it's "safe" to talk here since it's where we had that meeting about the letters; maybe it feels as though here they have some breathing room from the official church body. I don't know. It baffles me that they come here at all. It's not like I have some beautiful apartment: it stinks, any decoration is utilitarian at best, and it's located in a terrible part of town. I know Judah's not crazy about it.

"We should be meeting at the church," he's always griping. "We should be drawing people to the church where they can be nurtured and become a community. We shouldn't be forced to skulk around (yes, he actually said skulk) like criminals meeting in the slums." He'd shot me a guilty look and said, "You know I love you, Brooke, but you don't exactly live in a nice neighborhood. My place is a little better, but it's way too small."

I'd tried to convince him that maybe it was best, that we were like the early church, meeting in homes and spreading the gospel. There is no arguing the fact that God is blessing the meetings; every time we meet there are more people than the time before. Maybe there is a reason we are being driven from the church and out into the community . . . even if we don't know what that reason is.

The thing I really like about the meetings is how much the Spirit of God seems to be present. I feel as though I'm in the upper room with the disciples after the resurrection. We pray together; we sing; we praise God. People share what God has taught them during the week. We pray for each other's burdens and the difficult situations we face.

The meeting is in full swing when I hear a knock on the door. Everyone is singing and I only hear it because I happen to be standing near the door. I open it cautiously; the meeting has been going on for at least a half hour now, and I don't expect anyone else, but someone could be running late. My mind flashes back to the last time there was an unexpected knock on the door during a prayer meeting, and I'd opened it to find Kyle and Sadie on my doorstep. I do quell a moment of panic at the thought that it could be the TAOs, but then I realize I would probably have heard them coming by the screams and yelling that usually precedes them.

In the hallway is a woman I recognize, but don't know, flanked by her children ranging in age from the toddler in her arms to a teen a little younger than Rocko. I count quickly: five children. I know she lives on my floor, but I don't know exactly which apartment. The kids are often racing around unsupervised and the teen usually hangs out with a rough crowd. I'm pretty sure the mother drinks or does drugs, but she seems sober right now.

My first thought is that they're here to complain about the noise, but I wonder why they felt they had to come en masse; then I notice they don't look hostile. I realize I'm staring at her and that I haven't said hello a half second before she finally gives up waiting for me to greet her. "Hello," she says with an accent I can't identify, "we . . ." She looks around nervously at the children as if for support. "We have heard your music from next door." She blushes and I think she might worry that I suspect her of eavesdropping, but she hurries on before I can assure her that it's fine. "The songs, they are Christian songs, yes?"

"Yes," I say quickly. "Yes, they are. Would you like to come in?"

"We would be welcome?" She peers longingly past my shoulder into the room where someone is reading a Psalm aloud and with great enthusiasm. "Everyone sounds so happy," she says wistfully.

"You would be more than welcome," I assure her. I open the door as wide as the crush of bodies beyond allows. "Come in."

The children stick close to their mother at first, but then the teen girl spots Rocko, and she makes her way over to him where they do some teen greeting ritual I've seen on the streets. They appear to be acquainted. I don't remember Kyle being near the door when I went out, but he's there now and he draws me aside, using his body as a shield between me and the new arrivals.

"That's a pretty rough crew," he says in an undertone, jerking his head at the woman who is engrossed in what someone is saying about how God directed them that week. "The boyfriend beats her up a lot, judging from the amount of times we've 'dropped by' and she's covered with bruises. The oldest girl's been arrested a few times for petty larceny, but she's headed for much worse. The mother makes the little kids panhandle on the street."

"*She* does?"

He shrugs. "Could be the boyfriend, but . . ." He leaves his thought hanging.

"Then I'm even more glad they're here," I tell him with conviction. It occurs to me that if this prayer meeting was taking place at the church they wouldn't attending it; they wouldn't have been drawn here by the sound of the music and the joy. Maybe it is a blessing in disguise holding them in my dilapidated apartment. I make a mental note to mention this to Judah.

"Yes," Kyle agrees, "me, too." He takes my hand and gives it a quick squeeze. I know that, like me, he's looking at that woman and her children as souls that have just been snatched from the jaws of eternal death. "Praise God for bringing them here," he says fervently. "Make sure you give them some of those gospels of John you've got before they leave," he suggests. He moves off into the crowded room, keeping his face averted, and it occurs to me that he may not want my neighbor to recognize him. I wonder how much of a risk it is for him that she's come over.

I notice several of Professor McCormick's zombie prepper students—minus their usual walking dead costumes and makeup—across the room enthusiastically trying to join in the singing even though they clearly don't know the words, and I wish fervently that the professor was here, too. I decide I'm going to ask him again. Maybe this informal setting won't bring out the contrariness that blinds him from the message God so obviously has for him.

Later, the meeting is beginning to wind down when Judah makes the announcement about an alternate meeting place in case of emergency. We decide on a signal—if it's not safe I'm supposed to hang a "welcome" sign on the door, how's that for irony? Judah encourages people to contact each other to prevent everyone from having to come all the way to my apartment only to find that the meeting has been relocated. Sarah offers her home as a relocation spot, and I get the distinct impression she seems to feel it's her duty. Or maybe having Evie and the kids stay with her has made her realize how much she misses having people around. I know that hosting the meetings has done that for me; I have slowly begun to feel like part of something larger than just myself, part of a community of like-minded believers, if not exactly a family yet.

Having people come into your home and bring all that spiritual energy is incredibly uplifting. I find myself remembering scenes from the previous meeting, picturing people in various spots around my apartment, and I am moved to pray for them throughout the week even though sometimes I know only their faces and not their names. I often find myself humming snatches of the songs we sing or remembering someone's praise of God or chasing down the fragment of a Bible verse that's floating around in my head so I can look it up and study it more fully.

People slowly begin filtering out, and I find Sadie playing in a small open space behind the sofa. She's found some friends; someone else has brought their children along. They appear to be twins, towheaded boys about Sadie's age, maybe a little younger. A woman I take to be their mother because of her matching hair color is chasing them around, scooping up their belongings which are strewn from one end of my apartment to the other. "Honestly, boys," she's saying with amused exasperation, making a noise that's halfway between a giggle and a patient sigh, "did you have to take *everything* out of the play bag?"

I stoop to help her, and she catches my eye with a smile. She sticks out her hand. "Hi, I'm Theresa. I'm sorry about the mess."

"That's okay," I assure her, shaking. She has a firm, strong grip. "I'm Brooke."

"My husband was supposed to be watching them, but . . ." She trails off and gives me a conspiratorial female look. "You know men."

Not really, but I don't say that.

"Thanks for having us over," she continues while I'm trying to think of a suitable reply. "I enjoyed the fellowship. We've been looking for like-minded believers for some time. Our church wasn't exactly . . . accepting of us." I'm not sure if I should ask why, but before I can decide, a man ambles over with a sheepish grin. "Sorry, babe," he says.

She smiles. "Think nothing of it." She bends to collect some more toys and her husband turns to me.

"I'm Stephen," he says, extending his hand. As we repeat the introductory process I can't help but gape at him. His voice, his mannerisms . . . this man is gay. He has to be gay. *All right, he's effeminate,* I tell myself. *Plenty of men who are effeminate aren't gay.* "What?" he asks curiously. "Have we met already and I forgot?"

"No," I say hurriedly, "no, I'm sorry. It's just that you seem . . ." I want to say it, but I just can't, and I'm about to finish with "familiar" but I don't have a chance.

"Gay?" he supplies for me.

I swallow hard. I can't trust my voice so I nod.

"It's okay," he assures me. "I get that a lot. I *am* gay . . ."

"*Was* gay," Theresa corrects from her bent over position. "Was gay, honey."

He grins. "I *was* gay. But God convicted me, saved me, and changed me. That's a simplistic summary, I know, but that's my story in a nutshell." He spreads his hands to indicate his little family unit. "And God's blessed me with so much. He replaced the years the locusts ate. He is so awesome, isn't he?"

I'm speechless. "But that's impossible," I protest once I've found my voice.

Stephen seems amused. "That God is awesome?"

"No, no," I correct hastily. "Of course, he's awesome. It's just that, it's impossible to stop being a homosexual . . . isn't it?" I falter. "I mean, that's what I thought. How can God change your orientation like that? It's not as if it's the kind of thing you choose yourself."

Theresa and Stephen exchange a look, and it occurs to me that maybe he doesn't want to talk about his sordid past with a stranger, but apparently I've mistaken what passes between them because Theresa diverts the children and lures them away to give us some privacy while Stephen opens his Bible and invites me to take a seat at the kitchen table. I glance around. Almost everyone is gone, but there are still a few knots of people chatting. No one seems to need my services as hostess, so I allow myself to be led to the table and drop into a chair next to Stephen.

"Brooke, would you mind if I pray before we talk?"

"Please," I say by way of invitation.

We bow our heads and Stephen says, "Dear Heavenly Father, *thank you* for second chances. Thank you for your relentless, unfathomable, limitless love for us that you would rescue us from the bondage of Satan and give us a place in your kingdom. Thank you for redeeming us all from slavery to sin and giving us complete freedom in you. Thank you for not only rescuing us in our sin, Lord, but for giving us your power, your *grace*, to live in obedience to your perfect will for our lives, to live the very best version of our lives. Please guide our conversation tonight, and show us your truth. In Jesus' name, amen."

"Amen," I repeat. When I look up Stephen is smiling at me. "Can I ask you a personal question?"

"Shoot."

"Were you born gay? Or did something happen to you that . . ."

"That made me gay?" he supplies. "Or encouraged my own natural, hereditary tendencies?" He's quiet for a moment, probably considering how much he's willing to tell me. "No, I had a wonderful childhood, actually. I was always considered a bit of a sissy, but I wasn't abused or anything. There are a lot of circumstances that factored into my orientation. I won't bore you with them. Let's just say that I was exposed to a lot of questionable media when I was growing up that led me to have a rather 'rich' fantasy life. It all just snowballed into my first sexual encounter when I was in high school and the rest is history.

"So do you want to start with the clobber texts?" he asks. "Or with the definition of grace?"

"Clobber texts?" All I can picture is someone being thumped over the head with a Bible. "What are those?"

"Oh, well, you may not have heard them called that, but you know which ones they are, trust me. They're the texts in the Bible that either do, or don't depending on where you stand, condemn homosexuality. They're called clobber texts or clobber scriptures because Christians use them to convince—or "clobber"—homosexuals with them."

"Oh, *those*." Yes, I'm very familiar with those. They would be the texts my father shouted at me when I came out to my parents. At the time I didn't pay much attention, but later I did study them out with Judah. "I'm not in the lifestyle anymore," I tell Stephen, then hurry to add, "and I'm grateful for that. It's just that I feel as though I'm always struggling with the same old thing. It's frustrating," I haven't admitted this to anyone so it feels awkward admitting it to a stranger, "to be a Christian who used to be gay because you're stuck in this kind of limbo where you aren't gay anymore, but you aren't straight, either. You're just kind of . . . nothing."

Stephen nods. "I hear you," he says. "And I have good news for you."

I stare at him blankly. "You do?"

"I do. Listen, what you're talking about is nothing new. Look at King Manasseh. Here's this king of Israel—*God's chosen people*—and when this guy gets elected as king what does he do?"

I shake my head, not familiar with the story.

Stephen flips open his Bible and reads, "He did evil in the eyes of the Lord, following the detestable practices of the nations the Lord had driven out before the Israelites." He looks up and starts ticking points off on his fingers. "He worshiped the stars, built altars to Baal, practiced sorcery, consulted mediums and fortunetellers, built pagan altars *in the Lord's temple*, sacrificed his own son to the fire, and he killed so many innocent people that the Bible says Jerusalem was filled from one end to the other in blood. I mean, those are just the highlights of what this guy did."

"He sounds lovely," I murmur, wondering where he's going with this.

Stephen is on a roll, his voice animated with excitement. "Doesn't he? I mean, this guy was a real piece of work. Finally, God had enough. He allowed the Assyrians to come in and capture King Manasseh. They put a hook in his nose, hog-tied him, and carted him off to Babylon." He picks up his Bible again and reads, "In his distress he sought the favor of the Lord his God and humbled himself greatly before the God of his ancestors. And when he prayed to him, the Lord was moved by his entreaty and listened to his plea; *so he brought him back to Jerusalem and to his kingdom.*

"Can you even imagine that? I mean, God didn't just say, 'Okay, I believe you're sorry. Go on home now and try to keep your nose clean, but your days of being a king are over.' No, he gave him his kingdom back; he *restored* him. And Manasseh wasn't just a figurehead for the rest of his reign; he was a force for good in Israel. He got rid of all the pagan altars he had built and commanded all of Israel to worship God. So tell me, what made the difference between the monster we see before his repentance and the godly leader we see after his repentance? Do you think that Manasseh was able to change himself? To bring it a little closer, do you think someone like Hitler could decide to become someone like Mother Teresa if he wanted to?"

"No, not a chance," I reply.

"Tell me, Brooke," Stephen says earnestly, "would you think God was loving and kind if he asked you to do something, but withheld the power to actually do it?"

I shake my head. "I guess I never thought about it like that."

"Why do you think Jesus came to earth?" Stephen asks.

"To save us from our sins," I say. "To die for us on the cross."

"Yes." Stephen is nodding. "But also to show us how to live *by the power of God*. Jesus is able to understand our weaknesses because he was tempted in every way that we are, but he did not sin. Jesus was God, but he was also man. He was born with man's nature *after* the Fall; he was born to Mary in Bethlehem, not Eve in the Garden of Eden. The only way he was able to overcome temptation and not sin is the same way *we* are able to overcome temptation and not sin: by the power of God. Tell me, Brooke, do you find a list in the Bible of sins that God is able to help us overcome and a list that are beyond him?"

I know it's a rhetorical question, really; he's trying to make a point. But my mind darts through the Bible like a mouse looking for cheese. I come up empty. "No."

"The amount or kind of sin doesn't matter, God gives us the grace—*the ability and the desire to do what he asks us to do*—to overcome sin and live in obedience to him. The Bible says, 'But when sin grew worse, God's grace increased.' No matter how 'worse' your sin is, God's grace has you covered."

"But if that's true, why am I still tempted?"

Stephen looks amused. "The Bible doesn't say anywhere that God will save us from temptation. Even Jesus wasn't spared temptation. But God promises us that he will give us the power to *resist* temptation. Look at it this way, if you're experiencing temptation and not giving in, then God is giving you His power to overcome it."

I feel a *whoosh* of relief that's so strong I'd want to collapse onto a chair if I wasn't already sitting in one. "You mean . . ."

Stephen nods. "If you aren't giving in to temptation, you are living a life of victory over sin. Praise God!"

I fix Stephen with an accusing look. "It's still unfair, though. Why me? Why do I have to struggle with this?"

Stephen regards me thoughtfully for a moment. "Oh? I didn't know there were 'fair' sins in the Bible. Are other sins 'fair' then? Pornography, maybe? Is struggling with pornography fair? How about pedophiles. Do you think they'd say it was fair that they struggled against their 'natural' thoughts and actions? You know, homosexuals aren't the only people to struggle with forbidden sexual attractions; heterosexuals struggle with it, too. I doubt anyone plagued with lustful thoughts feels that it's fair for them, either. Or, maybe you're thinking of drug addicts, fighting with their addiction every moment of the day.

"We all struggle with something. It's a sinful, broken world. Some people suffer unjustly from its effects; they are born blind, maimed, paralyzed, or with incurable diseases. Some are struck down by accident or illness; they may be tempted to think God doesn't love them or that he's punishing them. They may be tempted to give up their faith and curse God, as Job was. It's an unfair world, Brooke. We're all dealing with the effects of sin. But we all have the same power to overcome in Jesus. That's the important thing.

"Honestly, what's the point of Christianity if God can't change people? It certainly doesn't win us any popularity contests. If I didn't believe with absolute certainty that God could change me completely into a new creature, then what would be the point of being a Christian? Why would anyone willingly follow a set of rules and live by standards that are impossible for humans alone to attain and keep? You'd have to be a masochist."

"So," I say slowly, trying to come to grips with what he's told me and the fact that by simply existing he is proving his own testimony. Obviously, it *is* possible for God to change your orientation, no matter how you arrived at it. And let's face it, the Bible does says 'all have sinned' and not 'some have sinned.' It isn't like any of us are unique in our sins. We may sin differently, but we all sin. "Do you think it's possible for me to live a normal life?"

Stephen barks out a laugh that surprises me into smiling myself. "What's so funny?" I ask curiously.

"Honey," Stephen calls, beckoning Theresa over, "would you say I'm normal?"

She rolls her eyes at him and then tells me in a conspiratorial tone, "I don't know what he's been telling you, but if he's claiming to be normal, don't believe him." She leans down and gives Stephen a kiss.

"Probably best not to shoot for normal, then," he tells me, keeping his arm around Theresa and hugging her close to him. "Seriously, though," he says, "God doesn't call any of us to live a 'normal' life. He's called us to live an extraordinary life. But if you're asking me, can you get married, have kids, join the rat race, I guess I'd have to say I'm living proof. If that's what God has in store for your life, then I wish you all the best. But I wouldn't go out and get married just to prove that you aren't a homosexual any more. You can be 'normal' without being married—whether you're an ex-gay like us, or a heterosexual."

I digest this thought as Stephen offers a quick prayer before turning to help his wife corral their children. Almost everyone else is gone, but I notice Kyle sitting not far away, absorbed in thought. He's clearly close enough to have heard every word we've said, and I wonder if that's what is occupying his thoughts.

"I thought you'd be gone," I tell him.

He drags his attention to me and slowly registers what I said. Then he smiles gently. "Sadie wouldn't leave until she'd given you a hug goodnight."

I grin. *That's my girl,* I think as I look over at her. She happens to glance my way at the same time. "Brookie!" she shrieks, hurtling across the room and throwing herself into my open arms. As I hold her close, I feel my spirit become so light I feel as though I could float. God has saved me, and he's given me power to overcome any temptation. I feel as though I just stepped out the doors of a prison and into freedom.

Chapter Fifteen

After my talk with Stephen, it's as though scales have fallen from my eyes, just like Paul on the road to Damascus. It takes me a long time to process what he told me, most of which I spend on my knees and in my Bible. The "clobber" texts have lost their teeth. After years of thinking of myself as an abomination, I can see that there are plenty of things heterosexuals do that are abominable to God, too. We're all just sinners in need of a savior. And while, since becoming a Christian, I've always believed that, always known that, always said that, it settles into my heart in such a new way that I can really understand now that we weren't meant to stay in the sins God rescues us from any more than we'd be expected to stay in the burned out hulk of our sinking ship at sea. We'd let go of the charred spar we were clinging to and climb into the boat of our rescuer. We wouldn't expect them to toss us provisions every now and then to keep us alive while we floated there in the midst of our destroyed life. We would expect them to take us back to shore where we'd board a brand new boat and begin a brand new adventure in our life.

Judah keeps looking at me funny and says he's trying to figure out what's different about me. I think he's just teasing me, but I do feel different. He knows what Stephen told me. He was already gone when we'd finished talking, but I filled him in later. Not that I was checking up on Stephen's facts—okay, I was checking up on Stephen's facts— but Judah confirmed that grace meant exactly what Stephen said it meant and that it did what Stephen said it did. He said he'd been trying to get me to understand that himself, but apparently he hadn't done as good a job as Stephen. Personally, I think that my understanding came exactly in God's time and that I needed to be at a place in my life in which I was able to understand it and accept it.

"You could have explained it perfectly," I'd assured Judah, "but unless God had prepared my heart to hear it, I still wouldn't have been able to understand it."

Judah had conceded that I was right, but he still insists I look different.

If I do, there are people at church who haven't noticed. Mr. Nash eyes my head every time he sees me as if he's worried that my hair will miraculously grow back as dreads or that I'll shave off the short hair that's taken the place of the dreads. When it became clear that I had no clue what to do with my quickly growing hair, Sarah dragged me to a beauty salon where I endured the first haircut I've had since I was a teenager. She said the result was a pixie cut, the best we could hope for given the length we started with. Apparently I'm "waiting for some regrowth" to "shoot for a layered bob" next. Personally, I miss my long hair, and that's what *I'm* shooting for. In any case, Mr. Nash—and many others—are still not impressed.

It's stupid, I know, but I feel like a major disappointment to them, an embarrassment even. Although I've done what they asked and even, with Sarah's help, bought a few nice (though plain) dresses to wear to church in actual colors besides black, I feel as though I'll never quite measure up. My close relationship with God, and even my obedience to their demands, doesn't seem to factor in to their overall opinion of me. I feel like a kid who is constantly striving for parental approval.

"Just let it go," Judah tells me. "If you are right with God, that's all that matters."

He does seem to live by his own advice. Having gotten over his little hiccup at college, he's back in college now that classes have started up again and still shooting for a career in ministry. "Wherever God leads," is his standard reply when asked which branch of the ministry he hopes to enter when he graduates in the spring. He's been a little quiet, brooding over the breakup with Marissa I suspect, but as far as I can see, he did everything he could to repair the relationship before calling it quits. As he said, "Some things were just never meant to be. And this, sadly, is one of them."

Kyle has begun coming openly to church. He says he's doing it for Sadie, because Sadie loves the children's classes. When I asked him if it was dangerous for him, because he was still a TAO, he looked at me for a long moment before he said, "Yes." But he didn't elaborate.

He's changed over the last few months. He is calmer and stronger. On the days I watch Sadie, we usually have a chance to talk in the morning while I make breakfast. Kyle often surprises me with his knowledge of Scripture. He's only been reading the Bible for what? Six months? And sometimes I think he knows it better than I do. When I asked him about it, he smiled serenely and said, "I read my Bible a *lot*."

When I questioned him further, he showed me his notebooks. He had to get them from their hiding place somewhere in his room (a precaution, he explained, in case the TAOs decided to inspect his home), but he brought them out to the kitchen so I could see them. The stack was almost as long as my arm. "I'm reading through the Bible again," he explained (for the seventh time, I learned later), "and this time I'm writing each verse down in a notebook and taking the time to let God speak to me through it. Then I write what he says to me." He shrugged. "When I fill a notebook, I start another."

We talk about the TAOs sometimes, too. He says he's waiting for God to find him a way out. And if he has to stay, well, he says then God must have a plan for him, a reason he needs to be there. "In the meantime," he said, "I'm using whatever knowledge I have about what's going to happen in order to help people." He shrugged. "Sometimes they take my advice, and I can prevent a tragedy; sometimes they ignore me." Then he'd looked at me very seriously and said, "Brooke, I want you to promise me something. If anything happens to me, you'll look after Sadie. Like a mother would. Will you promise me? I want to make it legal, but I wasn't sure how to ask you."

I promised him that I'd be honored to look after Sadie and both of us seemed to know that unlike most promises lightly given this one might eventually require fulfillment. I look over at her now, head bowed over her cereal bowl. "Like a mother would," Kyle had said. And instead of the phantom children pain I used to have, I feel a strong sense of love and belonging. I *have* grown to love Sadie as if she was my own child, and I think she loves me. She's very comfortable with me now, and we have our own little rituals and games.

Before I bring Sadie to school we all have "family" worship. That's what Kyle calls it, even though I'm not family. It does *feel* as though we're a family though, and on the days when I'm at my apartment instead of staying the night with Sadie I miss our morning "family" times together with Kyle's calm, sure presence and Sadie's boundless energy.

Breakfast seems pretty dreary when you eat it alone, I'm beginning to realize. I miss the conversations I have with Kyle who is generally quiet in the mornings as he tries to separate himself from the work he had to do the night before. He seems thirstier for the spiritual conversation we have than the freshly squeezed orange juice I make for breakfast. I miss making Sadie's school lunch and answering her impossible questions: "Brooke, why didn't God make the sky pink? I like pink." And "Brooke, can I have a bunny? Because I really want a hippopotamus, but Appa won't let me."

"Do you have family worship with the other sitters before they leave in the mornings?" I ask Kyle shyly, just as I'm leaving.

"Yes," he replies, and I feel the disappointment like a punch in the abdomen. I don't know why I thought I was special. "We always invite them to join us, and sometimes they do. But we don't call it 'family' worship then . . . It's just worship." He smiles sweetly. "See you tomorrow, Brooke," he says and closes the door gently behind me.

I realize I'm grinning like an idiot when a TAO gives me a stern look as I step onto the platform at the metro station. I try to stop, but honestly, that was just so sweet. Finally, I manage to pull my face into appropriately suitable, stern lines. As the train nears my side of town, that's not so hard. While the situation around the world in general has gone steadily from bad to worse, the situation in my part of the city has just gone from worse to even more worse. Professor McCormick is the only person I know who seems to get happier the more conditions deteriorate. His whole attitude projects, "I told you so."

But he's different in other ways as well. Attendance at his zombie prepper meetings has quadrupled, and after the night he let me speak that first time, he often asks me straight out for the biblical take on end-time events. At the "official" meeting it's just an "alternate" perspective. But he even lets me invite the students to the Wednesday night prayer meeting for "more information" if they're interested—more than that, he encourages attendance. And the meeting has relocated, conveniently enough, to the college—although the college doesn't know that.

Apparently, Athenaeum University has grown since its humble beginnings as a public high school. When it was a high school, its architecture was considered advanced because a lot of it was subterranean. But when the old buildings eventually needed repair, it was deemed cheaper to build over many of them rather than repair the existing structures. Some of which are still perfectly sound, just not very aesthetically pleasing. Professor McCormick had already explored them extensively as possible places to hole up during the apocalypse. In fact, the last class of each semester is a flashlight-only tour of all the buildings that aren't condemned, at midnight, wearing full zombie makeup. I haven't attended, but I gather it's pretty scary stuff.

One of the buildings the professor discovered was an old gymnasium. The door to the surface is conveniently located in a narrow alley between two of the new university buildings and looks like the entrance to a storage shed, which most people who discover it probably think it is. It's the perfect spot for our meetings because it's easily accessed, and the front of the alley is screened by shrubbery. Any foot traffic wandering by won't even notice people entering the alley and not returning; it will only seem as though they're taking a shortcut to another part of the campus.

We aren't there officially, of course. It's a secret that everyone who attends is expected to keep. Professor McCormick often shows up, but he told me that if push comes to shove he'll say he just discovered us himself and was going to report our illegal use of the place. He's smiling when he says it, but I don't know . . .

Fortunately, my apartment building is no longer under such strict security. I can get in and out with no problem. Not that they've rebuilt the burned down sections or improved it in any way. They simply boarded up the sections that are no longer livable, leaving those tenants with no place to go. I've seen some of them on the streets, holding signs identifying them as "victims of the city's stupidity" (only the signs use other, coarser words) and asking for handouts. Some have made their way to the shelter, which is now so full that they're in danger of being shut down if anyone discovers just how over capacity they are.

I see Rocko there sometimes, mostly visiting Sibby and other friends, but he lives on the streets now . . . by choice. He hangs out with a group of other like-minded Good Samaritan young men who call themselves "The Disciples." They preach on street corners, minister to the homeless both at the shelter and on the street, and try to live as the apostles would have lived. They have no possessions and no income and rely on God for everything they need. And he provides it. I asked Rocko once if he'd come back to church, but he'd looked down at his clothes (basically rags) and smiled. "Do you really think they'd let me in?" he'd asked sadly.

On the way to my apartment, I stop and tap on my neighbor Frieda's door. When she opens it, I marvel again how much she's changed. She looks tired, but there aren't any bruises on her face and she's not under the influence of anything besides the Holy Spirit. The "boyfriend" left when she "got religion" which was a blessing, and she found a job waitressing which was another blessing. The children are soaking up the new atmosphere in their home and are much calmer and happier. I hold out the bag of oranges Kyle sent me home with.

Fruit, of any kind, has gotten to be a real treat because some sort of fungus-based disease has wiped out many varieties and others are critically endangered. Oranges are one of the last kind you can still get in some parts of the city without having to go through the black market. Kyle, of course, being a TAO, is still able to get whatever he wants.

"For you," I say, smiling.

Her eyes light up. "Thank you so much! The children will be so happy."

"Make sure you get to eat one as well," I tell her, knowing that her guilt over how she's treated her children in the past tends to put her in danger of spoiling them and punishing herself at the same time.

My apartment no longer feels like home. It's started to seem like a place I store my things. I'm gone so often that it has a neglected smell, like stale air. Frankly, it's depressing. Glancing at my watch, I see I have an hour before I need to leave for class and all my papers are graded. I decide it's time to freshen the place up. I'm elbow-deep in a bucket of hot, sudsy water which smells so strongly of lemons that it's making my mouth water, when my phone rings. It's Judah.

"Have you heard?" His voice sounds strange, sort of strangled.

"Heard what?" I race through the possibilities in my mind, but nothing comes close to what he says.

"Diana Wallace is dying."

"Dying?" My mind goes blank, and it feels as though time has stopped. "Of what?" I ask stupidly.

"Cancer. She has lung cancer."

At the word "cancer" things start to fall into place in my mind. Diana's ashy complexion lately, the times she's seemed "ill," the way she's brushed me off when I've asked if anything was wrong. If I really think about it, I've known for months that something was not right with her. I just didn't know what it was. "Is it . . . Can it be cured?"

"No, apparently it's spread. It started out as lung cancer, and she went for chemo or whatever in the beginning, a few months ago, but it had already moved to other organs, and it didn't help much. She's in the hospital now, and I wondered if you wanted to go with me to visit her."

Does Diana want *me visit her?* I want to ask Judah. I honestly feel terrified even thinking about it, imagining a scene at the hospital in which Diana uses the last of her feeble strength to haul herself off her death bed and chase me out of her room. It won't be the first time I've tried to comfort Diana and been rejected. I don't want to impose on her final moments on earth just to make myself feel good about doing my "Christian duty." My silence apparently drags on long enough for Judah to feel the need for additional prompting.

"She's asked for you particularly," he says.

"She *what?*" This I can hardly credit. Why would Diana *ask* to see me? I can't believe that even she is vindictive enough to want one last chance to ridicule or belittle me.

"She wants to see you, Brooke," Judah says quietly. "Will you come?"

"Yes," I say. "Of course, I'll come. How . . . long does she have?"

His voice is sober. "Not long."

I finish my scrubbing quickly after I hang up with Judah, my mind racing. I don't think it's an understatement to say that I'm terrified about the upcoming visit. Judah has promised to meet me at the hospital after my last class, and we'll go in to see her together. In the few minutes I have before I leave to go to class, I drop to my knees and pray fervently for God to go with us. I pour out my heart to him, knowing that he understands how troubled my relationship with Diana has always been and that I don't want to cause her further pain simply by existing, but that I'm willing to be obedient and go to visit her. I beg him to relieve her suffering and to help the visit to go smoothly.

In response, a verse from Isaiah comes into my head. "So do not fear, for I am with you; do not be dismayed, for I am your God. I will strengthen you and help you; I will uphold you with my righteous right hand."

"Thank you, Lord," I breathe.

I try to keep my thoughts on my classes, but find them drifting to Diana in the hospital. I wonder why she never asked anyone at church to pray for her. I can't imagine facing what she's going through without the support of the people I love. As this thought passes through my mind, I suddenly feel as though a bucket of cold water has been dumped over my head. *The people I love . . .* I'm shocked to realize that there actually *are* people I love, and I sincerely believe they love me, too.

I try to pinpoint exactly when this transformation took place, when this miracle happened. When did I go from being a complete outcast with a handful of people who tolerated or pitied me to being someone with real friends whom I love and who love me back? It happened so gradually that I didn't even notice, but now, the realization is so overwhelming that I have to take a few minutes in my personal storage room where I work sometimes to pull myself together. I'm so full of praise and love and gratitude to God for changing my life in this way that when I return to class I feel as though I'm floating. It's as though he's saying to me, "I love you so much, Brooke, that I've given you these people who can demonstrate my love for you. But I love you so much more than that even if every single one of them deserted you, my love for you is still greater than you could ever comprehend."

Love has been a scarce commodity in my life, and even a little bit is enough to bowl me over. But this, this feels like a tsunami. And it is floating along in this blissful knowledge that I make my way to the café where I'm meeting Judah. We decide to take a bus to the hospital since he's left his car parked about the same distance away in the other direction. Driving around the city has gotten to be quite a challenge, and he says he's not sure how much longer he'll be able to do it anyway.

"Public transportation isn't such a bad thing," he says bleakly as we board one of the city's few remaining dilapidated buses. Most people traveling above ground take the new Hypertube: elevated and enclosed, it looks a bit like a rollercoaster in a tube. But it travels in fixed routes, like the metro, and doesn't have a stop close to the hospital yet. Despite the huge outcry about the wasting of public funds when it was installed, it's skyrocketed in popularity to such a degree that buses and taxis are only barely hanging on. Promoted as allowing commuters to reach their destinations at "hyperspeed," the critics call it "hyperstupid." It's also "hyperlimited" as funds ran out causing its route to be somewhat abbreviated from the original plan.

The bus shudders to a stop and we disembark. Neither one of us is sure where to go, so we wander around until we locate a desk and ask someone which room Diana is in. We're walking down the hallway, counting off the numbers on each door when we see Diana's husband,

Trevor, barrel out of a room slightly ahead of us. His face is red, and he's breathing heavily.

"Trevor?" Judah says, moving to intercept him, putting a hand on Trevor's shoulder. "Hey, man, you okay?"

Trevor looks blankly at Judah as if trying to process who he is.

"We heard about Diana," Judah says gently. "There's probably a waiting room around here somewhere." He looks around. "Do you want us to find one, and we'll pray with you before we go see her?"

"What for?" Trevor asks belligerently. "God doesn't care, and he's not listening. If he was, she wouldn't be here right now." Trevor has never spoken directly to me, but he's never seemed particularly hostile toward me. Now that I think about it, he just treats me as though I don't exist. He doesn't speak directly to me now, either. He addresses himself to Judah, but he's staring at me. "If he won't listen to me, what makes you think he'll listen to you? And he's sure not going to listen to *her*."

Judah flinches at the malice in Trevor's voice. He shifts his position, physically blocking me from Trevor's sight as if that will deflect his hurtful words. "It's normal to be angry at God . . . " Before he can finish Trevor cuts him off.

"Is it? That's good then, because I'm angry all right. No just, kind God would do this to my wife." He shakes off Judah's hand and shambles down the hallway.

"Are you okay?" Judah asks quietly, staring after Trevor.

"Yes." I don't trust myself to say more. I just offer my hurt feelings to God knowing that he can deal with them. Judah takes my hand and gives it a reassuring squeeze.

"He's scared and sad and angry with the world," he says. "Don't take it to heart."

I nod. "I know. It's okay."

Cautiously, we enter the room Trevor left and find Diana propped up in a hospital bed, asleep. "Should we wake her up, do you think?" Judah asks uncertainly, but I don't know what to tell him. As we're trying to decide what to do, a guy in scrubs and a lab coat comes into the room and stabs at a computer set up near Diana's bed. He glances over at me, appears thoughtful, and then studies me.

"Well, hello again," he says, and I realize it's the med student I've spoken to here before. "I didn't recognize you without your . . ." He twirls his fingers around his head, and my hand immediately snakes up to my hair.

"Right," I say in sudden understanding, "You haven't seen me since I cut off my dreads."

"Looks nice," he says with a smile.

"Thank you." I'm still not used to receiving compliments, but I'm relieved that at least now I know how to respond to them. I used to blush and object, or change the subject until Judah finally got exasperated with me and said, "Brooke, it's not that difficult. Just say thank you." I wonder why he's in the oncology unit rather than the emergency room where I usually run into him.

As if he's read my mind, he says, "I'm filling in today. They're short-staffed. I'm glad I am. It's nice to see you again." His eyes shift to Judah, "I'm Patrick," he says, sticking out his hand, but grinning at me. "I'm a med student here. Your girlfriend used to hang out in the ER a lot."

Judah doesn't correct him. "Judah," he says, shaking Patrick's hand. "We were hoping to talk to Diana, but we probably shouldn't wake her up, huh?"

Patrick glances over at Diana's inert form. "She'll wake up on her own in a minute or two. We've got her on a little morphine to keep her comfortable."

"Is she in a lot of pain?" I wince.

"No, not yet. It's more to help the anxiety she feels because she's having trouble breathing. It's a small dose, but it makes her sleepy. She'll drift in and out of consciousness." Even as he speaks, Diana's eyes slowly open, and she looks around the room like a diver surfacing.

"And . . . she's awake," Patrick says triumphantly. "What'd I tell you?" He turns to Diana. "How are you feeling, my dear?"

She nods, but her eyes have settled on me, and she's not really paying attention to him. "Good," she whispers. "I want to talk . . . to Brooke."

"And I'm sure Brooke wants to talk to you," Patrick says without a clue. He gives Judah the high sign, and the two of them melt out the door leaving me alone with Diana. Her breathing is labored and rapid, but it's her eyes that make me want to hold my own breath. They are anguished, her torment right on the surface for all to see. She waits for the door to close before she speaks.

"I can hear him . . . taunting me: Satan, not God," she says in a hoarse whisper. Before I can respond she asks, "Do you want to know . . . what he says? 'Christian . . . where is your God?' " She coughs and I wait for her to be able to go on. "All those years I thought . . . I was doing God's will . . . by keeping his church pure. I've been trying . . . to remember all the verses I used . . . to justify my actions, but the only ones . . . I can think of are about love." She turns tortured eyes on me. "I . . . wasn't loving."

It's not something I can dispute. And yet, who am I to increase her suffering? I'm just a forgiven sinner, no worse, no better. "It's not about what we were. It's about who we are in Jesus. That's all that matters. He offers us forgiveness before we even sin. All we have to do is ask for it."

"Your hair," she sighs with an exhalation that's heavy with regret. It's hard to wait for her breathing in order for her to finish her sentences. I want to jump in and finish them for her, but I force myself to wait. To let her say all of what she wants to say herself. "I'm so sorry . . . I know it's a lot to ask . . . but will you . . . forgive me?"

I swallow hard. "I forgive you," I assure her softly. "I forgave you a long time ago. I pray for you a lot, actually."

She smiles faintly at this. "Do . . . you?" she murmurs. "I guess . . . . I'm not surprised. When I . . . get well . . . I'd like to . . . get to know you . . . better."

I'm not sure how to respond to this. Does Diana not know she is dying? (Patrick later tells me that it's common for people who are dying to be in denial.) But then I decide that it doesn't matter. Diana *will* get better. God promises all his children healing. Psalm 41:3 says, "The Lord will give them strength when they are sick, and he will make them well again." Some of us will be healed while we're on earth, but all of us will be healed at the resurrection. Not only will we be healed, we'll be given completely new bodies that won't be subject to any of the physical infirmities we suffer on earth. So one way or another, Diana *will* get well, and we *can* get to know each other better.

"Yes," I agree. "I'd like that."

Diana closes her eyes and leans back against her pillows with a quiet sigh. For a moment I think she's fallen asleep. Then her eyes open. "Will you . . . pray for me?"

"Of course." As I bow my head I feel her hand rest gently on my scalp. It feels like a benediction.

Chapter Sixteen

I never have the opportunity to speak with Diana again. At church the next day they announce that she's slipped into a coma. We have a special prayer time for her. Elder Fortin walks around looking shell-shocked; he's lost his greatest ally. I see him and Mr. Nash speaking earnestly in a corner after the service, and it's not hard to figure out what they're probably discussing. Someone will have to take over Diana's duties and people who feel as they do—people who agree with the church board's recent actions—are few on the ground.

Many of the people they've offended have left. We still see most of them at prayer meeting, but they don't attend church. They say they don't feel welcome. Other people at church are so new they're not really ready to be leaders. Those of us who stuck around through the board's "purgings," as we like to call them, aren't the sort of people they want to see in leadership. That leaves them with slim pickings.

I can't even remember exactly what I'm thinking as I step outside the church. It could be something Judah said to me or it might be the fragment of a hymn or maybe I'm still pondering what will become of church leadership. Whatever it is flies away the moment I register her face. It's Lily. She's standing all hunched over, kind of folded into herself as though she wants to implode. I stare at her stupidly for ages before I manage to find my voice. One word comes out as a squeak. "Lily?"

"Brooke," she sobs and the next instant she's got her arms wrapped around me, and she's weeping on my shoulder.

I pat her back awkwardly, in the cautious way you'd touch a live wire if you were forced to. As desperately as I want to wrap my arms around her and comfort her, I know down that road lies destruction. As I'm wondering what to do, I become aware of something I hadn't noticed before. Lily has a pregnancy bump, her stomach protruding enormously in front of her.

"Lily, you're pregnant," I say, too dumbfounded to even realize I'm pointing out the obvious.

She pulls away from me, scrubbing at her face with her hands to wipe away her tears. "Yeah, six months, and I'm big as a house. Guess that doctor who told me I wouldn't be having any kids because of that botched abortion didn't know what he was talking about." She smiles wanly.

"Why are you here?" I know what she's going to say even before she says it.

"Brooke, I need help," she whispers, choking up again. "I got kicked out of my place at the women's shelter when I got knocked up."

"The baby's father?" I ask stupidly.

Her eyes shift away from me, not embarrassed, I realize, but secretive. "I dunno," she mutters. "I mean, obviously I know who the contestants are, but I don't know which one of them hit the jackpot." Her attempt at a joke falls woefully flat. "None of them want anything to do with me, although one of them told me to come back when I had the kid, and he'd be happy to sell it for me on the black market."

I know she's trying to shock me, to play on my sympathy, to force my hand. If I didn't know better, it would work, too. There is no way Lily would sell her own child. At least, I don't think she would. "Lily, come with me; come inside with me," I urge, wanting to reach out and grab her and pull her into the church.

She backs away from me. "Are you out of your mind?" she spits angrily. "If it wasn't for Christians, we'd still be together. I don't want anything to do with them."

"I have friends," I insist. "They can help."

"Oh, yeah, I'm sure the only thing your 'Christian' friends will like better than your bisexual ex-girlfriend is your knocked up bisexual ex-girlfriend," she scoffs. "I'm sure that will go over really well. They may even burn me at the stake this time instead of just ridiculing me and ruining my life. No, thanks."

I stand there uncertainly, not quite sure what to do next. I'm painfully aware of what Christians have done to both of us, and like Lily, I know that it's all my fault. I was the one who wanted to go see a nativity play that Christmas. I dragged her to a nearby church blinded by nostalgic memories from my youth. (It seems unbelievable now, but at one time I had played Mary in a living nativity put on by my own church when I was a teenager.)

That single episode awakened in me a yearning for God that was almost a physical need. It was like I'd taken a hit of some drug and couldn't get enough. I got hold of the church's calendar and kept making excuses to go back. I dragged Lily with me even though it was the last thing she wanted to do. I was so focused on my need for God that I completely ignored all the warning signs until it was too late.

One night it got ugly, things were said to us and about us that still make my heart bleed. Lily swore she'd never go back and she never did.

I'm not sure if I would have either except that was about the time I met Judah. He offered to study with me. One thing led to another. The more my life changed the angrier Lily got and the less she wanted to be around me. To punish me, she started staying out later and later every night; some nights she never made it back home. She was doing drugs, and I was pretty sure she was cheating on me. By the time I became convicted that my lifestyle was not God's best plan for me, that I was living in opposition to his direct commandments, I thought she'd be almost glad to be rid of me, but she wasn't. We had a vicious fight the night I moved out, and I was pretty sure that as much as I wanted us to remain friends, it would never happen. And it never did.

I felt horrendously guilty for months knowing my present happiness and growing relationship with God came as a direct result of wounding the person I loved most in the world and the only person on earth who even loved me. I almost felt as though I'd committed murder. Nothing had ever been resolved between us and, in a way, it was still like an open wound. I had realized that only God could heal it, and I'd left that up to him, accepting that there might never *be* any resolution in this life. Now I wonder if he's giving me a chance to have one after all.

I blink at her stupidly, trying to clear my memories as I realize this is the first time we've really spoken since we broke up. I want to reassure her, to tell her that it's okay, these are not the same folks who were so awful to us, but who am I kidding? Just because some of these people have come to accept me, to tolerate me, I have no reasonable expectation that they'll accept Lily. As much as I want to believe they'll treat her the way Jesus treated Zacchaeus or Mary Magdalene, I know the more likely scenario is that they'll just reinforce Lily's already jaded view of Christianity.

I'm not sure what to do. For a second, just for a second, I toy with the idea of bringing her home with me, letting her stay for awhile. I could give her the bed and take the couch for myself when I was home. It would be just like old times, except completely platonic. We could raise her baby together. I have one ridiculously intense flash of longing as I see myself holding the hand of a small child, bringing her or him to church, listening to a childish voice lisping the words of

"Jesus Loves Me" before I come crashing back to earth. If I brought Lily back to my apartment, it would be like dumping a box of rattlesnakes on the floor. Eventually, despite my best intentions, I'd get bit. Sin's like that.

So I do the only thing I can think of: I bring her to my parent's house. We barely speak on the trip across town, and then I make her stand outside with me across the street until we can be sure that my father is not at home. She's cold, hungry, angry, scared, and she has to pee. I'm beside myself with apprehension. I keep telling myself this is not as crazy as it seems. My mother works for a crisis pregnancy center. Surely, she'll be able to help or know what to do.

I'm so distracted that once, without thinking, I grab Lily's hand and started to pray out loud. She snatches it away and curses at me. After that, I pray silently, but I don't stop. I haven't seen my parents for quite a few years. The house looks the same though. It could use a coat of paint, but then no one is keeping up appearances as much as they used to before materials got scarce. This side of town isn't quite as nice as where Kyle lives, but it's still far above what Lily and I are used to.

"Lookit," Lily says finally, "are we going in or not? Because if we're not, I'm going to have to find some other place to go."

"We're going," I say mustering as much determination as I can.

I knock tentatively on the door while Lily jigs in place trying to talk herself out of the need to pee. A woman opens the door a crack, not far enough that I can see her face and I wonder, belatedly, if my parents have moved. "Can I help you?"

"Mom?"

The woman's sharp intake of breath is the only warning I get before she flings the door open and throws herself at me. "Brooke!"

With my mother clinging to me, I'm hardly in a position to make introductions. I pat my mother's back as she sobs and stare helplessly at Lily. There isn't a thing I can do. Finally Lily has enough.

"This is very touching," she snaps sarcastically, "but if you don't want a puddle on your doorstep I need to know where the bathroom is. This kid is parked directly on top of my bladder."

My mother waves her hand in the direction of a hallway behind her. "Second door on the left," she says, her voice muffled in my neck. Lily's gone a long time and my mother manages to pull herself together and invite me into the house before Lily's done in the bathroom. Mom bustles around the kitchen putting on the kettle, pulling out muffins and cookies, and placing them on the table where I'm seated. Between the unexpected encounter with Lily and this one with my mother and fear that my father will pop out of the woodwork and start screaming at me, my stomach is so upset that I couldn't eat a mouthful.

"It's good to see you, Brooke," Mom says. Her eyes seem to drink me in, and I feel badly that I've stayed away so long. But it's impossible to know when I might encounter my father instead, and I've never felt brave enough to risk it.

"Thanks, Mom. It's good to see you, too. How's Dad?" I manage to ask politely, but deliberately refrain from asking about Neil. It's not that I don't care how my brother is; it's just that I don't need to know. I've forgiven him, but I haven't forgotten what he did to me. Just because I don't want to kill him any more doesn't mean I want a relationship with him, either.

"He's fine. He misses you, of course," she lies smoothly. I know she's lying because she won't look at me when she says it. "He got promoted at work, so he's pretty happy about that. He's finally a supervisor. I think he's been dreaming about that position since before we even met." No matter how high up in his company my father rises he'll never outshine my hotshot lawyer brother, and I know that has to rankle him. Position to my father is everything. That's one reason Neil is his favorite even though Neil could care less whether he was alive or dead.

"And Neil has two children now," Mom continues without missing a beat.

She's still talking, but I can't hear what she's saying. I'm imagining my brother as a father. He wouldn't molest his own children . . . Would he? I feel cold all over. I'm wrestling with this sick feeling when Lily wanders into the kitchen.

Mom's voice trails off, and she looks expectantly at Lily. "You must be a friend of Brooke's." That's what she says, but I know she's trying to work out the situation. The last thing she heard me say before I left home was that I was gay. She never met anyone I was "dating," and yet, here I am in the company of a girl. But this girl is pregnant which is clearly against the laws of nature. I can see the thoughts rocketing through her mind: Is Lily my "girlfriend"? Is Lily just a friend? Exactly how are we connected? And why are we here of all places?

Lily's eyes shift to me and then back to my mother. She shrugs. "You could say that. An old friend."

I introduce the two of them, but I don't elaborate on our relationship. It's too complicated and frankly, since I am no longer in the lifestyle, for myself anyway, except in the sense that God has forgiven me from it, it's irrelevant to me. Lily pulls up a chair at the table with us and begins to methodically work her way through the food. I can't choke down a mouthful, but it seems like she hasn't eaten for weeks. My mother politely ignores this breach of etiquette, and I suspect that she deals with enough desperate, pregnant, young mothers at the clinic that she knows one when she sees one. She manages to keep up a stream of small talk that almost makes it seem as though the three of us are having a conversation, though I can't keep up my end of it and Lily makes no attempt to keep up hers.

After Lily's polished off every morsel of food and three cups of steaming tea, she begins to sag in her chair. Her eyes are slowly closing and every now and then they snap open, and her head jerks up. She tries to look interested, but I can tell she's just about to give up, put her head down on the kitchen table, and fall asleep.

"Mom," I say, heading her off, "we were wondering if Lily could stay here until the clinic opens on Monday. She doesn't have anywhere she can go, and I thought . . ." It's obvious what I thought, but I can't bring myself to say it.

I know my mother well though, and she's a hospitable soul who would never turn anyone away. She looks brightly at Lily, "You're welcome to stay here, of course. You can stay in Brooke's old bedroom. It's vacant." She gives me a dubious look. "You're not staying as well, are you? Not that you wouldn't be welcome," she hastens to add. "It's just that I've been keeping your room as a guest room, but I remodeled Neil's room and made it a library." She looks uncomfortable, not having managed to clear up the nature of our relationship. "You couldn't stay in the same room." She pierces me with a look. "Your father would have a fit," she adds meaningfully.

"It's okay," I assure her. "I'm not staying. "I have to take care of a little girl tonight over in Lex." I purposely mention Kyle's subdivision knowing it will impress her, which it does.

"Oh? That's nice. You should tell me about that later. First, let me go get your . . . friend . . . settled in your room before she passes out. Tired, aren't you, dear? Making babies takes a lot out of a woman."

Lily heaves herself up from the table and shuffles down the hall after my mother. She doesn't even say good-bye to me. After they leave I glance around the kitchen. It hasn't changed much. I always liked the kitchen. In fact, I probably hung out in the kitchen more than any other room in the house. It was safe here.

Dad spent most of his time at home in the living room watching sports on television. I tended to avoid going in there mostly because it was so noisy I couldn't think. When I had free time, I usually had my nose stuck in a book, and I couldn't read with him yelling at the players.

I didn't like to hang out in my room because of Neil. Even when he wasn't sneaking into it, bad memories choked the space. I am so glad my mother hadn't invited me along to help get Lily settled. It's a relief to be spared seeing it again.

I used to sit at this very table and do my homework, I think. *And my mother used to be right over there by the stove, cooking.* She was a great cook, my mother. Really, she was the only person in my entire family who made me feel loved. Sometimes I wish I'd had grandparents who lived close by, but they didn't. Mom's parents lived a few states over, and we hardly saw them. Dad's were divorced. I'm not sure he knew where his father was, and his mother got Alzheimer's at an early age and didn't know any of us anyway. I remember visiting her once or twice when I was little, but then she passed away.

I'm spared more thoughts of my painful childhood when my mother returns to the kitchen talking a mile a minute as though she'd never left. As she talks, she cleans up the empty dishes, wipes down the table, makes a fresh pot of tea, and digs around in the cupboards until she finds more cookies, store-bought this time, not homemade. "I'm sorry," she apologizes, "but your friend ate all of the ones I made." Finally, my mother falls quiet. The sudden cessation of her chatter seems like the eye of the storm, and I regard her warily, sensing it coming.

"Why haven't you come back before now, Brooke?" she asks, and though I sense accusation in her tone, I can also hear how hurt she is.

"I wasn't sure I'd be welcomed by . . . everyone," I reply, hedging, but she knows full well what I mean.

"Your dad loves you," she says stoutly. I don't believe her, but I nod anyway. "He even prays for you. We both do. Every morning."

I expect these prayers go something like, "Dear God, please save our heathen daughter and rescue her from the clutches of Sodom and Gomorrah." But I'm touched. I would never have believed my parents had been praying for me. And I *had* been saved. A shadow passes over my mother's face.

"What is it?"

She looks at me with tears in her eyes. "I'm just so sorry that you won't be in heaven with me, baby."

I flounder for a moment, trying to understand what she means. And then it hits me. Of course, she's the one who's been doing all the talking. How can she possibly know that my life has completely turned around? How can she know that I'm saved? "Mom, it's okay," I reassure her. "I've given my life to Jesus. I'm a Christian now."

She shakes her head. "The Bible says that homosexuals won't inherit the Kingdom of God," she objects. "I've read the verse, Brooke. It's in the Bible."

"Will you show it to me?" I ask gently.

Mom gets up from the table to retrieve her Bible from the living room. When she returns, she pages through it until she finds what she's looking for. Sadly, she pushes it across the table to me and points with her finger. I pick up the Bible and read aloud, " 'Don't you realize that those who do wrong will not inherit the Kingdom of God? Don't fool yourselves. Those who indulge in sexual sin, or who worship idols, or commit adultery, or are male prostitutes, or practice homosexuality, or are thieves, or greedy people, or drunkards, or are abusive, or cheat people—none of these will inherit the Kingdom of God.' "

"You see?" Mom says bleakly. "I told you it was there."

"Mom, it says 'practicing homosexuality.' I'm not practicing homosexuality anymore. God set me free from it."

She leans forward and says insistently, "But Brooke, you're still a . . ." she drops her voice to a stage whisper, "homosexual. That sort of person can't *change*. It's who they are, and God can't let homosexuals into heaven."

"There's a whole list here of people who won't be in heaven, and God can, too, change people," I want to say. Instead, I continue on to the next verse, " 'Some of you were once like that. But you were cleansed; you were made holy; you were made right with God by calling on the name of the Lord Jesus Christ and by the Spirit of our God.' "

Mom's eyes widen. "Read that last part again. I don't remember that." Her brow furrows in concentration as I repeat verse eleven of First Corinthians 6. "I don't remember that part," she says, but she continues to look skeptical. "But if you're not still being a, you know," she's clearly uncomfortable with the word, but since I do know what she means I don't supply it, "than what are you doing with," she jerks her head in the direction of my bedroom where Lily is probably at this moment blissfully snoring.

"Trying to help," I say simply. "Lily wanted me to take her in, but I . . . couldn't do that. I didn't know where else to bring her."

My mother's eyes tear up. "Are you only here for that reason, Brooke?"

"I wanted to come back, Mom," I say, "but I was afraid of . . ." Before I can finish I hear an ominous sound that makes my heart leap into my throat: a key in the lock, the hinges squeaking as the door swings inward, shuffling on the carpet. My dad's voice.

"Margaret? Where are you?"

I'm frozen with fear. Illogically, my brain is wildly suggesting that if I don't make any sudden moves he won't see me. O, he'll see me and forget about our last encounter, forget about driving me out of the house. Of course, neither of these things happens. What happens is that he rounds the corner and comes to an abrupt halt the instant he sees me. It takes him a few minutes to process who I am. While he's doing that, my mother rises cautiously from her chair.

"Graham, look, honey. Look who came to visit. Isn't this nice? Brooke, say hello to your father."

"Hello, Dad." I have to force the words between my lips. I brace myself, not knowing what is coming next. I realize I'm tensed up in my chair like a runner in the blocks at the starting line just in case I have to make a quick getaway.

Dad doesn't speak to me, though his eyes are riveted on me. He looks older than I remember with more wrinkles and gray hair, and shrunken somehow which makes him seem frail, but his voice is plenty strong. "What is she doing here?"

"Brooke brought her friend Lily to visit . . ." Mom begins, but immediately senses she made a tactical error and tries to correct course, but it's too late. "Not that kind of friend, Graham . . ."

"You brought one of your sick girlfriends to *my house*?" My father snarls. "Is this a joke? What were you thinking?"

"Lily isn't my girlfriend," I object. No need to tell him she used to be. What matters right now is the present situation. "She needed help, and I thought . . ."

"You thought what? That you aren't welcome here, but she might be?" He turns on my mother. "Margaret, I want her out of this house immediately. Where is she?"

"Graham, you can't," Mom protests. "And keep your voice down. She's asleep. And she's pregnant, so she needs her rest."

"Pregnant?" My father clearly can't compute this tidbit of information. "How can she be . . . never mind. We'll deal with her later. You *can* leave, so go," he says to me, raising his hand to point toward the front door.

"Graham," Mom wails, "nooo . . ."

I rise on unsteady legs, give my sobbing mother a hasty hug, and sidle past my father. "I wish . . ." I whisper, then break off knowing it will do no good to finish that sentence.

"What do you wish?" he demands.

I screw up my courage, bracing myself for impact. "I wish you wouldn't judge me because I sin differently than you."

He presses his lips together so tightly they are outlined in white. "Do. Not. Ever . . . put us on the same level," he hisses. "Ever. I sin, yes, everyone does. But you're a monster."

Every time my father says something cruel like this I find myself wishing he'd just hit me instead. A bruise, even a broken bone, would heal faster than the deep cuts his words make on my heart. Each one is still as fresh as the day he inflicted it. To be fair, he isn't often mean, my father. It usually happens when he is provoked—justly or unjustly. And it's usually a flash and then it's gone, rather like a snakebite. He seems to forget all about it soon afterward. I only wish I could.

As I leave the house, a feeling of déjà vu passes over me. Behind me I can hear my mother sobbing and my father is screaming at her. Just like the last time I left this house. All the way to Lex, I pray that Lily will be okay there. I leave her in God's hands; there's nothing more I can do.

Over breakfast the next morning, Kyle asks what's troubling me, and I tell him. He always listens patiently and never sits in judgment, which is something I love about Kyle. I don't know if it's because he feels a deep sense of God's forgiveness toward himself that makes him so compassionate toward others, or if he is just a very empathetic person, but I appreciate it. As I finish speaking, my phone rings. The caller ID says it's my mom.

Yesterday I had reluctantly given my mother my phone number. She'd asked for it, and I couldn't think of a way to politely refuse. Plus, I wanted to know how Lily made out at the crisis pregnancy center. It wasn't that I didn't want to talk to my mom; I was just afraid my dad would get hold of it, and I was terrified of having more encounters like the one we'd had the day before. When the phone trills, showing my mother's number, I'm not exactly surprised, but I am a little nervous when I answer.

"Your *friend*," the icy way she emphasizes the word "friend" implies that she considers Lily anything but, "is gone."

"Gone?" I repeat stupidly. "As in left?"

"Yes, left," my mother confirms frostily, "with all the cash she could get her hands on and every electronic gadget she could carry. She even took the soap and my special shampoo out of the tub! *And* she swiped the fruit from the back of a cupboard where Dad had it hidden so she wouldn't eat it all. He was *not* happy about that."

No, I thought, *No, I'll bet he wasn't.*

"I'm so sorry, Mom. Do you . . . do you have any idea where she might have gone?" I hesitate, hardly daring to hope. "Did she leave a note, by any chance?"

"Note?" my mother mutters sourly, "we're lucky she left the silverware. No, there was no note."

"If she comes back or shows up at the pregnancy center, will you let me know?"

Mom's voice softens. "I'll let you know." She hangs up and I'm left to wonder why Lily would leave such a good thing if she was really as desperate as she had claimed to be.

Kyle has been watching my face. "She ran off?"

I nod.

"She'll turn up again," he says confidently. "There are limited resources in this city. She's bound to show up somewhere. She may even approach you in a few weeks and try to reconcile," he warns.

I shake my head. "That's not an option." I look him directly in the eyes. "You know that I have no desire to return to that lifestyle, right?"

"I know," he says. His look is compassionate, not judgmental or disbelieving. "And you're fortunate that you don't have to."

"You'll be out soon," I say, hoping to make him feel better. Despite the good he is able to do, remaining a TAO is dangerous for him, personally, every minute he's out there. And although he's never talked about it again, I'm sure that he is often forced to do things that he is strongly against. But unlike me, he doesn't *have* a choice. I know that before each shift he prays for God to use him for his purposes and not for Satan's. I know that because I help him pray for exactly that before he leaves the house every evening that I stay with Sadie.

"I know." He forces a smile.

Together, we pray for Lily's safety and that she'll find God out there on the streets. Then Kyle surprises me by praying for my parents, especially my father. When we're finished praying, I look at him with tears in my eyes, touched that he cares so much, grateful for his friendship and his support. Kyle surprises me by pulling my head forward gently and kissing my forehead, the kind of kiss you'd comfort a child with. "Stay safe and go with God," he says to me as I turn to leave. It's our standard parting.

"You, too," I reply and slip out the door.

Chapter Seventeen

One morning I hear sirens shortly before Kyle usually arrives home. It's not just one, there are many of them, some short and piercing and some with long-drawn-out wails. Distracting Sadie, I turn the television on with the volume low. I don't want to worry or upset her, but I need to find out if anyone is reporting what's happening. Whatever it is, it can't be good.

Bomb, I find out, or rather, bombs. Apparently there have been more terrorist attacks on my side of the city, and they've come perilously close to this side of the city as well, which seems to be what all the news reporters are concerned about. This side has been relatively conflict-free, not safe, exactly, but with the appearance of safety at any rate. I turn the television off; I've seen enough.

According to the ticker tape that was running at the bottom of the screen there are cancellations all over the city, Sadie's school being one of them. I know she's going to be thrilled, not understanding the reason for an unexpected vacation day. Knowing that Kyle will most likely be late, I fix breakfast and try to hide my anxiety from Sadie. We pray for Kyle, who I have explained to Sadie is just "running late" this morning, but after she goes to her room to play, I find a quiet spot and pray earnestly for him and for everyone else who will be affected by the attacks.

It's late morning before he shows up. There are dark circles under his eyes and he's covered with soot and smells like smoke. We exchange a look, but Sadie has heard the door and bolts into the room before we can say anything. "Appa! You're home!" she screams. "I gotta day off! Let's play."

Kyle holds her tightly for a moment before she squirms from his grasp. "Yucky, you smell."

He forces a smile. "I know. Sorry." Over her head, he meets my eyes. "I'm going to go take a quick shower. Don't leave just yet, okay?"

I nod. "Okay. I'll wait for you."

While he's gone I warm up the plate of breakfast I put aside for him. I know he'll be hungry. But when he returns he ignores the steaming plate and draws me off to the apartment side where Sadie can't overhear him. "It's bad, isn't it?" I ask, fear making my voice come out in a choked whisper.

"It's bad," he confirms. "There are hundreds dead. These were big bombs. A religious group has already claimed responsibility. They released a statement, it's all over the Internet, something about being the arm of God who is seeking vengeance against the sinners. They targeted a synagogue, a mosque, a methadone clinic, an abortion clinic, and a halfway house."

Before I can manage even a gasp of anguish, he continues. "The worst of it is, because of the victims, the city isn't expending much manpower to save them. Firefighters are on standby, but they're just watching to be sure the fires don't spread. There are perimeters staked out around the individual sites, but law enforcement is just trying to keep the peace, not track down those responsible. They're not even worried about preserving evidence at this point. The victims who survived are being transported by ambulance, but after they found out who they were transporting the ambulances refused to run their sirens. From what I heard, the consensus is that these people didn't get anything more than they deserved."

"That's awful!"

He nods and slumps a little. "I know. I did everything I could, but they dismissed most of us with just a couple hours overtime."

"I'm so sorry, Kyle." It's inadequate, but I don't know what else to say. The magnitude of what's happened is more than I can process. I want more than anything to stay with Kyle and Sadie. To pray with Kyle and seek comfort from God during "family" devotions, but I need to get back to my apartment in case they shut down transportation between my side of the city and his as they were threatening to do. "I need to go," I say, "before they shut down the trains."

"You can't," Kyle says. He looks shocked, as if the thought hadn't occurred to him.

"What do you mean? Of course I am."

"You're not going back there," Kyle insists. "It's too dangerous."

"But I have to go back. My apartment . . ."

"Brooke, please, who cares about the apartment? Just leave it. There's nothing for you there anyway. Let it just sit empty. Squatters will break in eventually, and they'll be happy for a roof over their heads."

"Leave it? *Forever*? But where would I live? I can't live *here*," I protest. "What would I do when the sitters show up? Just try to stay out of their way, pretend I don't exist? I can take care of Sadie myself, but then what would they do? I don't want to put them out of a job."

"I hope they're going to be out of a job anyway, one way or another," Kyle says.

"What? I don't understand. What do you mean?"

Kyle looks conflicted, but as I begin turning to leave he grabs my upper arms to stop me. "Look, I was going to wait. I was hoping for a better opportunity, the right moment."

"Kyle, what is it? I have to go. Who knows how long the trains will keep running?" I can feel panic start to rise in my chest. I don't want to go back, but if I have to, then I need to go while I still can. I'm so distracted that I don't notice Kyle is cupping my face with his hands until he forces me to look directly at him. In that moment, I know what's coming, and the whole world seems to stop. I'm not even sure I'm breathing.

"Brooke, will you marry me?" he asks. He is searching my eyes as if he's hoping to be able to guess what I'll say, so he can fortify himself if I'm about to turn him down. "I know I'm no prize . . ."

"*You're* no prize?" I blurt out incredulously, shaken out of the frozen moment by the ludicrous thought.

"You don't have to rub it in, Brooke." I can sense he's teasing, but there is no teasing in his voice. He's truly worried that I'll say no. Having never prepared for this moment, for this *question*, I don't know what to say. I'm scared, as scared as if I was standing on a precipice contemplating the vast, unknown space in front of me and considering whether or not to step off the ledge and jump into it. What if I say yes and then let Kyle down? What if I let myself down? What if I say yes, but then I break Sadie's heart if it turns out that deep down inside I'm really no different?

You are *no different*, a voice says, not in an accusing way, but in a compassionate, loving way that sends reassurance flooding my being. *I, inside you, make the difference. I am the difference you see; I am the difference you are. Without me you can do nothing; with me, all things are possible. My grace—the power I give you to overcome all your weaknesses—is enough for you.*

I close my eyes and feel gratitude filling me. God's grace is not changeable like I am. It isn't imperfect like I am. God isn't capable of deceit like I am. I may be able to fool myself into believing that I have changed, that I'm a better person than I was, that the abuse in my life is past, that I have moved beyond it, that now I have a chance for true happiness because I know how to "handle" my sin problem. I could convince myself of that in my own humanness.

But I am not capable of making it come to pass, of making it reality. I can't *handle* my sin problem. Only God can do that. Only God can truly heal me. Only God can make me whole and give me the strength, the tools, and the desire to go forward acting in obedience to his perfect will. Only God can make all things new. If I want to receive his power to complete the changes he's been making in my life, I need to give every part of my life—especially *this* part—to him.

And then a miracle happens. Kyle leans closer and places his lips gently over mine, and I don't want to throw up, or gouge his eyes out, or run away from him. It feels perfectly . . . normal. I swallow a sob that wells up from the depths of my being, and before I know it, I'm crying and Kyle is holding me and kissing my face over and over. I'm so grateful to God for healing me, for giving me a second chance and the strength to take it, that I don't even know what to do or what to say. Kyle leads me over to the couch, and we sit down together. He puts his arm around me and holds me until I'm all cried out. All I can think is *I love you, I love you, I love you,* and I don't know if I mean God or Kyle.

As if he's reading my mind, Kyle says, "I love you, Brooke."

"I love you, too," I say shyly.

"You never answered my question."

"Ask me again?" Now that I know what to expect and I'm absolutely certain what my answer will be, I find that I'm longing to hear him ask me again so I can answer properly this time.

Kyle smiles, takes my hand in his, looks deep into my eyes, and asks, "Brooke Merrill, will you be my wife?"

"Yes," I say, practically before he's done speaking. "I would be honored."

There are a lot of things we need to work out, the most important of which is where I will live. Being engaged, and not just the hired help, means that living in the same house is out of the question Kyle and I agree. Although the apartment would be perfect, if I lived in it full-time, rather than just using it as a base when staying with Sadie while Kyle is away, we would be leaving the door open for Satan to tempt us physically, and we agree that neither one of us wants that.

"Everything needs to be completely above board," Kyle says, and

I agree with him. "There must be some place you can stay without having to go back to that apartment." He rubs my hand thoughtfully. "How about Sarah? Do you think she's got enough room?"

I've been to Sarah's a few times and even with Evie and the kids staying, I could probably bunk on the couch or in a corner somewhere. The nice thing is that she lives on this side of town, not far from Kyle's. I nod. "I'll go over later and ask her."

Kyle's eyes are troubled. "I want you to know, Brooke," he begins, and then corrects himself, "no, I *need* you to know, that I'm not always able to be true to my convictions at work." He shifts his gaze away from me. "There's a chain of command. I do the best I can, but, I have to obey direct orders." He spreads his hands helplessly. "You know what the TAOs are like. I just want you to know what you're getting into, what . . . who . . . you're marrying. I don't want to deceive you. You've been able to walk away from your sins. I'm still carrying some of mine around even though I don't want to, and I hate myself for it."

I put my arms around him and hold him close, as though I can protect him somehow with my embrace. "Kyle, I know your heart, maybe even better than you do because I can see the man you're striving to be. I know that with God's help you'll become the man you want to be. I believe that God honors your intentions and that someday he'll give you the opportunity to make a stand for him." As the truth of my words sink in I feel a cold flash of fear as I realize that from this moment on I am linked to that possibility as surely as if I'd just chained myself to Kyle with actual chains. Whatever happens to him will affect me, too.

We spend the day with Sadie, playing games, doing whatever silly thing she suggests, our hands locked together the whole time like drowning victims clinging to each other. I don't know which of us is more afraid this is all a happy dream we'll wake up from, Kyle or me. Sadie herself is eminently practical when we finally sit her down to tell her we're getting married.

"No more babysitters?" she asks hopefully.

"No more babysitters," Kyle assures her.

She turns to me. "And you'll be my new mommy?"

I nod. "Your other mommy," I say, not wanting to take Sylvia's place.

"I would rather have a mommy than babysitters," she replies

firmly, settling the whole matter in her mind in quick order.

It's not my turn to babysit tonight, so I get my things together when Elena arrives. Kyle, dressed in his TAO uniform, follows me out the front door so we can have a few minutes alone. "If Sarah can't take you in, come back here tonight," he instructs.

"I will," I promise, though I'm sure Sarah will let me stay.

"I'll swing by your apartment and check it out. Is there anything you want me to pick up for you?"

I shake my head. After what happened the last time with my building, I've taken to carrying my essentials—Bible, school books, Professor McCormick's paperwork—on my person, just in case. "There's nothing I need there."

Kyle seems relieved. "Okay. I'll feel a lot better if you stay on this side of the city from now on."

"I have to go back for classes," I protest.

"Just there and back again," Kyle says firmly. "But not tonight."

"No, they're closed down today because of the attacks. Professor McCormick's disaster preparedness training class was tonight, but I'm sure that's been canceled, too."

"Good. Go to Sarah's and stay there. I can't remember the schedule. Are you coming back tomorrow night to stay with Sadie?"

I nod.

"We'll talk more then," he promises. "We'll make some plans. Decide on a date. Okay?"

I nod again. "Okay."

Kyle tips my chin up with one finger and kisses me. "May the Lord watch between you and me when we are absent one from another," he says softly. "Stay safe and go with God, my love."

"You, too," I reply, kissing him back. "God protect you."

I tear myself away and hurry down the sidewalk. At the corner, I turn to look back. Kyle is still on the stoop, watching me go. I lift my hand and wave. His own lifts in reply and then he turns to go back into the house. I miss him already.

It's amazing how the city changes within just a few blocks. Sarah's apartment is in a nice part of the city, though not as nice as Kyle's despite the fact that it's only blocks away. Her section of town is still nicer than my parents, though more urban and not as green. In this neighborhood, people prefer their dwellings to lawns. There are a few potted plants to brighten things up, but for the most part it's all sidewalk and brick buildings. Many of the buildings have wrought iron balconies, but they appear to be more decorative than functional, though some of them seem to be used for storage of outdoor items.

In happier times, the city spruced the place up with cheerful iron sculptures. There is a now faded "flower garden" in one park filled with metal flower sculptures. The flower's faces were once painted bright colors, but have since dimmed from the effects of pollution and sun. Their rusting heads bob on coiled wire when the wind blows, creaking a little. Some of the other metal sculptures are interactive, meant for children—and curious adults—to push, twirl, or bend, setting them in motion. Most are now corroded and I wonder if they are even capable of movement anymore.

Sarah answers the door and looks questioningly from my face to the bulging backpack in my hand. "Oh no," she gasps with sudden understanding, "your building was bombed in the attacks?"

"Close," I say, "I'm getting married."

She blinks at me stupidly. "Come again?" she says. "You're *what*?"

"Let me in, and I'll tell you everything."

"Okay," she says, "but remember, you asked for it."

I can't make sense of this cryptic welcome until I follow her into the living room area which looks like the scene of an army hospital. There are blankets and ratty sleeping bags stretched out on every available inch of floor space. Dirty, but tidy, possessions are bundled up next to each makeshift bedroll. The smell is more than a little overpowering, and I try not to breathe through my nose. We pick our way around this setup as though we're walking through land mines to the kitchen from which I can hear the soft murmur of many voices.

Evie is at the stove flipping homemade tortillas in a skillet while one of her older children stirs a pot of beans and rice on another burner. About fifteen young men are wedged into the small space. Judah is holding court from a stool at the kitchen counter. He sees me and waves enthusiastically but doesn't stop talking. A few of the young men's heads turn to see who has entered the room, but they are too caught up in what Judah is saying to pay much attention to me. Only Rocko detaches himself from the group and makes his way over to me, surprising me by giving me a warm hug.

"Hi, Brooke," he says. He seems less hectic somehow. Maybe it's that he doesn't seem like a powder keg waiting for a spark to make him blow up. The quick anger that has always been inside him seems to have evaporated. "It's good to see you."

"You, too," I say. When he wanders over to give Evie a hand, I hiss out of the corner of my mouth to Sarah, "What's going on here?"

Her laugh is a whisper. "This is Rocko's Posse," she replies *sotto voce*, and then hastily adds, "but don't refer to them as that. They call themselves the Disciples." She steers me away from the group into another room, some sort of study or library. There are floor to ceiling shelves stuffed with books on two of the walls and some overstuffed chairs, but there is also a desk and filing cabinets.

"This was Morgan's 'office,' " she explains in answer to my unspoken question. A couple of Evie's smaller children are in here building something with plastic blocks. They don't look up from their play when we enter the room. Sarah and I curl up opposite one another in the chairs which are as comfortable as they look. My day has been such an emotional whirlwind that I feel as though the world is spinning around me, and the moment I stop moving it mercifully begins to slow down.

"The Disciples?" I ask. "That's Rocko's group, the one he was telling me about at the shelter one night. They're the young men who live on the streets and witness and preach, right?"

"They do," Sarah confirms.

I'm confused. "So what are they doing camped out here?"

"Oh, this isn't *all* of them," Sarah says, her eyebrows rising in surprise. "These are just the new ones. They come here a couple nights a week for Bible study with Judah or Rocko or a couple of the 'older, more mature' Christian men. They take showers here and sleep on the floor and then they leave the next day. Evie and I feed them while they're here. It gives them a bit of a break from being on the streets all the time," she explains, "while they're so new at it."

She's thoughtful for a moment. "Plus, I think it helps Evie. She's made it her mission to 'mother' them. We feed them pots and pots of beans and rice and tortillas. It fills them up without bankrupting us. They call her *mamacita*." Sarah grins.

Little mother? I think, picturing our pastor's tall, willowy, blonde wife. "Has *anyone* heard what's happened to Pastor Javier?" I ask. As far as I know, there's been no word since he was taken. At great risk, Kyle once tried to look in his file, but there wasn't one. That in itself was odd, he'd said. Even if Pastor Javier had been executed or died in prison there should still be a record of him in the TAO database. There wasn't even an entry for his arrest on the night it occurred. It was as if the event had never happened.

Sarah shakes her head. "No. Evie has been down to the official TAO headquarters; she's been to the police station; she's even written to the mayor. No one claims to know anything about him. It's as if he vanished." To distract us from this bleak thought, she looks at me and says, "Your hair is cute that way. What do you call it? Bed head?"

My hand reaches up automatically to my head. Now that my hair has grown out, I'm apparently supposed to be fussing with it all the time. "Not fussing," Sarah has explained numerous times, "it's called styling, Brooke, and you only have to do it once, in the morning. At the very least, run a brush through it." I can feel a snarl on one side of my head, and I suppose it must be sticking out in places. "I never had this problem with dreads," I mutter. "They were wake-and-go."

Sarah chuckles. "So did I dream you said you were getting married? Or did you say you were getting harried?"

"Married," I say automatically, but my voice is full of wonder. *I'm getting married.*

"He finally asked you then?"

"You *knew*?"

She shrugs. "No, not really. I mean, it's not like he said anything to me. But I have eyes. I could tell he cares for you a great deal. I just didn't know . . ." She shrugs again. "I didn't know if you were . . . willing."

I know what she means is more along the lines of "able." Sarah has proved many times that she's my friend, but I know she still struggles to accept what I *was* in light of who I *am* in Christ. I know she believes I *want* to change, but she's not sure I actually *can* change. Catching glimpses of her struggle used to frustrate me and, frankly, hurt my feelings. But then I realized that she's trying, and no matter what she thinks about my past life in light of my present life, she's willing to accept me unconditionally as a friend, as a sister in Christ, even. And that's what is important. "You *are* talking about Kyle, right?" I say, more to distract me from her doubt in me than because I think there are other men who could possibly be attracted to me.

"Of course I mean Kyle," she laughs. "Who else follows your every move with his eyes? Who else put his own neck on the line to make sure you were safe? I think he loved you before he even *knew* he loved you," she muses.

I feel a warm flush of gratitude at her words. Has it been that obvious, and I never even suspected?

"When is the big day?"

"We haven't set a date, yet," I tell her. "I'm watching Sadie tomorrow night. Kyle asked me to come by a little early so we can make plans."

"You're wearing a dress," Sarah informs me and her voice brooks no argument.

"I guess." I hadn't thought about that part. Brides are usually decked out like big, frothy cakes, practically swaddled head to foot in lace. Not exactly my style. I feel a slight stab of panic at the idea of being covered in ruffles and frills.

"Don't worry," Sarah assures me, no doubt seeing the slightly terrified look in my eyes. "We'll find you something even *you* can't object to." She eyes my plain jeans and black long-sleeve shirt meaningfully which makes me giggle with nervousness. All I can picture is Sarah finding me a fingertip-brushing, floor-grazing, chin-high black dress. *Actually,* I think, *that wouldn't be half bad. Except that black isn't exactly the joyful color you naturally associate with weddings.*

"So is it okay if I stay here on the nights I'm not watching Sadie? Just until the wedding," I hastily add. My dubious gaze is drawn in the direction of the kitchen where sounds of singing are now beginning. "I'll understand if you say no. I didn't realize you were practically a hotel now."

"I don't know about that," Sarah replies mildly, "but I have to say I am enjoying all the company a lot more than I ever thought I would. I didn't realize how lonely I've been since Morgan passed away until the house was full of life. I haven't even had a pet." She shakes her head at her own folly. "Why did I wait so long to invite people into my life?"

I have no answer for her.

"I'm sure you don't want to bunk with the guys." She waves her hand around the office. "No one is staying here. It's all yours. I may even have a cot around here somewhere that we can set up so you don't have to sleep on the floor."

I get up and put my arms around her shoulders. She returns my hug. "Thanks, Sarah. I really appreciate it."

"I'm glad to have you here," she says. "And congratulations. Really, Brooke, I couldn't be happier for you."

As we make our way to back to the kitchen she turns to me with a twinkle in her eyes. "I hope you like beans and rice!"

Chapter Eighteen

It's not exactly the wedding of my dreams: there is no big church ceremony, there are no elaborate, staged wedding pictures, no entourage of attendants, no beaming parents (my mother would have come, but my father forbade her and Kyle's aren't in the country.) But considering the fact that I *am* getting married, something I never thought possible, to a man I deeply respect as well as love, with the free blessing of God, our wedding is more than I ever could have dreamed it would be.

We've got a total of two witnesses, if you don't count Sadie who is present in a dainty lacy dress that is prettier than my own though she actually looks comfortable in hers: Sarah and Judah. We don't really call them the matron of honor and the best man, but I suppose that's what they are. They're both dressed formally. Judah and Kyle must have coordinated beforehand because they are both in dove gray suits with bow ties the exact blue of lapis lazuli. Sarah is smiling through her tears and trying not to fuss over me even though I can tell she really wants to.

My dress was a struggle. It's not that I didn't want to wear a dress, exactly. I just couldn't bear the thought of being encased in frills. Finally, exasperated with me, Sarah had dragged me to a small used clothing shop I'd never heard of and made me try on a few wedding dresses. She proved that she knew me pretty well when I found myself modeling streamlined sheaths of satin without a ruffle or geegaw in sight. I finally found one I liked: a sleek, but not form-fitting, column of satin with yards of fabric in the back, giving it fullness without the pretension of a train (at which I drew the line.) It has three-quarter-length sleeves and the only bit of ornament is a touch of patterned silver ribbon at the waist.

I don't feel stiff in it, but it's a far cry from my usual jeans and T-shirt, even if my T-shirts now include a few tasteful, low-key colors. But when Kyle's eyes meet mine, I forget all about the dress. I could be wearing a burlap sack for all I care. The only important thing is this man and our commitment to each other and to God. I know our life together isn't going to be without struggle, but we'll be facing it together now, and that's what matters.

The city clerk's office is all high ceilings and cold stone which makes cavernous echoes and amplifies the slightest sound. The city clerk himself is a thin, wan man who looks at us dubiously. "The rest of your people coming soon? I've got a schedule to keep up."

Kyle glances over our little group and assures the man, "This is all of us. We're all here."

He sniffs incredulously. "That so? All right, then. Let's get to it."

As I sign paper after paper, I wonder what our wedding might have been like if we'd been able to have it at the church with Pastor Javier officiating. The thought of a big, elaborate service makes me more nervous than this does, but at the same time, I feel slightly wistful. It would have been nice to be surrounded by people you know wishing you well and praying for your union. I almost snort at this thought. There are very few people left at our church who would approve of our union, much less pray God's blessing on it or wish us well.

No, Kyle was right. This is better. We'll go out to celebrate once the official obligations have been met and Sarah snaps some pictures of us.

In a quiet moment after the ceremony, while Kyle is speaking to the clerk and Sarah is showing Sadie how to operate her camera, Judah pulls me aside. He gives me a long hug and then holds me out at arm's length. "Look at you," he says, the admiration in his voice nearly choked by emotion. "You're beautiful, Brooke. Inside and out. I am so proud of you, girlfriend."

I smile, not sure what to say to this. I've never seen Judah get sentimental before. "Hey, you aren't giving me notice as your friend just because I'm a married woman now, are you?"

His laugh seems to shake him free from the danger of getting mushy. "I should say not," he assures me. "I expect I'll see you more than ever now that you're not getting ready for your wedding, and we're on summer break. I've got plenty for you to do helping out with the Disciples. In fact," he glances over his shoulder at Kyle who is still deep in conversation with the clerk, "I was wondering, now that you won't be needing Kyle's apartment, do you think we could use it as a gathering place? It's not so much that they've outgrown Sarah's place as that we're spilling out of it."

I think of the motley group of youth Rocko has collected who spend all their time doing inner city mission work. I don't have to ask Kyle; I know he'll say yes. And, I realize, the apartment is now *my* apartment, too. But before I can give in to the temptation of speaking for my new husband, he joins the conversation. Kyle readily gives his consent, and I feel a slight frisson of pleasure that I knew what he was going to say before he said it. But I can't shake a vague conviction that it is his place to say it and not mine.

"Are we ready to go?" Sarah asks, her eyes shining with happy tears. "Why are you still in that dress? Go change. We can't go out to eat with you looking like a bridal fashion plate. For one thing, there isn't a restaurant in the city with a booth big enough to accommodate the size of that train."

"It's *not* a train," I insist. "It's just a full skirt."

"Whatever it is, it won't fit into a booth," Sarah persists. "Here's your case." She hands me a small travel suitcase we packed with a change of clothes, still dressier than what I normally wear, but more appropriate for going out to eat.

"Wait!" Sadie says, tugging on Sarah's sleeve. "You forgot the pictures," she says in an accusing tone.

Sarah rolls her eyes. "What an idiot I am. Thank you, love, I did."

She groups us together in various configurations, taking pictures until my smile feels frozen on my face. She even talks the dour clerk into taking some pictures of all five of us together. Finally, she's satisfied and gives me a shove toward the ladies room so I can get changed. As I peel off the beautiful dress, I hold it up for a moment and just stare at it, trying to wrap my head around the fact that I'm a married woman. My wonderful husband is right outside that door, waiting for me—and doing it poorly if I know Kyle at all. My beautiful daughter is probably asking Sarah a million questions right now about outrageous things no one can possibly know the answer to.

I feel like the most blessed woman on the planet. I bury my face in the soft, silky fabric and breathe my gratitude to God not only with words but with my whole being. When I think about how bleak my world was and how full it is now, I want to cry. But Sarah made me wear makeup—"Just a little, Brooke, it won't kill you. I'll make it look natural, I promise."—and I'm afraid I'll spoil it. Instead, I finish changing as quickly as I can because I don't want to spend one more second parted from either of them.

"Mama!" Sadie squeals, hurling herself at me when I emerge from the restroom. I set the suitcase holding my dress on the ground and gather her up. Her small body feels so solid and warm in my arms. A rush of maternal possessiveness sweeps over me and then, for the first time, it occurs to me to wonder whether Kyle and I will have a child.

I find myself smiling at the thought. Not only because I would love to have another child, but because I know Sadie would be thrilled to have a sibling.

If we could have gone anywhere to celebrate, Kyle told me when we were planning the wedding, he would have wanted to bring me to a fancy restaurant called LaSalle. Being a TAO has many perks, both monetary (socially speaking, Kyle and other TAOs live in as grand a style as they like, many of them in far grander style than Kyle does) and in the form of "favors" (basically, getting anything they want just because they are TAOs.) If Kyle wanted to, he could simply have ordered the restaurant to block off an entire dining room for our personal use (even though there are only five of us) and provide whatever food he wanted whether it was on the official menu or not.

But there's one thing even a TAO can't do and that's reopen a restaurant that's boarded up and deserted. LaSalle closed several months ago, not because they weren't still doing a booming business, but because the owner, who was a kind, generous, Christian man, happened to be on my side of town when it was bombed. No one knew he was delivering leftover food to a halfway house that was targeted in the attacks. Rescue personnel assumed he was a former convict and let him bleed to death as the ambulance took its sweet time getting to the hospital. The restaurant closed shortly thereafter.

So instead of LaSalle, we find a little hole-in-the-wall noodle joint and cram ourselves into a single booth. In the steam filled air, we laugh ourselves silly and order a table full of dishes, sharing them all. I am so unused to laughing that by the time we leave my ribs are aching. Kyle and I hug Sarah and Judah, thanking them for spending our special day with us, but as we prepare to leave them to return home, Sarah bends down next to Sadie and says, "Sadie, honey, how would you like to have a sleepover at Auntie Sarah's?"

"Sarah, no, it's fine . . ." I protest.

She's speaking to Sadie, but giving me a look over Sadie's head. "Mommy and Daddy need some special time alone, and you and I can make moon sand. Would you like that?"

Sadie's eyes grow as big as saucers. "Moon sand?" she breathes in awe. I am positive she doesn't even know what that is. Frantic, she turns to Kyle and asks breathlessly, "Appa, can I go sleepover at Auntie Sarah's and make moon sand?" I stifle a giggle at how desperate she is. Was I ever that full of wonderment as a child? I can't remember.

Kyle laughs. "If you really want to . . ."

"I do! I do!" Fickle Sadie lets go of my hand and makes a lunge for Sarah.

"Her things . . ." I begin, but Sarah cuts me off.

"Snuck some of her stuff to my house yesterday. Go. Don't worry."

"But if she doesn't last the night," Kyle says, "call us. We'll come get her. She's not used to being away from home."

Sarah nods. "I will. Now shoo!"

Watching Sarah, Judah, and Sadie move off down the sidewalk as if they are a family gives me a strange feeling. I'm on the verge of hollering, "Stop!" when Kyle takes my hand. "It'll be fine," he says, watching my face. "She'll have too much fun to be homesick. You'll see. She's a brave little thing." He gazes after his daughter, his look equal parts wistful and proud. Then, it's like a door closes, and he turns to me. "Would you like to head home, or see some more of our fair city?"

I smile at the thought; the "fair city" is a sad shadow of its former glory. "I want to go home," I say firmly. And for the first time in what could be my entire life, more than anything, I *do* want to go home. The joy I experience at the sense of belonging I feel as we turn to head home—to *our* home—makes me feel giddy. I couldn't be more grateful to God for giving me a home and a family. I couldn't be more grateful to Kyle for making me a wife. And I couldn't be more grateful to Sadie for making me a mom.

We take the Hypertube—my first time ever—but Kyle is noticeably agitated in the station while we're waiting for our cars to pull in. He watches the other passengers warily and tightens his grip on my hand. There are more TAOs than usual patrolling the platform.

"Maybe we should take a taxi," he says. "I don't like this. Something feels off."

A TAO approaches us with measured steps. I think he's going to pass us, but he stops next to Kyle and acknowledges him with a nod.

"Captain Huang," he says quietly. "Off duty tonight, sir?"

Fascinated, I can't take my eyes off him. It's the first time I've heard a TAO (aside from Kyle) speak in a civilized tone of voice, not issuing a command or insolently ordering someone to do something.

It's amazing how much it humanizes him.

"Yes, Sergeant," Kyle replies crisply, his whole demeanor becoming more rigid and controlled, more . . . commanding. "I was married today. Allow me to introduce you to my wife."

The TAO's eyebrows rise in surprise, and he peers around Kyle so he can see me properly. "Mrs. Huang, congratulations, ma'am."

"Thank you," I murmur, suddenly aware that I'm staring. I manage to find something else to look at while the men continue their quiet conversation.

". . . whole unit is on alert," the TAO is saying, "but they're pretty sure it's just an idle threat. No one is really concerned. Tightened security though. Don't be surprised if they call you in."

"Better not," Kyle says grimly. "I've got a week off, and I'm taking the whole thing. It's my first vacation since I returned from my deployment. I think I've earned it."

The TAO smiles broadly. "Yes, sir."

Our cars pull in and the TAO glances up and down the platform at the other passengers. His partner is standing near the open door of the tube. He gives Kyle a modified salute and begins to walk away. I am just stepping over the threshold of the door into the car when a loud, masculine voice in the station behind me shouts, "Hit the ground!"

Kyle reacts so fast that I find myself on the concrete floor shielded by his body before my brain even registers what the voice said. I hear screaming and a muffled explosion. Kyle shifts his weight and lets me up enough that I can draw in a deep gulp of air which I immediately regret. Smoke from the explosion sears my lungs and starts a coughing fit. Kyle pushes me behind a large column and wedges his body on top of mine. Minutes feel like hours. Every now and then I hear a burst of gunfire punctuated by screaming and sobbing. I'm starting to feel claustrophobic in the enclosed station, physically trapped by Kyle, smothered and incapable of taking a deep breath of fresh air in the smoke filled tunnel, unable to see what's going on. Why won't he let me up?

Panicking, I start to wriggle, hoping to break free of him so I can make a run for the fresh air outside. He places one strong hand on my shoulder and hisses, "Be still. There's a sniper out there."

I freeze, wondering if my next second will be my last. Is any part of me sticking out past the column? Suddenly, I understand why Kyle is using his own body to cover me. He's a human shield. As the minutes wear on, I calm down enough to think logically again, and I begin to pray: for Kyle, for myself, for the innocent people the sniper is targeting, even for the TAOs who are trying to protect us.

"Captain," a hoarse voice rasps. By levering myself slightly I can see the TAO Kyle was talking to before the attack. He's lying on the ground not far from the column that is shielding us. I can't tell if he's wounded or not, but I assume he wouldn't be lying there if he had the power to move. "That sniper is taking out civilians. You have a better chance of hitting him than I do." Wincing, he holds his assault rifle out to Kyle.

What happens next takes place so fast that it's all a blur. Pushing me back further behind the column, Kyle uses the resistance to propel himself across the concrete in a tucked up somersault that lands him next to the downed officer. He snaps the gun up to his shoulder and fires at almost the same instant. It doesn't seem possible that he could hit a building under those circumstances, let alone a sniper hiding somewhere out in the smoky haze beyond, but he does. There is a loud thump followed by a TAO yelling, "Target acquired, target acquired. Stand down!"

By this time reinforcements have arrived, and they begin shepherding us all to safety. People are covering noses and mouths, but almost everyone is coughing and choking from the smoke. After assuring himself that I'm not injured, only frightened and coughing, Kyle reluctantly leaves me in the custody of a young TAO with instructions to have me checked out by medical personnel. Then he strides off to give a brief after action report to a superior officer and check on the condition of the sergeant whose rifle he used.

"He's a hero, your man," the TAO says. His face is expressionless, but he sounds a little awed as he watches Kyle gesturing as he explains the sequence of events to a scowling officer.

"I know," I reply, but I doubt we're talking about the same thing.

"He saved my life once."

"Me, too."

He looks at me and grins. "Busy man. Did he tell you he holds the record for the highest number of confirmed kills in our country's entire history?" Seeing my astonishment, he goes on. "Nah, he wouldn't. Too modest. He never brags about himself, but me? When I grow up, I wanna be just like him."

I shudder, but the TAO doesn't notice. When Kyle is finished, he comes to claim me. He leads me outside to the sidewalk where he wraps his arms around me so tightly I have trouble breathing. "Thank God you weren't hurt," he murmurs into my hair. "Thank you, God."

"You were amazing," I tell him. "What you did in there."

He releases me, his face grim. "I killed a man. I don't call that amazing."

"But you saved a lot of people." I have a feeling that I could talk all night and he'd still be castigating himself for his actions.

"Let's go home." It takes awhile, but Kyle finally hails a taxi. Huddled in the back seat, he clutches me fiercely. I've never seen him this shaken except for the time he came home following my first night babysitting Sadie, the night my building was burned. But this time he seems more in possession of his senses.

"I hate my job," he says in an undertone. "I hate it."

"I know." I wonder what it must feel like to have someone's blood on your hands. Kyle is close-lipped about his military work for the most part, but he's said enough that I know he's killed many people. A great many, if the young TAO can be believed. Piecing things together, I've figured out that his work as a sniper landed him in an elite Special Forces team when he was deployed, and those same skills have made him a valued asset to the TAOs. Unfortunately, they are skills that, while he once might have taken great pride in them, Kyle now finds repulsive. He's told me more than once that he feels like a monster.

I get my first taste of just how much those "confirmed kills" prey on his converted mind when he wakes me up that very night in a cold sweat, screaming as though someone is jabbing hot pokers into his eyes. In an unfamiliar place, an unfamiliar bed, an unfamiliar room, I don't even know where the light switch is. I blunder around running into things before I stumble across it, my heart hammering in my chest from the shock of being woken from a deep sleep by the sound of a man in such distress.

As light floods the darkness, I see again the strangeness I had my first glimpse of last night. Kyle's room looks like a military barracks. All it's really missing is the metal cot, though the full-size bed isn't a big improvement. There are a couple of army green, metal folding chairs, a large matching locker that takes up half of one wall, and some sort of gun rack or case that holds not only guns, but an arsenal capable of taking down a small city. Flak jackets, entire suits of camouflage, something Kyle calls a ghillie suit that looks like a pile of dead branches and grass, and another large metal locker that he tells me is an "ammo can" which, in civilian speak, is where he stores his ammunition.

He seemed surprised when he registered my shock. Looking around and seeing it through my eyes, he immediately told me that I was free to decorate it however I like. "I'll move all this stuff into one of the spare rooms. I've been on my own for quite awhile," he'd said by way of explanation. "It was just easier this way."

Now, he is staring around wildly in the bright light, his chest still heaving as though he's just run a marathon in record time, but the screaming has stopped. There is a vacantness to his eyes that tells me mentally he's still not in the here and now. I climb back into bed and tentatively put my arms around him. I have no idea if he will become violent or welcome comforting. He grabs me as though I'm a life preserver, and he's drowning.

The deep gasps eventually taper off and become sobbing. When he has calmed down, I slip out of bed to retrieve my Bible. Plumping the pillows up behind us, we cling together as I read Bible promises aloud, one after another, until the darkness recedes and it is light, both in our hearts and in the room. We have no place to be and nothing to do, so instead of getting up and muscling through the day, we snuggle together. Kyle drifts off to sleep again before I do. When his eyes close, I trace the dark smudges beneath them with my thumb. With all my heart, I look forward to the day when Jesus comes back, and Kyle will be released from all his demons and welcomed into the loving arms of our Savior. That happy thought is the last thing I remember before falling asleep.

The strange thing about married life is that it doesn't seem strange at all. The situation around the world is so unsettled and volatile that we don't even attempt to take a honeymoon. Instead, Kyle has taken a week off from work, and we hang around the house playing with Sadie, talking, and making a mess in the kitchen. It is, hands down, the most fun I've ever had.

Sadie has a few sleepovers with Auntie Sarah who teaches her, in addition to moon sand, how to make a "stained glass" kite from colorful tissue paper and black construction paper, funky little bugs from painted rocks and pipe cleaners, and a lion mask that turned her into a lion that hid and "pounced" on us most of one day. I'd had no idea Sarah was such a fount of children's crafts. By the end of the week, I'm getting a little jealous of Sadie and the fun she is having at Sarah's. When things settle down, I plan to join them.

The first day Kyle has to head back to work I feel a sick, leaden weight in the pit of my stomach. Seeing him in that awful black uniform just seems wrong. I want to wrap my arms around him and refuse to let go so that he can't leave for work. Instead, while he's helping Sadie with something, I slip into our room and onto my knees for a quiet word of prayer. Committing him to God's care and safekeeping gives me a sense of peace so that when I give him a hug and kiss goodbye, I can do it with a generous spirit.

We have family worship before Kyle leaves. After, I follow him out to the stoop. As he begins to run lightly down the stairs, he turns and gives me a wide smile. "I miss you already," he says.

I smile back. No sense letting my downhearted face be the last thing he sees in the morning. "I miss you, too."

I go back into the house and lock the door behind me. I've got a lot of furniture to order, I remind myself. And then I have to figure out how I'm going to continue going to school while caring for Sadie.

"Quit," Sarah says later when she drops by to help me cook for some of the Disciples who are staying in the apartment temporarily while they learn how to give Bible studies. Judah is supposed to be dropping by any minute to teach them.

Quitting had actually never crossed my mind, but now that the suggestion hangs out there between us, I can't find any reason *not* to quit. Professor McCormick can easily find another teaching assistant. I won't even have to miss him because he's a regular attendant at our midweek prayer meeting at the college. (He still won't admit he's a follower of the Jesus he used to scorn, but he's an active participant and seems to know his Bible better and better each week. I figure it's only a matter of time before he confesses to the rest of us what we can plainly see with our own eyes: Professor McCormick has become a Christian.) Over the last few months, current events have made me question more and more the need for a degree in economics; surely raising a child is a more worthy occupation. I glance around me at my newly acquired "wealth." And it's not like I need to earn my own living any more.

"I guess I don't see why I shouldn't," I say slowly, letting the simple solution sink in. I was never one of those people who wanted a degree just to say I had one. I actually needed a career before, but now . . . well, now, I guess I have one. "You're a genius," I tell Sarah.

"I know," she jokes with false modesty. "It's a burden I try to bear with grace." Then she becomes serious. "So how's married life? Is Kyle still having the nightmares?"

I blink at her. "How did you know he has nightmares?"

"Sadie," she replies. "She doesn't miss a trick."

I wince, thinking about Sadie being woken by Kyle's screaming. I'll have to have a talk with her later. "Ah, what does Sadie say?"

Sarah shrugs, the rhythm of her knife a rapid staccato as she chops carrots for the soup. "Just that he's woken her up a few times. Scared her a little. Apparently, she spied on you two once after it happened, and you were reading the Bible to Kyle." Sarah sneaks a look at me sideways. "She said that made her feel better and after that, when she hears him scream, she takes out her Bible and 'reads' Bible verses herself."

This is a new development because until the wedding, Kyle had been sleeping during the day while Sadie was at school. At night, when *she* was sleeping, he was at work most of the time. On his days off, he'd told me, he kept the same schedule as much as possible so he wouldn't mess up his internal clock. Now that we are married though, he'd put in for the day shift and easily gotten it. He was going to be home at night more often. We hadn't been married long enough for me to know yet how often these night wakings were going to happen.

"I'll talk to her," I tell Sarah. "It doesn't happen every night, but it is pretty terrifying at first when it does."

"I'll bet," Sarah agrees. She doesn't ask me why someone in Kyle's position wakes up screaming in the night, and I'm grateful.

One of the young men interrupts us, poking his head tentatively into the kitchen. "Can I help?" he asks politely.

"Thanks," says Sarah, "but we're all done." She brushes another pile of carrots off her cutting board and into the big stock pot I pulled out to use hoping it would be big enough to satisfy the boundless appetites of the boys staying in the apartment. If they are anything like the ones who stay at her place, she assures me, they'll be ravenous.

"They never ask for handouts," she told me when the first of them moved into the apartment a few days ago, "but don't be surprised if you find yourself cooking up big pots of soup or pasta to feed them.

That's what happened at my place. Food was never part of the arrangement, and then it was. We tried different meals at first, but Evie finally said that they needed something that would fill their bellies on the cheap. So we settled on beans and rice. Kyle's got a little more means, so maybe you can feed them soup. Get some veggies into them."

Judah steps around the kid and comes into the kitchen. "Something smells wonderful," he says, staring longingly at the pot simmering on the stove.

Sarah laughs. "You're always hungrier than the kids," she teases him.

"Yeah, well, I'm not such a good cook. There's only so much mac-n-cheese I can heat up before I get really sick of it. I haven't had homemade soup in . . . well, longer than I can even remember."

"Well, you're going to have some tonight," I say. "And homemade biscuits, too."

Judah high-fives the kid. "Soup *and* biscuits," he whoops.

"Shoo." Sarah waves her hands at them. "We've got this covered. Go start your study. We'll tell you when it's ready." She rolls her eyes at me and says with mock exasperation, "Men."

Judah grins. "Yes, ma'am. Come on. You heard the woman. Let's go." He herds the kid ahead of him toward the apartment. "We've got a Bible study to start," we can hear him saying.

"One thing they never do," Sarah points out with a grin, "is complain about the food."

Not only do they not complain about it, I find out later, they devour it at lightning speed. And I have to say, it gives me a good feeling to be able to serve them in this way.

Chapter Nineteen

Judah's sitting at our kitchen table, nursing a mug of tea. His eyes are troubled, but he hasn't yet spilled what he's obviously concerned about. I'm hoping he'll get to it soon because I still have to get changed before prayer meeting. I've been moving furniture all day. The new pieces have finally arrived, and I'm beside myself with pride at how transformed the master bedroom is. It no longer looks like a room in an army barracks. Kyle will be pleased because it's not full of froufrou, either.

Instead, it has clean lines of crisp, warm white with furniture of honey colored wood. There are accents of a shade of blue I remember from visiting an aunt and uncle at their beach home on Cape Cod when I was a little girl. Just seeing it brings back memories of that happy time and makes me think of the sun and the ocean.

The only thing that hasn't changed is the size of the bed, though I did get a new one that has an actual headboard rather than metal bars. My physical presence seems to soothe Kyle at night and the close quarters of the full-size bed force us to sleep very close together. Kyle keeps his arm draped across my body all night long. It was difficult for me to learn to sleep that way at first, but the nightmares tapered off rapidly, so it's been well worth the learning curve.

I can't wait for Kyle to see the room. He's still at work and called me shortly before Judah arrived to tell me a "situation" has come up that requires his expertise and that he isn't sure how long he'll be, but he'll try to get home as soon as he can. If he doesn't arrive before Sadie and I leave for prayer meeting with the others, I'm to go on ahead and he'll meet me there.

Judah sighs and says, "The thing is, I'm not sure how safe we are at the college anymore. Ever since they started cracking down on organized religion after those religious groups started setting off bombs . . . well, Kyle knows as well as I do, if they find us it won't be pretty."

He's right. The fanatical religious groups trying to get the world to repent by setting off bombs, not only in our city but elsewhere across the country, have caused the government to crack down on religion. It is only legal to assemble for religious purposes within the four walls of a recognized religion that has been duly registered with the proper authorities (recognized before the bombings, not formed after them.) There hasn't been a violation, yet, so no one really knows what will happen if a non-sanctioned religious group—like ours—is found meeting outside a church.

"I was thinking, maybe we should start meeting at the church again. The place is like a ghost town." A few of the people who meet weekly for the underground prayer meeting at the college also attend the church services, like us, but not enough to fill the pews. He shrugs helplessly. "I just don't know if they'd welcome us or not. What do you think?"

This is something I've been studying in my own Bible study time and have discussed at length with Kyle who also believes we should be meeting at the church (partly because he says it's just not wise to go against the law and partly because he believes the Bible confirms that God will have a church in the last days—which he is convinced we are living in—and that we should be an active part of it.) Everything I've studied agrees with Kyle's position, and I tell Judah this.

"The verse God has lead me to lately is in Ephesians," I say, quoting, " 'Now, therefore, you are no longer strangers and foreigners, but fellow citizens with the saints and members of the household of God, having been built on the foundation of the apostles and prophets, Jesus Christ Himself being the chief cornerstone, in whom the whole building, being fitted together, grows into a holy temple in the Lord, in whom you also are being built together for a dwelling place of God in the Spirit.' It seems wrong to be fractured away from the church, despite their hostility toward us sometimes."

"I know," he says, nodding, "I've come to the same conclusion. Maybe it was okay in the beginning, maybe it gave us enough distance from the church's stranglehold to build a body of believers, but it seems more and more like it's time now to return." He looks at me, worry in his eyes. "I just don't want to lose any of our precious members to the hypocrisy and judgment we escaped by starting to meet outside the church walls in the first place. But if we're going to be in the household of God, we should be meeting at His house if we possibly can."

"Are you going to tell them tonight?"

Judah shrugs. "I probably should." He grins. "No time like the present, right?"

A look at the clock tells me I'm going to be late if I don't get a move on. "I've got to go get changed," I glance upward even though I can't see my hair on top of my head, "and do something with my hair before I leave. Will you wait for Sadie and me?"

Judah swigs back some tea which must now be stone-cold. "Of course I will. Where's Kyle?"

"Work," I toss back over my shoulder, heading to the bedroom. "If he's not back before we leave, he said he'll meet us there."

It's a beautiful autumn evening as we make our way to the college, and after the coldest, rainiest summer on record, it seems even more spectacular than it might in an ordinary year. Even the sight of the bristling TAOs and the increasing dirtiness of the city as we move from our nicer section to where the college is located can't completely blot out the beauty of the sky filled with the burnt orange and purple of a gorgeous sunset, or block the gentle fragrance of mums spilling out of cement planters that some far-sighted city planner placed along the sidewalks of the college. Sadie is between Sarah and I who each have one hand, and she's forcing us to swing her even though she's almost too tall for that game anymore.

We take turns, in small groups, meandering nonchalantly into the opening of the alley that leads to the door of the underground gym where we meet. Inside there are probably a hundred people already. Judah is right, I think, we should be at the church. Not only is it the right thing to do, but our numbers have crept up so high that even if we wanted to keep meeting here it's getting far too dangerous. Sooner or later, someone is bound to find us, and I don't even want to think about what would happen then.

I see Professor McCormick and break away from Sarah and Sadie to speak with him. "Hi, Professor, have you found a replacement for me yet?"

He glares at me from beneath his bushy eyebrows. "Brooke, you're one of a kind. I can't replace you," he says mildly.

I grin. If he's teasing me, he must not be upset with me for quitting anymore.

"But I did find someone who can perform your job adequately," he admits. "Though I really don't appreciate having to train someone else. Especially someone who doesn't seem to understand the volume of work my classes tend to produce. And it's harder for me to present a Christian perspective at the prepper meetings without you there to help bring the topic of conversation around that way."

"Maybe I could drop by sometimes," I suggest, my eyes roaming the crowded gym looking for Kyle. I don't know if he'll still be wearing his black TAO uniform, which could startle some people, or if he'll have changed. I know he keeps some clothes at the station in case he doesn't have time to make it home to change before going out somewhere in public after his shift.

"Looking for someone?" Professor McCormick asks laconically.

"Sorry," I say, chagrined. "I am, actually. Have you seen Kyle yet? He hadn't made it home before we left, so I'm expecting him to meet us here."

Professor McCormick shakes his head. "Haven't seen him."

Someone starts the singing. We try to keep it low so we won't be overheard outside. It's lovely, actually. A quiet, hushed melding of voices that can almost make you believe you're in a cathedral with the volume turned down. I wave my hand at Professor McCormick and weave through the crowd until I find Sarah and Sadie.

After the singing we break up into small groups to pray for each other. Ever since we got to be such a large group we've done it this way. It's easier to pray effectively for each other in small groups like this. First, we offer up our prayer requests. Then, we take turns praying for each other. We keep our prayers short, a sentence or two, so that everyone has a chance to pray. The appointed leader prays at the end, closing our time of prayer.

I'm waiting for my chance to pray when I see a flash of black near the door out of the corner of my downcast eyes. Kyle's here, I think, looking over to the door to wave him over to our group. But my hand freezes halfway up. It's not Kyle. Or rather, it's Kyle and five other TAOs. I'm so scared and confused that at first my mind tries to convince me that Kyle's converted some of the other TAOs and that they're here for the meeting. I know it's ludicrous, but I'd rather believe that, I'd rather believe anything, than the obvious truth: they're here on official business.

Will they arrest us? I don't want to go to jail. They won't send the children to jail, too, will they? Sadie! Will they let me keep Sadie with me if they send us to jail? I lunge at her just as most of the rest of the crowd becomes aware of the presence of the TAOs. There's a collective gasp followed by a sickening hush as everyone realizes the worst has happened: we've been discovered.

Grabbing Sadie, I push her behind me. Sarah edges in next to me, and we exchange grim looks. I try to telegraph her my thoughts: If anything happens to me, take care of Sadie. She nods almost imperceptibly, and I hope she knows what I want.

"Who's in charge here?" one of the TAOs barks. He must outrank Kyle. My husband remains quiet, slightly behind and apart from the other TAOs. Even from this distance I can see that every muscle in his body is tense. His eyes are scanning the crowd, looking for me and Sadie no doubt, but I can't risk drawing attention to us by trying to catch his eye.

There's a second of hesitation before Judah steps forward, spreading both arms to show he's unarmed or as a sign of surrender, I'm not sure. The TAO brings back his bully stick with lightning speed and swings it at Judah's head so fast he doesn't even have to time to speak or react before he crumples into a heap on the floor. I scream, but I only know this because Sarah grabs me and claps a hand over my mouth, pinning me between her own body and the wall. I don't know if she's truly stronger than I am, or if she's being given supernatural strength to prevent me from going to help Judah, but I'm trapped there, straining to get away while I'm forced to watch the TAOs begin to beat Judah so hard I can hear his bones breaking.

"Officers, I can explain," Professor McCormick says in his most pacifying voice, hurrying forward. But before he can do anything of the sort, another TAO turns a powerful stun gun on him and he falls, his body jerking wildly, to the ground next to Judah.

"Stop!" a strong, calm voice commands.

"No," I moan. I know that voice even before I see Kyle break away from the other TAOs. He takes out his gun, but tosses it away. He doesn't take down the officers who continue to beat Judah, which I know he could easily do even without a weapon. Instead, he physically gets between them and Judah and the professor who both lie unmoving on the ground. He's holding up his hands in a placating gesture, but they don't even hesitate. In unison, the two who are closest to him swing their bully sticks at him. He doesn't even try to defend himself. He simply bows his head and takes the abuse until he, too, lies bleeding on the ground beside Judah. The last thing I can remember is two TAOs picking him up and dragging him away, his legs trailing through bloody smears on the floor. And I only remember that after Sarah has nursed me back to consciousness because I faint dead away.

"What happened?" I ask her weakly, before it all comes flooding back.

Sadie is at her elbow, her face pale and concerned. "Mama?" she asks, giving my arm a little shake. "Mama, are you all right?"

Sarah gives me a significant look before saying, "We're safe for the moment. They let most of us go."

"Most?" I lick my lips. "Where is . . ." I don't want to ask her where Kyle is in front of Sadie. Frankly, I don't want to ask her at all. I want him to be looking over her shoulder at me and say something like, "That was quite a trick I pulled, don't you think? Had you fooled." I look around trying to figure out where I am.

"We're at your old apartment," Sarah explains. "It was closest. Some of the Disciples helped me carry you here. They scattered after we got you up all those stairs. They'll meet us back at the house if they don't take to the streets for the night. It's okay. You can relax. We're safe for right now."

I sit up gingerly and notice immediately that there are obvious signs a squatter has been using my apartment in my absence, just like Kyle said they would. "We can't stay here."

"No," Sarah agrees, scanning the room as though noticing the signs of use for the first time. "Looks like you've had visitors while you were away. Do you think you can walk?"

I nod. "I'm fine. I just . . ." I want to send Sadie into my old bedroom to play while I grill Sarah about Kyle, but I can't. Who knows what's in there now: used drug needles? Guns? Whoever has been using this place could be back any minute.

"Let's go then," Sarah urges. "It's getting so late I'm almost afraid to try and make it home at this time of night. But I don't know where else we could go. You and Sadie should stay with me until we . . ." Her eyes flick to Sadie. "Until we know more," she finishes lamely.

"No, we're going home," I tell her firmly. There's no way I intend to be gone if Kyle shows up at our house. Who knows what kind of state he'll be in? And surely, he'll turn up in the next day or two, maybe even in the next couple of hours. He'll explain he was stepping in to protect civilians rather than because he is in any way connected with our religious group at the gym. They'll apologize and release him. Tell him to take a few days off to recuperate. He'll come home, and everything will go back to the way it was. Suddenly, having convinced myself this is how events will play out, I have to be home.

"Let's go."

Together we wedge Sadie between us, both keeping such an iron grip on her that she protests once and without thinking I unkindly tell her to shush. The last thing I need is for us to get arrested as well and end up in the same jail cell as Kyle, Judah, Professor McCormick, and anyone else the TAOs hauled away tonight. Kyle would not thank me for that, I think. He's a soldier. He would order me to get Sadie home safely and then stay put and wait for him to return. So that's what I'm going to do.

I have no idea how we elude observation, or perhaps it's only my imagination that anyone gives us a second glance. But just before midnight we finally let ourselves in the door of my house. The apartment is dark and empty, too. Apparently none of the Disciples dared to return. We go around the house throwing on every light switch to drive the darkness away. And light a beacon for Kyle to come home to, I think hopefully.

I sit by Sadie's bed for a little while after I've given her a warm shower and some chamomile tea. She's sleeping peacefully, and I wish I could join her. Combing my fingertips through her hair, I feel a surge of protectiveness grip me. Pity is close behind it. Poor Sadie, to lose first your mother and then your father.

Kyle is not lost, I tell myself sternly. He's temporarily gone. That's all. I won't even let myself contemplate an alternative. In a few hours, or a few days, tops, he'll come back home. Maybe this is the way God has chosen to get him out of the TAOs; maybe this is part of God's plan to get him out early. This could be a blessing, and we don't even recognize it.

I've pretty much convinced myself of this by the time I join Sarah in the kitchen. She's sitting at the table, a mug of untouched tea in front of her, staring. Her hands are clenched in her lap and for the first time I notice she has blood on her snow white cardigan. "Are you bleeding?"

She follows my gaze to the blood on her sleeves as if just noticing it herself. "No, it's not mine. Zach, one of the Disciples, I don't know if you've met him, he helped us carry you. They smacked him around a little before they let him go, split his lip."

I pull up a chair and sit down, trying to stay calm. "Tell me what happened. Tell me exactly what happened."

Sarah, who always looks so confident and competent, stares at her lap. "After they dragged . . . After that they made us all give them our names for their records. They questioned a few people, but there were just so many of us and so few of them. And I think they felt they'd made their point. I mean, what does it say about them that they turned so easily on one of their own for getting in their way?" She shudders.

"Kyle said they've been having trouble making arrests because the facilities are so full of people already. There's so much overcrowding that they sometimes have to wait for some room to open up." I glance at Sarah swiftly to gauge the effect of my next words. "He says they're secretly preparing more holding places around the city: reinforcing abandoned warehouses, putting up makeshift 'camps' outside the city limits."

Sarah sighs quietly. "It wouldn't surprise me." She fidgets with a corner of her bloody cardigan. "After they had us all accounted for, they released most of us. They kept a few people, as examples I think, just to scare us. They said that if they caught us there again they'd throw us all in jail. You can't imagine how fast the place emptied out when they said we could go. It was like being caught in a stampede. I don't know what I would have done without the Disciples. Some of them helped me carry you and keep track of Sadie.

"Evie wanted to come with us, too, but I sent her home with her kids. Some of the Disciples went with her to make sure she got there safely. I don't know if they stayed with her or if they headed back to the streets. Their only protection, really, is the fact that the TAOs can't find them easily with no permanent home address." Sarah suddenly looks all done in, as if in retelling she's relived the entire evening and it's taken all the strength she had left right out of her.

"Why don't you go sleep in my room?" I suggest gently. "I'm going to stay up until Kyle gets home."

The look she gives me is so full of pity it brings tears to my eyes, and I realize with a start that Sarah doesn't think Kyle will be coming home. I swallow hard and force myself to smile. "In the morning, you can tell me if you think the mattress is soft enough. The whole thing is brand new. I was going to surprise Kyle tonight . . ."

The next minute I'm sobbing, and Sarah shoots out of her chair to hug me and sob just as hard on my shoulder as I'm sobbing on hers. It's actually comforting to have a companion in your grief, to know someone shares your pain even though they can't do anything to lessen it. In that strange way incongruous thoughts pop into your head at moments of great distress, I can't help but think how even a year ago the thought that Sarah and I might be the kind of friends who could cry with each other would be absurd. Only by the grace of God have we become close . . . as close as sisters, I think, though I don't have any biological sisters I can compare Sarah to.

Before she agrees to go lay down for awhile in my room, Sarah and I sink to our knees right there on the tiled kitchen floor and pray so fervently that I imagine I can see a band of angels surrounding us, holding us up, lifting our impassioned requests up before the throne of God. Surely they are present. I feel such a relief as we pray that I can barely tear myself away after we've said our "amens" despite the pain beginning to manifest itself in my knees.

When Sarah has gone to bed, I curl up on the couch so I have an unobstructed view of the front door. Kyle won't be able to sneak in and decide not to disturb me if I should happen to fall asleep. I'll hear the door and know the instant he's home again. Opening my Bible on my lap, I turn to the Psalms, in which I always find great comfort and settle down to wait.

I'm aware of footsteps and the murmur of low voices in that vague, far-off way that makes it seem like part of your dreams. They go on for quite some time before I am close enough to the surface of my sleep to instinctively bolt upright with the sudden knowledge that I've fallen asleep without meaning to and may have missed what I was waiting for. Sunlight is pouring in the windows. Kyle is home!

I untangle myself from the afghan someone has kindly placed over me while I was sleeping and head for the sound of voices. I find Sarah and Sadie in the kitchen cooking something. "Where is he?" I blurt out, looking around for Kyle. "I can't believe he didn't wake me up. Is he in the bedroom laying down? He must be exhausted. I don't know how he got past me. I must have fallen asleep." I slowly taper off, realizing I'm babbling.

"Appa's home?" Sadie asks in confusion. "Where is he?"

Sarah slowly shakes her head, answering Sadie and also me. "No, baby, Appa isn't home yet. Mama just had a dream. But I'm sure he'll be here soon."

I slump against the kitchen counter. I'd been so sure Kyle was here, that I'd heard his voice with theirs in the kitchen.

Zach comes in, holding out a container of something. "Is this enough? It's all we've got over there." He notices me in the doorway.

"Oh, hi, Mrs. Huang. How are you feeling?"

Zach. It was Zach's voice I'd heard. Zach's voice that had dragged me from my sleep thinking I'd heard Kyle. I swallow hard before I can reply evenly. "I'm okay, Zach. Thanks. And thank you for helping me last night."

He looks abashed. "No problem."

"How is your lip?" His lower lip is still swollen with a crusted over scab where it split.

He touches it self-consciously. "It's fine. Doesn't hurt much unless I talk. I'm really sorry about Mr. Huang," he says after a moment's pause during which he seems to gather up his courage. "It was very brave of him to try to stop them."

"Yes, it was. Thanks."

Sarah is looking at me sympathetically. "Why don't you go get a shower? By the time you're out, Sadie and I will be finished making lunch."

"Breakfast," Sadie corrects.

"Brunch," Sarah compromises. "You'll feel a lot better once you've cleaned up and eaten something."

I nod slowly and turn to do as she suggests. I don't feel like eating, but I know she's right. I have a feeling I'm going to need my strength for the next few days. If nothing else, I have to keep going for Sadie's sake. Kyle entrusted her to me, and no matter how hard my life becomes in the next few days, weeks, or months, I refuse to let him down.

To locate Kyle, I try everything Evie tried, in fact, she comes with me. She doesn't say much, Evie, but her quiet presence bolsters me up. Unlike Pastor Javier who seems to have just vanished, Kyle is actually in their system. They know where he is. They just won't tell me. When I ask how long he'll be held, the woman at the desk actually snickers and tells me not to hold my breath.

I try asking about Judah and Professor McCormick, too, but they inform me that prisoner information can only be released to a prisoner's family which, they pointedly remind me, I am not. I'm not sure Judah's family knows that he's been arrested, and I don't even know if Professor McCormick has family. He never spoke of one. I never saw anyone else visit him when he was in the hospital, either. Probably sensing we're not going to get anywhere, Evie urges me away from the desk before I can be tempted to try and make a case for being Professor McCormick's long-lost daughter or Judah's sister or something.

"God knows," Evie is saying to me under her breath. "God knows where they are, all of them, and he will watch over them." In the next breath, she is praying. "Please, dear heavenly Father, keep them safe. Give them our love. Comfort them with your presence. Please bring them back to us if it's your will."

"Even if it's not your will," I want to scream, but I know that's my humanity speaking. God, help me to trust you. Help me to submit to your will, no matter what. Give me the spirit of Christ who was willing to follow your will to his death on the cross, I pray silently. Even though they tell us the same thing every time, we continue going back every week.

Sarah persuades me to pack up anything I can't live without and move to her place with Sadie. "They'll come here eventually," she warns. "They're bound to. What if they arrest you and Sadie, too?"

"They wouldn't do that," I say quickly, but then I think, wouldn't they? A stab of fear shoots through me. Already I've discovered that Kyle's bank accounts—our bank accounts—have been frozen. I destroyed our Universal Credit Cards, the only form of currency anyone accepts anymore, after the first time they were declined because Sarah was worried they'd track us through them. We've gone through most of the food I had stocked in the house. Is there anything really left here that's worth the risk of staying? If Kyle does come home and he doesn't find us here, surely the next place he'll look is Sarah's.

"You're right," I agree finally. "They probably will come here eventually, if only to repossess the house. Clearly, whatever perks Kyle had as a TAO have ended, and I have no assets of my own." The enormity of this dawns on me. "I have no assets of my own," I repeat. "Sadie and I will be a burden on you."

Sarah puts her hand on my arm and squeezes tightly. "You're not a burden. And anyway, you aren't my burden; you're God's. He's been taking care of us all this time. I trust him to continue to provide for us. All of us," she finishes meaningfully.

I pack light for myself and Sadie, but I have no idea what Kyle might need when he comes home, so I insist on bringing several boxes of his clothes. We leave the arsenal as it is. Surely the TAOs will find it when they get around to confiscating the house. No need to make off with it and give them a reason to come look for us.

At Sarah's, Sadie and I get our own room—a small space in a biggish laundry room. It is barely large enough to hold our twin-size bed. We stack our boxes on top of the washer and dryer. Even this is a luxury as Evie and all her children share the master bedroom, a rotating roster of Disciples are camped out on the floor, and Sarah herself sleeps on a fold-out bed in Morgan's office. Everyone cheerfully makes room for us and welcomes us and Sarah is right; God provides for all of us.

After months of punishing defeat and endlessly facing Sadie's pitiful inquires about where Appa is and when he'll come home again, I begin to wonder why bad things happen to good people, why I spend so many days crying, but then I read the verse that says, "He will wipe away every tear from their eyes," and I think, shame on me for wanting to be someone with no tears to wipe away. Ultimately, that's what gives me the courage to go on: knowing someday all of this will be over. There will be no more suffering, no more pain, no more separation. Someday Jesus will return and all this agony will end. That day can't come soon enough for me.

Chapter Twenty

I'm walking Sadie home from school, wondering how much longer it will be safe to even do that, when I spot a homeless man heading toward us on the sidewalk. My stomach gives a lurch of pity; his clothes are in tatters and his bare feet leave bloody footprints on the frozen sidewalk. He's in rough shape, and I'm just mentally going through the boxes of Kyle's clothes I hauled to Sarah's wondering what I can pilfer to give to this man, when Sadie bolts away from me down the sidewalk toward him. Before I can react, the man stops and kneels down, opening his arms wide. She hurtles into them, and I slowly realize this sad wreck of a man is my strong, handsome husband whom I last saw being dragged away bleeding and unconscious to prison.

"Kyle," I hear myself whisper incredulously as I stagger forward in disbelief. "Kyle!" Somehow I trip, skin the heels of my hands on the sidewalk, trip again in my haste to reach him, and end up crawling the remainder of the distance on my hands and knees. I reach him, throwing my arms around his neck, clutching him in a vise-like grip, and when I finally calm down enough to know what I'm saying I hear myself repeating over and over, "Thank you, oh, thank you, God, for giving him back to us. Praise God! Praise God!"

Kyle is slumped against me, and I'm shocked at how bony he is. Slowly I realize that he's also bleeding, but I can't tell where he's bleeding from. We need to get him home to Sarah's; he needs medical care and, obviously, food. "Sadie, honey, help me get Appa up. We're going home."

Kyle is able to help us very little, and I wince each time he puts a foot down on the cold sidewalk. When we arrive at Sarah's, I detach the death grip Sadie has on her father and convince her that Appa needs me to help him right now, and he needs her to go find Auntie Sarah and tell her that we need help. Just knowing that practical, efficient Sarah will help gives me enough confidence to begin to assess Kyle's injuries. As Sadie rushes off importantly to fetch Sarah, I strip the bed and lay down a clean sheet my husband can bleed on while I try to figure out where the blood is coming from.

I help him over to the bed and ease him onto it gently. He lays back and closes his eyes. I'm not sure whether he's resting, asleep, or unconscious. I don't want to wake him to find out. Carefully, I go over his body looking for wounds and patching them up with the supplies I send Sadie to fetch when she knocks on the door and tells me she can't find Auntie Sarah because she's gone grocery shopping.

Kyle's emaciated body is crisscrossed with old scars and fresh wounds. The most critical seems to be a deep laceration across one shoulder that is causing the confusing blood covering his torso that seems as if it could be coming from any one of the more superficial wounds. I deal with this biggest wound first. It's a nasty gash, but it doesn't seem to have gone through the muscle layers though I can see muscle fiber beneath the gaping edges. It probably needs stitches, but since they are beyond the scope of my medical knowledge I pull the edges of the wound together and tape them firmly.

Kyle grunts as I tug the sides of the wound together. As I work, I have to wipe tears off his skin where they drop from my burning eyes. *How could anyone do this to him?* I'm asking myself over and over. Kyle's body is so damaged that I'm afraid I'll hurt him more by trying to dress him again in fresh clothes. Instead, maneuvering awkwardly in the small space, I gently roll him from side to side in order to replace the bloody sheet beneath him with a fresh one, and then I settle another carefully on top of him.

His eyes flicker open for a moment as if he can feel me staring at him. They are deep, dark, dead orbs, but in their depths a light flickers, giving me hope. With great effort, his parched, cracked lips part, and he utters the first words he's spoken since we found him. "God is good," he croaks. Then he shuts his eyes again.

I reach out and caress his forehead, my own throat constricting with emotion. "Yes, he is, love. And he's brought you home. Thank you, God."

Gathering my strength, I go in search of Sadie, proud of the self-control she's shown by leaving us alone so I could doctor Kyle.

"Sadie?" I poke my head in the office where she likes to play with Evie's kids, but am met only by the sound of the room's silence. One by one, I search each room in the house. No Sadie. By the time I return to the kitchen I'm in a panic. A few of the Disciples are eating at the kitchen table, and one says he thought he saw Sadie leave but assumed she was with me.

He gives me a puzzled look. "Why would Sadie leave by herself? That's not like her."

"No," I agree, fighting to control my rising hysteria. "No, you're right. It's not like her."

"Where would she go?"

And the moment he says it, I know where she'd go: to fetch Sarah. Praying fervently to beat back the thousands of awful possibilities that rush into my mind, I tear out the door only vaguely aware that some of the young men follow me out. I make it two blocks before I spot them: Sarah has shifted all her grocery bags to one hand so she can grip Sadie firmly with the other, and they are moving as fast as Sadie's little legs will allow. As soon as she sees me, Sarah sets down the bags in her hand and waves. I manage to lift my hand in response before slumping against a nearby building as my legs begin to wobble. I'm still thanking God she's safe when they reach me.

"Sadie Huang, don't ever do that again!" I grab the bewildered child and smother her in a bear hug. "You scared me so much."

"But Mama, I brought my whistle," Sadie protests, distressed that she's displeased me. She holds up the brass ring with a whistle on it that Kyle gave her to carry when she's away from home "in case of emergencies." If she needs help, she's supposed to blow on it. Of course, what Sadie doesn't know is that Kyle and I had no intention of her ever being away from home *without one of us with her*. "And," she says triumphantly, "I had all my angels with me, too."

I laugh in spite of myself. "I guess I can't argue with that. But," I shake my finger under her nose, "don't ever leave the house again unless a grown-up is with you."

Even though she's really too big for it, I pick her up and carry her all the way back to the house. Sarah meets my eyes as we walk, but we don't speak until we're back at the house and I've explained to Sadie that Appa is taking a nap and she needs to go play while I talk to Auntie Sarah.

"How is he?" Sarah asks as soon as we're alone.

"Bad," I reply grimly. "I've patched him up as best I can, but he really needs a doctor."

"Until we know more, it would probably be a good idea to lie low," Sarah cautions. "Did he tell you why they let him go? Or did he . . . escape?"

I shake my head. "He's said precisely three words since we found him: God is good."

Sarah looks as touched as I feel. "Indeed he is," she agrees huskily.

She clears her throat and becomes practical. "First things first, has he eaten anything?"

"No, and he looks like a holocaust survivor. I know you have to feed people slowly if they haven't eaten in a long time. What do you think we should give him?"

"Broth seems safe," Sarah says.

At first, Kyle doesn't speak at all. But when I am in our room straightening things up in the small space, checking his bandages, or spooning broth—and later a thin gruel of oatmeal—into his mouth, his eyes, which have lost their dull flatness, follow me like an embrace. I try not to chatter mindlessly, though my anxiety for him makes it tempting. Instead, I speak to him in low, soothing tones and tell him what Sadie is up to, recite Bible verses, or pray with him. I comment matter-of-factly on the weather or how his healing is progressing.

It isn't until he's been home for nearly a week that he finally has the strength to speak. I'm sleeping by his bedside, my cheek pillowed on his hand which I've been holding, when he reaches over tentatively and strokes the hair out of my face. It's grown long now, and Sarah is always telling me to do something with it—so I usually put it up in a ponytail. I think I must be dreaming, but then I hear Kyle say, "Brooke," and I bolt upright, suddenly wide awake.

His voice is a raspy whisper, but after the endless days of silence it sounds like a shout. "How are you feeling?" I ask, putting my hand on his forehead to check for warmth, which is silly because he's injured, not sick. But then, I'm not thinking too clearly.

"Blessed," he says, after a pause during which he seems to gather up his strength.

"Kyle, are you safe? Will they come looking for you?" The question has preyed on my mind from the moment Sarah brought me back to earth by asking me if Kyle had escaped, something that had never occurred to me. For all we know, there is a warrant out for his arrest. Though after the first few days of expecting to hear an official knock on the door, we've begun to relax a little.

Kyle's head rolls from side to side. "They let me go. Miracle . . ." He begins to cough, which shakes his entire body.

As much as I want to hear more, want to hear him speak, need him to answer all my questions, I force myself to tell him to rest. There will be plenty of time to answer questions later. He closes his eyes. At first I think he's going to ignore my advice and continue to try to tell me what happened to him, but after awhile I realize he's asleep.

I get the whole story over the course of a few days. The next time he attempts to speak, his voice doesn't sound as rough, but he's still forced to pause frequently. Eventually I piece together what happened. For Kyle's sake, I try not to react too violently to what he says, though there are times when every part of me just wants to fall to pieces. Especially when he tells me that Judah didn't survive his first night in jail.

Judah never regained consciousness, apparently. Kyle says that Professor McCormick—he calls him Mac and says that's what everyone at the prison called him—helped them both. He doesn't remember much about what happened the first night except that when he woke up Judah was gone and Mac told him that he'd passed away and the guards had removed his body. He was in so much pain himself that, at the time, Kyle thought he might very well be next.

"Every time I woke up, Mac told me to hang on. He prayed with me. Whenever I woke up during the night, he was praying still."

He tells me that the overcrowding was unimaginable. "In certain parts of the prison, it was so packed with bodies that you could fall asleep standing up and not fall down. By morning, several men would be dead from being trampled or suffocated." The food was virtually non-existent and doled out in such a way that the strongest got the most to eat.

"If you weren't fast, you missed out. And if you were fast, but not strong, others would take your food away from you." His eyes grow distant as he remembers. "Or you were like Mac, and you gave your food away."

"Why would he do that?" I can't imagine Professor McCormick giving food away that he needed to survive. It went against every disaster preparedness training principle he'd drilled into the heads of his students meeting after meeting: be prepared, be strong, be ready to defend yourself against everyone who is not prepared and not strong. It is such a clear indication of the condition of his heart that if I didn't want to interrupt Kyle, I'd start praising God out loud.

"He said it was what Jesus would do." Kyle rests for a minute.

"Did they let him go, too?"

"No. He's still there."

Even the small amount of talking he's done has made him out of breath. When he can go on, I ask him if he ever found out why the other TAOs had turned on him so quickly at the time of his arrest.

"Apparently, I'd been under surveillance for quite some time," he responds slowly. "I should have known. There were instances. People had begun treating me differently. It doesn't seem to have been any one thing, just a bunch of little infractions. They found out I'd helped people avoid arrest, that I'd been snooping in records where I shouldn't have been. They flagged me and I didn't even know it. They were just waiting for me to mess up. I don't think they would have even given me that much of a benefit of the doubt except that my skills were so useful to them. I may have gotten off with a lesser punishment, or even a warning, if I hadn't stood up to them at the prayer meeting. Too public."

I shudder, remembering how he'd gone down when they attacked him.

His eyes roam around the room. "Where are we?"

"At Sarah's," I explain. "We didn't dare stay at the house." I'm not sure how much I should tell him. The last thing I want is to upset him. I don't think he's strong enough to take the loss of his whole life in one blow. Not yet.

He nods, accepting this news with equanimity. "I should have known."

It's another few weeks before Kyle is able to sit up in bed, propped up on pillows, and then hanging his spindly legs over the side, and then standing with Sarah and I supporting him on either side. Once he gets this far he insists on standing more often, even if we can't be with him; he exercises by clinging to the walls and furniture like a toddler and creeping around the rooms. Just being up and out of the tiny room and interacting with the Disciples, Sarah, Evie and the kids, Sadie, and I as we go about our daily duties seems to inject him with hope and strength. It isn't long before he's doing actual exercises, trying to rebuild his wasted muscles.

"You're going to eat us out of house and home," Sarah laughs in exasperation one day as he scoops beans and rice into his bowl. "I never knew a man who could eat so much."

Kyle's eyes cloud up with concern, as if it is only just occurring to him that we're living on charity. "I'm sorry," he says, attempting to spoon some of the food back into the pot.

"I'm kidding," Sarah protests, blocking his arm. "Eat. You, of all people, need it."

"But it's true," Kyle says, sitting down next to me at the counter. "Isn't it?" He looks over at me and Sadie as if he's calculating in his head the amount of food it takes to feed the three of us. "I didn't think . . . I didn't realize . . . I'm so used to having whatever I need, whatever I want. I'm . . . this is all new to me. I don't like it."

"What? Being poor, or relying on God?"

"I don't mind relying on God," Kyle replies slowly, as though he's trying to figure out what the two things have to do with each other.

"Then you shouldn't mind being poor," Sarah says matter-of-factly, "because God doesn't waste resources. He only gives us as much as we need." She waves her hand over the big pot. "He gave us this. And tomorrow he'll give us whatever we need to live on. Like the Israelites in the desert. He sent just enough manna to feed them for that day. When you think about it, who needs more than that? As long as you have enough, technically, you're rich." Sarah looks pleased with herself at this little bit of philosophizing, but Kyle pales slightly.

"Are you saying this," he indicates the pot of beans and rice and the pile of tortillas fresh off the grill, "is all the food we have *in the house*?"

Sarah nods. "That's what I'm saying."

"And the fruit and oatmeal we ate this morning?"

"Arrived this morning. One of the Disciples brought them. I believe it was a donation someone made."

Kyle lets this sink in slowly. "I'm . . . I'm . . ."

"Overwhelmed?" Sarah suggests gently. "We all are. We've just had more time to get used to it than you have."

I place a hand on his arm comfortingly. "God will provide for us, Kyle, no matter what. He's been so faithful. If I started counting our blessings right now, I wouldn't finish for a week."

"For awhile, after you were arrested, some of us still had jobs," Sarah explains. "We felt confident when we were able to make ends meet. It was always rough, none of us are professional anythings, so money was always scarce. But we made do. We stretched what we had. At least, we thought we did. Really, God was doing all the stretching. We found that out when the jobs dried up, and we suddenly found ourselves with zero income and still a house full of mouths to feed."

"And God took care of us," I put in, taking up the story.

"Sometimes food or other necessities show up just hours or even minutes before we need them, but they always show up. In the beginning, we were scared. We tried to trust God, to rely on him completely, but it was difficult." I exchange a look with Sarah who nods in agreement. "The adults understood that any food would be given first to the children. If there was a shortage, we'd feel it the most." I shrug. "But there never was. Every single time there was enough for all of us, but rarely any extra."

"Eventually," Sarah continues, "we got used to trusting God. And now you'll have to learn to trust him, too."

"That shouldn't be too difficult," Kyle says quietly, "after trusting him with my life . . . and my family. And I still have both of those."

" 'Those who are honest and fair,' " quotes Sarah, " 'who refuse to profit by fraud, who stay far away from bribes, who refuse to listen to those who plot murder, who shut their eyes to all enticement to do wrong—these are the ones who will dwell on high. The rocks of the mountains will be their fortress. Food will be supplied to them, and they will have water in abundance.' "

"That's us," I say, taking Kyle's hand and giving it a squeeze. "Our bread and water will be sure."

"And our beans," pipes up Sadie.

Kyle smiles, one of the first times I've seen him smile since he came back to us. "And our beans," he agrees, lifting a spoonful in salute and making her giggle.

It seems like it's always the middle of the night when the TAOs act. Kyle and I are shaken awake by a young man whose face seems familiar, but whose name I can't recall. We're sleeping in a dog pile on our tiny bed: Kyle, me, and Sadie. She groans in her sleep and wedges her elbow into my side, leveraging for more space.

"What's wrong?" I hear Kyle ask.

"TAOs," comes the terse reply. "They're banging on doors up and down the street, rounding people up. Grab your stuff. We're leaving."

I bless Professor McCormick and his disaster preparedness training. Thanks to him, it's the work of a few minutes by muffled flashlight to gather our already assembled possessions. Carrying Sadie because Kyle's not strong enough yet, I follow him out into Sarah's living room where the rest of the household is gathered. The young man tells us all in a hush that we're going to move to one of the Disciples' hiding places. He instructs us to be quiet and to stay together. Then he leads us out the back way.

I'm wondering how long I will have to carry Sadie and if I'm strong enough to do it, when she begins to stir in my arms and soon wants to be put down. Her eyes are wide in the illumination of a nearby streetlight as I whisper to her that we're on an adventure and that we must be very quiet and stay with the others. She obediently takes my hand falls into step beside me like a trooper.

I lose track of the alleys and streets we traverse to reach the new hideaway. I'm surprised that Kyle's strength has held up so well, but when we arrive and I can see his face more clearly in the lighted area where we gather upon arrival, I can see that the long walk has taken a big toll on him. He looks as though he's just run a marathon with the flu.

"You'll all be assigned sleeping quarters," Zach, who met us at the new facility, is explaining. "Actually, it's more like an assigned place on the floor to set up your bedrolls, but whatever. Go back to sleep, if you can. We'll brief you all on procedures in the morning." As they get us all signed up, I'm impressed by how organized everything is. I had no idea the Disciples had become such a well-run group.

Our little family unit is one of the last to be assigned. As Sadie and I begin to follow Kyle and one of the Disciples to our assigned "space," I notice a walking skeleton dressed in clean, but threadbare rags. There's something about the man that seems familiar. Just before I turn away, it hits me. Those bushy eyebrows. "Professor McCormick?" I blurt out, dropping Sadie's hand and taking a few tentative steps toward him.

The skeleton stops shuffling forward. Slowly a grin stretches across the gaunt features. "Brooke!" His eyes, in the cavernous hollows of his sockets, glow like coals of fire. "Call me Mac; we're not in college anymore, Jesus Girl."

"You're alive! You're . . . here." I can't believe no one told us he was here. "How long?"

"Only a few hours. I've been at a different 'facility.' " The Disciples have people in hideouts all over the city. Whereas I used to know most of the young men on sight, now there are so many I'm not sure *anyone* knows all of them.

"The TAOs released you then?"

"In a manner of speaking," he replies thoughtfully. "They thought I was dead." At my look of incredulity, he adds, "It's a long story.

Why don't I tell you some other time?"

I glance behind me to find that Kyle, not recognizing Mac, has gone on ahead of me with Sadie to set up our new lodgings. "Okay, I'd like that."

"This is the beginning of the end, Brooke," he says, his face alive even though his skeletal frame seems undecided. "We've got a lot to do and not much time to do it in."

Joy and excitement crackle through my body as I realize what he means. Instantly, I'm so charged with energy, I feel as though I've been electrocuted. "Amen!" I exclaim, suddenly so anxious to leave this dark, dreary, scary world behind that I can't wait to get started. We're going home soon to be with Jesus! "Amen to that!"

> "Now to Him
> who is able to keep you
> from stumbling,
> And to present you faultless
> Before the presence
> of His glory
> with exceeding joy,
> To God our Savior,
> Who alone is wise,
> Be glory and majesty,
> Dominion and power,
> Both now and forever.
> Amen."
> Jude 1:24, 25, NKJV

Acknowledgments
Explanations
Resources

Since this is a work of fiction, I wanted to explain a little about Brooke and her transformation. I know some people will accuse me of "curing" her homosexuality, as if I was taking the "easy" way out in dealing with homosexuality by making her a heterosexual with a wave of my pen. When I started writing, I didn't even know if it was possible for homosexuals to "change" their orientation. About halfway through, God led me to the book *Strait Answers to the Gay Question* by Pastor Ron Woolsey who writes under the pen name Victor J. Adamson. Pastor Woolsey was a homosexual who was saved by Jesus and experienced a transformation in his life. He has been happily married to his wife for 22 years at the time of this writing and has a ministry to homosexuals at www.victorjadamson.com. He is also the author of *"That Kind Can Never Change" . . . Can They?*. I highly recommend both books and all his resources to anyone who is searching for further insight into this subject.

I was introduced to Pastor Woolsey's book at the exact point in *The Shaking* when I needed to know that, indeed, God *can* change a homosexual's orientation. I began the book knowing that God could save homosexuals if they were willing to abandon their sin (like anyone else), but I didn't know if people could be "born gay" or if their orientation could be changed. I assumed their only choice was a lifetime of celibacy if they were Christians. Pastor Woolsey's book helped me to understand that God gives salvation to *all* people, *all* sinners, and He is able to *change every heart* as long as we are willing for Him to change us.

That hope is the whole point of the gospel. What kind of God would we be serving if He left us just as He found us, stuck in our sins, and didn't give us the power to overcome them? "Therefore, if anyone is in Christ, he is a new creation; old things have passed away; behold, all things have become new" (2 Corinthians 5:17, NKJV). If all things have become new, change is not only possible, it's guaranteed. Believing anything else is "having a form of godliness but denying its power" (2 Timothy 3:5, NKJV).

For those interested, Judah's "knowledge" of Greek comes from the wonderful book Sparkling Gems from the Greek by Rick Renner which was a gift from my dear friend Michele. It's been an incredible blessing to my life as well as a valuable resource. I get goose bumps reading it, but then, I'm a word nerd.

I would like to thank Ron Woolsey for his ministry and his courageous testimony. And my friend Michele Deppe for her willingness to read this book, give me honest feedback, and answer the millions of questions I had about the whole process of getting what I'd written into your hands. I'd like to thank Tim Morgan for telling me why I needed to care what an SEO was and (I hope) helping me figure out how to make a book trailer. And thank you to J.P. Choquette (who happens to be my sister) for all the help figuring out how to create my website. I would also like to thank the ladies of the Singing Hills Fibers of Faith Retreat for their encouragement.

And thank *you* for giving *The Shaking* your time. I hope you were not disappointed. For all the latest news about what I'm working on and which books are scheduled to be released next visit my website: cperrinowalker.com. If you enjoyed *The Shaking,* please consider leaving a review wherever you bought it as well as Goodreads and wherever else you like to socially network. If you Tweet about it, please use the hash tag #TheShaking and tag me @CelestePWalker.

"I pray that your hearts will be flooded with light so that you can understand the confident hope he has given to those he called—his holy people who are his rich and glorious inheritance. I also pray that you will understand the incredible greatness of God's power for us who believe him. This is the same mighty power that raised Christ from the dead and seated him in the place of honor at God's right hand in the heavenly realms. Now he is far above any ruler or authority or power or leader or anything else—not only in this world but also in the world to come. God has put all things under the authority of Christ and has made him head over all things for the benefit of the church. And the church is his body; it is made full and complete by Christ, who fills all things everywhere with himself" (Ephesians 1:18-23, NLT).

Additional Resources:

For articles about overcoming homosexuality, go here: http://www.victorjadamson.com/articles2/

For the complete Victor J. Adamson website loaded with resources go here: http://www.victorjadamson.com/

If you would like to contact Ron Woolsey directly, e-mail: vja@victorjadamson.com or narroway@windstream.net.

If you would like to sign up for my (very infrequent) newsletter, go to the bottom of the "About the Author" page on my website: cperrinowalker.com

Questions for Book Clubs or Small Group Discussion:

Do you think Brooke should have made more of an effort to conform her outward appearance to what a majority of people consider normal?

Do you think her appearance hindered her testimony?

How vital do you think Brooke's relationship with God was in helping her deal with persecution?

Do you think Brooke would have been any less deserving of God's love (and the love of the Christians in the book) if she had continued to practice her homosexual lifestyle while getting to know God better?

If your church required you to conform to a particular mandate, would you react as Brooke did? Or as Judah did? Explain your answer.

Is it our role as Christians to convict or love sinners?

How do we balance our Christian beliefs and our own personal convictions about someone else's sin with God's mandate to love sinners?

Is it ever our duty to confront non-Christians with their sin? How about Christians? What makes the difference?

How can we help new Christians overcome the stigma of their past? (Read Acts 9:26-30.) How do we know what sin is?

Do we ever make up our own criteria for sin and compare people to our made-up rules?

Who is responsible for convicting people of sin? (John 16:8-15)

Do you think we judge each other because we "sin differently"? How so?

Do you know any "Brookes"? How do you treat them?

Bible Texts

To facilitate your own Bible study, the following is a list of all Bible texts quoted, or alluded to, in this book. (Except for the verse from Job. I can't remember why I put that in here, but it's a good verse, so it's staying.) For copyright information for a particular Bible translation, please see the copyright page.

"His servants then asked, 'Do you want us to go out and pull up the weeds?' 'No!' he answered. 'You might also pull up the wheat. Leave the weeds alone until harvest time. Then I'll tell my workers to gather the weeds and tie them up and burn them. But I'll have them store the wheat in my barn' " (Matthew 13:28-30, CEV).

"Don't have anything to do with foolish and stupid arguments, because you know they produce quarrels. And the Lord's servant must not be quarrelsome but must be kind to everyone, able to teach, not resentful. Opponents must be gently instructed, in the hope that God will grant them repentance leading them to a knowledge of the truth, and that they will come to their senses and escape from the trap of the devil, who has taken them captive to do his will" (2 Timothy 2:23-26, NIV).

"If I go and prepare a place for you, I will come again and receive you to Myself, that where I am, there you may be also" (John 14:3, NASB).

"After I have done this, I will come back and take you with me. Then we will be together" (John 14:3, CEV).

"Anyone who can be trusted in little matters can also be trusted in important matters. But anyone who is dishonest in little matters will be dishonest in important matters" (Luke 16:10, CEV).

"Sing to God, sing praises to his name;
    lift up a song to him who rides upon the clouds—his name is the Lord—
    be exultant before him.
Father of orphans and protector of widows is God in his holy

habitation" (Psalm 68:4, 5, NRSV).

"Who remembered us in our lowly state,
　For His mercy endures forever;
And rescued us from our enemies,
　For His mercy endures forever" (Psalm 136:23-24, NKJV).

"For all have sinned and fall short of the glory of God" (Romans 3:23, NIV).

"There is therefore now no condemnation to those who are in Christ Jesus, who do not walk according to the flesh, but according to the Spirit" (Romans 8:1, NKJV).

"For God so loved the world that He gave His only begotten Son, that whoever believes in Him should not perish but have everlasting life" (John 3:16, NKJV).

"For where two or three are gathered together in My name, I am there in the midst of them" (Matthew 18:20, NKJV).

"We know that anyone born of God does not continue to sin; the One who was born of God keeps them safe, and the evil one cannot harm them" (1 John 5:18, NIV).

"Stay away from stupid and senseless arguments. These only lead to trouble" (2 Timothy 2:23, CEV).

"We love because he first loved us. Whoever claims to love God yet hates a brother or sister is a liar. For whoever does not love their brother and sister, whom they have seen, cannot love God, whom they have not seen. And he has given us this command: Anyone who loves God must also love their brother and sister" (1 John 4:19-21, NIV).

"If it is possible, as far as it depends on you, live at peace with everyone" (Romans 12:18, NIV).

"Make every effort to live in peace with everyone and to be holy; without holiness no one will see the Lord" (Hebrews 12:14, NIV).

"The start of an argument is like a water leak—so stop it before real trouble breaks out" (Proverbs 17:14, CEV).

"Do not let any unwholesome talk come out of your mouths, but only what is helpful for building others up according to their needs, that it may benefit those who listen" (Ephesians 4:29, NIV).

"I am the resurrection and the life. The one who believes in me will live, even though they die; and whoever lives by believing in me will never die" (John 11:25, 26, NIV).

"Jesus answered, "I am the way and the truth and the life. No one comes to the Father except through me" (John 14:6. NIV).

"Repay no one evil for evil, but give thought to do what is honorable in the sight of all. If possible, so far as it depends on you, live peaceably with all" (Romans 12:17, 18, ESV).

"You will keep him in perfect peace, whose mind is stayed on You, because he trusts in You" (Isaiah 26:3, NKJV).

"But I say, love your enemies! Pray for those who persecute you! In that way, you will be acting as true children of your Father in heaven. For he gives his sunlight to both the evil and the good, and he sends rain on the just and the unjust alike. If you love only those who love you, what reward is there for that? Even corrupt tax collectors do that much" (Matthew 5:44-46, NLT).

"We ask God to give you complete knowledge of his will and to give you spiritual wisdom and understanding. Then the way you live will always honor and please the Lord, and your lives will produce every kind of good fruit. All the while, you will grow as you learn to know God better and better. We also pray that you will be strengthened with all his glorious power so you will have all the endurance and patience you need. May you be filled with joy, always thanking the Father. He has enabled you to share in the inheritance that belongs to his people, who live in the light. For he has rescued us from the kingdom of darkness and transferred us into the Kingdom of his dear Son, who purchased our freedom and forgave our sins" (Colossians 1:9-14, NLT).

"For I know that this will turn out for my deliverance through your prayer and the supply of the Spirit of Jesus Christ" (Philippians 1:19, NKJV).

"I will exalt you, my God the King;
    I will praise your name for ever and ever.
Every day I will praise you
    and extol your name for ever and ever.
Great is the Lord and most worthy of praise;
    his greatness no one can fathom.
One generation commends your works to another;
    they tell of your mighty acts.
They speak of the glorious splendor of your majesty—
    and I will meditate on your wonderful works.
They tell of the power of your awesome works—
    and I will proclaim your great deeds.
They celebrate your abundant goodness
    and joyfully sing of your righteousness.
The Lord is gracious and compassionate,
    slow to anger and rich in love.
The Lord is good to all;
    he has compassion on all he has made.
All your works praise you, Lord;
    your faithful people extol you.
They tell of the glory of your kingdom
    and speak of your might,
so that all people may know of your mighty acts
    and the glorious splendor of your kingdom.
Your kingdom is an everlasting kingdom,
    and your dominion endures through all generations.
The Lord is trustworthy in all he promises
    and faithful in all he does.
The Lord upholds all who fall
    and lifts up all who are bowed down.
The eyes of all look to you,
    and you give them their food at the proper time.

You open your hand
   and satisfy the desires of every living thing.
The Lord is righteous in all his ways
   and faithful in all he does.
The Lord is near to all who call on him,
   to all who call on him in truth.
He fulfills the desires of those who fear him;
   he hears their cry and saves them.
The Lord watches over all who love him,
   but all the wicked he will destroy.
My mouth will speak in praise of the Lord.
   Let every creature praise his holy name
   for ever and ever" (Psalm 145, NIV).

"Come now, and let us reason together," says the Lord, "Though your sins are like scarlet, they shall be as white as snow; though they are red like crimson, they shall be as wool" (Isaiah 1:18, NKJV).

"Anyone who belongs to Christ is a new person. The past is forgotten, and everything is new" (2 Corinthians 5:17, CEV).

"He was oppressed, and he was afflicted, yet he opened not his mouth; like a lamb that is led to the slaughter, and like a sheep that before its shearers is silent, so he opened not his mouth" (Isaiah 53:7, ESV).

"But whoever has been forgiven little loves little" (Luke 7:47, NIV).

"But He answered and said, "Every plant which My heavenly Father has not planted will be uprooted" (Matthew 15:13, NKJV).

"And just as each person is destined to die once and after that comes judgment, so also Christ was offered once for all time as a sacrifice to take away the sins of many people. He will come again, not to deal with our sins, but to bring salvation to all who are eagerly waiting for him" (Hebrews 9:27, 28, NLT).

"You were dead because of your sins and because your sinful nature was not yet cut away. Then God made you alive with Christ, for he forgave all our sins" (Colossians 2:13, NLT).

"Always be prepared to give an answer to everyone who asks you to give the reason for the hope that you have. But do this with gentleness and respect, keeping a clear conscience, so that those who speak maliciously against your good behavior in Christ may be ashamed of their slander" (1 Peter 3:15-16, NIV).

"For with God nothing will be impossible" (Luke 1:37, NKJV).

"Be sober, be vigilant; because your adversary the devil walks about like a roaring lion, seeking whom he may devour" (1 Peter 5:8, NKJV).

"I am Yours, save me; For I have sought Your precepts" (Psalm 119:94, NKJV).

"I am yours; rescue me! For I have worked hard at obeying your commandments" (Psalm 119:94, NLT).

"Surely the arm of the Lord is not too short to save, nor his ear too dull to hear" (Isaiah 59:1, NIV).

"For 'Everyone who calls on the name of the Lord will be saved' " (Romans 10:13, NLT).

" 'I give them eternal life, and they will never perish. No one can snatch them away from me, for my Father has given them to me, and he is more powerful than anyone else. No one can snatch them from the Father's hand' " (John 10:28, 29, NLT).

"Therefore, if anyone is in Christ, he is a new creation; old things have passed away; behold, all things have become new" (2 Corinthians 5:17, NKJV).

"I have fought the good fight, I have finished the race, I have kept the faith. Finally, there is laid up for me the crown of righteousness, which the Lord, the righteous Judge, will give to me on that Day, and not to me only but also to all who have loved His appearing" (2 Timothy 4:7, 8, NKJV).

"Love suffers long and is kind; love does not envy; love does not parade itself, is not puffed up; does not behave rudely, does not seek its own, is not provoked, thinks no evil; does not rejoice in iniquity, but rejoices in the truth; bears all things, believes all things, hopes all things, endures all things. Love never fails" (1 Corinthians 13:4-8, NKJV).

"Be strong and of good courage, do not fear nor be afraid of them; for the Lord your God, He is the One who goes with you. He will not leave you nor forsake you" (Deuteronomy 31:6, NKJV).

"For My thoughts are not your thoughts, Nor are your ways My ways," says the Lord. "For as the heavens are higher than the earth, So are My ways higher than your ways, And My thoughts than your thoughts" (Isaiah 55:8, 9, NKJV).

"For if you remain silent at this time, relief and deliverance for the Jews will arise from another place, but you and your father's family will perish. And who knows but that you have come to your royal position for such a time as this?" (Esther 4:14, NIV).

"You, Lord, are my shepherd.
   I will never be in need.
You let me rest in fields
   of green grass.
You lead me to streams
   of peaceful water,
   and you refresh my life.
You are true to your name,
   and you lead me
   along the right paths.
I may walk through valleys
   as dark as death,
   but I won't be afraid.
You are with me,
   and your shepherd's rod
   makes me feel safe.
You treat me to a feast,

while my enemies watch.
You honor me as your guest,
   and you fill my cup
   until it overflows.
Your kindness and love
   will always be with me
   each day of my life,
   and I will live forever
   in your house, Lord" (Psalm 23, CEV).

"So do not fear, for I am with you; do not be dismayed, for I am your God. I will strengthen you and help you; I will uphold you with my righteous right hand" (Isaiah 41:10, NIV).

"Jesus understands every weakness of ours, because he was tempted in every way that we are. But he did not sin!" (Hebrews 4:15, CEV).

"The Lord will give them strength when they are sick, and he will make them well again" (Psalm 41:3, NCV).

"Don't you realize that those who do wrong will not inherit the Kingdom of God? Don't fool yourselves. Those who indulge in sexual sin, or who worship idols, or commit adultery, or are male prostitutes, or practice homosexuality, or are thieves, or greedy people, or drunkards, or are abusive, or cheat people—none of these will inherit the Kingdom of God. Some of you were once like that. But you were cleansed; you were made holy; you were made right with God by calling on the name of the Lord Jesus Christ and by the Spirit of our God" (1 Corinthians 6:9-12, NLT).

"For our high priest is able to understand our weaknesses. He was tempted in every way that we are, but he did not sin" (Hebrews 4:15, NCV).

"But when sin grew worse, God's grace increased" (Romans 5:20, NCV).

"So Satan left the Lord's presence. He put painful sores on Job's body, from the top of his head to the soles of his feet. Job took a piece of broken pottery to scrape himself, and he sat in ashes in misery. Job's wife said to him, "Why are you trying to stay innocent? Curse God and die!" Job answered, "You are talking like a foolish woman. Should we take only good things from God and not trouble?" In spite of all this Job did not sin in what he said" (Job 2:7-10, NCV).

The whole story of King Manasseh: 2 Chronicles 33 and 2 Kings 21.

"He did evil in the eyes of the Lord, following the detestable practices of the nations the Lord had driven out before the Israelites" (2 Kings 21:2, NIV).

"In his distress he sought the favor of the Lord his God and humbled himself greatly before the God of his ancestors. And when he prayed to him, the Lord was moved by his entreaty and listened to his plea; so he brought him back to Jerusalem and to his kingdom" (2 Chronicles 33:12, 13, NIV).

" 'I am the vine, and you are the branches. If any remain in me and I remain in them, they produce much fruit. But without me they can do nothing' " (John 15:5, NCV).

"I can do all things through Christ who strengthens me" (Philippians 4:13, NKJV).

"But he said to me, 'My grace is enough for you. When you are weak, my power is made perfect in you.' So I am very happy to brag about my weaknesses. Then Christ's power can live in me" (2 Corinthians 12:9, NCV).

"Jesus looked at them and said, 'With man this is impossible, but with God all things are possible' " (Matthew 19:26, NIV).

"Then He who sat on the throne said, 'Behold, I make all things new.' And He said to me, 'Write, for these words are true and faithful' " (Revelation 21:5, NKJV).

"May the Lord watch between you and me when we are absent one from another" (Genesis 31:49, NKJV).

"Now, therefore, you are no longer strangers and foreigners, but fellow citizens with the saints and members of the household of God, having been built on the foundation of the apostles and prophets, Jesus Christ Himself being the chief cornerstone, in whom the whole building, being fitted together, grows into a holy temple in the Lord, in whom you also are being built together for a dwelling place of God in the Spirit" (Ephesians 2:19-22, NKJV).

"He will wipe all tears from their eyes, and there will be no more death, suffering, crying, or pain. These things of the past are gone forever" (Revelation 21:4, NKJV).

"Those who are honest and fair, who refuse to profit by fraud, who stay far away from bribes, who refuse to listen to those who plot murder, who shut their eyes to all enticement to do wrong—these are the ones who will dwell on high. The rocks of the mountains will be their fortress. Food will be supplied to them, and they will have water in abundance" (Isaiah 33:15, 16, NLT).

"All glory to God forever and ever! Amen" (Galatians 1:5, NLT).

"I pray that your hearts will be flooded with light so that you can understand the confident hope he has given to those he called—his holy people who are his rich and glorious inheritance. I also pray that you will understand the incredible greatness of God's power for us who believe him. This is the same mighty power that raised Christ from the dead and seated him in the place of honor at God's right hand in the heavenly realms. Now he is far above any ruler or authority or power or leader or anything else—not only in this world but also in the world to come. God has put all things under the authority of Christ and has made him head over all things for the benefit of the church. And the church is his body; it is made full and complete by Christ, who fills all things everywhere with himself" (Ephesians 1:18-23, NLT).

"But know this, that in the last days perilous times will come: For men will be lovers of themselves, lovers of money, boasters, proud, blasphemers, disobedient to parents, unthankful, unholy, unloving, unforgiving, slanderers, without self-control, brutal, despisers of good, traitors, headstrong, haughty, lovers of pleasure rather than lovers of God, having a form of godliness but denying its power. And from such people turn away!" (2 Timothy 3:1-5, NKJV).

Also by This Author:

Digital:

Eleventh Hour (Updated version)
Midnight Hour (Updated version)
Prayer Warriors
Guardians
Prayer Warriors: The Final Chapter

Print:

Prayer Warriors
Guardians
Prayer Warriors: The Final Chapter
The Third Coming
Eleventh Hour
Midnight Hour
Joy: The Secret of Being Content
Making Sabbath Special
I Call Him Abba
Adventist Family Traditions
Making Holidays Special
Banza's Incredible Journey (and other stories from ADRA)
Playing God
Sunnyside Up
Juventud y Alegria
Jenny's Cat-napped Cat
More Power to Ya
iChoose Life

"All glory to God forever and ever! Amen" (Galatians 1:5, NLT).

Made in the USA
Coppell, TX
30 September 2021

63243182R00134